THE
REVENANT
GAMES

THE
REVENANT
GAMES

MARGIE FUSTON

SIMON & SCHUSTER

First published in Great Britain in 2024 by Simon & Schuster UK Ltd

First published in the USA in 2024 by Margaret K. McElderry Books,
an imprint of Simon & Schuster Children's Publishing Division,
1230 Avenue of the Americas, New York, New York 10020

Text copyright © 2024 Margie Fuston

1 3 5 7 9 10 8 6 4 2

Simon & Schuster UK Ltd
1st Floor, 222 Gray's Inn Road
London WC1X 8HB

Simon & Schuster: Celebrating 100 Years of Publishing in 2024

www.simonandschuster.co.uk
www.simonandschuster.com.au
www.simonandschuster.co.in

Simon & Schuster Australia, Sydney
Simon & Schuster India, New Delhi

A CIP catalogue record for this book is available from the British Library.

PB ISBN 978-1-3985-3464-3
eBook ISBN 978-1-3985-3466-7
eAudio ISBN 978-1-3985-3465-0

This book is a work of fiction. Names, characters, places and incidents are either
the product of the author's imagination or are used fictitiously. Any resemblance
to actual people living or dead, events or locales is entirely coincidental.

Printed and Bound in the UK using
100% Renewable Electricity at CPI Group (UK) Ltd

MIX
Paper | Supporting
responsible forestry
FSC® C171272

For my sisters, Jenny and Stacie –
I'd fight a vampire to save you.

ONE

HUNGER DROVE MOST PEOPLE TO THE EDGE of the forest. Bly felt it too, but hers wasn't the grumble of an empty stomach. Dreams fueled her hunger. They burned in her belly, and sometimes she thought they'd turn her to ash from the inside out if she didn't at least try to make them a reality.

She stood there often, staring at the spot where the trees grew thick and what lay beyond them rested solely in her imagination. But it was time to see what was really out there.

She tensed at the sound of shoes squishing in the mud behind her. Only one person knew of her plan. She turned and smiled at Elise. Her sister brushed at the sun-blond strands of hair that had escaped her practical braid. A frown pulled at her round cheeks, and her fawn-brown eyes crinkled in the corners with worry.

"I knew you'd come," Bly said.

Elise bit her lip and glanced back over her shoulder at the village. Smoke curled from every chimney now, rising into the pale sky.

Longing and a little bit of regret filled her sister's expression. Bly had a feeling that Elise was imagining sitting in front of the fireplace, enjoying a slice of warm bread that she'd baked, sipping mint tea and preparing for a day of work with either their father or mother.

Bly stared at the rows of wooden houses and wished she could feel what her sister did. It'd be easier, but all she saw when she looked at her home was cold that choked the lungs and muddy streets that never dried.

Bly didn't feel longing until she turned back to the maze of oak and pine trees in front of her. Yes, these woods were dangerous. They lived in one of the human villages in the Gap, caught between the city of Vagaris, ruled by vampires, and the city of Havenwhile, ruled by witches. Vampires and witches didn't agree on much, but neither would harm a human so long as they remained in the Gap.

The forest honored no such rules.

But Bly wasn't foolish enough to crave danger. She wanted what you could get if you faced it, and she was brave enough to do it.

Elise didn't understand that.

How could they be so close, yet so different?

Elise would never follow Bly beyond the woods, and Bly would never stay. They'd both have to break the other's heart a little to feel whole. But in this moment, Elise was still here for her.

"Will you at least tell me why we're going foraging?" Elise glanced at Bly's thick wool pants that had already been patched at the knees multiple times. "Do you need money for clothing?

Are you cold? I'm sure we could skip a few meals this week and pay for something new. Let me ask mother."

Mother never said no to Elise. Her sister rarely asked for anything though. The original cloth of Elise's skirt ended half-way up her shins. Instead of asking for more clothes, Elise kept stitching new material along the bottom and somehow, she'd managed to make it look beautiful and intentional, like a quilt of woodsy colors. The way Elise took what she had and made it something lovely was a type of magic, but not one that Bly envied.

Bly didn't want to skip a meal for new, practical clothes.

Bly wanted more. She wanted a full belly and skirts in different colors and ribbons for her hair.

She *wanted*.

Elise didn't. She was content. Bly had already listened to her lecture on how they had everything they needed; how this was a risk they didn't need to take, which was why she hadn't told Elise exactly why she wanted to forage for food to sell.

She knew her sister would follow her anyway, even without an answer.

Bly moved to take the first step, but Elise grabbed her arm.

"You could sell blood instead. It's safer."

Blood was the most valuable thing any human possessed.

The vampires needed it to live, and the witches needed it to cast their spells.

But she shuddered at the thought of getting poked by a needle and watching a red stream leave her body. "I hate blood. You know that."

"I'll sell some of mine then."

"No," Bly said. She'd already anticipated that Elise would make that offer, but Bly wanted to start her new life right. If she couldn't be bold enough to wander into the woods for a day, then how would she ever step into them without looking back?

She'd been dreaming of this adventure forever. She and Elise and their friend Emerson had been coming to the woods since they were kids. They'd wander inside but only so deep, making sure they could still see the village, since vampires and witches rarely bothered with people who kept to the edge.

While Elise and Bly climbed the pines, Emerson would stand watch below. Elise always gathered the needles that they could chew on later, but Bly would sit on the highest branch she could and stare out into the trees. There were stories of people who lived far away, past the woods that were caught between Havenwhile and Vagaris, surviving off the land and living better lives than the ones in the Gap. Some people said they built their homes in the trees, hiding from anyone who might hunt them, and Bly loved the idea of living close to the sky with only the branches closing her in.

Then a couple of years ago, she grew too heavy for her favorite branch. It split while she was daydreaming, as if it couldn't hold the impossible weight of everything she wanted. She'd fallen, banging herself up a little on the way down, but she hadn't hit the ground.

Emerson caught her.

It was the first moment she saw him differently.

Every dreamer needed someone grounded to catch them if

they went too high. Alone, she didn't think she could do it, but with practical Emerson at her side, she knew they'd make it. They'd do more than that—they'd thrive. Her dreams shifted from half-formed thoughts and whimsical imaginings to something that felt possible. It'd be a simple life, but that was exactly what she wanted. She'd always been envious of the witches with their orchards and fields beyond the walls of Havenwhile. She loved the idea of being able to spend each day working in the dirt with the sun on her neck or climbing apple trees to pick the food she'd eat and share. Emerson would spend his days woodworking, which she knew he loved more than the metalwork he did now. He'd build beautiful tables they'd trade with others who lived near them for clothes as rich in color as the fruit Bly grew. When she came home, only after the sun began to fall, Emerson would be there waiting. He'd brush the dirt from her cheeks and grumble about it, then kiss her anyway. They'd make dinner, and it wouldn't feel like a chore because the food would have come from her own hands, and she'd have the sunburn on her skin to prove it. *That* would feel like a home.

The problem was that Emerson never looked at her the way she looked at him. She'd been his friend for too long. But he just needed one moment—like she'd had when he caught her—to make him see her as someone to chase a different future with. And making sure Emerson came with her was the first, most important part of her plan.

So, trembling from a little bit of fear but mostly excitement, Bly stepped out of the mud and into the soft crunch of newly fallen leaves.

She didn't turn back to see if Elise followed, but she heard her trailing behind as she moved.

They walked straight out for a while, weaving between the trees that hid the sun and let the cold creep in even more. Even a half-hour walk from the edge of town, the forest was completely scavenged: acorns and pine cones collected from the ground, pine needles cleared from the lower branches, bark for teas and medicines stripped from the trees. It would be like that for miles. They had to go deeper.

And they had to choose a direction: head toward Havenwhile or Vagaris.

The basic things anyone could gather in the forest wouldn't fetch a high enough price. But mushrooms grew in abundance the closer you got to Havenwhile, and berries thrived the closer you got to Vagaris. There was a catch, of course. There always was. The vampires hunted here, snatching humans they'd drink to unconsciousness—maybe you'd wake up or maybe you wouldn't. And witches put spells on some of their mushrooms, sleeping curses that would let them take blood from people— maybe you'd wake up or maybe you wouldn't.

Bly turned toward Havenwhile. She wasn't about to risk a vampire's bite—she'd much rather have her blood stolen while she was unconscious. But Elise grabbed her arm for the second time, fingers digging in a little too hard. "It's not too late to go back."

Bly tugged away from her in answer.

"At least tell me what you need the money for," Elise said.

Out here with nothing but the trees watching them, the

words wanted to leave Bly's lips. This was a place to whisper about secrets and desires. "I need a fancy dress I saw in the market."

Elise blinked. *"What?"* She leaned toward Bly like she hadn't heard her correctly.

Of course, it sounded foolish unless Bly told Elise everything—how that dress would set off each step of her plan.

"I want to leave," Bly added. "For good."

Elise didn't look surprised. More resigned, like this was a moment she'd already played out in her mind and knew she couldn't stop. Bly had talked about it since she was old enough to imagine things she couldn't touch.

Her sister remained silent for a long time. When she spoke again, resolve hardened her face. "Then we need to start cutting back on meals, drying apples to pack, saving up for jerky. You do need warmer clothes. We'll have to start selling blood—at least some. You'll never get enough supplies without trading for it, even if you survive the forest."

Relief flooded Bly's chest, and just a little bit of hurt. Elise knew her too well to beg her to stay. That made it easier and harder all at once.

"Wait . . ." Elise paused her list of things Bly'd have to do to leave her forever. "Why do you need a dress? New wool pants to wear under a skirt would be better."

Bly's cheeks burned in the cold kiss of the breeze ruffling her curls. "I'm asking Emerson to come with me."

Elise's lips parted in surprise. *"Our* Emerson?"

Bly bristled at *our*. Of course all three of them were close, but

Bly and Emerson had met first, on the edge of this same forest, where Bly had come to wander and Emerson had come to gather sticks to whittle into slender knives. At first she'd just watch him, imagining that he was carving swords and dreaming of battles and heroes, and she filled him into the stories she made up. They always walked the same section, where the oak branches grew out farthest over the empty field. He didn't notice her until she started following him around, and then she finally worked up the courage to ask him what all his knives were for. He'd said practice. His father was the bladesmith, and he wasn't old enough to work with him in the forge yet, so he practiced by carving miniature swords and knives. Bly's stories about him were more entertaining, so Bly told them to him, and he'd laugh at all the silly adventures she made up. He'd laughed more back then—it was a big, bold sound that always caught her by surprise because he looked so serious most of the time.

She'd held onto that original fantasy—Emerson could be the hero in a world that belonged to her.

They were friends for an entire year before Elise joined them, since she was a whole year younger and rarely left the village. Bly would always sneak out in the mornings before her parents could ask her to work, and Elise would stay home baking and cooking. Elise preferred it that way. In the afternoon, she'd even meet Bly where the edges of the houses touched the field to give her a warmed slice of bread and jerky so Bly wouldn't have to come home for lunch and get dragged with their healer mother to stitch up someone's injury. Elise loved working with their mother. She had the stomach for it, and she'd told Bly once that healing felt magical. But one day, Emerson came to pick up Bly's lunch with her, and the next day, Elise had brought a little for him too, and the day after that, Elise packed her own lunch as well and ate with them at the edge of the forest. Bly enjoyed sharing that time with her sister and seeing Elise love a little bit of what she did.

But it also made her jealous to share someone else with Elise, because Elise had their parents in a way that Bly didn't. Their father was a tanner for the vampires, and Elise also thrived at assisting him as much as she did their mother. Both made Bly nauseous. At dinner, their parents were always arguing about who'd get to take Elise with them for the next day, and whoever didn't win would look at Bly as if they wished she were another Elise and not a girl who wanted things they couldn't give. She'd overheard them arguing about what to do with her—how she'd survive. They hoped she'd marry someone with a good job, and then she'd be their problem. She wanted to be someone's solution, but she couldn't be that in this world.

"I want him to be *my* Emerson," Bly said. "I thought you knew that." She'd never actually said the words out loud, but surely it was obvious to her sister that she wanted Emerson to be more than a friend, even if Emerson never seemed to notice.

Elise flinched back. She swallowed, looking around the forest as if it had shifted and left her lost.

"I just . . . Emerson didn't seem the type to leave. I had no idea he wanted to," Elise said. She was silent for a moment, looking everywhere but at Bly. When she finally spoke again, her voice was firm. "But I *want* him to go with you. It'd make me feel better."

"Well, I haven't asked him yet," Bly admitted, hating the worry that immediately crossed Elise's face at her words. Clearly Elise didn't think Emerson would go with her.

"That's why I need the dress," Bly reminded her. "I need him to see me differently when I ask him." When she'd seen the sapphire-blue dress in the market yesterday, she couldn't help but go up to it and run her hands across the silk bodice and the velvet skirts. It was the type of dress that'd get ruined in minutes where she lived, but she hadn't thought of that. She'd pictured herself wearing it on the balcony of a tree house with her legs dangling off the edge, watching a fire-orange sunset with Emerson at her side. Her dress would be the perfect contrast to the sky. If Emerson saw her in that dress with a matching ribbon holding back the dark brown hair that she usually left wild, he wouldn't see the little girl with leaves tangled in her hair. He'd see her as she was now. He'd be able to picture the same future.

But Elise didn't seem to see the possibilities that Bly saw. Her sister just looked sad.

Was Bly's dream sad? It seemed romantic to dress up before you asked someone to run away with you. She should have known that Elise wouldn't understand—even in the morning forest that seemed to glisten with lost magic.

"Can we just go?" Bly asked.

Elise looked back the way they came for a long moment before taking a deep breath and nodding.

Bly took another step toward Havenwhile.

"Wait," Elise said. "Why don't we go toward Vagaris instead?"

Bly spun back around. "I'd rather take a nap than get bit."

"The vampires aren't all bad," Elise said, staring down at her fingers. "I've worked in Vagaris with father for a while now. They usually send the worst ones to the village to deal with the humans to make us think they're all horrible—to make us afraid. A lot of them in the city are . . . nice."

Bly shook her head. "Don't let Emerson hear you say that."

Emerson's older sister foraged in these woods once, and she never came back. They found her body tangled in the berry bushes, clothes stained red from the crushed fruit and neck stained red from the blood. Emerson had been twelve. He'd rarely laughed after that. Sometimes Bly felt like she was searching for the boy he used to be. She doubted she'd ever find him again while they still lived in the Gap.

"I just mean that maybe we'll run into one I know," Elise said. "They'd probably just let us go."

"You sound like you think they're your friends."

Elise shook her head but she didn't meet Bly's eyes, and Bly couldn't tell if she was denying being friends with them or protesting Bly's hatred of them, but finally she sighed, walking past Bly in the direction of Havenwhile. She paused once, though, to look over her shoulder in the direction of the vampires.

But vampires were a more familiar danger to Elise—people always chose the fear they knew over the one they had yet to face. That was all.

The forest grew denser as they walked in silence, until eventually the trees started to thin again, and bright white glistened ahead.

"Snow?" Elise paused and squinted.

"No." Bly grinned and sped up, ignoring the worry on her sister's face.

Elise caught her just at the edge of the small clearing where grass grew wild around moss-covered stones and white mushrooms sprouted everywhere.

"Beautiful," Bly breathed at the same time Elise whispered, "Poisonous."

Bly laughed. "Beautiful things should be."

Elise looked nauseous, but Bly bent down and found them two long sticks. "It's totally safe if we're careful." Everyone knew the undersides would have faint blue lines that indicated a spell hidden in them if the witches had cursed them. They just needed to flip the mushroom over with the stick first and make sure there were no marks. If not, they were fine to touch.

Bly poked one, revealing the clean belly. Elise took a sharp breath as Bly's fingers closed around the velvet-soft mushroom. Bly grinned up at her, running her fingers over it. It felt like touching clouds. Almost magical. She dropped it in the sack at her waist.

Elise stood watching for a while, shifting back and forth from one foot to the other until Bly turned around. "I'm not cursed yet," she said. "It'd go faster if you helped."

Elise bit her lip, but she bent down and used her stick to flip a mushroom, staring at it forever before pulling up the front of her skirt and plopping it there.

With both of them collecting, perhaps Bly could get enough for the dress *and* some supplies.

It wasn't long before Bly's bag stretched with enough to buy what she wanted. She was about to turn and tell Elise they should head home when she heard the soft thud.

Bly's heart gave one matching thud before it seemed to stall out. It must have kept beating. She was still breathing, but she couldn't feel it anymore.

"Elise?" she whispered.

Silence answered, and then her own foolish heart roared back, racing too fast, thrumming too loud in her ears, knowing already what she didn't want to see.

She turned, somehow moving too quickly and too slowly all at once.

Elise lay on her side, golden blond hair fanned across the ground, brown eyes open and vacant. Sleeping didn't look like that.

How could eyes empty so quickly?

Bly dropped to her knees beside her, reaching to knock free the mushroom still clutched in Elise's hand. She barely caught herself. Her fingers shook so badly that it took her several tries to push it free with her stick.

The faintest blue streak ran along the stem. Easy to miss.

Bly shook Elise.

She was warm. It'd be okay. She could drag Elise away, hide before the witches found them, and wait out the sleeping curse.

It was only a sleeping curse. Only a sleeping curse. Just sleeping. But each time she told herself, it felt more like a lie.

Sleeping didn't look like that.

Bly poked the mushroom again, and then she saw it: the tiny pinpoint of brown that marred the smooth white top of it. She crushed it, the flesh crumbling easily to reveal a tiny nightshade thorn. Her throat closed at the sight of it. She knew the spell such a thorn could hold. It was a death curse hidden inside the sleeping-spelled mushroom. She hadn't considered the need to be afraid of a trap within a trap. Her stomach twisted at the evilness of whatever witch had done such a thing.

And then black veins began to crawl from Elise's fingertips, webbing upward and across her cheek almost instantly, the sign of a death curse. But how long did Elise have? A year? A week? Only moments? Every death curse was different, and Bly clung to the fraying shreds of her hope until Elise's lips turned a startling shade of blue, and the sound of voices forced her to look up.

She couldn't see them yet, but the witches were coming.

She leaned close to Elise's lips, holding her own breath as if denying herself could make her sister breathe again.

Nothing.

Laughter sounded closer in the woods.

It was so light and cheerful, and hearing it while she stared at her sister's empty eyes made her want to cover her ears and scream and never stop, but she didn't have time.

The witches were coming. People always said they knew somehow when a human had touched one of their curses.

Bly pushed Elise from her side to her back so she could try to grip her under her arms. Elise's head flopped, cheek squishing more mushrooms, and a sob tore from Bly's throat at the lifelessness of the movement. Wrapping her arms under her sister's, she dragged her a few feet and then a few more. But even though Bly was taller and older, Elise had always been stronger, with hard muscles under her full curves.

There was nowhere to go.

The voices grew louder.

Nothing existed in Elise's still-open eyes.

Dead. The word filled up every inch of Bly's thoughts.

Elise was dead.

Bly might be too if she didn't give up her sister's body.

Elise would want her to run. A body was just a body, she'd say, not a person to be saved.

Bly gently laid her sister back on the ground. She pressed her fingers against Elise's eyelids, soft like the mushrooms that killed her, and closed them. She didn't want the witches to see the color of her sister's eyes. They didn't deserve to.

Elise would've yelled at her for that if she could. So impractical.

Bly ran until the trees thickened. She should've kept going, but instead she pulled herself into the branches of a black oak, the kind she'd dreamed of living in, and hid in its dense foliage.

The witches wore a combination of soft browns and greens that blended in with the forest, so Bly didn't even see them until they stepped into the clearing. Greenery clung to their hair in wild crowns, and they walked with a slowness that made them seem like ancient trees made human for only a moment.

There were three of them. Their eyes flashed as they glanced around. Bly had always liked the deep blue pool of a witch's eyes, but now the color seemed garish.

They moved with fluid steps that somehow never broke a

mushroom until two of them lay a burlap stretcher next to Elise, and the other bent down and pressed fingers to her throat. They rolled Elise onto the stretcher. One of them pointed at the drag marks on the ground, and they all glanced around again.

Take me too, Bly thought, but she didn't say it.

That would be the easy way out.

They didn't bother looking for her anyway, but as they picked up the stretcher and melted back into the trees, Bly felt the most important part of her go with them. The part that hoped.

She clung to the tree for hours, blinking again and again and looking at the spot where Elise had fallen as if time would make her reappear.

The air heated slightly in the afternoon and cooled again, and still she clung there, legs numb from the branch digging into her thighs. For the first time in her life, her mind was painfully blank: no dreams, no plans. Until her thoughts came back and caught on the moment of her sister falling. Then they spun into every second leading up to it—all the chances Elise had given her to stop. To go back. Every moment that could have changed what had happened.

Her throat burned.

The sky turned a horrible bluish black. She used to love the color of the time between day and night, but now it reminded her of the quick spread of poison under Elise's skin.

The steady crunch of leaves distracted her. Maybe they'd come back for her body too. She felt dead enough.

"Bly?"

Hearing her name jarred her. How could they know it?

"Bly?"

This time she recognized the voice through her haze.

His voice made everything feel a thousand times better and a thousand times worse.

Emerson.

She tried to move out of the tree and fell. She hit something hard, but not the ground. He'd caught her, just like he had when they were younger, but she didn't deserve to be saved anymore. She pushed away from him so violently that he dropped her. The ground hurt. The pain made her feel better.

She looked up into a face that felt like home: dark brown skin with darker brown eyes, always furrowed brows, full lips that pressed together when he was thinking—and he was always puzzling something through.

Even now.

Emerson yanked her to her feet.

"Bly? Bly?" He wouldn't stop saying her name as a question as he ran his hands across her face. Finally, he paused. "Where's Elise?" His eyes left her and roved over the darkening forest. "She left me a note. I came as soon as I found it. How could you two be so foolish?" His eyes came back to her face and darted away again. "Where's Elise? Bly?"

She saw the moment he knew—that slow breaking apart of one reality as another awful one takes hold.

He looked the way she'd felt when she'd turned around and saw her sister motionless on the ground.

Somehow, it felt even worse seeing the expression on him.

Emerson's lips moved again, but she couldn't hear a thing.

His hands wrapped around her arms, but she couldn't feel that either. Her head wobbled, and she was vaguely aware that he was shaking her.

Eventually he let go of her and moved away to the spot she couldn't pull her eyes from. She watched him pace back and forth, hands running over and over again across the dark brown curls he kept cropped close to his head.

She had to look away. She used to love the way he'd run his hands over his hair while he was thinking. It usually made her want to grab them and put them in her own hair while she kissed him, but she'd only ever thought about it and never actually did it. And looking at him now, that desire was already gone, stripped away from her the instant she'd heard that thud.

Her chest ached with the realization of everything she'd lost; not just Elise but herself too. She already felt like a person who didn't know what dreams were, who went to sleep at night and saw only the dark, who moved through each day thinking only of surviving the moment they were in.

It terrified her.

And then guilt swallowed her terror. Even now, she was worried about her own dreams while Elise's had been stolen from her because of Bly. What had Elise really wanted for her life? Bly had never asked her, just assumed that Elise was satisfied because she always wore a soft smile on her face no matter what she was doing.

Bly was a terrible sister, and not just for bringing Elise to the forest, but for all the times she'd never turned to Elise and asked her what *she* dreamed of.

She sat down and curled her legs up to her chest, making herself as small as she felt.

She couldn't go home. She couldn't stand the thought of seeing the horror on her parents' faces when she told them, and then underneath it, she'd see their regret—that it was Elise who was dead and not Bly. She felt the same, but she didn't want to see it reflected back at her.

Eventually Emerson came back, and he stared down at her for so long that she dropped her head onto her arms so she wouldn't have to look at him and all the pain on his face. Unforgivable pain.

She felt deep inside that he would leave her, but he didn't. Not yet. He scooped her up and carried her home. The dark had swallowed everything by the time they got to her house where her parents were surely wondering where Elise had been all day—their daughter who never wandered.

Emerson didn't speak when he finally did leave her at the door, and the only good thing was that the dark didn't let her see his face.

In the morning, Bly realized she still had the bag of mushrooms Elise had paid for with her life. She took them to the market. She didn't buy the dress, but she did buy the blue ribbon that matched it, and she wrapped it around her wrist tight enough to make her eyes sting.

Then she started planning, but not for the dreams she'd had before.

Those had died with her sister.

TWO

ONE YEAR, FOUR MONTHS, AND ELEVEN days after she killed her sister, Bly stood on the edge of the forest again. Fear always haunted the woods, even when her dreams had lived beyond them, but these days, the shadows between the trees held her guilt too. Fear could be pushed down out of necessity, but guilt was a starving wolf always looking to consume. She could only run for so long. It gnawed on her now as she stood there, unable to take the last step from the muddy path to the crumbling leaves and fallen pine needles. Maybe she didn't need to go foraging. She should at least try to sell more blood first. She could practically hear Elise suggesting it.

For once, she listened. Turning away, she imagined the branches reaching for her, attempting to drag her to where she deserved to be. But she was being ridiculous. Her guilt didn't live in the forest.

It lived in her bones.

She tugged at the fraying blue ribbon around her wrist as she walked the path through the field of patchy dead grass that led back to the villages. She tried not to think of her sister, but not thinking of her only made the guilt more ferocious, and she had to stop for a moment and breathe before she became a curled-up ball of remembering. Then she'd be no good to anyone. And for the second time in her life, Bly had a real plan instead of just dreams.

This time was different. She wasn't a child anymore. Before, she'd been selfish with too many wants.

Her heartbeat slowed and her breathing steadied. She was faint and darkness lingered around the edges of her vision, but that was from blood loss, not losing herself to her pain, and she'd gotten used to that dizzy feeling of not enough—too little blood in her veins and too little food in her belly, so when she started walking again, her steps were mostly steady. She focused on her brown boots sinking deeper and deeper into the mud until she reached the edge of the worn wooden houses where the road became wider, but even more precarious, with puddles that looked small but would swallow half your leg. Though once you stepped in one, you didn't forget, so everyone wove around them except for the kids who were young enough not to be bothered with the cold yet.

Bly remembered being that young—even though she wished she didn't. She and Elise and Emerson used to collect sticks from the edge of the forest and tie them together with pine needles that were still fresh enough to bend without breaking, and then they'd set sail their contraptions in the deepest puddles and weigh them down with rocks to see whose was the strongest. Emerson and Elise both had a knack for practical designs, so Bly always lost. She wanted hers to be beautiful while it sank.

She'd always been too vain.

She touched her ribbon, wondering if she'd tied it more harshly than usual.

Pulling herself from those dangerous memories, she focused on the weary people with dim eyes walking by that had long forgotten a time they'd felt joy at puddles. Their world was harsh. Cold. Unforgiving. It was not a place for dreamers, but Bly had one more dream to hold onto before she let herself succumb to the same fate.

And she needed money to make it happen.

The Gap was long and narrow, made of little villages divided by markets that were run by the vampires and the witches. The houses got nicer the nearer you got to a market. They belonged to the people who worked closest with the vampires and witches— spies who'd report if someone disappeared for too long so a hunting party could be gathered. They couldn't make it too easy to leave, which made Bly even more certain that there was another world beyond the one trapped between Vagaris and Havenwhile. But Bly was probably lucky she'd never gotten the chance to leave herself—all her plans had been for after she'd escaped. Sometimes she was astounded at how careless she'd been.

Finally she reached the market next to her village, which was kept much nicer since vampires and witches traded there as well. While they couldn't care less about the squalor they forced most humans to live in, they had certain standards for themselves, and the difference was stark and immediate as Bly stepped from the mud to a road of smooth multicolored pebbles. At one point, they'd tried to make the road from shiny white stones, but the humans tracked too much dirt with them, so instead of fixing the constantly wet roads through the villages, they'd changed the color of the rocks.

Bly didn't have time to be angry about little things like the road—not anymore. She was just grateful her feet weren't as cold here.

She kept her head down, pulling her gray cap low on her forehead and tugging her brown curls free to frame her face as she walked past the booths owned by humans. They were simple wooden tables with an array of foraged mushrooms and berries, or odds and ends that people traded back and forth. Then there were the booths owned by vampires or witches, run by humans too. Witches controlled all the food that couldn't be gathered because nothing grew in the sodden fields the human villages wallowed in, so they supplied bread, potatoes, apples, and other rarer foods like oranges. The scent of citrus in the crisp air almost always made Bly stop. It smelled like her distant dreams, and sometimes she'd still let herself linger and remember how bursting with hope she used to be, but today she didn't stop. She moved past the booths stocked by the vampires that held meat, cloth, and metal pots and knives. Humans worked to produce all of these things for them, and then humans sold the harvest of their labor, all while the vampires and witches kept most of the profit and gave the workers just enough to survive and nothing more. They needed them hungry enough to sell their blood.

For a second, an old rage surfaced. Humans were the ones the vampires and witches couldn't live without, so why did they deserve to be the poorest? After Emerson's sister had died, she and Emerson had spent many days sitting on the edge of the forest, chewing the ends of pine needles and letting their anger bubble over about how unfair it was—how they should rise up and take control of their own lives. But ultimately, Emerson said they were too weak to win any type of uprising. They'd tried plenty of times in the past, and it never ended well. Why repeat a history that only ended in more death? They needed to stop pretending. Bly could see the fear in him, and he'd buried his rage beneath it—he couldn't stand to lose someone else he cared about, and he'd live a quiet life if that's what it took.

Bly would've followed him into a revolution if he'd asked, but he'd probably saved them with his practicality. Just a few years ago, a group had tried smuggling people through the forest. Rumor had it they'd even been successful a few times before they were caught and murdered. People said the group had been led by vampires, but most people didn't believe that. What motivation did a vampire have for setting free its food?

Everything had been set up just right, so humans didn't go extinct, but they didn't get to really live either.

Life wasn't fair. Neither was death.

But that was the way their world had worked for as long as anyone could remember.

They had a story, of course, of how things used to be, and how it ended up the way it was now. The story was undoubtedly made of both truth and lies, and what was true changed depending on who told it, but most things stayed the same.

Once, there were no witches or vampires, just people living

in a world that bloomed magic. A lily petal made into tea would make your hair shine; water from a certain stream would cure a cough; a golden berry from a far-off bush would add a year to your life. Anyone could use the magic, combining ingredients for spells to create whatever their heart lusted for. And perhaps everyone could have remained happy and content, but there was always one more thing to be had, and pretty soon the golden berries vanished, lilies didn't bloom, and a leaf that once gave strength to whoever crumbled it in their hand became nothing but crushed wants.

Magic disappeared.

But it had to exist somewhere, and nobody wanted to live without it. They named it the Hallow Pool, and people searched far and wide until they found a deep pool in a lonely forest that shimmered with too many colors not to be magical. People traveled to sip from it in hopes of recapturing a tiny bit of the power that had fled them, but it didn't have the same effect on everyone. Some people came away from the pool as witches, with eyes like deep water and the ability to put spells back into the objects that used to hold them. Others came away as vampires, with eyes as dark as gray oak bark after the rain and raw power in their bodies: speed, strength, healing, immortality. Yet others seemed to come away with nothing. Or so they thought.

When the last drop from the pool was swallowed, people began to experiment with what they'd been given. The vampires' new power began to fade until they succumbed to their cravings for human blood. The witches instinctually tried mixing spells, combining their ingredients with their own blood, but nothing worked until a human suggested they try human blood. The witches had laughed in their face at first—after all, humans were the ones seemingly rejected by the magic—but finally a witch tried it and it worked.

The very people who'd thought the pool had given them nothing held the key to unlocking magic.

In a different world, it might have made them gods. Bly used to enjoy imagining that other life.

But instead they became like the leaves, the grass, the flowers—all the things that got trampled before.

Witches and vampires began hunting humans for the blood they needed, all while fighting each other, each side believing that the magic had blessed them more than the other, so they should rule.

Eventually they realized they were evenly matched, and the one thing they both needed to survive was becoming extinct: humans. A truce was called that split the power between vampires and witches and protected the humans as well.

Bly shivered. Saved from open slaughter, but not from the cold.

Not from a life of misery.

The markets were a place for peace, where they could all trade without fear. For the most part.

On one side, Vagaris guards lounged between the booths, dressed in their bloodred uniforms with high black boots that gleamed like hungry eyes. On the other side, Havenwhile guards mingled, wearing dark brown cloaks and belts around their waists with dozens of pockets for spells. They were supposed to intervene if anyone illegally touched a human.

Bly had only seen it happen once: a woman bumped into a vampire, who turned around and tore into her neck before she could even scream. The Havenwhile guards were on the vampire a second later, subduing him with spells and dragging him off toward their city. That was their punishment—the other side could take you. The vampire had screamed the whole way, and the sound might have haunted Bly except that the woman he'd bitten was already dead on the ground. *That* was the thing that haunted her. A life gone for a bumped shoulder.

Bly reached the witches' section that sold goods they didn't trust humans to handle. Bly hated this area and the blue eyes that matched the ribbon she wore on her wrist; their eyes reminded her of poison and the tint to Elise's lips that day.

Her heart stuttered, but she gritted her teeth as she approached the witches' blood booth. Aside from the people who worshipped vampires and witches in hopes of one day being like them, almost everyone had a side they detested more than the other. Vampires were brutal and bloodthirsty, but at least they'd wound you straight to your face. They were like mountain lions, incapable of hiding their true nature. It was visible in the flash of their fangs when they smiled. But witches hid behind their spells. Pretending not to be bloodthirsty while lying in wait was worse. Bly had fallen for it once, but now she knew better. The greater evil was the one that smiled without the warning of fangs.

But she'd already sold blood to the vampires today.

The witches' booth grew out of the ground, a thick bush with branches that wove together in an unnatural checkered pattern, creating the semblance of a tabletop. It was the work of spells, of course. Nothing grew here naturally. A young man leaned against the top, plucking a green leaf that grew back as fast as he could pull it. His dark brows furrowed in anger as it sprouted once more, and his expression didn't change as he looked up at Bly. His eyes, the same lake blue of every witch, trailed from her mud-caked shoes to the deep purple circles under her dark green eyes. She knew she looked painfully human.

"Don't waste my time," he said as he went back to his leaf.

"I want to sell some blood."

"No."

"Why not?"

He sighed and straightened, waving her forward with two fingers.

As soon as she closed the gap between them, he grabbed her hand and jerked her forward so roughly that the stray branches from the table scratched her through her skirts. She bit her lip as he yanked her sleeve up to her forearm, revealing a blue line on her wrist. When a human gave blood, they marked their arm with a spell, and it would fade as soon as it was safe for them to give more. They needed blood, but they also needed humans to still be alive to sell it.

The witch's lip curled into a slight sneer as he stared down at her. "You think I can't spot someone who's already been bled out from a mile away? Take your desperation somewhere else."

He let go of her so quickly that she almost fell as she stumbled back.

She wanted to challenge him, force him to come out from behind the booth so she could draw some of *his* blood, but he was back to the leaf, which was more of an inconvenience than her. He could cast her aside much more easily. Her face heated. A few people gave her sad looks, and she wondered what they thought. Her parents had better jobs than most. They weren't starving, so why was their child selling so much blood? They'd all be guessing the same thing.

More blood than usual got sold this close to the Games.

She smoothed out her skirt like that would distract people and headed toward the vampires. If she were lucky, Osmond wouldn't be working anymore. Usually she wanted him to be the one to take her blood—she liked him, for a vampire—but he wouldn't let her give more blood than legal. The other vampire who sometimes ran the booth was a different story. Rumor had it that Victor would take as much as you'd let him and dump your body on the edge of town if things went poorly. More than one starving person had gone that route.

The vampires' booths were made of stone pillars topped with cold steel that glistened in the rare peeks of sun. Victor lay stretched out on top of the booth, arms tucked behind his head, bathing in the light. Only well-fed vampires could stand the sun. Their bodies didn't work like those of humans or witches. Their hearts didn't even beat—something the witches claimed was a sign they were abominations. All it really meant, though, was that magic kept them alive. But that magic grew weak if it wasn't fed, and their bodies would start to fail. Victor clearly ate and ate well. The thought turned Bly's already rolling stomach. Even a year later, she hadn't gotten used to selling blood.

Victor didn't open his eyes as she stopped in front of him. Her insides pinched again, but she needed the money, and it was this or the woods.

She cleared her throat, and he turned his head, opening one dark gray eye slowly.

He barely glanced at her before closing it and turning his face to the sun. "You'll die." His voice was bored.

"You didn't even check for a mark."

"Don't need to."

"Please." She let her desperation leak into her voice.

He sighed and sat up, spinning around so his legs dangled off the edge of the table. "Me and my bleeding heart." He smiled, but it didn't reach his eyes. "Let's see." He waved for her arm.

She gave it to him, and his cold hands pulled up her sleeve. One of his fingers covered her mark. "Look at that. My mistake." His smile morphed into a grin, and the excitement in it scared her. He loved this—taking too much blood and gambling a life that wasn't his.

She supposed she should be grateful, but a little bit of hate crept in too. He didn't care why she needed the money badly enough to risk her life. He only cared about his momentary thrill.

He hopped down and waved her around to the wooden stool. She stuck her arm out on the table and rolled her sleeves up, revealing the soft, bruised flesh in the crease of her elbow. This was going to hurt, whether he was gentle or not. Victor grabbed an empty bag and tube and leaned over her with a needle. His eyes lit up at the state of her arm, and he plunged the needle in without warning. He bit his lip at the little gasp she couldn't keep in, and then he yanked the needle out again.

Blood leaked down her arm.

"Sorry. I missed." His pupils had turned a solid black like all vampire eyes did when bloodlust filled them.

Tears stung as she turned her head to the side. He didn't miss. He just wanted to stab her again, but she couldn't do anything about that but try and deny him the pleasure of another reaction.

She closed her eyes and waited.

"You're not supposed to be here." The voice was worse than a needle prick.

She opened her eyes as Osmond yanked the needle out of Victor's hand. Osmond was short and burly and loved to wear bright yellow shirts that sometimes got spotted with red from his work, but still somehow looked pretty against his warm brown skin. He always smiled with his mouth closed, so you didn't have to look at his fangs when you felt the pinch of the needle, and Bly always wondered if he was attempting to hide his true nature or just trying to be kind.

But she didn't need kindness right now.

"Didn't you check her mark? I maxed her out earlier." Osmond threw the used needle onto the ground.

"Oops." Victor shrugged.

"I need this," Bly said.

Osmond gave her a sad look. "There's nothing you need enough to die for."

Not true. Not true for a lot of people: there was plenty in the world to die for.

Some of those reasons were horribly pointless.

But it could be a worthy death if it meant correcting your mistakes.

"Please . . . ," Bly started.

"No." Osmond's voice was harsh, his eyes hard. Whatever niceness he showed the people who bled here, it only went so far. It was probably an act.

He was still a vampire, and he lived by their rules. They only broke them to hurt, never to help.

Bly stood up, knees shaking so badly that she knew she would have passed out and Victor would have dropped her body in the frozen mud behind the town. She'd probably have died, depending on how much blood he'd continued to take after she was unconscious. Emerson would've mourned her. Even though they weren't as close as they once were, he'd still have taken a moment to remember her. Maybe he'd have even felt guilty about the distance between them.

But she wasn't dying today. At least not here.

She checked the sun in the sky. It wasn't even noon. She still had time to travel deep into the woods and get back before dark.

She had to if she wanted any hope of winning back her sister's life in the Revenant Games.

THREE

THE GAMES STARTED SOON AND BLY WASN'T ready. She felt comfortable enough with a blade in her hand—Emerson had given her one after Elise died, and even though he'd never taught her to use it, she'd practiced holding it and running through the moves she made up. But one blade wasn't enough. She'd also spent more than a year studying spells but knowing how to use them would mean nothing if she didn't have enough of them. And a heavier winter coat could mean the difference between freezing in the forest and winning. Plus, she needed time to get stronger, too, but that wasn't an option. She couldn't live through another year of her parents looking at her and wishing she were someone else. Another year of Emerson being cold and distant. She worried that she'd run out of hope if she kept waiting.

Her steps quickened as she wove back through the village toward the woods. Mud splattered the hem of her skirt, but she didn't care.

The Revenant Games only happened once a year, and this year had to be it for Bly.

The Games were another part of their world meant to keep peace because the original truce wasn't enough. The story was that with the human population almost extinct, it didn't take long for vampires and witches to try each other's blood. The vampires quickly discovered that witch blood was a delicacy and increased their powers tenfold; meanwhile, the witches found that vampire blood could be used to concoct more powerful spells, including one for immortality—the one thing the vampires possessed that the witches were jealous of. Chaos descended again, and with the vampires and witches killing each other, the humans revolted and almost won.

Bly smiled anytime she thought of that part. They'd been so close to winning, to proving humans were just as strong. She wished she could have seen it, but that had happened so long ago that the tired faces of everyone she passed in the village held no memories of it. The power they'd almost taken had become a cruel myth.

The threat of human victory had been enough for the vampires and witches to unite once more. Stricter rules were put in place, and they weren't even allowed to sell their own blood to each other—too much access made their bloodlust turn frenzied, but they also needed an outlet for their cravings, so they devised the Games.

For two weeks at the start of winter, the Games were held. Humans who wanted to play would pick a side: while both sides promised wealth, the witches would also raise one person from the dead for whoever brought them the highest-ranking vampire, and the vampires offered immortality to whoever brought them the most powerful witch.

They called it the Revenant Games—the witches brought someone back to life and the vampires saved a human from a life that was as good as death.

Plenty of humans grew up dreaming of playing the Games. And then others, like Bly, had nightmares they needed to undo.

Vampires and witches couldn't participate themselves. After all, witches couldn't be turned into vampires and resurrection spells only worked on humans. Some people said that was a gift to humans from the magic because it'd given the witches and vampires so much already. But it wasn't like humans could create the spell.

A gift held in greedy hands is nothing but a curse.

Bly felt the full weight of that curse. For a second, she stopped her march to the forest. A cold breeze nipped at her ankles as she breathed deep, trying to quiet a familiar rage. The worst part about this whole thing was that she *needed* a witch to get Elise back. She needed the help of the very people who'd stolen her.

Because even though they couldn't win the prizes, vampires and witches still loved to play within the loopholes. Days before the Games would start, the vampires and witches would open their cities to humans under the guise of luring them to play for their side. But along with the lavish parties and feasts they'd throw for the humans, they also held trials for humans to prove their prowess. From those trials, any vampire or witch could choose a human to sponsor—which Bly knew was truly the key to winning. She'd need someone powerful on her side if she had any chance of coming out on top, because sponsors would do just about anything to help their humans since that also meant they'd win their own prize: an endless supply of blood for a year.

And even if a human didn't want to play for the vampires or the witches specifically, they could still participate in the Games as bounty hunters. Both sides would pay a reward to anyone who could take out players from the opposing side.

For vampires and witches, it was the only way to get the blood they craved most—and it also gave them a way to hurt each other without starting a bloody war that would leave humans with the upper hand again. Plus, it fixed the pesky problem of humans rebelling against them for better lives. Revolutions were hard to plan when most people were focused on winning the Games. After all, it was easier to lift just yourself out of poverty than try to change the entire world.

But for Bly, the Games just meant hugging her sister again.

If her sister would hug her at all after what Bly had done.

So by the time Bly reached the edge of the forest again, she'd pushed aside her fear and called on her guilt to draw her in, not keep her out.

She walked, tugging her scarf tighter around her neck as the forest grew denser. Eventually she stopped. It looked like the same spot where Elise had begged her to turn around one more time. Too late for that now.

The cold suddenly became too much. Bly's breath puffed in short white clouds, making her panic visible. But what was the point of panicking at a memory? It wasn't practical. What was done was done. It made more sense to be fearless, to forget the past and focus on what she had to do. But cruel memories clung harder than good ones. Only a little more than a year later and already Bly struggled to hold on to some of the little ones, like the exact shade of her sister's brown eyes—were they a darker muddy brown or more like a tanned deer hide? Why was that so hard to remember when her death haunted Bly's every thought?

So standing there again, it was an easy choice: she headed toward the vampires.

It was a two-day journey—one and a half if you didn't rest—to the walls of Vagaris, but it'd only take a few hours to reach the first of the berry bushes. And it'd be faster if she ran. She might not have been that great with a knife, but when Emerson and Elise had raced her around the edges of the village as kids, she'd always won. And in the past year, she'd honed the skill further while foraging, tearing through the woods and darting around trees with a speed she liked to imagine rivaled a vampire's. She knew, of course, that a vampire would be faster, that she didn't actually stand a chance if they spotted her, but something about being fast enough to feel a breeze against her cheeks made her feel safer.

Her only regret was the full skirts she wore today instead of breeches, which were easier to run in, but skirts were better for hidden pockets of spells. Breeches required a belt with pouches, and flaunting your collection so obviously was just asking to be robbed, so she'd taken to skirts lately. Her parents thought she was trying to look prettier—her mother had even mentioned how she was pleased to see her trying to attract a husband. In reality, her skirt just made her deadlier. Nobody could see the spells she carried: three acorns for strength, two blue jay feathers for speed, sharpened birch twigs for binding, a lump of coal for warmth, a satchel of herbs for energy, and a few dead fireflies that would light the night around her in a pinch. Hopefully she wouldn't use any of those today, though—she needed them for the Games.

Bly tried to make her mind as numb as her toes as she sped through the trees. The past was her motivation, but she also couldn't let it distract her from the task at hand. It sometimes felt impossible to balance those two things.

She slowed, dropping her skirts back around her ankles, when she reached a small stream. The frozen mud around the edges cracked like glass as she approached it. On this side, there was nothing but the same picked-over forest, but on the other, bushes hugged the edge of the water, crawling up the sides of trees, consuming the already dense growth. It wasn't like the water was some type of boundary the vampires wouldn't pass, but they didn't really need to bother.

Anyone willing to come this far was probably going to keep going.

And all the bushes nearest to the water had been stripped of berries already.

Bly took a deep breath and jumped to a clear section on the other side. Her boots slipped on the ice, and she teetered backward as her hand shot out on instinct, gripping a thorny branch. She hissed but held on long enough to balance herself before letting go and pulling off her ragged glove, glancing down at the wells of blood across her palm. At least she didn't fall in the stream. Walking back wet in the near freezing cold could be a death sentence.

But so could fresh blood. Vampires had a heightened sense of smell.

Kneeling, she plunged her hand into the icy stream before taking it out. It stopped the bleeding, but blood stained her glove. She hung it on the branch that had bit her and moved away, wrapping her hand in the tail ends of her scarf to muffle any lingering smell. It'd have to be enough. There just wasn't time to go home and come back another day.

The bushes were somehow both wild and tamed. The branches reached chaotically in all directions, attempting to draw more blood, but clear paths also wound in all directions.

Everything about it seemed like a trap: a place you could easily get lost. A place you could easily bleed.

Fear pulsed in her chest, the faint sting of her hand reminding her that she already had one mark against her. With any luck, there wouldn't be hunting parties out today, not when the vampires opened the gates of their city tomorrow to hold a trial for people seeking a sponsor for the Games, but she needed to hurry regardless.

She crept deeper into the brambles until she finally caught the first glimmer of red and stepped into a small clearing of grass surrounded by deep green branches laden with berries that hung like drops of blood. Rumor said that the vampires watered the fruit with their own blood, and that's what kept the plants growing through any weather. People even thought the berries had healing properties because of it, but Bly didn't believe that. Her mother didn't use them. But truth didn't matter—all Bly cared about was what people would pay for them.

She removed her remaining glove before grabbing the pouch she carried at her waist. Holding it in the hand still wrapped in her scarf, she started gathering as quickly as she could. The soft skins of the berries burst easily, and it wasn't long before her fingers turned red from the juices, but so many grew in this clearing that a few damaged ones didn't matter.

This would be easy. She wouldn't have to travel deeper.

It was just like her world for one positive thought to curse her.

"Caught you." The cold air of the vampire's breath hit the sliver of bare skin at the back of her neck.

Bly spun, her bag slipping from her fingers as she scrambled back, but thorns pressed into her, each pinch reminding her that she had nowhere to go.

That's why there were so many berries here. Seasoned foragers would know better than to enter somewhere with only one exit.

And that exit was blocked by a startling array of vampires.

The five of them filled the clearing, shining like sharply cut jewels in richly colored velvets and extravagantly patterned brocades. It almost hurt to look at them, like stepping out of the dark and into the sun. Despite the fact that vampires never got cold, they all wore capes with plush collars hugging their chins.

Bly focused on the one right in front of her. He had a square jaw and thin, smirking lips. His red hair was one shade lighter than the berry juice stains on Bly's fingers.

He tapped the glove she'd abandoned earlier in his leather-clad hands. "I bet you thought that was smart. Leave a bit of blood to send us off course." He lifted her glove to his nose and sniffed. "Just made me hungrier. And angrier. I don't like wasting my time—no matter how much of it I have."

He stepped closer. Bly's heart ricocheted against her ribs. His gaze dropped to the movement of her chest, and his eyes seemed to warm at her discomfort. "She looks like a rabbit," he said over his shoulder.

Some of the other vampires laughed: a short girl with white-blond hair and two twin boys with black hair pulled into matching ponytails. The only one who didn't laugh was the most extravagantly dressed of the lot. He looked like he might be the brother of the vampire holding her glove. His hair was red too, but more coppery, like it had been faded in the sun, and his features were sharper except for the round pout of his mouth. He wore black leather boots that went to his thighs, green velvet pants, and a silky pink shirt that opened to reveal a scarf embroidered with wildflowers. Over all of it was golden cape that brought out the threads of blond in his hair. Bly couldn't imagine putting on such an impractical outfit—even if she were a vampire—and she was someone who admired pretty things. Or rather, she used too. This vampire wasn't even looking at her, though. He eyed a circle of vultures above—his pretty mouth curved downward.

"Did you hear me, Kerrigan?" the vampire in front of her snapped. "We caught a rabbit."

The pretty one, Kerrigan, glanced down, his stare settling on the other vampire. "Funny, Donovan, I thought you preferred drinking from humans."

Donovan, the one in front of Bly, scowled, but Kerrigan went back to admiring the sky above them. He hadn't even acknowledged Bly.

Her attention darted back to Donovan when he bent down and grabbed the bag of berries at her feet. He wrinkled his nose as he held them up. She couldn't stop herself from reaching for them, but he tossed them over his shoulder, and they landed at the feet of Kerrigan, who still stood back at the entrance to the clearing. The others had stepped closer.

Donovan grabbed her still-reaching hand. She tensed but didn't pull away. This was the price—allow them to drink her blood. She agreed to it the moment she stepped into the woods. But her blood was weak in her veins. Osmond had been right. If she let them drink from her, she might never wake up. And with five of them, the odds seemed high that they wouldn't be satisfied with the little blood she had left to give. And then who would save her sister?

Her mind tumbled over itself as she tried to decide on a spell to use, but she couldn't get past the cost of wasting one that she didn't have time to replace. And she couldn't spell five vampires without her throat being ripped out after the first one. When she'd thought through what she'd do if she were ever caught, she'd always imagined a single foe, not a group of them.

She only had one choice—be like the rabbit they thought she was: bite and run.

Her free hand closed around the hilt of the knife she always kept at her waist, and she jerked it out and upward, slicing through the wrist of the vampire. She didn't wait to see the look on his face, though she would have liked to.

She bolted the minute his hand released hers, darting to the left like she'd run straight into the brambles before turning sharply for the door of her cage. She ducked just before the vampire girl grabbed at her, sliding under her arm.

Kerrigan's gleaming boots still hadn't moved from his place by the entrance. Her eyes landed on her bag of berries at his feet. If she made it out of here, she'd have to waste a speed spell to run as fast as she could, and she wouldn't be able to risk coming back for the berries she'd need to buy another spell.

She lunged for them.

"Grab her, Kerrigan!" the girl's voice screeched.

Her fingers grazed the bag as a cold hand wrapped against the scarf at her neck and dragged her upright.

Bly let out a scream that shook her. It sounded like an animal with its leg in a trap, but it also sounded like a release of all the pain she'd gathered in the past year. A few tears leaked out of her eyes, but they weren't from weakness; they were from anger. Hands spun her around, grabbing her wrists in a firm grip. She blinked away her blurry vision, expecting to see Kerrigan, but it wasn't.

Donovan glared down at her.

She stared over her shoulder at Kerrigan, who watched her with his head tilted slightly as if she were an animal he'd never seen before. He hadn't moved an inch, as if he'd never even attempted to stop her. The sack of berries still lay at his feet.

The other vampires were at her back—she could feel them there, as dangerous as knives.

Donovan growled, tightening his grip on her wrists until her tears flowed from pain instead of anger. "You *are* a rabbit," he said. "Bolting instead of accepting your fate. Pathetic. And now your paw's stuck in a trap."

Kerrigan bent down, plucking from the snow the knife she hadn't even realized she'd dropped and holding it in the air, staring at the blade as if admiring the blood streaked along the edge. He met Bly's eyes as he spoke. "I don't know . . . she fights like a wolf. She made you bleed, didn't she?"

If Donovan tightened his grip on her any more she feared her wrists would shatter.

He pushed her back until the thorns scratched against her again, probably to make her feel more trapped and vulnerable. And it worked. The other vampires, except Kerrigan, closed into a semicircle behind the one who held her, and she wasn't sure what was worse: not being able to see them at all or seeing them with their eyes black with hunger.

"Just bite me and be done with it," she spit.

Kerrigan's eyes widened. A small chuckle left his lips.

But Donovan didn't bite. He looked at her stained fingers.

"I want to taste *these* instead." He said it like a statement but looked at her like it was a question.

The ones at his back laughed.

"No," she croaked out. Those weren't the rules. Of course, she'd tried to break the rules first, but that didn't mean they could do it in return.

"Don't be crass," said Kerrigan.

Donovan's expression darkened. "You're one to talk, brother."

Kerrigan grinned as he strode forward, stopping just beside Donovan.

Bly couldn't decide if that was a good thing or a bad thing. Probably bad. Now she had two vampires peering down at her—one looking like he wanted to eat her and the other looking like this was all a delightful game. Then Kerrigan dropped his grin so quickly that Bly jerked back, but he turned the hard expression on his brother. "My playthings come to me willingly. There's a difference." He reached a hand out and pressed it against his brother's chest, pushing him back.

Donovan scowled but didn't protest. He released Bly's wrists.

So Kerrigan was in charge.

Good. He seemed more reasonable. Bly could pay her price and go. Maybe she could even leave with what she came here for in the first place.

She tried to keep her voice steady and icy when she spoke. "Take whatever blood you want. But please let me keep the berries."

Kerrigan's dark stare flitted back to her bag a few feet away. Some of the fruit had burst, staining the bottom and turning the snow around it a violent red that looked like a warning that came too late.

The berries weren't the only things here that were going to bleed.

She swallowed, and multiple pairs of eyes tracked the movement. Not Kerrigan, though. He stared at her face as if he could read her life's story there. She'd almost rather him look at her neck. It made her even more uneasy to think that he was feeding on something else—whatever pain he saw in her.

She took a step back, ignoring the nip of thorns. They all shifted in response, like instinct demanded they get ready to pounce if she was going to bolt again.

But Kerrigan took one long stride and picked up the bag before moving back and holding it out to her.

Her fingers felt too frozen to take it. He only waited a moment before his eyes drifted down to her waist and the tie there. He reached out slowly as if he didn't want to spook her. Long fingers plucked the end of the tie from her skirts, and before she could even register what he was doing, the bag hung against her again, heavy with berries.

This time it was he who stepped back.

"Kerrigan, get on with it," said the girl. "I'm starving."

"We're not drinking from her." Kerrigan didn't look away from Bly as he spoke.

Bly couldn't quite breathe. Surely he was toying with her. A vampire wouldn't let her go without paying. Elise had thought one might, that day in the woods, but Bly hadn't believed her. She still didn't.

"What?" Donovan snarled.

"Look at her. You know as well as I do that there's not a spare drop in her. She'll black out before your teeth break skin." Kerrigan chuckled like they were sharing a laugh at Bly's expense, but the look on his face was hard and uncompromising.

Donovan's eyes flashed with anger.

The girl bared her teeth like she wanted to rip into Kerrigan instead. "I don't think it should be *your* call."

Kerrigan moved in a blur. When he stopped, he had his hand wrapped under the girl's chin. "Watch yourself. I still outrank you."

"Maybe in name. Not in respect," she ground out.

"Jade." One of the twins finally spoke. His voice held a soft warning, but he glared at Kerrigan.

Jade looked like she was going to spit in Kerrigan's eye anyway. "Donovan should be calling the shots and you know it."

Kerrigan dropped his grip on her, and Jade turned to Donovan. "Why did you invite him, again?"

Donovan glared at Bly like she were at fault for whatever weird power play was happening. But none of this was about her. Not even Kerrigan's insistence to let her go—he was clearly doing it to infuriate the others, remind them who was in charge. It made Bly feel better, actually. Vampires still fit firmly in the category of evil—Elise hadn't been right that day. There was no way to know if her sister would still be alive if Bly had chosen berries over mushrooms.

Kerrigan's face shifted to a grin as he leaned back on his heels. The easiness he suddenly exuded seemed calculated. "Anyway," he purred, "I prefer my drinks dressed in something gold. This one definitely doesn't suit me." His eyes flicked back to Bly and away again. Dismissive. Or at least meant to seem that way. But something about every look he gave her seemed deeper than that.

"Let's just get out of here," Donovan said.

"A wonderful plan, brother." Kerrigan turned and strode away.

The other vampires shared a look that seemed like an unspoken question of whether they'd listen, but eventually they trailed behind him, including Donovan, who shrugged and didn't even glance her way as he left, like he'd lost interest altogether.

Kerrigan never looked back. Jade did, though.

She held Bly's stare for so long that it felt like a promise.

When she finally turned and didn't look back again, Bly spun on the heels of her boots and took off.

She moved haphazardly at first, her only thought about putting distance between herself and the vampires, until she stumbled, catching herself on the wet bark of a tree that gave way beneath her fingers. She fell. The faint heat of blood on her knee drew her back to her senses, and she pulled herself to her feet, fishing her compass out of her pocket. It was an old thing, rusted around the edges, but it worked. Emerson had given it to her on her fifteenth birthday. And she'd thought it was a sign that he shared the same dream as her: to run away and let the compass take them to some far-off place that had to be better than here, but then he told her it was so she could always find her way back. At the time, she hadn't wanted a way back; she'd wanted a way forward.

But she was grateful for it now.

She held it up in the dim forest light and started moving in the right direction.

A branch snapped behind her and she spun, finding nothing but tree trunks.

She glanced at her feet. She was being too loud, imagining her own footsteps chasing her.

Cold, delicate hands clasped her upper arms.

Bly's head snapped up.

Jade's mouth stretched into a grin wide enough to show both her upper and lower fangs. "I changed my mind," she whispered, like someone would care and come to Bly's rescue. But there was nothing to rescue Bly from. She'd pay the price this time. She had a feeling that Jade would snap her neck if she fought back.

Bly wanted to nod but didn't trust her head to do what she ordered.

"Wrist?" the vampire asked, raising snow-white brows.

Bly swallowed, and the vampire's eyes darted to her neck, but Bly lifted the sleeve of her shirt, exposing the blue veins beneath the pale white skin of her arm, and the vampire took her wrist so quickly that Bly didn't even feel the prick of her teeth—only the throbbing that came after.

Her vision swam. She hoped the vampire would honor their rules and stop feeding when she passed out because it wouldn't be long.

Bly closed her eyes. All she could do was hope, and she didn't have much to spare, but she didn't have to think about that for long because pretty soon she felt nothing at all.

FOUR

SHE WOKE TO SOMETHING DIGGING INTO her stomach. Her head throbbed as if she were hanging upside down. Blinking to ease away the blurriness in her vision, she made out the ground moving beneath her. *Curses.* They weren't supposed to take her blood and take *her*, too, but Jade seemed like the type who laughed at rules. She'd chased Bly down, after all.

Bly squirmed, hands pushing against a broad, muscled back that didn't feel like it belonged to the girl.

"Put me down," she croaked out.

They stopped. The arms pinning her legs to a hard chest shifted, and then she was sliding down the front of someone.

She half expected a redheaded vampire—maybe the one who'd pretended to be kind had come back to fix his mistake.

Instead, she got a face she knew well: Emerson frowned at her, and somehow he made it feel like he was frowning *down* at her despite the fact that he was barely taller than Bly.

"What are you doing out here?" he asked, right before the same question left Bly's lips.

She hated when he beat her to something. "I could ask you the same."

"You couldn't. Because I'm looking for you, so my reason's tied to yours."

She also hated when he talked like that: logic that sounded like a riddle.

"I'm foraging."

His expression went blank. "You wouldn't." He'd gotten good at showing nothing on his face, but the pain in his eyes wasn't as easy to hide.

She didn't answer. It wasn't a question anyway. She should know better than anyone what a risk it was, and she did know— it just didn't matter.

"Why?" he asked simply.

"It doesn't concern you," she said, moving to step around him, but Emerson caught her arm.

"Don't you know better than to be out here?" His voice broke as a little bit more of his mask slipped.

His words held too much and echoed the questions she'd refused to answer after Elise's death.

She'd never told Emerson why she'd talked Elise into gathering with her in the woods that day. She couldn't. Emerson loved for things to make sense, and risking too much for something so silly wasn't a concept he'd understand. Plus, then she'd be admitting what she felt for him, and he'd hate her even more than he did now. He'd only see the foolish heart that had wanted too much when all he'd ever done was push her to be content with what they had.

But she didn't even have *him* anymore.

Their friendship hadn't been the same since Elise had died. After all, her sister had been his friend too. And Bly had held back the one thing Emerson needed most: a reason—something to force the loss to make sense. They'd never found out why *Emerson's* sister was foraging in the woods the day she died. They didn't even know if it was her first time doing it, and Emerson had spent months after her death wondering. He'd even ask Bly to come up with stories to explain it, but whatever she came up with—his sister earning money to help a sick friend, to run away with a lover, or maybe even to enter the Games—Emerson would just shake his head at it. Because what could make sense of death?

And Elise's death had bought something so frivolous that the truth would be worse than not knowing.

She stared down at his hand, wrapped just above her wrist, inches from that cursed ribbon and above a thin strip of cloth covering where the vampire had bitten. He had his sleeves rolled up because he was always hot, even with snow on the ground, and the hem of his shirt was loose and ripped. That little bit of care for her made her want to lean into him, tell him everything, but that wouldn't be best for him. She needed to push him away a little bit longer.

"I have my reasons," she said. "They don't belong to you."

He dropped her arm as if she'd burned him.

The look on his face made her stomach twist. She took another step and stumbled into a slender pine, barely big enough to catch her, wincing as the bark scraped a layer of skin from her already cut hand.

"You need me to carry you," Emerson said gruffly.

She took another step in answer, and her legs wobbled like branches in a storm. Emerson barely caught her before she went down. He moved like he'd heft her over his shoulder again, but she shook her head. "I'm going to puke if you do that."

He hesitated and then bent, scooping her up behind the knees with one arm and catching her back with the other. She ended up cradled against his broad chest like a child.

She stiffened. This felt too intimate. They'd never been the type of friends to hug or hold hands or share any of those tender types of moments. So now the contact made her cheeks heat.

Emerson, ever stoic, looked straight ahead and started walking, and for a moment she relaxed into the steadiness of his arms around her, which managed not to tremble for quite some time. But even Emerson, whose arms ripped through one of his own shirts several years ago when he first began forging metal, couldn't carry her forever. Even if she sometimes dreamed he would.

Though in her dreams, she always felt lighter.

The longer she stayed in his arms, the more it seemed like stones were collecting in her heart, weighing her down until she was sure he'd drop her and she'd sink through the forest floor and become tangled in the roots of the trees.

"I'm fine to walk now," she said when she felt the first tremble in his arms.

He looked like he'd argue for a minute. But he didn't.

She wasn't sure why that hurt.

He held onto her for moment longer though. "I'm glad you're okay," he said gruffly as he let her go.

They continued in silence with him walking in front of her, just out of arms' reach, but occasionally he'd turn and look back at her with worried eyes.

When they broke through the trees and into the field of mud that surrounded the village, he stopped, and for a second she just watched his broad back as he stared at the ground.

Then he turned. The sadness on his face added one more pebble in her chest, but that was the one that made it too much.

She looked away.

She sensed him still standing there, watching. His solid presence felt like the same question that was always wedged between them.

Not why she was in the forest now—why *they* were there on *that* day.

But there was another reason not to tell the truth.

He'd blame himself if he knew she was out there trying to get him to look her way with something besides friendship in his eyes.

And she couldn't let him carry around that guilt. He'd overthink it, wondering why he didn't see her feelings when he was so good at analyzing things. He'd replay their conversations for moments he could have acted—told her how he felt one way or the other.

Even though it wasn't his fault, she should've just said something instead of concocting some elaborate plan to get him to notice her.

Had she lost her sister because she was afraid of starting one conversation? That was the question that haunted her. She'd thought she was so brave that day, stepping into danger to get what she wanted, but in reality she'd been running away. She'd been a coward.

But what was the point in having that conversation now? It'd only tear wider an already open wound.

Emerson hadn't moved, but he still said nothing, probably too tired to actually voice the question again.

When it had first happened, he'd asked her again and again why they had risked going so far into the forest that day, and every time she didn't tell him the truth, she'd felt it—that little bit of distance widening between them—but she thought it was better than the rip that would happen if she were honest. But little bits add up, and eventually the gap between them had become immeasurable.

Telling him now would fix nothing.

Getting her sister back would, though. It was the one selfish dream she'd managed to keep: bringing back her sister could bring back Emerson too.

She stepped to go by him, pausing for a moment with their shoulders almost touching. "Thanks for carrying me," she said softly. It was all she could give him. The market closed soon, and she needed to make her trade.

She made her way to the many spell booths, stopping at the one almost nobody came to that held the more dangerous spells. Most of the people who came to this shop were entering the Games, selling and trading whatever they had for a chance to win.

And most of those people would end up dead or worse . . . alive with nothing to their name because they'd sold it all here.

Bly had been more careful though. As much as she wanted to,

she didn't enter the Games right after her sister died. Instead, she did what she'd thought Elise would do: took her time and sold as much blood as she could to buy the spells she needed. But she needed one more spell, and it was an expensive one: a branch that would bind a vampire.

An older witch with honey hair that fell in tangles to her waist eyed Bly as she scanned the table. Witches tied spells to objects that held similar magic once upon a time. They used their blood plus human blood—and sometimes vampire blood as well—to put the magic back where it belonged. Only witches could create a spell, but once placed, anyone could use it with the right command. Whisper "health" and eat a spelled apple to heal your cold; murmur "grow" as you buried the right seed in your garden; sing "sleep" as you crushed a dried mushroom into a cup of tea.

Or say "bind" as you stabbed a vampire with a branch from a birch tree.

Bly avoided looking at the dried mushrooms laced with sleeping spells. She knew they wouldn't be enough after hearing terrible stories of unconscious vampires waking up and killing their capturers in previous Games. The length of time someone would stay asleep was too unreliable. People tried them every year, though. They were cheaper and could even be foraged for free if a person was careful enough.

Bly's stomach clenched with nausea.

Her eyes settled on the slender shoots of birch carved to points. One would bind two limbs and buy you twelve hours of safety. She needed at least a dozen: six for the feet and six for arms. Three days of binding to make it from Vagaris to Havenwhile with a vampire in tow. And that would be assuming everything went perfectly. More would've been nice, but she didn't have time to secure a safety net. She had eleven. This was the last thing she needed.

She pointed at the birch. "One of those." She looked up at the witch's skeptical expression before reaching deep into her skirts and pulling out the bag of copper coins that she always kept on her. She dumped them out on the table.

The witch counted them before shoving the coins back. "Not enough."

Bly already knew that. She'd tried to barter with a different witch this morning. She reached for the berries tied to her side and held the bag out as well.

The witch's eyebrows raised in a way that felt promising— that made Bly want to take a deep breath for the first time in a year—but then the witch frowned and tossed the bag onto the table. "Most of them are squished. Useless for spells." To emphasize her point, red bled from the corner of the bag onto the wood of the table. Witches usually loved these berries. People said they put longevity spells in them, but they never had such a thing for sale in the market.

The deep breath Bly had taken a minute ago rushed out of her, and she had to remind herself to keep drawing in air. She wouldn't wilt in front of this witch. She snatched up the bag and her coins. She knew better than to cry or beg. Vampires might not have beating hearts, but witches didn't have them at all.

She stepped away. The vampires' trial for sponsors began

tomorrow, but she still had time until the witches' trial began.

She could sell more blood in the morning and then go back to the woods tomorrow. In the meantime, she'd trade these berries for some extra food to get her strength up. She could eat them herself, but she'd get more food if she sold them. They wouldn't go to waste just because the witches wouldn't take them.

A hand grabbed her forearm.

She spun and faced Emerson. From the look on his face, he'd seen what she'd tried to buy.

"Tell me you're not that foolish," he said.

"I don't know what you're talking about."

Emerson closed his eyes for a second, like he couldn't even stand to look at her. When he opened them again, he shook his head. "Stop lying."

"I've never lied to you."

"Silence is a lie."

Bly bit the inside of her cheek. She agreed. It sure felt like one, but she kept her plan to herself, chose the easier path—or the harder one; she really wasn't sure anymore.

"You shouldn't have followed me."

"It was the only way to get an answer. You won't talk to me anymore. Do your parents know?"

"No. They can't stop me anyway." That wasn't the real reason she hadn't told them. She was worried they wouldn't even try. If she kept it from them, then she didn't have to face that truth.

"You're going to get yourself killed."

"But the prize is worth that risk, isn't it?"

His brow furrowed. It gutted her that he had to think about

it the same way he thought through everything, weighing her life against the chance to bring Elise back. But she knew what his answer would be. No. He'd come to the same conclusion when his sister died, and Bly had asked him if he would enter. Emerson hated the Games. He saw them for what they were: a chance for the vampires and witches to use humans as toys, just like the rest of the year when they used them as bags of blood. And even greater than his morals was the fact that his family needed him and the income he would bring when he started metalworking. His parents wouldn't survive another dead child, and that was the most likely outcome of the Games. But maybe he understood what Bly did—that a dreamer didn't bring any real value to a family in the Gap, and dreaming was all she'd ever been good at. She was expendable.

"Let me play instead of you," he finally said.

His offer made the world spin too fast beneath her.

He was willing to ignore all his careful reasoning and risk his life instead of hers. The realization that he still cared that much for her made her eyes sting.

But there was no way she'd say yes.

He'd die, and she'd have two deaths on her selfish hands— the two people she cared about the most—and even though Emerson barely bothered with her anymore, she couldn't live with herself if he were lost too. Sometimes in the past year, she'd imagine him working in the shack behind his house with his father, heating metal and beating it into something useful, and the thought would warm her like she were standing there, watching like she used to in the only place she ever felt like the winter couldn't touch her. Without him existing, the world would be too cold. Too terrible to endure.

She couldn't let him do it. For him. But for her too.

"No," she said simply and turned from him.

To her surprise, he didn't follow as she moved away and stopped in front of the apple stand.

Ackley nodded at her from behind his overflowing baskets of apples. He wore soft leather clothes that most humans couldn't dream of affording. He was in his fifties with gray in his black hair and a round belly that he sometimes rubbed absently. He didn't talk much. He'd won the witches' prize twenty years ago, though. People said that before his sister died, before the Games, he was the type of person who never stopped telling jokes and laughing. Bly didn't think she'd ever seen him really smile beyond maybe the ghost of one when he looked at the sister whose life he'd won back. Mabel was behind him, sorting apples into bins. Bly tried not to stare at the deep scar on her neck. Being raised from the dead didn't erase everything.

She'd asked Mabel once, when Ackley wasn't there, if she was glad to be back. Mabel had hesitated far too long before shivering and answering yes.

Of course, it was yes. And now she farmed an orchard with her brother in the witches' city. They were together again, *and* they had a better life on top of that.

Ackley cleared his throat. He didn't like people staring too long at his sister. Bly passed her berries to him, and he glanced inside. "Six apples of your choice," he said gruffly.

Bly looked at him in surprise. That was more than a fair trade. It felt like a gift.

He turned away before she could question it.

Bly stared at the apples. Her favorites were the sweet reds, but she picked up a bright green one and turned it over absently in her hands.

"Your sister was always buying those."

Bly jerked her head up. Mabel gave her a sad smile. But Bly hadn't been remembering her sister, who'd used to buy baking apples for her bread. Emerson was the one always eating the too-sour apples out of the bin. Her chest pinched with guilt. Nothing had changed. She was still thinking of him over her own sister.

Her cheeks burned with shame.

Mabel studied her as she placed a few new apples into the bins. Bly had a feeling they knew what her plans were. From their vantage point, it wouldn't be hard to put together if they saw her selling blood every week for the past year and visiting the spell booths.

"She wouldn't want you to do it," Mabel said.

So they did suspect it.

"You said before that you were glad to be back," Bly pointed out, but Mabel had gone silent, her eyes distant as if lost in the morning fog. Her hand squeezed the apple in it so tightly that juice leaked out of the broken skin.

"Mabel?" Bly said.

The woman didn't answer. Ackley turned back around, and a broken look flashed across his face as he hurried over, murmuring in Mabel's ear and gently prying her fingers away from the damaged fruit.

Mabel's eyes cleared.

Bly let out a soft breath. She'd heard that those who'd been resurrected sometimes suffered moments where they seemed to go back—as if their souls weren't quite tethered to their bodies.

But as long as they had someone who loved them to bring them back again, then surely it was okay. It *had* to be okay.

Bly started to say thank you for the apples, but a scuffle down the street drowned out her words. She didn't think too much of it. Plenty of people were hungry enough to steal and suffer the consequences, but she turned her head to glance over her shoulder. The commotion was at the spell booth—the one she'd just visited.

The one where Emerson now stood with the witch's long fingers wrapped tightly around his wrist.

Bly stopped breathing.

Emerson pulled against the witch's grip but got nowhere. The witch had probably used a strength spell on herself, making her stronger than even Emerson. Reaching out, she plucked a white branch of birch away from him and tossed it back on the table. She still didn't release him.

The witch glanced around at the people who had stopped to watch. "It's been a while since I made a real example of someone."

Bly dropped her apple in the mud. A human caught stealing could be punished in any way they saw fit. The guards wouldn't intervene. The witch could kill him, and there would be no punishment.

Bly started to move. Emerson caught her eye and shook his head, but she didn't stop.

The witch's hand hovered over her wares. "What shall it be?" she asked. Grinning, she plucked a sharp black thorn from the table. She struck like a snake, pricking Emerson's arm and letting him go.

The witch began straightening her spelled items with a slight smile on her face like all was right in the world. And for a second, Bly thought it just might be okay—even though Emerson hadn't walked away, even though he wavered on his feet.

She lied to herself until he hit the ground on his knees before slumping backward. Until she slid to the ground beside him.

Until she saw the black veins crawling down his arm.

FIVE

BLY TRIED TO THINK. SHE NEEDED TO BE stronger than she was before. She needed to act, but her mind split between the past and the present. Her chest tightened and her vision blurred. She could practically feel the leaves and sticks under her knees, the soft give of crushed mushrooms, her sister's warm hand in hers. Black vines grew across her vision as if *she* were the one who'd been cursed.

But she wasn't. She was the one who needed to do something.

The hand she felt in hers squeezed back. Elise's had never done that. Emerson groaned, and Bly focused on the sound as her vision started to clear. He wasn't Elise. He wasn't dead . . . yet. Death curses could be instantaneous, or they could set a time limit on the person's life. Emerson was still here.

His dark brown eyes met hers. "I'm fine," he said, his voice surprisingly steady.

"You're not," she croaked, dragging a deep breath into her belly and holding it, making her heart beat even more sporadically. When she let it out, she focused on the witch.

The woman stood once again behind her booth, straightening her collection of spells with the calmness of someone who didn't care one bit about the lives of the people in front of her. Bly's whole body buzzed with the urge to rush forward to that table, grab every death curse on it, and stab every witch she could before they could stop her. She pushed the desire away. Revenge wouldn't help Emerson, and it wouldn't bring back Elise, either—no matter how much she wanted to give the witches a taste of their own ruthlessness.

"How long does he have?" Bly's voice came out strong enough to shock her. She knew better than to ask her to undo it—there was no such spell, or at least so they claimed.

The witch didn't look up.

Bly tried to rise to her feet, but Emerson's grip on her hand tightened.

Don't leave him. Her mind threatened to take her back again to the moment she ran and left her sister's body to the witches.

But this wasn't that.

She pulled free of his grip. Her legs shook so badly she didn't dare take a step.

"I'm talking to you." Her voice was a roar in her ears. Had she really been that loud?

The witch's eyes flicked up at her before she fiddled with an arrangement of leaves on the table.

Bly took a step and another with legs that wanted to fold in and give up. She stumbled and caught herself on the witch's table, shaking the spells the woman had so carefully straightened.

Her lips tightened with annoyance as she finally gave Bly her attention.

Bly swallowed. "How long? A day? A week?"

Please let it be longer.

The witch eyed her wares, and Bly knew that she was dangerously close to being cursed too.

Strong arms closed around Bly's waist and pulled her back from the table.

"I'm fine," Emerson said again. "Let it go." His chest felt firm and solid behind her. She could feel his racing heart, and she wanted to let that comfort her, but she tried to push away instead.

"I don't want to know," he added.

She stilled. How could he not want to know? What if the curse wouldn't strike for twenty years? How could he live each day wondering if it was his last? How could *she*?

Bly wanted to scream her question at the witch again, but Emerson had shifted her against his side. He was walking away, and she was stumbling along beside him, her throat burning with the pain of the past and the future.

"Enjoy your last year together," the witch called behind them.

The words stole the air from Bly's lungs—no, it was Emerson's arm around her, tightening. He'd stopped walking.

She turned to stare up at him. He had her supported against his side, and she squirmed in his iron grip so her arm could go around him as well. He didn't look at her, just took several deep breaths before he started walking again, pulling her along beside him without looking back. Bly turned her head as they went, though.

The witch smiled.

She hadn't thought her heart held more room to hate the witches.

She'd been wrong.

Her eyes watered with frustration as their feet sunk into the muddy streets of home. She wished she had the power to go back and confront the witch, to give her a taste of the pain she'd caused, but there was nothing to be done that wouldn't end with Bly cursed too.

Emerson let go of her just long enough to roll down his sleeves, covering the mark of the curse before pulling her toward his house. It was slightly bigger than some of the other houses in the village because the vampires valued metalwork above all else and paid well for it, but nonetheless, it was made of the same rough wood that stayed stained with rainwater throughout the entire year.

Bly stepped toward the front door, but Emerson pulled her around the side instead.

Of course he wouldn't want to see his mother yet. Emerson's mother was a frail woman who coughed like fog lived in her lungs, and she'd almost certainly be at home. She used to work selling potatoes for the witches in the market, but she'd quit as soon as Emerson was old enough to start working with his father and bringing in a second income that was double hers anyway.

When she saw Emerson's curse . . . she'd almost certainly have a coughing fit. Bly already knew that Emerson would keep this from her for as long as possible. His curse wouldn't impact just him. His parents would lose another child. Just thinking about that made Bly's legs turned to lead. Only Emerson's grip on her kept her going.

Behind Emerson's house stood two small sheds. Emerson pushed her past the largest of the two, the forge where he worked the scraps of metal his father brought home from Vagaris, and he pulled open the door to the woodshed before steering her inside. He kept the door open slightly so that a stream of dim light highlighted his stoic face as he stared at her.

"Are you okay?" he asked.

"I'm not the one with a death curse." Of course she wasn't okay because he wasn't okay.

She couldn't see the marks of the curse on his arm, but she stared anyway. She could feel them as if they were wrapping around her skin instead of his.

"Why did you do it?" she finally asked.

"Because if you're going to play in the Games, then you need the best chance you can get. Everyone knows you need binding spells, and if you were still there bartering this close to the start of it, then you're clearly not ready."

"I was handling it."

"By letting vampires feed on you in the woods?" He reached out and grabbed the sore wrist the vampire girl had fed from. His thumb pressed a little too hard into the wound, and she flinched. "Elise wouldn't want that for you. *I* don't want that for you." The fear in his voice was too much. She hated making him feel that way.

She tried to jerk away, but he held fast.

"Elise doesn't want anything for me because she's *dead*. I'm trying to change that."

He let go of her, and she instantly regretted her words. His touch had been gone from her life for so long that she was desperate for it—even if it hurt.

"I needed to give you a chance," he said.

"All you did was ensure that if I do win, and if Elise comes back home with me, we will both get to watch you die. And then what? I grieve you until I can't take it anymore, and I enter the Games again? For you?"

"You wouldn't dare," he whispered.

"Of course I would." Her own voice was hushed and hesitant. It was what someone did for the people they loved.

"Bly . . ." He took a step toward her, and his hands closed around her upper arms, squeezing gently. "You know that's not what I would want."

She cried then. The tears came hot and familiar like a friend she knew well but hated to see. She sniffled, and his hands tightened their grip on her as if trying to staunch whatever had broken. Emerson wasn't one who liked emotions. Even when he'd silently held her while she cried about Elise's death, she could feel the stiffness in his body, the desire to be anywhere but confronted by her tears. So she made herself stop. He was the one who needed her to be brave. She had no right leaning on him in this moment.

He shook her gently. "Promise you won't try to save me." He drew in a deep breath. "And if you do win, don't let Elise enter the Games to bring me back either. I'd never forgive either of you for risking your life for mine."

Bly didn't want to promise anything at all. If she didn't die trying to bring Elise back, if she by some miracle won, she'd come home and only have months before she replaced one hole in her heart with another.

The thought almost brought her to her knees.

So she didn't answer. Instead, she shook her head. "I doubt I will come home anyway. I still don't have what I need to win, but I have to try. You understand why I have to try, right? I know why you never entered, but I'm not you. I don't care about being their entertainment if they give her back to me."

Emerson dropped her arms. They tingled as the blood rushed back to where he'd been holding her too tightly, but she still missed his grip on her. He'd felt solid and strong and not at all like a boy who would be dead within the year. She resisted the urge to reach out and touch him again. If she was holding him, he wouldn't be able to leave her. The thought wasn't rational, but she had to clamp her hands together just to stop herself.

When she finally focused again, Emerson was holding a fist out in front of her, and she watched in confusion as he unfolded it and revealed what lay in his palm.

A slender shoot of birch gleamed as the light from the door caught it.

She sucked in a breath. "You got one."

"I went for two at the same time. The odds were that she would only see me grab one."

"You knew you'd get caught," Bly accused.

He didn't answer.

"I could've gotten it. I still had time to go back to the woods before I had to leave for the witches' trial."

"And you would've gotten yourself killed."

"So you got yourself killed instead?"

His eyes flashed, and she saw the rage in him that he always kept buried under his practicality. He'd slipped up and become the boy who'd just lost his sister, who wanted to burn their world down regardless of the consequences. She wasn't sure if she was glad to see that side of him again or afraid of the risks he'd continue to take.

Her fingers reached for the small, precious stick in his hand, because despite the cost, she needed it to have a chance of bringing back her sister.

But Emerson's fingers closed back over it. Her hand hovered above his as she glanced up at him.

His eyes bore into her. "Let me go instead," he said.

"I already told you—"

He cut her off. "That was before I had nothing to lose."

"Don't say that. A year's not nothing." Her throat burned as she spoke the words, though. A year wasn't nearly enough. Even if she did win, even if she did get her sister back, she still wouldn't get that last little thing she'd hoped for: a future with Emerson.

"You have a full life, and I only have a year." His voice took on a sense of urgency that surprised Bly. Emerson was nothing if not always stoic. "Please, Bly. Let me do this for you."

She realized with horror that he'd done this on purpose. Emerson didn't make rash decisions. He wouldn't have tried to steal the spells without thinking through all of the possible consequences. He knew it might end with him being cursed, and he knew he could use that to get his way.

But with all his logic, he'd failed to account for one thing. She couldn't live without him any more than she could live without her sister.

He'd tried to be noble, but he'd taken away her one chance at regaining happiness. That was the reality she was facing.

Unless she changed it.

A new idea gripped her by the throat—one that was so foolish and reckless and hope-filled that only she could have come up with it. Just the possibility brought the flush of feeling back into her numb fingers.

"You *should* enter," she said.

Relief flashed across Emerson's face, quickly followed by wariness. He knew her too well, even after their time apart, and she was giving in too easily.

"You need to win the vampires' prize," she said firmly.

Emerson frowned. "We need the witches' prize to bring Elise back . . ." He trailed off as he realized what she meant.

There was exactly one way to void a death curse: become immortal. And for humans, there was exactly one way to become immortal: win the vampire prize. Vampires rarely turned humans—it was against their laws to turn one without the approval of the vampire council. Everyone knew they only changed humans who had been raised with the vampires since they were children, because changing humans who came from the Gap created vampires who were too sympathetic to the humans' plights. The one exception was the Games.

Emerson did need to play, but he needed to win a prize for himself.

"You can't be serious." He spoke with enough venom to make her backstep.

She swallowed. She was asking him to be one of the creatures that killed his sister—she understood better than most how revolting that would be.

"What's the alternative?"

He shrugged. "I die."

"And leave your parents? Your mom will have to go back to work, and you and I both know she won't survive it." Her words were honest but also cruel. The odds of them winning were slim, and she was forcing him to see the pain that lay ahead for his family. "If you're a vampire, you could actually give them a better life."

She saw the sliver of a crack in his resolve, but he still shook his head. "They're evil. I don't want to be like that."

"Maybe some of them aren't."

He frowned.

"Okay . . . most of them probably are, but the ones turned as adults who weren't raised by them seem better. Remember the boy who won the Games from one village over—his parents live in the nicest house there, thanks to him. It didn't make him evil."

"You don't know what he's really like now—just because he doesn't rip his parents' throats out with bloodlust doesn't mean he's good."

Bly bit her lip before blurting, "Elise told me some of them were nice."

Emerson's face went blank. "She wouldn't say that."

"She did. The day she died—she wanted to go foraging near Vagaris because she thought vampires were nicer, but I wanted to go toward Havenwhile." Bly sucked in a breath at the confession. It was the most she'd ever told him about that day—a little piece of her guilt. Maybe her sister had been right. Kerrigan had let Bly go, after all.

Emerson looked broken.

"I don't think they're all the same," Bly said. "Even if the kind ones are rare."

He said nothing.

"And if you're on the inside, maybe there's something you can do to help more humans. You could patrol the woods yourself and protect them. You'd have power."

She saw it again—that old gleam in his eyes when he'd talk about revolution. He could see the good he might do, and he was selfless enough to turn into something he hated if it made sense.

She was surprised when he still shook his head, running a hand across his short hair. "I want to play so you don't have to."

Lifting her chin, she met his stubborn stare with her own. "We enter together, and we'll go after both prizes. We'll capture a vampire to bring Elise back, and we'll capture a witch to save you."

"That's a death wish, and you know it."

She shrugged. She couldn't deny it. Nothing in the rules prevented someone from going for both prizes, but it was also twice as dangerous. Humans were branded on their wrist to mark whatever side they were playing for, and if you chose both, you were twice as valuable to the bounty hunters. They'd kill you and deliver one of your arms to the witches and the other to the vampires and pocket the money before your body turned cold.

The Games were ruthless.

"It's the only way I'll let you play with me."

He hesitated. She could see him thinking through all the odds, calculating whether it would be safer for her to play by herself and go for one prize or play with him and go for both. She wasn't sure what the answer would be.

Finally, he sighed. "Fine. I'm in."

He unfolded his fingers from the shoot of birch and offered it to her like a pledge.

She took it.

✦

Bly left Emerson at his front door with a pained look on his face that twisted her gut. She couldn't imagine the horror of having to tell parents that adored you and relied on you that you only had a year to live unless your desperate gamble in a game where most humans died paid off.

She knew his mom would cry. His dad was stoic like Emerson was, but she had a feeling that this would be a moment that broke that.

Tears rimmed her eyes as she turned away and headed toward her own home. A deep ache of dread filled her stomach, but it wasn't that she feared her own parents' tears when she revealed her choice to gamble her life. Rather, she didn't want to see their dry eyes.

In front of her house, her foot slid into a small puddle that she normally dodged on instinct. She barely noticed the cold seep of water in her boot as she put her hand on the doorknob.

The door creaked as she stepped inside, and she cringed. The sound always felt like a condemnation. *Your wayward daughter is home. The one who never wanted to be here. The only one who's left, who'll never be the dutiful daughter you lost.*

Not that she hadn't tried. About a month after Elise had died, Bly woke up and decided the right thing to do was to try to fill the hole Elise had left in their parents' lives, so she'd asked her father to let her work with him for the day. She should have known by the pained look on his face that it was a bad idea. Why had she expected excitement from him when all she'd ever done in the past was try to avoid it? Of course he knew what she was doing—trying to appease her own guilt. Part of her had hoped that he would take her with him on one of his trips to the vampire city because he often traveled there to work for a week at a time, and Elise had even made the trip with him before. Bly wanted to see for herself if Elise had been telling the truth about some of the vampires in the city not being all that bad. But her father worked in a small shack behind their house most of the time, so on that day, he led Bly out there, but she hated the smell and feel of hides of things that had once been full of life. She didn't like wearing furs even in the dead of winter, and she tried desperately to hide her distaste, but her face had always been too open with her emotions. The few times she'd dared to glance at her father, his expression almost killed her. *You're not Elise*, it said. *You'll never be Elise*. He'd told her at lunch that they were done for the day, but she saw him go back to work afterward. Maybe that should have been enough, but the next morning she'd asked to go with her mother. At least her mom smiled at the idea, and Bly had diligently followed her through the village, dropping off medicine to those who needed it and biting the inside of her cheek to stop the nausea anytime her mom needed to treat a wound or stitch a cut. She'd thought she'd done better, but the next day when she'd asked her mother if she wanted her to come again, her mother had patted her hand and given her the same soft smile with a shake of her head. And Bly saw the soft smile for what it was: a shield. Her mother didn't want her to see the truth in her eyes—regret that Bly was not Elise. Of course, that feeling had been there her whole life, but without Elise there to carry their expectations, it only got worse.

Now Bly tried not to be home until her parents had gone to bed.

But leaving without saying anything would be a coward's move, and Bly had only been a coward once in her life and wouldn't be again.

Her parents didn't look up when she walked in. They sat hunched over plates of steaming potatoes at a table that only had two chairs. There used to be three, but never four, because the table was small, with one side pushed against the wall and only room for one seat on each side. A month after Elise died, the third chair disappeared.

Bly didn't say anything.

She was always taking her food outside to eat anyway. She couldn't even remember the last time she'd sat and eaten with the family before Elise died, but one day her mom caught her staring at the empty space and told her they'd needed to sell the chair for a little extra money that month, and that was that.

It didn't mean anything.

But she stared at the empty side of the table until her mother looked up. She seemed startled to see Bly, like she'd forgotten she still had a daughter. But in her defense, on any other day Bly would have drifted in like a spirit, taken an offering of food from the living, and faded away again.

Bly glanced toward the fireplace where she could see a cooked potato wrapped in a cloth, waiting for her. It was tempting.

"Is something wrong?" Her mother's voice held a trace of worry.

It made her father look up. Both parents stared at her, blinking like they were adjusting to the glare of something too shiny.

She opened and closed her dry mouth several times before speaking. "I just wanted to tell you I'm leaving."

"Oh," her mother said. "Food's by the fire." She turned back to her dinner. "Don't stay out too late," she mumbled like an afterthought—a reflex of what a caring parent should say.

Her father was already bent over his plate again, eating too fast because he always said eating wasn't to be enjoyed, it was just fuel to work.

The only time she'd seen him smile was while taking a bite of one of Elise's apple pies.

Bly had always planned on asking Elise to help her learn to bake, too. In her dreams of living away from here, she was always cooking marvelous things—things meant to be savored.

Her stomach twisted with emptiness.

"No," she said finally. "I'm leaving for the Games."

That got their attention. A fog seemed to clear from her parents' eyes when their heads snapped back up, as if they were seeing her for the first time in over a year. Seeing her as a daughter. As something to lose.

It felt terrible and wonderful all at once.

Silence stretched between them until the moment became unbearable.

"What?" Her mother finally spoke, her expression a weird mix of confusion and understanding.

"To bring back Elise," Bly said softly, as if there could be any other reason.

"You won't last a day." Her father shook his head and turned back to his plate for another bite, dismissing her as he had every other time she'd announced she'd do something just a little bit wild. Because she never actually did the things—just dreamed them.

Her mother still looked at her, perhaps sensing that this time was different.

"No," her mother said. "You wouldn't."

Those words stung—not that she shouldn't or couldn't, that she wouldn't do something like that. She wouldn't be brave enough or strong enough to follow through.

"It's my fault she's dead," Bly said.

Her mother said nothing.

Her father looked back up again.

But he said nothing.

Their silence ate at her until she felt like half a person. Half a daughter.

"You dying won't bring her back," her mother said softly.

"I'm not planning to die." She wished her voice held more conviction.

Her father snorted. "Grow up. Believing something doesn't make it true. Dreams don't make you invincible. Would've thought you'd learned that by now."

She flinched.

Her mother's eyes said she agreed even if she wasn't cruel enough to say it.

"You're better off just forgetting," her father went on. "Live your life. Let us live ours."

His last words held too much—a plea or maybe an order. *Leave us alone.*

They didn't want her dead, but they wanted her to move on. Marry Emerson. They'd mentioned the idea to her more than once since Elise had died—as if she were a burden he could take from them.

"What does Emerson say?" her mother asked, as if she could sense Bly thinking about him.

Her parents had no idea that they weren't as close anymore. She had no reason to tell them, but the question annoyed her regardless. She didn't need Emerson to weigh in on her choices, even if he wanted to.

"He's coming with me."

Her mother gasped.

Her father's fork hit the table. "I thought he was smarter than you."

Bly didn't answer. She wasn't going to admit that he *was* smarter than that—that the only reason he'd agreed to it was because her decisions had made him uncharacteristically reckless, and now he had no choice but to take the same gambles as her.

Instead, she said, "He believes we can win."

Her father shook his head.

Her mother looked grim.

"Please just wish me luck. You can't talk me out of it," Bly said, even though they hadn't really tried. Her father had made it clear that he thought her a fool, but he hadn't asked her not to go.

Her mother rose from the table and took Bly's hand, and she imagined her mother asking her to stay, telling her that she couldn't lose another daughter, but instead she pulled Bly into an impossibly tight hug. The kind of hug you gave someone you weren't going to see again.

Bly bit her lip to keep from crying.

Her father was eating again.

He didn't look up as she fetched her meal and left until she could creep back home to sleep for one more night in the cold silence that should've been her home.

SIX

BLY HAD ONCE DREAMED OF STEPPING into the woods with Emerson, but not like this. She had always imagined she'd be holding his hand when they left, not standing several steps away with cold night air between them. She'd thought they'd be focused on the life before them, not the death both behind and in front of them.

Emerson stared straight ahead as he took the first few steps without her before pausing and turning around. "I can still enter alone and go for the witches' prize." He said it halfheartedly. He knew she wasn't someone who changed her mind.

She shook her head and he kept walking.

She followed and didn't look back. Without Elise stoking the fire in their kitchen, it was even less of a home than before. She swore if she got Elise back, she'd find a way to be happy there. Make her dreams more realistic. Maybe she could find something to do that she liked just a little. A job selling oranges in the market. It would be close enough to her dream of having her own orange tree. And maybe one day Emerson would look her way and dream about her . . .

She looked at Emerson ahead.

It was going to be a long walk.

The vampires would open their gates for potential players at dusk with their trial beginning at midnight, so Bly and Emerson had left while it was still dark out. That would give them just enough time to walk there, but only if they used speed spells for the second leg of the journey. Bly had already lit the dark around them with two glowing orbs the size of her fist that floated around her head and drifted after her like the fireflies they were made from. And they'd certainly need an energy spell before the trial after walking for twenty hours without rest. It made her chest squeeze in panic at the thought of using so much before the Games even began, but what else could she do? They needed either a vampire or a witch sponsor to have the best shot at winning. Even though people didn't need a sponsor to enter, it was rare to win the prize without one. A sponsor provided guidance, but more importantly, they provided money, spells, food, and other supplies that humans never had enough of when they entered. And *most* importantly: protection against the bounty hunters. Vampires and witches couldn't harm each other in the Games, but human players were fair prey.

So they had to try. Especially when Bly was already burning through spells.

They weren't the only ones. The woods were busy. Bly rarely saw anyone when she went foraging, but now the woods flickered with the tiny glowing dots of others who'd cast their spells, turning everyone into weaving shadows, all of them with the same destination. Once in a while, they'd get close enough to catch someone's eye, and they'd nod, acknowledging whatever desperation had pushed the other to walk toward a city of vampires, but there were no waves or kind words between them. Whatever desperation bound them, it would also make them turn on each other the second it became necessary.

They all knew it.

They'd heard the stories: players who'd kill another and steal their captive to claim the prize as their own; teammates turning on one another so they didn't have to share; and of course, the bounty hunters who played against their own from the beginning.

Bly stared at Emerson's broad back. Despite whatever tension existed between them, she knew he'd never betray her.

Emerson hesitated when they reached the first of the berry bushes, and so did Bly. His shoulders lifted slightly, as if he were stealing himself against the past, and then he stepped in, pulling back a stray branch so that Bly could follow more easily. She shuddered at her own memory of being caged in them, surrounded by hungry vampires, and now she was about to walk into their *home*. But being afraid of a memory, however recent, made her weak, and the weak didn't survive the Games. They certainly didn't win.

"Do you need a break?" They were the first words Emerson had spoken since they entered the woods. He glanced at the bloodred berries around him, and his eyes flicked to where the sleeve of her coat hid the fresh scabs on her wrist. Understanding flickered in his eyes, but Bly stepped into the maze of thorny branches before he could say anything else.

His hand brushed her sleeve as she moved past him, and she froze like he was holding onto her even though his touch had been brief.

"Did you eat before we left?" he asked softly. "We'll move faster if we keep our strength up."

The suggestion was practical, but there was care behind it. She loved that about him—he'd hide his worry for people behind his logic. She saw through it though. She dropped the strap of her bag off her back as Emerson reached out and plucked a berry from the thorns.

"We should save the food we brought," he said.

Bly watched as Emerson collected a handful of berries. He paused when he turned back to her, taking in her own empty hands before holding out his full ones. Reluctantly, she pulled off her gloves before he gave them to her. The berries felt chilly against her skin. Staring at the handful of red, she tried not to think of redheaded vampires, but that felt impossible, so she focused on the one who returned her berries. Perhaps she had been wrong. Perhaps vampires could be kind without reason.

She shook her head. Better to not think like that—even if she'd tried to convince Emerson that it was true, she didn't need to drop her guard with them.

She glanced up just long enough to catch Emerson studying her. He didn't bother trying to hide it.

Dropping her head, she picked up a berry and plopped it in her mouth, trying not to gag on the sharp sweetness that broke against her tongue.

She ate them all.

Emerson said nothing.

He said almost nothing for the entire walk. All she got were basic questions: Did she need a break? Was she hungry? Was she too hot or too cold? She was grateful for whatever concern he showed for her, but she longed for the easy conversations they once had.

The first part of the journey seemed to take forever. An impossibly long day in a year of long days. But on the second leg, the speed spells were everything she'd hoped they'd be, and Bly worried she'd become addicted to the way the magic made her limbs feel weightless, how it made the forest a blur of color, and the refreshingly cold bite of the air against her flushed face. She'd always enjoyed running, but the magic made it exquisite. It also made her realize just how slow she really was compared to a vampire.

She was almost disappointed when Vagaris loomed before them.

The forest didn't yield to the vampire city. It grew right up to the edge of the stone walls that surrounded it. The wall had to be at least three people high. Moss hugged the stone so that it was more green than gray. Oaks grew against it—the branches draping over the top as if trying to drag the wall into the forest. Sections of the bottom had cracked around the roots that refused to be kept out, making the whole thing look as if it were on the verge of collapse.

"This way," Emerson said.

They walked along the green wall until they reached the gate that led inside. They weren't the only ones to pause in front of the daunting black iron bars. Normally they'd be closed—those that worked in Vagaris or Havenwhile were given bracelets made of metal for the vampires and wood for the witches and stamped with magic, leaving a glowing seal that couldn't be replicated, that would let in those who worked inside. Now they were swung open to welcome the players, but the sharp sword-like tips that fanned out in pointed arches at the top of each gate still seemed to scream at you to stay away unless you were ready to bleed. The threat rooted Bly for a moment, and she thought she might cling against the outside wall forever, like one of the trees. She'd never intended to compete for a vampire sponsor. She knew little about what the vampire trial *or* the witch trial would entail—former players rarely talked about the Games, especially since those who talked too much tended to disappear. But she knew the witches valued an understanding of their spells. She'd prepared for that. Vampires valued brute strength. She was *not* prepared for that.

The feeling that she would certainly bleed before the night was done sent a quiver down her spine.

Warmth encased her cold hand, startling her. Emerson squeezed her fingers. She glanced at him, but he wasn't looking at her. He was staring ahead, but she just needed his touch—the reminder that she wasn't alone.

He'd never been one for comforting words, but there were other ways to be there for someone. Not long before Elise died, she and Bly had visited Emerson in his forge. They'd both liked watching him work, creating something beautiful and deadly with heat and will. Elise had called it magic once, because she always saw magic in the ordinary. Bly had agreed. But what she'd loved the most was holding the finished products in her hands and imagining stories that were just as fanciful as the ones she'd made up when Emerson was only carving wooden blades.

On that day, Bly had picked up a long, slender sword, holding it with both hands in front of her. She'd said something silly about how no foe could stand in her way with such a noble weapon . . . or at least no tree branch. Emerson had looked up from his labor, face lit by the glow of the fire, and smiled, wide and quick like he used to. He didn't laugh, but even his smiles had become so rare in the years since his sister had passed that it had made Bly fumble the sword in her hands. On instinct, she'd reached out to try to keep from dropping it, and the sharp edge caught her finger, slicing it almost to the bone.

Elise had run for their mother while Bly sunk down to the dirt floor, blood pooling through the hand that cradled her finger. Her vision had blurred, and the only thing she could feel was the throbbing pain until Emerson had knelt beside her and placed a hand on her shoulder, squeezing hard enough to give her something to focus on besides the pain.

Elise had returned without their mother, who was gone on a house call, but she'd knelt in front of Bly and pulled her bleeding hand into her lap. She'd swallowed when she looked at it. "All the spells are with Mother," she said, and then she'd pulled out a thread and needle. Only Emerson's grip on her shoulder kept Bly from moving away. But Elise's fingers shook as she tried to thread the needle—until Emerson had shifted until he could lay a hand on her knee. Elise had looked up at him, and Bly saw the change in her eyes, as if Emerson's touch had forged steel in her. She threaded the needle and stitched Bly back together without another quiver. Emerson had held them both together.

Sometimes all you needed was the right touch to be brave.

So she took the first steps that led them inside.

The same coldness that haunted the human villages seemed to cling to Vagaris, but where the Gap's inhabitants had constant mud dampening their toes, bare ground didn't exist here. Everything was stone. Huge gray slabs with dark green moss growing in between the crevices made up the walkway beneath their feet, and ahead of them lay a city built with black and gray.

Stones made up the walls of every house they passed; the shades varied from the pale gray of morning sky to the deep gray of an almost black cloud. The only pops of color were the moss that clung to everything and the shutters of each house painted in berry reds and purples.

And the vampires themselves. Everyone knew vampires loved fashion. Their clothes were always frivolous and colorful, as if they owned all the brightness that existed in the world. They moved against their dreary city like flowers scattered in a storm, and some gathered on the sides of the street, their eyes tracking the entering humans with a sharpness that made Bly's pulse skitter.

But there were also vampire guards lining the street, dressed in red and holding unsheathed swords at their sides. She shuddered at the thought of why they needed the guards between them and the rest of the vampires.

Not to mention that the guards' eyes seemed to track them with the same hunger.

Finally, they arrived at a towering set of wooden doors built into the walls of a fortress that curved subtly to circle the lake at its center. Both Havenwhile and Vagaris were built around water. Towers rose from the fortress, each one a different height and design. Some were spirals of stones that ended in spiky crowns and others were so haphazard that it seemed like any rock at hand had been patched into them. Some were even built of delicate pebbles that wound in intricate designs with carefully carved gargoyles guarding the top. The inconsistency made the whole thing look like a mouth of jagged teeth biting at the sky.

It seemed very much like a vampire to change something to fit their mood every other second.

Unpredictable creatures.

Part of her liked it, though; perhaps each tower held its own unique adventure. She tried to shake her imagination. This was not the time for it, nor the place.

She glanced at Emerson's grim face, taking it all in. He liked order and sense. He'd been here many times for his work, but he'd probably never looked at it through the eyes of someone who might live here. He had to be thinking about it.

But she didn't dare bring it up. If she gave voice to his worries, it opened the door for him to back out.

She couldn't let him do that.

More people arrived behind them, pushing them closer to the door. Minutes ticked by, and it began to feel as if they were sheep in a pen. She shuffled her feet. She wasn't the only one who was fidgety. An uneasiness had begun to spread through the other gathered humans.

Vampires along the edges of the crowd shifted as if they could smell the stirring fear. Some of the guards tightened their grips on their swords, and Bly wondered if there'd ever been a massacre *before* the Games even started, because it felt like a possibility. But surely she would've heard of that.

Just when she thought they might all die right there, the wooden doors burst open and a sea of vampires dressed in gold poured out. They wove in with the humans, grabbing them and twisting them, before pulling them away into the fortress. The guards did nothing, so Bly tried to temper the fear in her. Clearly this was part of the process. Regardless, she was grateful for Emerson's hand still around hers. His hold shifted, his hand sliding up to circle her wrist, making it harder for them to get jostled apart.

Long fingers closed around her other wrist.

"I want this one," a deep and sultry voice said.

Bly spun awkwardly, still anchored to Emerson as a vampire with light brown skin and black hair that swung to her waist tried to pull her away. The girl had bright red lips, and her eyes were wide and intent as she stared at Bly. "Look at these cheekbones. I could cut myself on them." The vampire turned to another just behind her, a boy with lips painted the same shade and the same dark hair and brown skin.

The boy sighed. "She just looks hungry." The girl gave him a pout, and he seemed to soften. "But you're right. She's interesting. Her giant round eyes remind me of you."

The girl laughed. "She's gorgeous then. And look at this—she comes with someone who's terribly handsome as well."

Emerson's grip tightened, and Bly glanced at him. His face gave nothing away, but she could practically feel the tension rolling off him.

People around them were still getting whisked into the fortress by the gold-clad vampires. It seemed to be the only way forward.

"Time to go," the vampire girl said. She tugged at Bly's arm, but Emerson didn't let her move an inch.

The girl frowned.

"They're scared," the boy said to the girl before turning to them. "It's our job to clean you up for the party tonight. Think of us as your guides . . . and protectors." He flashed a fanged smile and looked them up and down. "I do think we should get started, though."

The vampire girl pulled Bly's arm again. She probably could've ripped Bly right from Emerson's grip, but she just applied pressure and waited.

Bly took a step and then another, pulling Emerson behind her like a weight until they were inside.

The same intimidating stone as outside made up every surface, but inside, golden sconces broke up the stone walls. Each one was slightly different in design, just like the towers outside, and Bly wondered if it was a product of immortality. You probably wanted something new to see at every corner or you'd be endlessly bored.

Doors lined the hallway as well, each one made of dark

stained oak. They stopped at one that seemed like any other and entered a small room where racks of clothes in dark red and purple shades lined the walls. In the center of the ceiling dangled a bright orb that glowed like a sun trapped behind frosted glass, undoubtedly powered by a witch's spell. Despite hating one another, the two sides traded with each other just as often as they traded with humans—just not for blood.

The girl dropped Bly's arm and twisted so her overflowing gold skirt shimmered in the light. She grinned at Bly watching her.

The boy rolled his eyes. "This is my sister, Seraphine, and I'm Sebastian."

"Please take your clothes off," Seraphine said.

"What?" Bly took a small step back.

"No thanks," Emerson said gruffly.

Sebastian sighed. It seemed like he was the kind of boy who sighed quite a lot. "What she means is that we need to get you changed for the ball."

"Umm." Bly glanced at Emerson, who was decidedly not looking at her. "At the same time?"

"Surely you've seen each other naked before?" Seraphine laughed. "And we've seen so many naked people that it's nothing to us." She shrugged.

Bly shook her head.

"You're not lovers?" Seraphine's eyes widened as her gaze raked over Bly and then Emerson. "Whyever not?"

Bly actually glanced at Emerson as if she were waiting for him to answer before flushing and looking at her toes.

When she looked back up, Sebastian winked at her. "Don't pry," he said to his sister. To Bly he said, "We'll do you separately." He strode to the back of the room and grabbed a golden curtain hanging against the wall and yanked it, splitting the room in two until he reached the point where Emerson still gripped Bly's arm.

He cleared his throat, and when Emerson still didn't move, he said, "You've got to let go of her unless you're trying to let her know that you *do* want to see her naked?"

Emerson blinked and then he let go of Bly so fast that she was a little bit offended. The curtain snapped shut.

Seraphine pulled her to the racks of clothes, running her fingers through them as she glanced back at Bly periodically. "Hmm . . . you'd look lovely in blood red."

Bly couldn't hide her cringe.

Seraphine raised an eyebrow. "Maybe a nice plum purple then."

"I need to keep my clothes," Bly said. She kept her hands still even though her instinct was to touch the spells in her skirts.

Seraphine saw through her anyway. "You are not allowed to keep any spells or weapons while you're here," she droned before flashing a smile. "But don't worry, you'll get them back. And I just like making people lovelier." She hummed to herself as she turned back to the clothes, flipping through them with a new determination. She pulled out a purple that was so dark that the folds of the dress seemed to hold the midnight sky. Seraphine thrust the dress into her arms. "That'll do perfectly." She stood, waiting, and then waved a hand. "Go on then." When Bly didn't move, Seraphine huffed. "You're awfully modest for someone who wants to be a vampire." She turned her back on Bly as she said the words.

Bly didn't correct her. Emerson's death marks were hidden under his clothes, and if he was too shy to change in front of Bly, she doubted he'd disrobe without making Sebastian turn around first. Nobody needed to know their motives.

The dress weighed down her arms, the material heavy but smooth and cool to the touch. It wasn't the sky-blue dress that she'd longed for in a different lifetime, but she warmed at the thought of putting it on, of being beautiful. And then she hated herself.

She wasn't here to be pretty. She was here to be fierce.

She yanked off her own clothes and pulled on the dress, trying not to think about the way it felt against her skin.

"I think you may need my help buttoning the back," Seraphine said.

"Okay," Bly said.

Seraphine had her buttoned up in seconds.

"Perfect!" She clapped her hands and spun Bly around to the thing she'd been avoiding: a tall oval mirror in the corner of the room.

Bly tried to keep her eyes unfocused, but she couldn't stop herself from looking. The top of the dress clung to her torso with sleeves that hung off her shoulders and pooled around her upper arms like spilled ink frozen in time. At her waist, the material fanned out, cascading to her knees where the purple skirt stopped, revealing folds of black lace in a leafy pattern.

"The lower half of the skirt rips off if you want it too," Seraphine said.

"I like it," Bly said. She didn't plan on baring too much skin.

Seraphine's hands reached into Bly's hair, pulling out the pins that held it in a loose bun at the nape of her neck and then restyling it into a high bun with loose tendrils of hair that looked like vines breaking free. Somehow the simple change accented the shape of Bly's face. She felt pretty. And guilty, again, but this was what she needed to do. If this was the part she had to play, then she would. It wasn't about her. She lifted her chin, noticing for the first time the bareness of her chest and neck.

"Well?" Seraphine asked. Her voice suggested she awaited Bly's praise.

Former Bly would have been gushing and twirling in the skirt and soaking it all in. This Bly touched her collarbone. "Maybe a scarf?"

"You'll attract more attention without it." That was probably their true purpose in dressing them—making them look appetizing, like pigs on a platter. She shouldn't mistake Seraphine's pleasant personality for anything other than a performance.

"That's exactly why I want the scarf."

Seraphine's voice dropped to a whisper, like they were plotting together. "You're here for a sponsor, right? This will help. You're pretty. You have a particularly long and lovely little neck, and if you let the right person take a few sips tonight, then it won't matter how you do in the trial. They'll pick you just for the chance to stay close to you in the game . . . to have a few more sips."

Bly watched in the mirror as her neck bobbed with a swallow. Maybe the vampire was right. Bly touched the tender wound at her wrist. It hadn't been that bad—she'd barely felt it before she blacked out, but if she didn't black out, would she be able to stand it? She hated seeing her blood leave her body when she sold it in the market. "I didn't know . . . I thought it was just the trial. I didn't know you have to feed someone."

"Oh, you don't have to," Seraphine said. "Some vampires choose the best team from the trial because they really want a chance to hurt the witches and win their own prize, but others just want a little bit of fun and free blood from a pretty neck."

She winked, and Bly fought the urge to cover her neck with her hands.

"Whatever you decide, my job tonight is to just make sure nobody goes too far."

"Too far . . . ," Bly echoed.

She hadn't truly considered the danger *before* the Games. The fact that this was more dangerous than wandering into the vampires' forest. The only thing protecting her here from a whole fortress full of fangs was a girl who liked to twirl around in her golden dress and had sharp teeth herself.

"Nothing to worry about," Seraphine said lightly.

"Are you ready yet?" Sebastian called from the other side.

Seraphine gave Bly one more up and down assessment. "More than ready."

The curtain pulled back, and Bly turned, still fighting the urge to cover her naked chest.

Emerson wore black breeches that looked an awful lot like

the ones he arrived in, but a new crimson shirt buttoned tightly across his broad chest. The top was open to reveal more skin than Bly was used to seeing. She finally glanced at his face, but he was looking at her practically naked chest too.

"I don't like this," he said gruffly.

She didn't know what exactly he meant, his outfit or hers, but she imagined he was talking about everything.

"Time to party," Seraphine said with over-the-top brightness.

Sebastian ushered them out the door, and they continued down the hallway until it led them into the biggest room Bly had ever seen.

The space felt both alive and cold at the same time, which seemed fitting. Large slabs of black stone formed the walls and ceiling and floor, but the walls were broken up by huge tapestries. Most of them showed scenes of battle: vampires latched onto the throats of blue-eyed witches as they stood on bodies strewn across the forest floor. But a particularly beautiful one showed a deep blue pool shimmering with threads of gold and silver. From the water rose a naked woman, her light brown skin shining with droplets, her black hair cascading tangled and wet down her naked front, her cupped hands brimming with water lifting to her mouth, her eyes the dark gray of a vampire. The vampires' lore claimed that *they* had been the first people to drink from the Hallow Pool and that was why they possessed raw and brute power. As more and more people partook of the water, the magic diluted and those people became the witches, and eventually the magic ran dry, leaving the rest of them human.

"What do you think?" Seraphine said.

Bly could only nod as she took the rest in—whether their lore was right or not, the vampires lived like they deserved to rule.

Chandeliers hung from every inch of the high ceilings, each one a gold tangle of vines that drooped down to hold orbs made of purple or red glass that glowed with soft lights, giving everything in the room a bluish blood tint.

The room itself was a maze of more golden berry bush statues, as if a section of the forest had been planted here and gilded. Bly stepped closer to one and inspected a jagged metal leaf and the shining purple and red jewels that hung in place of the berries. Deep within the golden vines were plates piled with food that looked different from anything Bly had ever seen back in the village.

As she stared, a human girl came up beside her. "Oh," the girl breathed, "these look amazing." She reached past Bly, plucking up a tiny golden cake topped with a creamy white frosting dotted with specks of berry red. "Ouch," she said as she pulled her hand back. She held the cake, but a thin red line of blood slid down the side of her hand.

Bly inspected the bushes again. The leaves were sharp, and golden thorns adorned each of the vines as well. And none of the platters of food were easily reached.

A trap.

Just like the bushes in the woods were.

She turned back to the girl, who was lifting the last bite of her miniature cake to her mouth just as a vampire appeared at her side. This vampire wasn't dressed in gold. He wore the same bright red as the line of blood on the girl's hand and on his head

sat a golden diadem shaped like a branch with a cluster of berries in the center. He was stunning to behold, with white-blond
hair and the type of perfectly sculpted face that seemed made to
be under the sun, not shadowed in the dim light. He took the
human girl's hand while her mouth was still full and turned it
over, inspecting the line of blood. "I can help you with that," he
whispered seductively.

When he looked up from the girl's open palm and caught Bly
staring, his lips curled. "Don't worry, dear. I'll come back for you
later." He winked at Bly as he pulled the wide-eyed girl away.

Bly spun to find to Seraphine and Sebastian still watching
them. "What's he going to do to her?"

"Heal her if she'll give him a taste," Sebastian said.

"A fair trade," Seraphine added.

It didn't feel fair at all. *We'll hurt you and then you can pay a
price for us to fix it.*

Bly glanced at Emerson's bleak face.

Sebastian noticed their unease, but Seraphine didn't. "And
look at you, already catching someone's eye," she said. "That
was Prince Benedict." She lowered her voice. "He doesn't usually play. He just likes the pregame fun. But you never know."
She cleared her throat. "Let me give you the lay of the land."
She waved a dramatic hand toward a balcony that hung over
the entire room. "Our kings and queens watch from above. You
are not welcome there. You'll be mingling with the princes and
princesses and royal children who are dressed in red and the
rest of the nobles who wear purple. Obviously a higher-ranking
sponsor is an advantage."

Bly nodded. She knew how vampire power worked. It was different than the witches, who passed power down to their children. Vampires had no children except those created with blood. The queens and kings were those who had drunk from the Hallow Pool. The royal children were those who had been turned by the queens and kings, and the nobles were those turned by the royal children. The further a vampire was removed from the original vampires, the weaker their power.

Bly glanced back up at the balcony. Behind the stone railing, total darkness reigned. All she could make out was the occasional flash of red clothing among the shadows. She had hoped to see the ruling queens. She'd always liked that bit of vampire history, whether it was true or not. The story said that the vampire royalty used to fight constantly to see which of them would rule, but the result was too many original vampires being killed, leaving them weaker and weaker with each death. So they held a tournament where they'd duel until first blood. Two queens made it to the final battle, but they loved each other and refused to draw blood. Instead they clasped hands in the middle of the arena and pledged to rule together with the other royals as their council.

Vampires were at least capable of love—if the story was true. She thought of reminding Emerson of it, but his expression said all he'd hear in the story was the blood and not the love that stopped its shedding.

She turned back to Seraphine and Sebastian instead. "Are you royalty or nobles?" If they were, then maybe Bly could just convince one of them to be their sponsor.

"We're but lowly city folk," Sebastian said, a hint of bitterness in his voice.

Seraphine bumped her shoulder into his.

"So you got forced to babysit the humans?" Emerson asked.

"We volunteered," Seraphine said brightly. "They always look for newly made vampires to watch out for the guests because they're less . . . cranky, and we only got turned a year ago."

"You volunteered us," Sebastian said to her pointedly.

"I wanted to come to the party." Seraphine glanced around like it was the most beautiful place in the world. "Can you blame me?"

Sebastian had a sour look on his face, but he said nothing.

"So you wouldn't be sponsoring?" Bly asked.

"Oh no," Seraphine said. "They reserve that for higher-ranking vampires than us, but we'll be keeping an eye on you, and if you win, we'll get a little cash bonus for picking the winning team. We do love our gambling." Her fangs flashed.

Emerson shook his head.

"We'll give you space to work the room, of course," Seraphine added with a wink at Bly before turning and winding away.

"I don't like her," Emerson grumbled as soon as they were out of sight.

"She's nice," Bly said, trying to push aside her own doubts as to what motives lay behind that kindness.

"She's a vampire."

Bly didn't answer. They needed to start looking for the good in them. Emerson had to become one, after all.

"Let's find somewhere less crowded," Emerson said. He

turned down one of the paths that wound through the golden brush, and Bly drifted behind him, trying not to let the needle-sharp leaves snag her dress or skin.

Eventually they made it to the center, where a large circle of clear space surrounded the centerpiece of the room.

Bly almost gagged. The golden fountain in front of them was somehow both beautiful *and* horrible. At the center was a lifelike woman cast in gold with her arms bent at the elbows and palms lifted to the ceiling as if in worship, but at each wrist was the mouth of another figure, and from her wrists a thick red liquid poured past golden lips and into a pool below.

Vampires stopped and filled stemmed glasses from the constant flow of red.

"I hate this," Emerson said. He glanced back to the tangle of vines they'd come from and winced. At least here they weren't in constant threat of cutting themselves.

"Let's just focus on us," Bly said, turning to face him.

They stared at each other, drawing painful awareness to the fact that they didn't talk anymore. The days of easy conversation between them were long gone. She searched the silence for something to say and found nothing. They couldn't talk about Elise. They couldn't talk about home. They couldn't talk about anything at all without picking at wounds they didn't want to make bleed, especially not here.

The only safe topic was strategy.

"Seraphine said that you don't have to do well in the trial to get a sponsor."

Emerson's eyebrows drew together.

"You can let one feed on you before they start, and then just agree to let them drink from you while you play in the game, which isn't that long when you think about it." She paused, noting the way his expression had tightened even more. She almost didn't want to say the next part, but she had to. It was her fault he had death in his veins. She had to offer it. "I'm used to giving blood."

"Absolutely not." Emerson looked sick. "And that's not the same as . . . letting one bite your skin."

"It wasn't that bad." Bly glanced down at her wrist.

"You were unconscious."

"I'd be in control."

"I'll walk out of here right now."

"Then go. I'll stay here and win the vampires' prize out of spite."

His jaw twitched as he ground his teeth.

In the past, she listened to him—that had been their dynamic. She was always taking one step too far into the woods, and he was always reminding her that it wasn't safe. But he'd left her alone this past year, and although she didn't blame him for that, she'd become untethered. She had to stay that way if she wanted to win.

This time, *he* listened to *her*. He didn't walk away.

She liked that change.

But she also had to admit she didn't *really* want to let one feed off her.

Emerson's eyes narrowed behind her. "It looks like you've caught someone's else's attention," he grumbled.

As soon as he said the words, she could feel it—a stare on the back of her neck. She didn't turn around for a long moment until it became almost unbearable, as if it weren't just a stare but the scrape of fangs against skin. Her stomach turned.

Ever so slowly, Bly turned her head to glance over her shoulder—and then froze.

Emerson's voice grew soft. "Was he the one that bit you?"

The vampire who watched her wore sky-blue breaches and a matching shirt that billowed in the sleeves and cinched at the wrists. A silky white vest with gold buttons broke up the color like a single cloud on a rare sunny day. He was one of the only vampires not dressed in rich reds and purples. As if he wanted to be the single sliver of brightness. He stood out. And something told Bly that was exactly what he wanted, given what he wore yesterday in the forest. She finally met his eyes. It was the copper-haired pretty one—Kerrigan. Of all the vampires that could've been staring at her, this one seemed like the best choice; at least he'd already refused to eat her once. Of course, that didn't mean she could trust him, but at least it gave her better odds of surviving whatever was going on in his head. He had to want something from her to be watching her so intensely.

A ring of gold crowned his head. A prince, even if he didn't wear red.

She searched his face for some type of emotion—hunger or interest or recognition—but found nothing. Maybe she was only a flicker in his memory that he was trying to figure out. Vampires probably didn't go out of their way to remember humans, even the ones they'd seen just a day before.

She turned back around to Emerson. He glanced at her face and made a sound that was half rumble and half sigh. "I'll kill him."

"Hush." Bly glanced around them. Everyone knew vampires had superior hearing, but who knew how good it actually was?

"I don't care," Emerson said, reading her mind.

"It wasn't him," Bly hissed.

"Sure looks like it was." Emerson stared beyond her shoulder where Bly was certain that Kerrigan's eyes were still on her. She could still feel that prickling on her neck. She reached a hand and rubbed the skin there as if she could brush away his interest.

"Stop that." Emerson's hand closed around her wrist and pulled her fingers from her back down to her side. "Touching your neck like that isn't helping anything. *More* vampires are staring."

"Don't we want that?"

"We want to work with someone who will help us win. Not someone who just wants to taste you." His eyes finally left Kerrigan and met hers again. "And definitely not someone who already has."

"I told you it wasn't him," Bly snapped. She hated when he did this, refusing to believe something if he thought he saw evidence otherwise. She had no choice but to tell him the whole story— she wasn't sure why she hadn't already—of how a vampire had been kind to her for whatever reason. It didn't mean anything. He'd probably been bored with cruelty for the day and decided to try something else for a change. Bly cleared her throat. "It wasn't just one vampire in the woods. It was a group."

A look of horror flashed across Emerson's face before she could continue.

She shook her head. "They didn't attack me. The one watching me now"—she hesitated to say his name—"Kerrigan."

Emerson's cheek twitched as if he were barely containing his disgust.

Bly swallowed. Why hadn't she just called him "the vampire"? It wasn't like they had exchanged names. She didn't need to admit to remembering it.

"Kerrigan noticed how weak I was. He called them off. He told everyone to let me go."

"I found you unconscious, Bly. And bitten."

"Not by him. The girl with him doubled back. She's the one that drained me."

"Looks like he has regrets," Emerson said.

Bly shivered.

Emerson's eyes narrowed, noticing everything.

"I should talk to him. Any type of connection could make us stand out in the trial."

"Do you *want* to talk to him?" Emerson's words were accusing, as if Bly had been in the woods throwing herself at the vampires, as if she wanted to feel fangs sinking into her neck, as if she wanted *any* of this.

She made her voice hard. "I think I have to."

He softened his own voice. "I just . . . want to keep you safe. It feels impossible here. I can't imagine you dying like . . ."

Like his sister.

"I'll be okay," she whispered. "We need this."

She stepped away without waiting for him to respond. She knew what he'd say anyway—that they didn't need to be here at all. He'd walk away and just lie down and die if she'd let him, but she was going to play this game whether he wanted to or not.

She pushed her way through the swirl of red and purple, lifting her chin as she walked, baring her neck with the confidence of someone begging for fangs against their skin. Because they'd dressed them like themselves, it was impossible to tell who was human and who was vampire until you were close enough to see the flash of someone's eyes on you, and by then you were close enough to see the hunger in them too. Even if vampires didn't all have gray eyes, their expressions when she passed with her neck on display would have been enough to give them away.

Her steps faltered as she neared the fountain. The familiar smell of blood rolled off it. She'd avoided that smell her entire life, dodging working with both her parents who dealt with it regularly. Even having given blood for the past year, she hadn't gotten used to the sight or the scent.

She dropped her chin and hunched her shoulders, trying not to breathe through her nose.

She didn't look back up until she spotted the flash of blue pants in front of her. Taking a deep breath, she raised her eyes and met the gray ones that were waiting for her.

She expected him to speak first, with the way he'd been watching her, but he silently sipped from his cup as his storm-cloud eyes held hers.

Maybe he didn't really recognize her at all.

Her cheeks heated. "I . . . I wanted to thank you."

He raised a single eyebrow as he lowered his drink. "For what? You're here. It seems I saved you from a few bites just so you could walk into a room full of vampires who want much more." He leaned in so close that she could feel his breath on her neck. "If you wanted to know what it's like to feel the prick of fangs sinking into you and the slow pull of blood leaving your body, then all you had to do was ask. I would have shown you right there. You didn't have to come under the guise of the Games just to get a taste of being tasted." He leaned back. His lips quirked into a half smile, the same charm he'd first shown in the woods that didn't quite meet his eyes. But even now, beneath his seductive demeanor, she sensed . . . annoyance . . . as if he really were disappointed to see her again.

"People come here just to be bitten?" she blurted. She knew some romanticized the vampires. And there were a handful of humans that lived in here, working as warm bodies that the richest vampires could buy for their meals. People called them bleeders. It was often the desperate who chose that life, along with a few who craved it, and there were strict rules in their treaty with the witches that said how many humans each side could employ only for their blood. The main source was still what got sold in the market.

But she couldn't imagine coming all the way to the trial just for *this*.

Kerrigan laughed. His voice turned throaty. "Plenty like it." His mouth parted slightly, and his tongue flicked over his fangs.

"Well, I'm here for the Games."

He shrugged. "My mistake. But you are dressed . . . like that." His gaze traveled across her exposed neck so slowly that she couldn't stop herself from wrapping her hand around her throat.

"I asked for a scarf," she said.

His expression shifted—he was still annoyed, but it didn't feel like it was directed at her anymore.

He held up his half-full cup to the side, and a gold-clad vampire whisked it away. Then he tugged loose his blue silk scarf. Closing the gap between them with a small step, he reached for her neck and slid the scarf around it. Her breath caught at the feather-light touch of the material, and she shivered as his fingers shifted to the front of her neck, brushing her skin as he looped the scarf around itself to tie a loose knot.

He paused, clearly noticing her reaction. His eyes darkened and lifted to meet hers. "Are you sure you don't want to be bitten?" Something had shifted in his tone—the seduction in it didn't sound fake like it had moments before. His eyes crinkled at the corners as if he were surprised by the change in him too.

Her mouth parted in answer and she meant to say no, but the word seemed lost in her throat. His gaze drifted down to her lips.

Emerson. Her mind practically shouted the name at her. He was watching. And even if he wasn't, she didn't want to flirt with a vampire—not yet. Only if she failed at the trial and had no other choice.

She shook her head.

Kerrigan cleared his throat, his eyes fading back to a lighter gray, his fingers finishing the knot against her neck.

"Settling on a plaything already?" The girl's light, cruel voice made Bly's blood dance with fear.

Kerrigan's hands froze again at her throat before casually smoothing out the details of the scarf, fingers lightly touching the sensitive area between her breasts and collarbone. "Just helping a young lady who's cold."

"No helping humans, Kerrigan. You already slipped up yesterday. So make sure that scarf is just a leash to play with later."

For a split second, Kerrigan's eyes darkened again, and his fingers tightened around the scarf now snug against her skin. His whole focus seemed swallowed by her neck, and her instincts screamed and told her he was imagining exactly what he might do with her in his scarf.

She leaned away and felt the pressure of the silk against the back of her neck.

He did have her trapped like an animal.

But he seemed to shake himself. He chuckled as his hands drifted away from her and disappeared behind his back. He flashed her a look that held . . . remorse?

"Watch yourself, Jade."

Bly glanced around for a way out. Jade stood slightly behind her. She hadn't seen Bly's face yet. If Bly took a step past Kerrigan and into the tangled maze behind him, then she wouldn't have to see those cold gray eyes ringed in blue, but the second she moved, one of those dainty viselike hands gripped her arm.

"Hold on now. Let's see what caught the traitor's eye."

The anger that flashed across Kerrigan's face was so startling that Bly might have run if Jade weren't behind her, gripping her arm.

"I don't care what you are to my brother, Jade. Call me that again, and I'll rip your tongue out."

"Try it," she said, and then she stepped around, positioning herself beside Bly. She wore crimson and the same diadem of gold as the rest of the royal children.

"You?" Jade blurted as soon as she glanced at Bly's face. She turned around to glare at Kerrigan. "Does this blood bag mean something to you? You know how that ends." Jade smiled. "I didn't rat you out yesterday, out of loyalty to your brother, but maybe I do need to tell the queens to keep a closer eye on you."

Kerrigan's gaze flicked to Bly for the briefest moment. "She means nothing. It's just a happy coincidence that she's here, and she seems slightly replenished now. Just look at that pretty flush in her cheeks." His voice turned into a seductive slither that tightened around Bly's throat and made it hard to breathe. He slid a finger under his scarf and pulled, and she took a stumbling step toward him.

Jade looked back at Bly. Her eyes sparked. "Well, I can vouch that she does taste particularly good."

"What did you say?" The shift in Kerrigan's voice was jarring. Gone were the coyness and games of a moment ago, sharp steel in their place.

Jade's head whipped back around just as Kerrigan's hand landed on her shoulder. "What did you say?" His fingers tapped as he repeated the question.

"I was hungry," Jade snapped. "I doubled back and took what was owed."

"After I said not to."

"So you *do* care." She smirked like she'd caught him in a trap. "Why?" She sounded genuinely baffled.

Bly was wondering the same thing. It made no sense at all.

And it was starting to attract attention. A few people nearby had turned in their direction. Kerrigan shifted slightly as he took in their audience too.

"I don't," he said slowly. "What I care about, Jade, is you ignoring a direct command. Maybe the queens should know about that."

Kerrigan's stance was still casual, but he gave off an air of power. There were clearly rankings among the royal children, and Kerrigan's had to be high.

The type of vampire that would win the witches' prize.

And Bly had at least caught his attention, even if what he said was true and he didn't care a wit about her beyond what was in her veins.

She didn't need him to. She didn't *want* him to.

His gaze flicked to her. "You may go."

Jade turned to her with a sweet smile as she dropped her arm. "Don't worry. I'll find you."

Kerrigan growled. "You will not ignore me again." He looked at Bly once more. "Go."

This time she didn't hesitate. She turned and scurried away with none of the confidence she'd pretended as she walked over.

She'd caught too much attention.

She didn't breathe until she reached Emerson again.

"Bly." Emerson said her name like a curse as he stared at the scarf on her neck.

Should she take it off? She didn't want to. The material pressed against her naked skin made her feel less vulnerable.

"I think it worked." Bly glanced back. Jade was nowhere in sight. Kerrigan's gaze was on her again. He didn't glance away in embarrassment. His expression didn't even flicker. He just stared.

"It worked too well. He looks like he wants to eat you even more." Emerson's voice was thick with disgust. "Half the room looks like they want to eat you."

Bly shook her head. "No. I don't think it's that—not with him." She remembered his hands tying the scarf. His dark eyes. "At least that's not all of it. That girl that approached us— *she's* the one who bit me. He made her leave me alone. He's . . . protective."

Emerson scoffed. "He's a vampire." He said it as if that alone were enough of an argument.

It was. It should have been.

Bly bit her lip as she held Kerrigan's stare. He'd protected her. Twice. And not the way Osborne had, who'd only been following the rules. Kerrigan had *ignored* the rules that day in the woods.

But Kerrigan's eyes still drifted to her neck way too often for his interest in her to be solely kindness.

Sometimes people protected you to prey on you later.

"Don't make up some fantasy about him." Emerson's hard voice drew her back.

Bly finally turned from Kerrigan to stare at Emerson. "I wouldn't."

"I know you, Bly."

But he didn't. Not all of her. He didn't know all her fantasies were built around him.

It hurt that he still didn't see that. She was standing here in a room full of vampires for him because she needed him to live. Otherwise, even if she got her sister back, all those fantasies would stay dead.

"What if I offer him a drink?"

"He has one," Emerson said.

Kerrigan had finally broken his stare to sip at his cup, which was somehow back in his hands again.

"Not that kind."

Emerson followed Bly's stare to a couple not far from them. At first glance, it looked like nothing more than a couple embracing, but one man had his face against the other's neck, and there was no movement of a tender kiss. He was latched on. Drinking.

"Not worth it."

"Anything is worth it," she said, her voice barely above a whisper.

Emerson's face softened for a moment. Pain shown in his eyes, and the vulnerability of it took her breath away. It made her want to reach for him, but he reached first, taking her smooth hand in his rough one.

"I don't want this," he said gently.

"It's fine. We don't have to make a blood deal."

"No." He squeezed her hand. "I don't want this life at all. Can you honestly imagine me living here?" He looked away from her at the room full of humans who were probably used to starving, eating tiny cakes while blood dripped from where they'd been cut just to reach them. Vampires hovered around like vultures, like the people in the room were nothing but carcasses they could scavenge.

No. She couldn't imagine it at all.

He'd never fit here.

"I'm sure you'll get used to it."

"Stop with the fantasies. Please. Can we just face reality for one moment?"

But she couldn't. "You don't even have to stay here. We can leave together. We can head out into the woods." She'd been talking of leaving forever, but she'd never suggested he go with her. She swallowed, waiting for his reaction.

"Not this again."

She jerked back. Emerson was always telling her she was foolish for wanting to run away from their life, but he'd always said it with a half-smile and a shake of his head, like it was one of her stories that he loved. Now his voice was harsh. Had he always felt like this? Annoyed by her dreaming?

"Please be logical." He gripped her hand tighter as if afraid she'd run into the woods right then and there. She felt his fear in the pressure.

But he was wrong. It was her dreaming that would save him. And Elise. The only way out of impossibly horrible situations were impossible dreams.

She straightened. "You'll be a vampire—it makes more sense than before. If you're with me, that would be added protection, and Elise will be with us too."

Emerson cringed at Elise's name, and Bly knew he didn't really believe they'd save her, either.

She wondered if he believed in anything at all.

She'd have to believe enough for the both of them.

"And what am I going to feed on in the woods, alone with you and Elise?" Emerson said.

"I would feed you."

He looked repulsed. She couldn't help but compare it to the way Kerrigan had looked at her moments before, as if he wanted nothing more than to put his mouth against her skin.

Her cheeks heated at his reaction because it hadn't seemed like the worst thing in the world to her, despite the fact that blood made her squeamish. It didn't seem that bad at all, really.

"And what about a vampire's control? What if I killed you by accident?"

"Why do you always have to think of the worst-case scenario?"

"Because you refuse to live in reality."

"And you refuse to want anything at all."

"There's no point in wanting things you can't have anymore."

Hurt crushed the air between them.

"Let's go home," Emerson said.

"Does it really still feel like home to you?" Bly asked. "Without Elise?"

He looked away from her. "Home is just a place, not a feeling."

"You're wrong," Bly whispered. "It *is* a feeling—we just have to find it."

Emerson sighed. "You're not leaving, are you?"

"Of course not, but I'd understand if you do." She could win the prize and then drag him here to claim it. He couldn't say no if she went through all that.

Emerson was silent for a long time. "I won't leave you. Either of you." He glanced around the room. "But Bly, this isn't going to be an ending where the three of us live happily ever after. We're not kids. There are no happy endings."

"But there are better ones than everyone dead while I'm stuck here without you both. Can we just . . . try?"

Emerson swallowed. She thought he might walk away from her.

"Okay," he said. "Okay." His voice was firmer. "But we do things my way, and we leave this party and wait for the trial to start, because what we're looking for isn't here."

"Leaving is not an option."

Bly jumped at Seraphine's voice at her shoulder. How closely had she and Sebastian been watching them? Bly hadn't even seen them.

Seraphine's voice was chilly as she continued. "Not unless you want to be escorted out of the city without a chance in the trial."

Sebastian appeared next to Emerson and put a hand on his arm, which Emerson shrugged off.

Sebastian smiled at the slight. "Not having a good time?"

"This isn't what we're here for," Emerson said.

"But the Games have already started," Seraphine said, her voice warm once more. "That's exactly why you're here." Her stare flicked to Kerrigan. "And Prince Kerrigan never actually plays. He pretends, but he's never sponsored a team before. You'd have better luck with his brother. I can introduce you?"

"No," Bly said a little too quickly.

Sebastian's eyes narrowed. Seraphine shrugged.

"Please try to enjoy yourselves," Seraphine said. She nodded at her brother, and they disappeared into the crowd again.

The night wore on. The heady smell of blood and alcohol draped the room. Bly's head began to swim. Eventually she tried to slither her hand between the sharp golden leaves to get something to eat. She captured a tart filled with cream and topped with white berries just as a golden thorn pricked her finger, making her bleed on top of the sweet. Pulling it out anyway, she ate around the stain of her own blood, and as she stared at her last tarnished bite, a hand snatched it from her. The handsome blond vampire from earlier stood in front of her once more—Benedict, Seraphine had called him. "I told you I'd be back," he said, winking at her as he popped the dessert past his fangs and into his mouth. He closed his eyes as he swallowed. "Delicious," he murmured before weaving back into the crowd.

"Gross," Emerson said.

Bly just stared down at her still-bleeding finger and back up at the vampire moving away from her.

The sugar helped. Her ears stopped buzzing, and she found herself searching for Kerrigan again. He sat on the edge of the fountain, laughing as he held his cup under the stream of blood, letting it fill before taking a few sips and putting it under again.

"You can't be serious," Emerson said, as if reading her mind.

"Relax," Bly said. "I'm not offering him blood, but he's a prince. We could use a prince."

Stumbling slightly, Kerrigan stood up and pulled a glass of thinner red liquid off a tray that was passing, downing it in one gulp. The food may have been hard to reach, but the vampires were generous with the wine, and it seemed Kerrigan partook more than most.

Kerrigan's stare connected with Bly as he raised the empty cup in her direction.

"He seems to have a drinking problem," Emerson said. "And not with blood."

Bly closed the narrow gap between her and Emerson. She didn't want Seraphine and Sebastian overhearing again. She didn't want anyone to overhear what she was about to say—the plan that had started to take shape as she watched Kerrigan. "We can use all of that in our favor," she whispered. "We get him to sponsor us, and then after he helps us deliver the witch here, we capture him. Whatever you think, he seems to like me. I don't think he'll see it coming. He's perfect."

Kerrigan sat on the edge of the fountain again, a girl on one side of him and a boy on the other. Both had their hands on his thighs. Perhaps another team pulling out all the stops.

But Bly had the advantage. They had a history, however brief. He'd pick her—all she and Emerson needed to do was impress him in the trial.

She looked back at Emerson.

Frustration pinched his face.

Because it was a good plan.

But Bly didn't get the satisfaction of hearing him admit that.

A clock struck midnight. Doors scraped open across the room, letting in a night breeze that left Bly shivering.

The vampires cheered.

SEVEN

THEY WERE HERDED OUT INTO THE NIGHT. Dim glowing orbs were suspended above them like miniature moons, casting everything in an otherworldly glow. People bumped up against one another as they were pushed together, making it hard to take in their surroundings.

Vampires filed in too, but most headed for stone blocks that were stacked like steps in a semicircle, and others stood on balconies built above those seats—an arrangement that gave them a clear view of the humans before them.

An arena. She'd seen this depicted on one of the tapestries inside—the same one the queens had made their legend in.

Bly turned to Emerson and followed his stare to where they'd entered. "I think we should . . . ," he started.

The doors slammed shut, and the scrape of bolts sliding into place made both the crowd and the players fall silent.

Emerson muttered a low curse, and Bly thought she saw panic on his face. Her palms began to sweat. When was the last time she'd seen Emerson panic?

Not since that day in the woods—that look on his face when he'd realized Elise was gone.

He grabbed Bly's elbow and pulled her closer to his side.

"Look at them bunched up like cattle," someone yelled from the stands.

Laughter bled through the crowd and set Bly's teeth on edge. Already this didn't feel like a simple showcase of skills for vampires to choose who to work with. It felt like a show.

"Spread out along the edges," another voice ordered.

For a second, nobody moved, but slowly the people packed around them began to shuffle to the right or the left.

Bly looked out at the arena that she could see fully for the first time, and dread filled her stomach. A stretch of open ground sloped before them, and the lake had to be beyond. She could feel the chill of night air wafting from it, but a barrier rose well before you'd be able to reach the water—one made of branches that were bound together haphazardly and grasping for the sky in points. Bly guessed there were more walls beyond the first— the vampires loved their mazes.

A vampire woman dressed in all red stepped out from a narrow gap in the first barrier. The same crimson shade stained the tips of her hair.

She grinned at their silence.

"Beyond these barriers, a witch waits." The woman's voice was sharp and high and jarring. "Working with a vampire in the Games is a great honor that's given to a select few humans, and we need to make sure that you share our hatred of the witches, that you have the strength and ruthlessness to live forever . . .

that you're capable of becoming one of us." She waved a hand at the vampires around them, none of whom seemed remotely bothered by what was about to happen. Maybe it was just the shadows, but their eyes were all black with what seemed like hunger.

"So kill the witch." Her command was casual, as if it were a simple request. A few players gasped. The rules of the Games stated that you had to deliver your captive alive to receive the prize. Of course that didn't mean the other side kept them alive after that, but murder was a step beyond what most of them had signed up for.

The vampire grinned, clearly enjoying the crowd's unease at becoming killers themselves instead of just people who would surrender their captives and pretend there wasn't blood on their hands.

But Bly wasn't squirming at the thought.

All she felt was a cold numbness, as if her bones had turned to ice. She'd dreamed of revenge before, death for death, but it had always been something that would only get in the way of bringing Elise back, given that she had to play *for* the witches. Except now the vampires were telling her that she *needed* to kill a witch. For all she knew, the witch on the other side of this was one of the ones that laughed as they rolled Elise's body onto the stretcher.

Those witches deserved the same fate as her sister.

She could do this.

Not because it was right, but because it was a fair price to save Emerson and Elise. A price she only had to pay because of the witches' cruelty. They'd set her on this path, and they would pay the consequences.

"The person or team that kills the witch will be sponsored by Prince Donovan himself, whose team won last year."

Bly's head snapped up, following everyone's stare to the vampire with the bloodred hair, but she only looked at his smug face for a second. Next to him stood Kerrigan, and his eyes were on her again, watching with a sharpness that seemed at odds with the stumbling, flirty drunk he'd been just moments ago. He didn't give any indication that he noticed her meeting his stare.

"You may begin," the woman said, heading to the crowd. Nobody moved, and she paused. "Oh yes, the rules: you can use any weapon you get your hands on—you're more than welcome to kill each other." Her teeth flashed. "*Any* draw of blood means you're out, but your teammate may continue on."

She stalked off as a blur of vampires dressed in dark gray darted onto the playing field. Metal clattered, and when they'd disappeared, they left behind a slew of swords and knives in their wake.

Nobody moved.

"Stay close to me," Emerson said.

"You're doing this?" She'd already decided she could, but she hadn't thought Emerson would.

"Of course not." His voice dripped with disdain. "But I'll kill anyone who tries to hurt you, and if we don't bleed, maybe that will make us stand out." He eyed the rest of the unmoving people and then the vampires. "And we should at least move. I don't want to see what they do to anyone who tries to refuse."

Bly glanced at the drawn swords of the guards behind them. There were more now, creating a line between the audience and the playing field.

"We should try to reach the witch," she said. "It'll make us look good to be the first, even if we don't kill them."

Emerson nodded.

She didn't mention that she actually planned to kill the witch. He didn't need to know. She didn't need him to tell her it was wrong. Right and wrong didn't matter when it came to witches. She needed to win.

Everything was silent until a girl with bright blond hair in a tight bun strode out from the edges and picked up a long knife that she spun quickly in her hand. Behind her came a tall boy with tan hair and muscled arms. He plucked a sword from the ground and swung it in a practiced arc as he turned and grinned at the other players. Some of the vampires cheered. A team— and one that had clearly been practicing. Not everyone entered the Games out of desperation. Some parents encouraged their children to dream of power and trained them for it.

They began striding toward the barrier's opening and for a second Bly thought nobody would challenge them, but an older man with a worn face and a beard reached down and grabbed a sword. His muscles bulged as he held it in front of him, accenting the black veins in his arm. Most of the people who entered the Games were younger—people who still hungered for a different life and weren't willing to accept the fate of being a human in their world.

But sometimes life left very little choice.

More people began shifting, taking tentative steps forward, most selecting weapons that looked uneasy in their hands; others handled them with practiced skill.

"We need to move," Emerson said. "We need a weapon just in case."

Bly followed. They reached a sword first. It was crude and dull compared to the weapons Emerson and his father made, but Emerson grabbed it and held it easily in his grip.

Nodding toward a small dagger to their left, Emerson slid in that direction, reaching the blade just as a small boy who looked a couple years younger than them tried to grab it.

Emerson held his sword out over the blade, and the boy stopped, eyeing the weapon as if wondering whether or not Emerson would really use it.

The boy decided not to move.

"Bly," Emerson said.

She knelt down and lifted the weapon. Even though she'd practiced with the blade Emerson had given her and usually carried it at her waist, the cold metal felt uncomfortable in her hand, too heavy, too real.

The boy sucked in his already hollow cheeks as he watched her, and her chest ached as if she'd stolen it from him, but these were the Games. They left no room for compassion. Their world left no room for it. But somehow, impossibly, Bly's heart still felt it, because this was a human caught in the same world with her, so she opened her mouth to tell him to stick with them.

Metal clanged against metal before she could say anything. She spun toward the sound. Emerson turned slightly while keeping his sword pointed toward the boy.

The bearded man and the tall boy who grabbed the second weapon had their swords locked against each other. And for a second, it seemed like the bearded man's bulking muscles would be enough to win, but the blond girl slid up next to them and thrust her long dagger hilt-deep into the side of the man's chest.

The clatter for weapons stopped.

The blade came out red and glistening.

The man dropped with a thud that seemed too quiet for the way his head bounced against the ground.

Everything was too quiet.

And then it broke.

People ran. Some of them seemed to sprint without thought; some grabbed the remaining weapons and swung them wildly in all directions; and yet others pushed toward the opening in the barrier. The vampire guards closed in on those still standing on the edges, forcing them into the mix with the tips of their swords. Something clawed at Bly's arm, and she spun to face the boy she'd wanted to help as he pulled at her, fingernails almost drawing blood as he clawed to get the blade in her hand.

Bly yelped and Emerson turned, swinging the sword with what looked like instinct. It cut into the boy's arm and he cried out, letting go. Emerson pulled back, and the boy whimpered as he gripped his bloody sleeve, and then a vampire dressed in gray appeared from nowhere, gripping the boy by the collar and darting away with him.

Pure chaos had descended. Some people still tried to run back to the door, but the vampire guards used their swords to draw blood, leaving the bleeding people to be swept away by the other vampires.

The guards pressed closer. The scent of blood clogged the air.

"We need to move," Bly yelled over the screams. When did people start screaming?

"Come on then!" Emerson tugged at her before letting go to hold the sword out in front of them.

They pushed forward, Bly hugging Emerson's back like a shadow, her hands clenched so tight around her dagger that she wasn't sure she was holding it at all. She couldn't even feel her fingers. The crowd thinned as vampires dressed in gray whisked in like smoke and carried away the wounded.

And the dead. She froze as she spotted a girl splayed on the ground with hair the color of her sister's. Blood leaked from a hole in her throat, feeding the red pool beneath her. Her eyes were open. Brown eyes. The same color as Elise's? Bly couldn't remember.

But the remembering still tried to swallow her. The color of Elise's eyes wasn't important in that moment, but it was all she could think about. *Elise. Elise. Elise.* Her eyes were lighter than the dead girl's, weren't they?

Bly was here to save her sister and Emerson, and all she was doing was cowering behind his back. It made her look weak. It made her *feel* weak, and it kept her from showcasing her actual skills. She was following behind Emerson because he was stronger, but that wasn't the only power vampires valued. She had a skill of her own to show them.

And with it, she could reach the witch first.

Taking a deep breath, she darted out from behind Emerson, sprinting away from him. He called her name, but she didn't have time to tell him her plan—she didn't want to when she knew he'd argue for the safer route—the one that kept her by his side. He'd only slow her down.

She let her vision blur. The weapons that tried to bite her flesh were only tree branches grasping in the wind. The bodies she leaped over were only fallen logs. At least, that was what she told herself. Deep in the back of her mind, she was screaming in terror.

She reached the first of the barriers. She hadn't aimed for the entrance, which was twenty feet away and bottlenecked by a group of people all fighting to be the first one in. Kicking off the delicate slippers Seraphine had dressed her in, she bent down and ripped away the bottom half of her skirt, finally understanding what Seraphine had done for her. She'd seen other girls trying to hack away at full ballgowns with their blades.

But she was free.

She clamped the knife between her teeth. Her hands wound around the bark and her feet found purchase on a wider branch, and then she was scrambling up, moving with all the ease of a girl who'd spent her childhood dreaming in treetops. Everyone thought she'd been wasting time, but now those days were the very thing that gave her the advantage.

The barrier swayed slightly as others tried her method, but she was already at the top, where some of the branches had been broken into jagged points.

Don't bleed. She let the words repeat in her head as she swung her legs over. She didn't climb down gently. She jumped, bending her knees and taking the impact. Above her, someone cried out, and she glanced back even though she knew she shouldn't. A boy straddled the barrier, a sharp branch piercing his thigh. Instinct called for her to help him, but the gray-clad vampires were already there, pulling him off as he screamed, and she forced herself to turn.

The door in the next barrier was right in front of her, and she tore through it, then sprinted along the length of the next one because she didn't need to climb if she was ahead.

Finding the next gap, she raced through. Were those footsteps behind her?

She tried to force herself to ignore what she heard, but the sound pounded in her, making her heartbeat thump along with it.

She reached a barrier with no opening and smiled. This would slow down some people but not her. She climbed easily, landing on the other side with a splash.

Cold bit her bare skin, but she barely noticed.

It was one thing to be told to kill a witch at the end of a maze. It was another to see her.

The witch stood waist-deep in the water with her hands tied behind her to a stake.

She wore a soft green vest over a flowy beige shirt. Her dark brown skirt swirled like mud in the water. She stood calmly with her chin lifted as if any fight in her had given way to silent dignity.

Bly hated witches, but the girl looked so helpless it made her stomach pinch.

The chill in the air had deepened next to the water. Or

perhaps it was because of what would take place here.

Bly took a couple of steps, the water sloshing up to her knees. Her ears roared as if the lake around her were churning and not eerily calm.

The witch's blue eyes met hers as Bly took the knife from her mouth.

She looked so young. Her hair was the same color as Elise's. Bly didn't know why she'd thought of that. What did it matter? She was a witch. She tried to imagine the girl laughing in the forest with Elise's body. She tried to stare at the girl and see everything that had hurt her.

Instead she saw the flicker of fear break through the witch's calm demeanor as Bly took a step closer.

She'd never seen a witch look afraid before.

The expression looked so . . . human.

Something thudded behind her, and Bly spun as someone splashed in her direction.

An arm slashed toward Bly, knife angled for her throat, but she dodged it, and the blonde who'd made the very first kill stumbled slightly. Bly shoved the girl in her side, sending the blonde careening into the water, where she scrambled onto her knees, clearly searching for the blade she'd dropped in the fall.

Bly moved toward the witch until they were face-to-face. Bly should have wanted her death—a witch's blood on her hands—but suddenly she realized that she didn't want revenge as much as she'd thought. She didn't want to be ruthless like the witches or the vampires.

She just wanted her sister back.

But she had to do this to make it happen.

"I'd rather a blow to the heart than across the throat." The witch spoke. Her voice was soft and sweet, and Bly's dagger trembled in her fingers.

She *had* to do this for Elise . . . but as she thought again about her sister, all she could hear was Elise telling her to stop. Bly heaved a shaky breath. "I'm not going to kill you—"

A blade sliced across the witch's slender white neck.

Bly's dagger dropped from her fingers, and she stumbled back as the witch gurgled, blood leaking from her throat and dribbling out her lips. A horrible way to die.

Bly couldn't look away.

The soaking wet blond girl turned and grinned at Bly—the witch's blood still gleaming on her blade.

Only when a vampire clad in gray grabbed her did Bly notice the sting in her arm.

The girl had cut Bly as well, but she'd been too caught up in the witch's death to notice.

The arms around her torso yanked her away.

She was dropped in one of the wooden pens that lined the arena, where a bunch of other bleeding people milled around like cows waiting for the slaughter. There were a few vampires in there with them, but she didn't bother wondering what they were doing. She pushed through everyone until she reached the wooden rail, scanning for Emerson.

She didn't find him.

"Would you like me to heal that?" A finger poked at the hand that held her wound.

She spun to face a pretty vampire with short hair and large angular eyes.

Bly's own blood heated her hand. She desperately wanted the sensation to stop.

But the vampire's sly smile stopped her from saying yes.

She glanced around the pen and watched another vampire lick at the wound on someone's neck before drawing their own vampire blood to heal them.

Her stomach twisted.

"As long as I give you a taste?" she asked. A vampire didn't need to drink a human's blood to heal them.

"Nothing is free." Their fangs flashed with their smile.

Blood leaked past Bly's fingers that were clamped over her wound. She knew as well as anyone that nothing came without a cost, and that cost was rarely a fair one, but a little blood for a healed cut that was bleeding way too much seemed fair enough.

A lot of humans were doing it.

"I will take care of this one." The voice was familiar, and Bly was surprised to find a bit of the tension in her shoulders relax at the sound of it. The pretty vampire darted away and Bly turned.

Kerrigan's solemn face stared down at her. He stood straight and tall with his hands folded behind his back as he looked at her arm.

"At least you're not dead," he said.

Bly was surprised at the statement. Where the other vampire saw blood, Kerrigan seemed to care about the actual wound.

"Would you like me to heal you?"

She hesitated. She imagined him leaning his mouth down to

her arm, and the thought made her squirm with unease . . . and not so much the thought of him doing it, but that she'd imagined it at all.

"You don't have to say yes," he said, "but I'll be quite gentle." His eyes shined with amusement.

It felt weak not to let him, so she nodded.

He reached out slowly, as if she were an injured fawn in the forest—as if she were the same girl who'd been cornered in the berry bushes and needed saving.

She was. She'd thought entering the Games would make her feel stronger, but she needed Kerrigan's help now more than ever.

He gently pried her hand loose, and the feeling of his fingers gliding through the blood on her skin made her want to grimace. Instead she drew in a deep breath and held it.

He glanced up at her face from where he'd leaned down to inspect the cut.

She looked away.

Her arm throbbed in pain as he ran his finger across the torn flesh.

She tensed.

"All done," he said.

She jerked her head back around. He was staring down at her again, arms behind his back.

"You didn't have a taste?" Her voice was startled.

He lifted an eyebrow. One side of his mouth quirked up. "Trust me . . . I thought about it. Consider this one a gift, but bleed in front of me again and I might not be so generous." His eyes darkened and darted to her mouth, and Bly licked her lips, wondering if she had bitten them in the fight and had blood there too that had drawn his stare.

She didn't.

"You could answer a question for me, though," he said.

She hesitated before nodding. She felt like she owed him, and not just for the blood.

"Why didn't you kill the witch?"

"I . . . couldn't." It was all she could offer. She didn't fully understand what had stopped her, but she was relieved. Her hesitation made her human.

He searched her eyes as if looking for a deeper answer. She expected him to ask for more, but he seemed satisfied with whatever he'd seen on her face.

It made her feel naked.

And then he simply turned away, pushing through the players who looked at him like a prize.

She probably should have thanked him, taken every last chance to make sure that he picked them, but the pen was being opened and they were being herded back onto the playing field. Some of the people tried to resist, and they were dragged out.

"Don't be cowards," someone yelled from the stands.

"You can't be a vampire if you're afraid of a little blood," someone else added.

They laughed.

But it was hardly a little blood. Miniature pools of it dotted the ground, staining everyone's shoes. And Bly had given up her shoes. The slickness on her feet made her gag.

"Line up as teams." The vampire who'd started the Games

stood in front of them once more. "Vampire sponsors will go down and choose the player or team they wish to work with."

Bly spun, searching for Emerson with her heart in her throat. She practically crashed into him. He'd already found her, just like he had the day Elise died, just like he had after she'd passed out in the woods.

Just like he always would.

She looked him over. A thin cut that hadn't been healed ran down the side of his neck.

"Is your arm okay?" he asked.

She followed his stare to the blood there, knowing the cut underneath was gone. "It's fine."

He looked closer at it and frowned.

She opened her mouth to say she hadn't made the trade, but saying that Kerrigan had healed her for nothing seemed worse.

"I'm fine," she said again.

He looked ready to say something else, but the first vampire sponsor walked down the line. Donovan. Bly almost cringed as he passed, but he didn't look at anyone. He barely paused in front of the winning team. "Come," he ordered. The couple shared the briefest look before they followed him.

A tall man with a narrow face and dark brown skin and hair came next. He wore deep purple and black and moved like he owned the air around him. He had to be another high-ranking prince. He didn't even pause in front of Bly and Emerson. He chose a single, older man with blood splattered across his face.

She recognized the next vampire—Benedict, the handsome blonde who'd eaten her bloody bite of cake. He smiled broadly as he sauntered down the line. The only time his grin faltered was when he reached Bly. His steps slowed, and his brows pinched together as he looked at her with a more thoughtful expression than he'd shown earlier. Perhaps he was taking her seriously now.

"What's your name?" he asked her.

"Bly." She pulled her shoulders back.

"Interesting."

She held her breath with hope. He'd probably want more from her than her skills, but she'd just have to deal with it.

"You should've killed her," he said bluntly. "You don't have what it takes." His cocky smile came back. "Tasty, though."

He moved on, stopping in front of a group of three men Bly hadn't noticed before. Their taut muscles looked formidable. The vampire waved at them. "Let's play, fellas," he said brightly.

The crowd murmured at the choice before there was trickle of laughter.

Kerrigan had stepped up.

A few people booed, and Bly couldn't help but wonder what he had done to earn it. Jade had called him a traitor. She seemed to hate him, but he clearly still held power.

The crowd didn't seem to trouble him though. He turned toward them and winked, and the laughter grew a little bit louder before his face turned serious. Seraphine had warned Bly that he never selected anyone, even though he pretended to be interested. Apparently it was some kind of joke among them.

But maybe this year would be different. He'd helped her three different times now, and that couldn't be just part of his game.

Kerrigan strode down the line, glancing at everyone in the peripheral without even turning his head.

It seemed he'd pass her by as well.

He took a single step past her before pausing and stepping back. His head turned toward her as he kept his stance facing forward.

Her heart beat a bit faster with hope.

He glanced down at the arm he'd healed and then at her face. He frowned before twisting on his heels and striding away.

"Such a tease," a vampire yelled.

The crowd chuckled.

Bly lurched forward, like she'd run after him and beg, but Emerson grabbed her wrist, anchoring her to his side. He leaned into her. "It's fine," he murmured. "There are other sponsors. And if we don't get one here, we still have the witches' trial."

Vaguely she was aware of Emerson's mouth close to her ear, how it might have made her shiver in another moment to feel his breath on her skin, but all she could focus on was Kerrigan moving away from her.

And just like that day in the woods, he didn't look back.

More vampires came down the line, and while a few of them hesitated in front of Emerson, they turned away once their eyes drifted to Bly. *She* was the weak link between them—the one who could've killed but didn't. It would've been better if she'd never reached the witch at all. Vampires clearly didn't value mercy.

But she'd been training for the witches' trial. That was where her past year of skills would be useful.

Emerson was right. Her plan would still work.

Get a witch sponsor. Catch a vampire to bring back Elise.

Betray the witch.

Save Emerson.

And she didn't need Kerrigan and his fake kindness to do it.

EIGHT

LUSH GREEN HEDGES GROWING UNNATURALLY tall and thick surrounded Havenwhile. Vines of morning glories, purple petals worshiping the early sun, wound up the wall of green. Bly hated how warm and inviting it looked. At least the vampires' thick stone wall and heavy black gate practically screamed that danger lived inside. The entrance to the witches' city seemed to promise happiness and light.

Lies.

Small doors punctuated the hedges. Each one had been made from manzanita branches stripped of their bark. The pale wood had been bound in chaotic designs that curved at the top.

Manzanita bark could hold a spell for forgetting. Perhaps the doors were a warning.

Emerson sensed her unease. His eyes kept sliding in her direction.

The doors were closed, unlike the open welcome of the vampires.

A few other people had popped out of the woods and stood

eyeing the entrance with them. Everyone knew not to touch the witches' things, even if no one knew quite like Bly.

"I guess we just go in," Bly said. Normally, there would be guards checking to make sure everyone who entered had the band on their wrist that said they worked there. But the witches were supposed to welcome everyone during the Games.

Still, Bly hesitated as she reached for the manzanita.

There was no doorknob, so she wrapped her hand around a curve of wood and shivered. The smoothness of it felt like a spell on her skin already. She pulled as other people on the edges of the woods watched.

It gave easily.

The part that was difficult was making herself enter.

Emerson stepped in first and turned back for her. He didn't rush her, just waited, his gaze steady and patient. Things had felt easier with him on the journey here. They still didn't talk much, but they'd walked side by side for most of the way, and the silence felt easier. They didn't need words for Bly to notice that Emerson was cold and give him one of her warmth spells. She didn't need to ask for him to offer her the water canister he carried. It was simple, even if it wasn't what they had before.

And he knew without words why she had paused now. But others were pulling open similar doors and walking inside.

She'd just run through a bloodbath—crossing a threshold shouldn't have made her feel like this. She forced herself to go in.

She hated it immediately.

It was a town built into the forest. A cobblestone road

stretched before them, but grass and flowers grew up from the cracks so that it was more wild than road. Mushrooms grew in clusters of milky white caps along the side. Bly tried to swallow down the panic that rose at the sight of them, but it caught in her throat, making her heart gallop until steady fingers pushed into the pulse at her wrist.

"I'm here," Emerson said. Not *it's okay* or *there's nothing to worry about*. She appreciated that he didn't say those things. He wasn't a liar.

She focused on the pressure of his fingers against the ribbon tied there, imagining that he could control her racing pulse.

It worked. She looked up and met his steady brown eyes. He waited patiently for her to take the next step. When she did, he dropped his grip on her wrist.

She wished for it back but didn't say it. Not yet. One day soon, though, she'd be able to—when she took off that ribbon.

Nobody greeted them as they walked, as if the trial weren't as big a deal to the witches. They just went about their business. Maybe their goal was to show what life was like here. It looked like the kind of life Bly had once imagined for herself—one that mingled with the forest instead of one caged by it.

The homes and shops were built around and into the trees as if to disrupt nature as little as possible. On their right, a house blended in with the low branches of an ancient oak. Beneath the sprawling branches were rows of garden boxes overflowing with leafy greens. A witch kneeled in the dirt, filling his basket while he hummed. On their left, they passed a shop built into the gap between two pine trees. The walls were made of wooden shingles in an array of rich browns that made it look like a patchwork quilt. Across the roof, the pine tree's branches had grown at odd angles, no doubt manipulated by magic, so that the roof seemed to be made of pale green needles.

An older witch sat outside next to a basket of bread that smelled fresh and sweet and made Bly's stomach grumble. A little boy approached, and the witch handed him a loaf after he dropped a coin into her hand. She smiled and Bly turned away.

She didn't want to see them happy and normal.

But as the sun continued to rise, more witches bustled about their village, waving and calling to each other, smiling and chatting . . . completely unlike the vampires' eerie stillness. They were acting almost . . . human.

Except they weren't human.

In the human villages, people rarely smiled. They moved with one quiet purpose: survival. In some ways, they were more like the vampires—driven to get what they needed to stay alive.

And Bly's village was almost always cold.

Subtle warmth mingled with the cool forest air, and Bly searched for the source. Lanterns hung from the tree branches that stretched over the road. Each one was a curving cage of branches painted in soft colors that had worn and chipped over time, so they looked as natural as the trees themselves. Light glowed in the centers—spells that must have been for heat as well as sight when darkness came.

How hard would it be to add those heat lamps to the streets in the Gap?

Some of the laughter that trickled through the town was

from the humans in awe of the place—maybe they were already dreaming of winning and being allowed to live here and forget the cold they came from.

Emerson wasn't laughing, though.

Bly knew he'd be thinking the same—that there was wealth here that was easily shared. And that if humans had more, then maybe his sister never would have been in the woods that day. Maybe she and Elise wouldn't have been either.

Bitterness filled her mouth and she welcomed it. She wasn't here to be charmed. A witch's life looking so much like the life she had once imagined for herself only made her angrier. Not only did they already have everything she'd once wanted, but they'd also stolen what little she had—a wisp of a dream that was similar to this.

They came upon a larger building where each corner was supported by a giant oak, its branches spreading out across the wooden roof so that it looked like a cloud of green hovering above the building. Older children milled around outside of it, and Bly stopped walking for a moment. Some of their faces held the same easy smiles as the rest of the witches, but others frowned, their brows creased. A girl who couldn't have been older than ten sat on a wooden bench out front, slumped over a book in her lap. Bly thought she might be crying.

She wondered how real the smiles were that they passed. Children didn't hide the truth as easily.

Unlike vampires, whose power was linked to the one who turned them, witches were born with power in their blood, and the strength of it depended on knowledge and practice. Spells could only be placed on certain objects, and each spell required witch, human, or vampire blood—or a combination of each—plus something more elusive: the witch had to command the magic back into the object. There were rumors that not everyone could do it. Some could only ever master a simple spell like a sleeping curse, and those who failed to master their skills by the time they reached adulthood were banished from Havenwhile to live off the forest beyond its borders.

Based on the faces of the children, it seemed true.

Bly tried not to have too much sympathy—at least they had heated lanterns on their streets.

Turning away from them, she kept walking because that was all she could do anyway.

Trails broke off from the main walkway, winding into the thick forest where she could make out more houses and shops, but they kept going straight because nobody told them otherwise. It was like the witches had been ordered to ignore them and carry on with their daily life.

In a way, it was a spell meant to draw them into this world that could be theirs. You could choose to live in Havenwhile if you won their prize. If she got Elise back, would she still want to escape into the forest? Or would she want to take the easier route and live here instead? Could she let the colors and smells of this dreamscape erase the nightmare they'd wrought?

A cluster of witches gathered outside of a shop with redwood shingles and warm yellow trim laughed louder than most.

Bly jerked to a stop again at the sound.

Emerson glanced around like she'd seen a threat.

She'd never told him how they laughed as they carelessly rolled Elise onto a stretcher, like she was nothing.

Just a body.

Her chest tightened and her head lightened.

Emerson's scanning eyes came back to her, as if he knew that the threat was inside her.

He was right. It wasn't the laughing witches in front of them, who weren't even looking at her. It was that memory. It lived in her—a monster in the cave of her chest that would rise at the slightest nudge to wrap its long claws around her lungs and squeeze.

Sometimes she could fight it off, but sometimes she lost.

Standing here in the blur of green and brown with the laughter in her ears, she thought her lungs might close up completely.

But fingers pressed against her pulse again like a weapon she could use to fight.

She focused on Emerson's strength, and she let it feed her own until the monster retreated back into the dark.

The world was light and bright and cheery again in the worst way.

"I hate them," she said softly.

Emerson's hand at her wrist squeezed in response before releasing her.

They walked on until the street narrowed to another trail, and they caught the shine of a deep blue lake winking like a witch's eye between the greens and browns of the forest.

And suddenly the witches began appearing along the edges of the path, smiling and nodding, holding out baskets of muffins that smelled of tart apples and fragrant blueberries, loaves of dark brown bread, gleaming piles of bright oranges. People began to fill their hands and mouths as they walked.

Bly took nothing. She tried to stare straight ahead to avoid those welcoming smiles, but the tang of citrus, sweet apples, and sugar-laced treats assaulted her senses, making her stomach turn.

"You need to eat something." Emerson held an apple in front of her. She hadn't even seen him grab anything, which she was glad for—she might have made a scene trying to stop him.

He held it out until it became awkward for her not to take it. She lifted her hand, staring at the unblemished red skin as if blue veins might suddenly appear on it, but even if they did, apples didn't hold curses. A spelled apple would only make your hair grow longer.

She didn't bite.

She held it in front of her like a snake as the trail spilled to the edge of the lake.

She didn't know whether it was a spell or luck, but the overcast sky that usually haunted the Gap was nowhere to be seen, and the sun shimmered on the blue water, creating its own magic. Tiny hexagon-shaped gazebos surrounded the lake. At each corner of a gazebo stood a tree trunk, still covered in dark green moss, that supported a thatched roof. Ivy twined up everything, and in the center of each platform sat wooden benches facing the lake and ceramic pots overflowing with flowers.

It was beautiful. It was the kind of thing that might once have made Bly's heart sing and dream and long.

But the only longing she felt now was to win, and it wasn't a pretty thing. Winning would be brutal and blood-thirsty and fit more with the vampires than this deceptively soft place.

One platform was on stilts, raised a few feet above the rest. On it was a chair of woven branches that fanned out toward the sky like a sunbeam, and in that chair sat a witch with a pile of dark red hair pulled up on her head and a circle of ivy on her crown. She wore a dress of tiny white petals that seemed to be held together by nothing but air—they shifted as if in a breeze as she stood. She was short and slight, but her shoulders were pulled back and her head tilted up in a way that made her appear taller. The crowd silenced with her movement.

Bly felt fear in that silence.

She had to be Halfryta, the head witch.

Once, the witches had been ruled by a group of elders led by *two* head witches, Una and Dyfed, a couple who'd been rumored to have been at the Hallow Pool. Witches with power and money could afford immortality spells, placed in golden berries that only grew far from this picked-over land. But unlike most immortals who hardened with age, Una and Dyfed had visited the human villages after years of leaving the management of humans to the elders. They were appalled at the conditions. They began making plans to improve the humans' lives, giving them spells for heat or to nourish food on their barren patches of land, but the elders argued against it. Giving humans anything risked everything the witches thought they deserved.

So the elders murdered Una and Dyfed, but they left alive their teenage daughter: Halfryta.

Like most elders, they underestimated youth and the pure,

unbridled fury they were no longer capable of feeling in their old age.

And Halfryta possessed one of the most powerful spells of all, left to her in her parents' collection: a vampire fang, spelled so that if it broke the skin, it would briefly give the user all the strengths of a vampire, including the power to heal. Armed with her fang, an invisibility spell, and a fistful of death curses, Halfryta tore through the night and murdered her parents' killers in their beds. When morning dawned, she stood bloody and fierce in the center of the city and declared herself the ruler. She appointed the children of the dead elders in their parents' places, even though she ruled completely. Nobody dared challenge her.

You might think that she'd have taken up her parents' cause to help the humans, but she was even crueler. She saw her parents' compassion as the flaw that killed them—a flaw she'd never share.

And now she stood in front of a group of humans, staring down her nose without bothering to conceal her hatred.

If she'd been the one tied to the stake at the vampire trial, maybe Bly could've actually killed her.

"Welcome to Havenwhile," Halfryta finally said as she scanned the crowd. Her eyes seemed to land on each one of them even though she couldn't have paused for more than a second. "We are grateful"—she paused to let the word drip with condescension—"that you've chosen to come to our trial. We relish the chance to work with you to capture the vampires— beasts who think they're better than us because of their brute strength when we all know that their powers are an abomination." She grimaced as if the very thought of them were repugnant. The witches' lore was unsurprisingly very different from the vampires' and claimed *witches* had been the first to drink from the Hallow Pool. Everyone came away with a witch's power until a fight broke out near the water and blood was spilled in it, tainting the magic, turning those who drank next into vampires, and leaving those who never drank as humans.

Halfryta smiled, but it lacked anything close to warmth. "But true power lies in the ability to create magic. We put things back as they once were, the way things were intended to be, but with all magic there is a cost, and that cost is blood. Ours, vampires, humans—we all need to play our part. We all need to give. You sell your blood to us because you understand that."

No. They sold their blood because they were starving. Or desperate for a chance at happiness. Some of the crowd shuffled. Emerson glanced at her, an anger she hadn't seen in a while flashing in his eyes, remembering all those conversations they'd had about how the world had been rigged against humans for far too long.

But nobody spoke up. Halfryta paused as if daring them to.

But they were all here because they needed something or longed for something so much that they were willing to play a game designed to use them like disposable playthings. None of them were revolutionaries. They were just desperate.

Halfryta nodded as if they'd shouted their agreement. "But the vampires are too greedy to trade, so we have to take."

She stopped again, taunting them, because that wasn't how

the story went, of course. Both sides had lost control . . . and almost let the humans rise up.

Bly stared down at the bloodred apple still in her hand. At least the vampires were open about their lust for blood. They didn't hide behind warmth and fresh fruit.

She sank her teeth into the flesh, holding the sweetness in her mouth until she almost gagged and had to swallow.

Halfryta clapped her hands. "And now we'll let you prove that you can take too." She lifted her hand and then turned slightly, blowing dust from her palm over her shoulder.

The lake quivered, and not just the water. It was as if the sunbeams and the air itself were shaking. Bly blinked. A few people gasped. A huge circular stage hovered above the lake that hadn't been there seconds before—or rather, hadn't been visible. A table sat in the center, and next to it stood a giant, empty wooden cage with a rope and a pully attached to a beam above it. On the perimeter of the circle stood another cage, but this one wasn't empty. It held what seemed to be a man, but Bly had a feeling he had fangs.

"Your task is simple. Incapacitate the vampire any way that you can."

Witches swarmed into the crowd, pulling people this way and that. A young girl with straight blond hair grabbed Bly's arm. "Do you have a team?" she asked.

Bly's ears buzzed. Every part of her zeroed in on the press of the girl's fingers just above her elbow.

The girl's mouth moved again. Her brow furrowed with annoyance.

"I'm with her," Emerson said, his deep voice drawing Bly back into herself.

The girl looked from Bly's face to her arm and then dropped it, as if she suddenly understood. Some of her annoyance faded, but Bly didn't want pity from a witch. She wanted to be fearless in front of them, but before she could collect herself, the girl was spinning away. "Follow me, then," she said over her shoulder as she moved through the crowd so quickly that Bly had to push through everyone to move after her. The witch led them to one of the platforms that lined the lake's edge. "You'll sit here, and when it's your turn, a boat will take you out to the arena." She started to turn away before she paused. "Good luck." Her words were bright and cheery but fell uselessly like stones in water.

Boats covered the lake, each painted a shade of blue. Some sat idly in the water, filled with witches looking for a better view. One was depositing a woman onto the stage already. A group of witches in a boat pulled the rope attached to the cage by the table, waving her inside. The woman only hesitated a second before stepping in.

"At least we're not first," Emerson said.

There was no time to answer. Bly couldn't look away as the cage began to rise again. The woman inside reached through the bars, grabbing for something on the table beside her. It had to hold spells. But whatever she wanted was out of reach. The cage rose slowly, but the vampire's cage lifted at exactly the same pace. The woman gave up trying to reach and dropped to her belly, waiting for the cage to lift enough to slide under.

Finally, she was free.

But so was the vampire.

Her hand closed around a spell as the vampire reached her. She was moving toward a second spell when the vampire snapped her neck. It didn't look like she'd had a chance to cast a single one.

Some of the witches booed and some cheered. Bly didn't know which was worse.

A group of six witches launched themselves onto the platform to detain the vampire, but Bly was focused on the two that approached the murdered woman. They grabbed her by the arms and pulled her across the platform with her head bobbing at a sickening angle.

"Did she pick up a binding spell?" Emerson asked. His head was tilted as he took in the scene, always thinking. "Couldn't she have spelled him before he snapped her neck?"

"I don't think the binding spell is on the table," Bly said slowly, forcing her eyes away from the woman's body thudding into one of the boats. "Look." She pointed but dropped her hand when she realized her finger was shaking. "There's a small metal cage next to where the vampire is released. I bet it holds a binding spell or at least a sleeping spell. They wouldn't make it easy. We have to reach that spell." Her voice quivered.

"You don't need to watch," Emerson said quietly.

But she did if she wanted to figure out how she and Emerson could survive this.

A group of three went next. One launched himself at the vampire without any spells at all. It gave the other two girls a chance to grab a spell each before the vampire was on them, their companion already nothing but a lump on the deck. One of the girls met the vampire with a raised sword. At least the witches weren't taking their weapons like the vampires had.

Even from a distance, Bly could see the girl's arms were muscular with training, but the vampire dodged her swing with ease. She'd probably used a strength spell but not speed.

The vampire was behind her in an instant. Her neck snapped with her sword still in her hand, ready to strike.

The other girl had gotten whatever was in the small cage. But she hesitated, eyes catching on the bodies of her companions, and turned and sprinted off the edge, swimming toward a boat with witches that dragged her up.

The vampire laughed, a loud, cruel sound that was at odds with the still woods that surrounded the lake. Bly shuddered.

"She had it," Emerson said. "Why'd she quit?"

"The strength and speed spells still don't make you *as* strong as most vampires, though it helps if you're already strong." She glanced sideways at Emerson's bulking muscles. "I bet there's one of each spell." She worried her lip, watching the witches rearrange the table. "Someone needs to use both spells and hold the vampire at bay while the other person gets the binding spell."

"The first woman barely had time touch them, let alone cast two."

"We have to be faster."

Emerson said nothing. She already knew he wanted an actionable way to be better, not just hope they would be.

Another duo took the stage. A boy and girl with the same dirty blond hair. They were both tall, with sharp features and wide-set eyes. Probably siblings.

Bly desperately wanted to not watch this one.

She willed them both to make it.

The cages rose. The boy met the vampire, swinging his sword with a roar that skittered across the lake. He carried through the swing in a full circle, stopping the vampire from getting to his neck, giving the girl enough time to spell herself twice. She charged the vampire, and he laughed as she swung an ax in quick, practiced arcs, forcing him to dance back. But she wasn't the real threat. The boy hadn't gone for the binding spell, like the vampire surely thought he would. He was still behind him, holding his sword in two hands, swinging it with all his might, and even human strength was enough to decapitate.

The vampire's head hit the wood. The crowd was silent for a moment before the witches cheered. And so did the humans.

It was possible.

But Bly was not that girl. She didn't even have a sword or ax, just a small knife.

"Your turn." Bly hadn't even noticed the boat that had pulled up to the dock that reached from their gazebo to the water.

Emerson looked at her, a question on his face: Did she still want to do this? They could play without a sponsor, after all.

But teams rarely won without one.

"Leave any of your own spells that you have on you. Failure to do so will result in disqualification. Human weapons are allowed." The man's voice was monotone.

Bly reluctantly laid her spells out on the bench beside her. The man barely glanced at them before waving them forward.

The boat wobbled beneath their feet as they stepped into it. Bly stared at the sky instead of the water as they rowed to the edge of the stage.

The witch offered his hand as she climbed out, but she didn't take it. He nodded at her like she'd done it to be strong, but she didn't need his approval. She smoothed out her gray skirt. It'd slow her down. She wished she could change into breeches instead, but it was too late.

Her eyes trailed to the fresh blood already staining the deck and then to the vampire cage that had been filled once more. Her stomach sank. The other vampire had been short and a little scrawny. This one was wider than Emerson and at least a foot taller.

She hoped he was slow.

The witch ushered her and Emerson under the cage.

Her eyes scanned the crowd as the cage lowered, as if she'd be able to spot the witches who'd actually plucked Elise from the forest.

"Bly," Emerson said softly. "I need you here."

Not in the past.

The past was her motivation, a weapon of sorts. It had gotten her here, but now she needed to put it away and focus on the weapons she needed to win. The witches' spells. The people she hated most were the key to getting Elise back.

She drew in a deep breath of the cold air that rose from the lake. She preferred it to the false warmth of the witches' spells on the shore.

"Bly," Emerson said again.

He thought she was still lost to the monster of her memories, but she wasn't. Not anymore. She was here, breathing deep and steadily. Bly knew the spells like the back of her hand. She'd spent hours lingering around the witches' booths in the marketplace, listening to them talk to customers, hearing them explain the spells in each object and the words needed to release them.

The problem was speed. How to get the spells activated before the vampire got you?

She scanned the table behind the bars. A speed spell and a strength spell taunted them just out of reach, while a bunch of other spells sat within reach that'd do them no good at all.

If Emerson charged and held off the vampire long enough for Bly to use the speed and strength spells on herself, would she be able to win against the vampire? The spells only amplified your own strength, and she wasn't the girl who'd just won, but if *she* charged the vampire while Emerson cast the spells, it'd certainly kill her before Emerson could reach her.

She wanted to cry. She had the knowledge, but why hadn't she spent more time making her body stronger?

Emerson shifted on his feet as if he were thinking the exact same thing.

She thought he said her name again, but she wasn't listening.

Her eyes landed on a bright green leaf with sharp edges. It was one she could reach through the bars.

The horn bellowed.

Emerson yelled her name as the cages rose. He was already on the ground, ready to crawl under the bars the moment they could fit. He tugged at Bly's skirts.

But she didn't need to be free to cast the first spell.

Her fingers closed around the leaf. Kneeling, she crushed it against the wooden planks at her feet as she shouted, "Grow."

A thick hedge unfurled in front of them and across the entire platform, so quickly that Bly fell backward as the branches sprang toward her.

The vampire howled on the other side as he crashed into it. If they were lucky, he'd impaled himself. But already the sound of branches snapping filled the air; she'd bought them time.

Their cage had risen, and Bly bolted and grabbed what she needed from the table. She pressed a blue jay feather into Emerson's palm. "Speed," she said.

He repeated the word as he closed his fingers around it.

"Strength," she said as she jabbed him with the sharp tip of an acorn.

His fingers tightened around the sword in his hand as the spells took him.

Another branch cracked, and then the vampire on the other side grew silent.

Bly plucked a smooth white stone from the table and hoped it was what she thought.

The vampire crashed through the remaining branches in the hedge.

Blood lined his face and arms from scratches that had probably already healed. His head swiveled from Bly to Emerson, and he shifted ever so slightly in Bly's direction before Emerson swung. The sword whistled toward the vampire's neck, and for a second Bly thought the blow would land—that she wouldn't have to keep fighting, and she held her breath with hope but also fear. She didn't want to see a head rolling at her feet, even a vampire's. She didn't want that memory. But she wanted to win.

It didn't matter.

The vampire moved as if casually stepping out of the way of someone in his path. The sword bit deep into the planks, and the vampire rushed Emerson before he could yank it free.

He lunged for Emerson's throat, and Emerson barely pulled the sword loose in time to swing it toward the vampire's side. But the blade never broke skin. Even with Emerson's enhanced speed and strength, he still didn't have the raw power of a vampire.

"Go!" Emerson hollered.

The vampire's head snapped in her direction. His pupils were black pits. Bly didn't wait to see if he would come for her. She bolted through the jagged hole in the hedge. Branches tore her clothes and ripped her skin, but she barely felt it. She barreled toward the cage on the other side, wondering the whole time if she'd be snatched from behind, if Emerson was holding his own or if the vampire had gotten him already. But for once, fear didn't freeze her limbs. She reached the silver cage and slammed the stone against the lock as she breathed, "Break." The lock clinked, and she swung the door open. Her fingers closed around two sharpened birch sticks just as hands wrapped around her head, one across her chin and one at the back. Her breath caught as one stick slipped from her fingers. Some distant part of her screamed for Emerson. But he'd never let the vampire get to her if he were still standing.

The vampire chuckled. They liked to play before they killed.

Everyone knew it. But that was a weakness.

"You lose," the vampire said at the same moment Bly whispered, "Bind," stabbing the birch stick into his arm. His hands tightened for an instant around her head before they fell away. A binding spell would act like a rope around his wrists, and it would bind them in front of him if that was the path of least resistance, which meant he could still kill her, standing behind her with fangs close to her neck.

But she already held another birch stick in her hand, pulled quickly from the cuff at her wrist. Because she hadn't relinquished all her spells. If the vampires and witches didn't play fair, why should she?

She spoke the spell again, jabbing it into his thigh, then spun as he dropped, his legs tangled together as if bound with invisible rope. As he snapped uselessly up at her, Bly knelt at his side as if she were brave and fearless and taking a moment to taunt him, but she said nothing.

Her hands felt across the ground until her fingers brushed the first birch branch that she'd dropped, now hidden just under the hem of her skirt. As she rose, she dropped it into her pocket. Perhaps nobody had seen her cheat, but she couldn't really bring herself to care if they had. Her heart was beating so hard that she was painfully aware that she was alive. But that wasn't the most important thing to her. She twisted in search of Emerson at the same moment he stepped through the torn hedge.

His fingers clutched his neck. Relief rushed over his face as he looked from her to the downed vampire. "You did it," he croaked as he took a step and teetered.

She reached him just before he fell. His weight crashed into her, and she wished more than anything that she had a strength spell for herself so that she could catch him, so that she could carry him to safety the way he had done for her.

Instead he pulled her down with him.

His fingers went lax on his neck, and she replaced them with her own.

His blood was so hot.

And then the witches were on them. They tried to pull him from her lap, and this time she screamed. She wouldn't let them take him. She wouldn't let them take anyone else from her. She clung and clawed, pushing them away until a hand clamped over her mouth, crushing something against her lips. "Sleep," a woman's voice said.

◆   ◆   ◆

Bly woke from an eerie emptiness. Blue eyes stared down at her.

"Get away from me." Bly sat up as the witch watched her. She was older, with dark brown skin and graying black hair that hung in tight ringlets to her waist. Her face looked tired.

"Where's Emerson?" Bly asked. She was back where they'd started, in one of the structures that surrounded the lake. Around them, a party had begun. People ate and laughed while music drifted from somewhere close by.

"He'll be getting healed and checked over the same as you," the woman said. "I'm Hazel, by the way."

Bly didn't answer.

Hazel smiled in response. "You don't like witches."

Bly startled at the blunt words.

"But you're here, so you lost someone—probably to us," the woman said with a nod.

"Are you reading my mind?" Bly asked.

Hazel laughed. "Just your face." Her expression turned sad. "I'm sorry for your loss."

Bly said nothing.

"I know it will mean little to a heart full of brambles, but we are not all alike. We don't all practice magic with blood from the murdered."

"But you do nothing to stop it," Bly retorted. She didn't like the way the older witch's presence comforted her. Maybe it was the look in Hazel's eyes—actual concern for her without any condescension.

"You know nothing about me," Hazel said as she stood and nodded toward a pile of clothes on one of the benches. "Those are here if you want to change, although I suspect you will not." She started to drift off into the party before turning back around. "If you survive this fool's game, come find me. Then we might be able to talk about what I do or don't do."

Bly stood, her head surprisingly clear, and glanced at the pile of clothes. A brownish green dress, from what she could tell without touching it.

She'd never wear it. She spun, looking for her spells, panic bubbling when she didn't see them. Her hands patted her skirts on instinct, and she felt them there. Hazel had repacked her pockets as she'd slept. Her panic spiked to fear as she as she pulled up her sleeve. The birch stick she'd hidden in her skirt was tucked snuggly in her cuff.

Hazel knew she'd cheated then. She scanned the crowds for her, wondering if she was watching and laughing, waiting to see Bly kicked out of Havenwhile or worse.

But nobody came for her.

Perhaps the witch had meant what she said about being sorry. Bly didn't want to believe that, but a sliver of gratitude snuck into her anyway.

She drifted into the party in her gray skirt. Only after attracting the stares of several humans and witches did she realize that Emerson's blood was a dark, angry stain across her thighs.

Her stomach pinched as she looked for him.

"Let me help you." The voice sounded smooth and flat like undisturbed water.

Turning around, Bly met blue eyes that matched the voice. The witch wasn't much older than Bly and just as tall, with strawberry blond hair that fell in loose waves to her waist. Her pretty face dimpled at the cheeks as she smiled, but Bly was caught in those eyes.

Eerie, like a still lake with horrible things lurking just beneath the surface.

Bly shuddered before she could repress it.

She could've sworn the girl's smile widened at her discomfort.

But maybe she was imagining the worst because all she'd seen was witches at their worst—except for Hazel. But she'd partner with any monster to have a better chance at bringing back her sister. Even pretty ones with deceptive smiles.

So she stopped herself just short of saying she didn't need help, but the girl didn't wait for an answer anyway. She bent down and crushed something against Bly's skirts, muttering softly. When she pulled back, the blood was gone.

"I'm Demelza," she said.

"Bly." Her name was all she gave. She wasn't about to be too friendly.

Demelza nodded like that was all she cared about anyway.

Bly turned to look for Emerson again. Cleaned clothing wasn't the help she needed.

"Emerson's fine. He's still getting fixed up," Demelza said.

Bly froze. "Emerson?"

Demelza glanced around as if looking for him. "You competed together, did you not?" Her blue eyes landed back on Bly. There was a glint in them—though of what, Bly couldn't say.

Bly nodded. But how had the witch known Emerson's name? Had she already spoken to him? Bly couldn't imagine him sending a witch to find her if he were really okay. But before she could ask, the witch spoke again.

"I'd like to sponsor you."

She almost let the word *no* leave her mouth—her gut response was to say no to anything a witch suggested. "I would like that," Bly said slowly instead. Excitement spread through her, mixing with her worry for Emerson, making her sick and giddy all at once. This was the moment she'd trained for, to snag the attention of one of these horrible creatures so that she could bring her sister back, and she'd done it.

"Here he is," Demelza said.

Bly spun around, barely stopping herself from jumping into Emerson's arms. She stared at his neck, perfectly unblemished, and relief crushed her so thoroughly that she thought she might faint from it.

"Someone wants to sponsor us," she blurted to stop herself from running her fingers across his neck, just to reassure herself.

She waited for him to show some emotion—relief if not excitement. This was exactly what they needed, but instead his brows were drawn together as he stared at Demelza.

"I know you," he said.

Bly glanced back and forth between them. Demelza's dimples deepened as her smile grew more genuine.

"Diana?" Emerson asked.

Her smile wavered for a moment before snapping back with a shake of her head. "Demelza."

"Of course," Emerson said. "Demelza. I . . ." He seemed to remember Bly and turned to her, and his face held something that Bly hadn't thought he was capable of having: a secret. He pressed his lips together like he wasn't quite sure how to let it out.

Part of her couldn't bear to hear it.

When they were children, she'd caught him hiding something at the edge of the woods, and he'd held it behind his back and told her it was nothing, but she'd only had to pout and tell him it'd hurt her feelings if he kept a secret from her to convince him to show it to her. It was a miniature horse he was carving for her birthday, and every year after, he'd carve her something else: a sword, a bird, a tree. But no matter what it was, he told her about it the moment he started the project. He'd let her sit and watch him work, and even though she'd been sad that she'd ruined her surprise that first year, getting to watch seemed like the better gift. It let her see the imagination he usually kept hidden and made her think they were more alike than they appeared. And it was an unspoken promise that he'd never keep anything from her again.

But what secrets had he gathered in the past year?

Her hand drifted to the necklace she wore tucked under her shirt. It was a tiny wooden rose on a string. The last birthday present he'd given her, before Elise died.

Her birthday this year had come and gone with nothing, even though she'd spent the day walking the edge of the woods, hoping.

Emerson stared at Bly's hand on her chest. Did he guess that it was the necklace she held in her fist?

Shaking his head, he turned back to Demelza. "Could you give us one moment?"

"Of course," she said, "but I need to know soon if you want to partner with me." She glanced at some of the other witches huddled around the teams that had excelled. "The players that have a shot get taken quickly."

Bly felt a little thrill at those words.

Someone besides Bly believed she could do this. She didn't even care that it was a witch.

Only Emerson's uneasy expression stopped her hope from soaring.

"Tell me," Bly said, because she thought he needed the little push, just like he had when he'd held her first birthday present behind his back.

He spilled just as easily.

"After Elise died, I came here." He looked past Bly instead of at her as he talked, another thing that was unusual for him. "The thought of them having her body ... draining it ... it made me sick. I needed to take that from them. The day it happened, after I took you home, I walked here. I carved my way through one of the hedges and just started wandering the streets. I kept cornering people and asking them where they kept the bodies they stole until eventually they sent some guards to deal with me. I saw them coming down the street toward me, and I . . . just didn't care. I turned around to wait for them when Demelza grabbed me and pulled me into a flower shop and hid me behind a cluster of roses. They smelled so beautiful that I threw up." He looked at Bly then, so she could see the pain in his eyes that he normally hid. The pain that matched hers. "Because she'd never get to smell roses."

Bly's heart squeezed. "You should have taken me with you," she whispered. All this time she thought she'd loved her sister best because she was the one trying to fix things, but Emerson had tried as well.

And he'd been rash and careless about it too.

The boy who always thought things through. She tried to picture him acting like that and couldn't, but it made her love him more that he'd done it.

For Elise. For *her*.

"I didn't want to put you through that."

"Did you find her?" she asked softly.

He shook his head. "Demelza took me to where they keep . . . their blood supply. She was already gone . . . sold." He choked on the word. "The bodies and blood collected in the woods belong to their leaders, but they sell it off to their citizens. And those are just the bodies. Some of their supply is . . . alive. They keep some of the vampires that get turned over to them in the Games and drain them when they need the blood."

That wasn't supposed to happen. The Games were supposed to put a cap on the blood supply, not make an endless one. The witches were breaking the rules. Bly wondered if the vampires were too. It'd make sense that the humans were the only ones who had to play fair—although Bly hadn't. Maybe there were no rules at all, just the appearance of them.

Emerson's expression darkened. "You know I loathe vampires, but the witches keeping them like that? It's cruel, and we're helping them do it."

"We're helping *Elise*," she said, but her stomach twisted.

He nodded, lips tight. "Then we should work with Demelza. She's not as bad as some of the others."

"A witch is a witch, just like a vampire's a vampire." She threw his own words back at him, even as her hand drifted to her binding spells, secure and safe thanks to Hazel.

"She helped me. She doesn't agree with how humans get treated or even the vampires kept in cages."

It was just like when Bly had said Kerrigan was different, but Emerson had insisted he couldn't be. She clamped her mouth shut against her desire to bring him up again. Besides, something else gnawed at her. "Then why would she be sponsoring someone to catch more vampires for them?"

Emerson frowned. It was unlike him to miss a glaring piece of logic.

"Perhaps she has her reasons just like we do. Either way, we need someone, right?"

She wanted to argue. "Yes," she said instead. She glanced around for Demelza and found her talking to two other competitors—the siblings who'd decapitated the vampire without going for the binding spell. Up close, they looked like twins. "We need to accept her offer before someone else does."

They walked over and Demelza beamed at Emerson. "You've decided?"

The twins stared at them with narrowed eyes.

"We'd like to work with you," Bly said, even though Demelza seemed to be waiting for Emerson to respond.

Demelza nodded.

Bly let out a relieved breath.

"Under one condition," Demelza added. She gestured toward the twins. "This is Nova and Vincent. I want them to join us. We'll have a better chance with a more solid team." She looked Bly up and down. "You're good with spells, but as you saw today, sometimes you need muscle to even land a spell. You don't have that, and I worry Emerson won't be enough." She gave him an apologetic glance.

"No," Bly said. "I need that prize."

"I know," Demelza said. And she did, of course. She knew they'd lost someone; she'd seen Emerson's grief. "But they want the prize money, not the resurrection spell. And prizes get split all the time."

Bly stared at the twins. Their clothes were threadbare and tattered. Their eyes had a hollow, starving look that went beyond the year-long hunger Bly had endured for the sake of saving money for supplies. Their desperation was altogether different than hers.

And the money meant nothing to her. It might have been nice, but she probably wouldn't have been able to stomach keeping the generosity of witches who'd only turn around and take more priceless things. And the longer she stayed here, the more she was certain she wouldn't be able to live here, constantly drowning in deep blue eyes that reminded her of her worst moment.

She nodded.

Nova gave her a sharp nod back. Vincent didn't even blink.

Demelza glanced between them all. "Then let's rest and plan tonight, because tomorrow we begin."

NINE

STEPPING BACK INTO THE FOREST WAS jarring—like leaving one nightmare only to find yourself in another one that was all too familiar. Had the mushrooms doubled overnight or was the path they took just denser? Bly couldn't take a step without feeling the soft crush of them beneath her feet. She tried not to look down, but she couldn't stop herself until she felt eyes on her and caught Demelza watching. Demelza gave her a sympathetic look. Bly kept her chin up after that.

Besides, she needed to watch for bounty hunters. The forest would be crawling with them now that the Games had started.

There were rules to make it easier for hunters to play their part in the slaughter. Competitors weren't allowed to use invisibility spells, and they weren't allowed to use speed spells to travel, only to fight, so the hunters had a chance to catch their fellow humans. And, of course, there were punishments if you got caught breaking the rules that ended with your blood drained from your body.

Bly tensed as the forest crackled with movement to their left. A group of a dozen witches wove in and out of the trees. The vampires would have similar groups on their side—not to interfere with the fair capture of one of their own, but to make sure the rules were followed and punishments delivered. They would also collect the bodies that the bounty hunters brought them or those killed to steal a prize. Bly grimaced as one of them nodded at Demelza before fading into the forest again.

They walked in mostly silence after that. Demelza asked Emerson questions at first, as if they were old friends catching up on lost time, but Emerson huffed out short responses, and eventually Demelza grew quiet.

Occasionally they heard screams. The kind of screams that created new nightmares.

"Should we keep strength spells on each of us?" Bly asked as the woods turned a liquid gold in the setting sun. Bly had always loved this time of day, but now it reminded her of the vampires' gilded city.

"I'm not made of spells," Demelza answered. "We need to conserve what I have, and you might panic and waste one when we don't need it yet."

"*We* don't panic," Vincent growled, making it clear that he only meant him and Nova.

Emerson said nothing. He radiated a cold confidence—nobody would look at him and think *he'd* panic.

"I've proven that I can handle myself," Bly said. She hadn't hesitated at the witch trial, unlike the vampire one, and they didn't know about that.

"Better to wait until we need them," Demelza said.

"Better for who?" Vincent asked. Bly was a little impressed at his willingness to talk back to her.

"Me," Demelza snapped.

Vincent didn't answer, but Bly saw his teeth grind on whatever he'd wanted to say. He knew what they all understood—Demelza was in charge here.

Last night they had gathered in a pub and sat around a wooden table with plates of warm bread and cheese and potatoes while they made their plan. But the plan seemed to be "follow Demelza's lead without question." Bly had asked what Demelza's arsenal was like, but all she'd said was "enough." It wasn't like witches had unlimited spells—it drained their energy to make them.

It made Bly uneasy trusting someone else. So she didn't let on that she had her own small arsenal. Most people entered the Games with some spells, but Bly had a feeling she had more than most. She wondered if anyone would notice if she reached for them—at least *she* could be prepared. But Nova and Demelza had both been eyeing her frequently, and she didn't like it. If they saw her collection, they might pressure her to share. Her loyalty to a team only went so far.

The one real plan they'd made was that if they were attacked, they should all gather around Demelza, who would swiftly give them what they needed. It wasn't lost on Bly that the strategy involved them putting themselves between whatever the threat was and the witch.

They were expendable. She was not.

None of them complained. Their world had raised them not to.

She didn't like it, but Demelza had to have more spells than Bly ever would've been able to collect on her own, and people rarely won without the help of magic. In fact, she'd only heard of it happening once before when a dozen players decided to team up together. They overpowered another team in the woods and stole their vampire to deliver him to witches, but some of them never saw the prize. The group turned on each other the closer they got to Havenwhile, murdering one another so that they wouldn't have to split the prize so many ways. Three brothers were the only ones left in the end. At least the killing had stopped with them.

Bly eyed the twins' backs ahead of her.

Blood always came first in this world, in more ways than one.

Perhaps working with a larger team wasn't smart, even if they wanted different parts of the prize.

But she wasn't without her own ally. You could form bonds that weren't built on blood at all, but hours of friendship that forged something else—maybe even something stronger.

Bly glanced over at Demelza, who had pulled her thick skirts up to climb over a fallen log with the ease of someone who spent a lot of time in the woods. But her clothes were nicer than those of some of the other witches; not in a way that was ostentatious, but in the little details that only someone who loved clothes would admire. And once upon a time, Bly had dreamed of clothing with such perfect lovely detail. Demelza wore a billowing white shirt with a vest over top that hung over her hips. She wore it open, and Bly knew it had to be loaded inside with pockets for spells, but the detail that caught her eye was the leafy pattern, stitched in multiple shades of green that rose like a column on either side of the vest. Plus her skirt was a stitched patchwork of green and brown materials with delicate designs, each piece a differently sized leaf, so she looked like a cascade of every lovely color the forest held.

All of it said more money than the average witch Bly saw in the market, which could mean a higher ranking, too.

Bly felt guilty about looking at Demelza and thinking of how she might betray her, but witches and vampires had come up with the Games and Bly was only playing them.

Demelza was choosing to play too.

Bly had to wonder why. Humans couldn't be the only ones with reasons, not when a lot of the vampires and witches that were captured in the Games were sponsors. But Demelza didn't look like someone who couldn't afford to buy blood, so maybe it was power and prestige, or maybe she was older than she looked and bored from years of partaking in immortality spells.

Demelza hadn't used a glamour spell to hide what she was, either—but most vampires and witches wouldn't since they couldn't directly kill one another in the Games, and if they didn't look like themselves, then all bets were off. They'd rather take their chances with the humans trying to capture them.

But why play at all?

Motives were important when death was on the line.

Bly drifted in Demelza's direction. The golden light of the melting sun made the red in her hair shine like threads of blood in honey, and something about her made Bly think she'd be better off as a vampire, that she'd meld into their city of gold and crimson.

"Why are you sponsoring?" Bly asked. "I don't mean us. I mean at all."

Demelza's eyes slid in Bly's direction. Whenever she turned her stare on Bly, Bly had to fight the urge to glance away from that deep blue color. She wondered if Demelza could sense the way her attention made Bly uneasy.

"It's not your concern," she said.

"But it is," Bly pressed. "You know why I'm here."

Demelza's gaze slid beyond Bly's shoulder. Emerson had drifted over to them, listening in as well.

Demelza sighed before staring straight ahead. "I come from one of the more powerful families, which means every year growing up, someone tried to come for us during the Games." Her voice grew cold. "Nobody ever got us, but I dreaded the Games and sitting in our home, wondering if that was the year someone would make it through our defenses, so when I was old enough, I decided to play. I'd rather be out here hunting the vampires than waiting for them to lead some blood-thirsty humans to my door." She paused, giving them a look that wasn't the least bit apologetic before adding, "No offense."

"None taken," Bly said tightly. It was her turn to stare ahead, because she couldn't conceal what had to be on her face: relief. Not only did they have a sponsor, but they had a one who could help them catch a powerful vampire and might also be powerful enough herself to win the vampires' prize when they betrayed her. Every piece she needed to win both prizes was falling into place.

She snuck a quick look at Emerson, but he was looking at Demelza.

"I'm sorry," he said to her. "That's no way to live."

Demelza's head jerked back in their direction. Her mouth was rounded in surprise. She looked away again just as quickly.

Bly gritted her teeth. He didn't need to say sorry to a witch whose ancestors had devised the Games in the first place. But something else needled at her. "Emerson said you didn't like keeping vampires imprisoned for their blood."

Demelza shot Emerson another, harder look. That clearly wasn't something any of them were supposed to know.

But he didn't owe her kept secrets.

"I don't," Demelza bit out. "I'd rather just see them dead."

"Seems fair," Emerson said darkly.

Bly let herself fall back. Emerson was only making nice with someone they needed, but it still stung. Witches didn't deserve pity.

But Demelza had helped Emerson before—had tried to help him find Elise.

So maybe she deserved some credit.

Darkness began to chase the gold away, muting the forest as Bly tried to focus on the threat that would bring and not her uneasiness with her own plan.

As soon as night completely overtook them, Demelza paused and passed out tiny vials of liquid that they dropped into each eye, letting them see in the dark—a spell that could only be made with dew collected from morning glories as they first opened to the light. The spell was expensive and reminded Bly exactly why they needed the witch. It would allow them to walk as far into the night as possible in hopes of gaining ground and getting ahead of those hunting for bounties without the danger that lights or flames might bring.

Bly finally found a moment to take out her own strength spell and quietly passed one to Emerson as well. Demelza might not want them to carry those spells, but Bly wasn't taking chances.

The night grew violent around them. Metal clanked and more screams echoed, and Bly had to wonder if they should have hunkered down in the shelter of the trees instead of moving. Movement could be heard.

A scream ripped through the night so close that the pain in it ricocheted through Bly's chest. All of them stopped walking, even Demelza.

"Should we stop here?" Nova asked.

Demelza shook her head, and Bly actually agreed with her. She did not want to rest where the sound of someone dying clung to the trees like a ghost.

Each of their steps seemed louder than the last and so did each of Bly's heartbeats. She'd never liked the dark, and even with the spell, the forest looked more like dusk right before night than walking in the day.

A hand grabbed her wrist, and she was grateful once again for Emerson, who always seemed to be able to hear the panic in her heart.

Until the hand squeezed so hard that it felt like their fingers were trying to rip her bones through her skin. Another hand closed around her mouth, catching the spell she was trying to utter as the fingers at her wrist dug in so excruciatingly that her fist opened.

The fragile acorn that held her strength spell dropped to the ground as someone pulled her sideways into the woods.

The hand muffled her scream as the trees began to swallow them. Why had she decided to walk in the back?

Emerson paused as if he'd heard. Nova's head actually whipped in Bly's direction, but the last things Bly saw were shadowy figures peeling away from the tree trunks.

Demelza yelled.

And then Bly saw nothing but the forest closing in as she was dragged deeper into the trees.

She heard the sound of metal against metal and shouts that didn't sound like the high-pitched keen of death.

Branches nicked at her skin, reminding her that she needed to fight too—whether she had the strength spell or not.

Or she'd become just one more echo of death in the forest.

Her legs kicked, landing blows against shins that felt like tree trunks. Instinct made her claw at the hand over her face.

Then she forced herself to stop. She was fighting like a human, but she still had the strength of a witch within reach. The spell she'd held was lost to the forest floor, but she had more.

She kept her legs kicking—a distraction as she reached into one of the top pockets of her skirt and pried open a small case inside. Her fingers withdrew the fragile piece of dried mushroom.

She needed to speak, but whoever held her knew that too, and the pressure on her mouth was unforgiving. Her kicking had done nothing to change that. Panic threatened to overtake adrenaline.

But she thought of Emerson fighting, probably already realizing that she'd been taken. He'd be distracted trying to reach her.

She threw out her legs once more, but this time she didn't kick back. She bent a knee, hooking her leg around the slender trunk of a small oak in front of her, trying to yank herself forward in a way that made her knee and hip scream. Her captor growled in confusion. Still, he didn't drop her, but his hand at her mouth gave way just enough.

She bit him, tasting dirt and smoke and unpleasantness. He snatched his hand back.

"Bitch," he growled, his hand trying to recapture her face, but it was too late.

"Sleep." She tried to make her voice a triumphant yell, but it came out like a croak.

It was enough, though. She crushed the spell into his palm.

He stumbled, his grip going limp just before he toppled onto her.

The weight of him forced the air from her lungs. Wheezing, she clawed at the leaves, digging her fingers into the soft dirt to pull herself forward until she could haul herself to her knees.

Something cold brushed her throat.

"What did you do to him?" a woman's voice asked.

Bly said nothing.

"Answer me." The blade pressed in, forcing her to confess as if she were spelled.

"Sleep," Bly said.

The woman actually chuckled, but it was harsh and mirthless. "You don't know how many times I wished I could use one of those on him." The blade retreated before coming back. "But I can't let someone else get away with doing that. Get up."

The blade rose, scraping along the skin of her neck as if it wouldn't stop once it reached her chin, and Bly scrambled to her feet, trying to keep it from nicking her. The second she found her footing, her hand drifted to the pockets of her skirt.

"No." The blade drew blood. "Hands in the air."

Bly obeyed, because it wasn't the woman giving commands at all, it was the knife.

A smaller dagger, the size of a finger, appeared in the woman's other hand. She lifted it toward Bly's wrist.

Bly tried to back away, but the knife followed.

"I have to check," the woman said. "We have a code, after all: check for the mark before we kill you."

The little dagger popped the buttons at her wrist, revealing the vampires' mark that they'd received before they left Vagaris: a red berry printed on their skin.

"Beautiful," the woman hissed. "I prefer dealing with the witches. Those icy bastards freak me out." She turned to the other wrist, and Bly tried to back away again. This time the woman pushed her against the trunk of a tree, the blade at Bly's throat drawing a thicker stream of hot blood, and she gasped. The other weapon ripped the opposite sleeve, revealing the mark they'd gotten before they left Havenwhile: a faint blue mushroom that Bly hated knowing was on her.

"Jackpot," the woman hissed. She opened her mouth, glancing toward the sound of fighting like she'd call out that she'd found a double bounty, and this terrified Bly more than the knife at her throat. It'd make the hunters fight harder to kill Emerson and the rest of her team. She threw her leg up, catching the woman between her legs, but all she did was let out a grunt as her head swiveled back to her. At least it stopped her from yelling.

"Well, I was going to kill you quickly, but just for that, now I'm going to cut off both your hands while you're screaming and then leave you for the wolves or the vampires, whichever animal gets to you first."

A branch crashed into the side of the woman's head and she toppled, jerking Bly to the ground with her before she went slack with unconsciousness.

A feral, snarling face loomed above them as hands pulled the woman onto her back. Nova kneeled down and plunged a dagger in and out of the woman's heart. Bly pushed herself up and away as blood spurted. The woman's eyes fluttered as if trying to regain consciousness just in time to die. Nova turned to the man, plunging her blade in and out of his back. The sleeping spell kept him from stirring as the blood poured out of him.

A scream bubbled in Bly's throat, and she clamped a hand over her mouth as she stared up at Nova's grim face.

"You're welcome," Nova said without even looking at her.

Bly pulled herself to her feet. "You didn't have to—"

"Save you?" Nova's raised eyebrows made her gaunt face harsher. "I know."

"Kill them."

"You wanted me to leave them so they could kill us later?" Nova's eyes cut to Bly's wrists that were covered once more. "To cut off *both* your hands while you screamed?"

Bly closed her mouth around more protests. Had Nova seen both her brands? She'd heard what the woman said, at least, and now she suspected.

"Then you're welcome," Nova said as she started to turn away.

Bly couldn't bring herself to say thank you, even though part of her understood the ruthlessness. She'd been teetering in that direction for almost a year, and where would she be in two years or three more if she didn't win this competition?

"The others?" Bly started to push past Nova, but the girl grabbed her arm lightly.

"They've got it under control. I ran after you as soon as I knew they'd be fine." She frowned a little bit, like maybe that'd been a mistake.

"Thank you," Bly said finally, the words wavering and unsure.

Nova gave a harsh laugh. "You're just saying that because I know your little secret."

Bly shook her head, but there was no denying it if she'd seen the marks. Bly glanced at Nova's hand still gripping her.

Nova let go, but she stepped in front of her, looking Bly up and down for a moment. A flicker of disgust flashed across her face. "You know, I thought we were the same. I'm only here because of my family. I've got a lot of siblings who don't eat unless Vincent and I feed them." She paused, glancing away and then back as if she regretted sharing something personal. "I agreed to play with you because Demelza said you had similar motives. I thought that'd make you stronger. But you're playing another game too. Maybe everyone else should know that. Does your boyfriend even know? Are you one of those people who like getting bitten? Is that it?"

Bly recoiled. "Of course not."

Nova folded her arms across her chest, and Bly sighed.

"Emerson's death cursed. We're going to save him too."

Nova's brows shot up.

Emerson called Bly's name through the trees as Vincent called Nova's, but neither of them answered yet.

"I need to save them both. I can't . . . I can't not try to save them both. It won't affect our arrangement. We'll hand over the vampire and won't make any moves to capture a witch until then. You have to understand."

Nova was silent for a moment before nodding. "I do."

"And I know I can do it."

"I believe you," she said, holding out her hand. "I'll keep your secret as long as it doesn't affect us."

Bly took it. Both their grips were firm and hard. Unbreakable.

TEN

THE SHIVERING SENSATION OF BEING watched made Bly search the trees numerous times on the rest of their journey to Vagaris, but each time she only found Emerson's eyes on her. He'd run to her when she stepped out of the trees with a blood-covered Nova. His hands had hovered over her body as if he wanted to run them across her skin to check for wounds. *I couldn't get to you*, he'd said. More than once. And she wanted to tell him that it was okay to touch her—to make sure she was in one piece, since she only really felt whole when he pressed his fingers against her wrist.

So she was glad for the way he kept watching her. Every time she turned from that feeling and caught him, a part of her that had felt dead before seemed to come back to life in a painful, tingling way.

But it wasn't time to get distracted. She had a whole future ahead of her to get lost in that feeling if everything went right. Assuming he still looked at her afterward. What if it was only the fear of losing her that kept his eyes on Bly? What if she did all this and he still only saw her as a friend once they were safe again?

She'd live with it.

If she could go back, maybe she could've just been happy with what she'd had—a beautiful sister and an overprotective friend. All that really mattered was having them both alive and with her. She'd learned her lesson about wanting too much.

Eventually, the gate loomed before them, the spikes on top making a deadly silhouette against the moonlit night. The twins took a step toward it.

"Not that way," Demelza whispered. "No need for extra eyes on us."

"Then how?" Nova asked, not even attempting to hide the annoyance in her voice. Bly could tell already that she was the type of person who faced things head-on: walk through the gate and deal with what was on the other side when you get there; stab someone in the heart to make sure they're not an ongoing problem.

Bly needed someone like that.

"Follow me," Demelza said as she turned.

They skulked through the trees, the wall to Vagaris a looming shadow at their side. Demelza's hands trailed along the bark of every tree she passed until she reached a small, scraggly oak and paused before turning and walking straight to the wall.

Bly placed her own hand on the oak as she passed and felt the faint carving of a star.

The wall here looked the same as the rest: stones upon stones overrun with moss. Until Demelza held out a hand against it, whispering something Bly wished she had heard. She blinked as she looked back at the wall. A sliver of jagged darkness had appeared. Demelza's teeth flashed white in the darkness as she smiled at them, and then she slid through the gaping opening in the wall. The twins glanced at each other and followed.

Emerson gestured for her to go next. "I don't want to leave you on this side alone," he said, so she turned sideways and slipped through the narrow crack. It took several steps to shimmy through the thick wall, while rocks scratched at her skin.

She stepped into Vagaris again. The backs of stone houses rose just feet ahead of them. They seemed to be in a dark, forgotten sliver of the city—the space between the wall and the buildings.

Demelza held a finger to her lips even though nobody had spoken. She cocked her head, listening. "I can hear a gathering not too far off. Teams rarely bring back a vampire of super high ranking. Most people will usually capture a guard. If we get a commander, it'd be almost a certain win."

Almost certain wasn't good enough. Bly didn't want any sliver of a chance that someone would beat her. She couldn't imagine losing and having to play again year after year. She thought of all the blood she'd already seen spilled, and her stomach lurched. Some people played every year, and they seemed to be hollow husks of humans—the desire to be something else had stripped away what they had of themselves to begin with. Most of them lived on the edges of the villages and didn't bother with the people around them anymore.

She didn't want that for herself.

"No," Bly said. "We need a royal. I won't risk losing." She glanced at Nova, who nodded her agreement.

The boys were sharing their own look. But Bly already knew Emerson was weighing the risks and deciding a royal wasn't worth it.

"I agree."

Bly's mouth popped open at the words, but they didn't come from Emerson. They came from Demelza. A fierceness flickered in her eyes, but she shrugged as everyone turned to her. "I want to win," she said, like it wasn't a big deal. Her expression had cooled, but something else lurked there. Bly'd seen it. Perhaps Demelza's hate for vampires ran even deeper than she'd admitted.

But Bly didn't really care as long as they were on the same page.

Demelza pursed her lips. "There will be a party happening in their fortress tonight. They'll let anyone walk in."

"Why would they do that?" Vincent asked. "It sounds like a trap."

"Because they're cocky bastards who think they're untouchable." She let out a soft little laugh. "Although the witches do the same. Of course, the problem isn't getting in, it's walking *out* with the prize. I've never been inside. I can't make a plan without knowing what I'm working with, but we don't have to make our move tonight. We can go in, have a look around, see if there's a weak point." She nodded. "That makes the most sense. We have time to be careful."

But Bly and Emerson didn't. She felt Nova's stare on her because she had to have realized the same thing—going for both prizes didn't leave room for days lost to planning. They needed to act now.

Bly glanced at Emerson, who shook his head ever so slightly.

They couldn't admit that they'd already been here. At least not completely.

"Emerson's been inside. He works as a bladesmith. I think he delivered a sword there." She turned to look at him. Thankfully, his face held no evidence of surprise at her lie. "Didn't you say something about the design? A long hallway with lots of doors off it that went into a ballroom?"

"Yes," Emerson said slowly.

A plan had taken root in Bly, twisting into her stomach and making her queasy. But it was a good plan.

"What if most of us hide in one of those rooms near the ball while one of us goes in and lures a vampire into the room to feed on them and the others ambush them? They won't see it coming, and it'll be away from the eyes of everyone there."

"You'd still have to get the vampire out of the room and out of the city," Emerson said.

Bly sucked in a breath. She hadn't thought that far ahead.

"I can make them invisible," Demelza said.

"You have an invisibility spell?" Bly asked. They were made from the opaque wings of dragonflies, but only ones that had drowned naturally—the magic wouldn't take if the insect had been killed for the sake of a spell, which made them so rare they weren't even for sale in the market.

"The bigger problem is who's going to be the alluring bait," Demelza said with raised brows. "They'll be feeding on people in the open . . . why would one follow someone to a room?"

Bly met Emerson's eyes. He was already shaking his head again.

"I met a prince in the woods while I was picking berries . . . and he liked me."

Demelza scoffed. "Vampires don't like *people*. They like open veins."

Emerson nodded slightly in agreement and Bly glared at him.

"He stopped the other vampires from feeding on me because I was already weak."

Demelza raised her eyebrows like she didn't quite believe that.

"It's true."

"So you're going to . . . what? Come back to offer him a snack as a thank you?"

Bly shrugged. "I think he wants one."

She met Emerson's eyes again. He'd seen the way Kerrigan had looked at her. The vampire might fall for it. However polite he was, his eyes had still darkened when she'd stood in front of him. If she was offering her blood willingly, she didn't think he'd refuse. In fact, he'd said he would have bitten her if that was what she wanted.

"Let her try." Emerson winced slightly as he said the words.

Vincent was shaking his head. "We don't have to do it tonight."

"It's a good plan," Nova said. "Why not finish quickly?" She turned to her brother. "If we hand over the vamp early, we can wait for the results back home."

The word *home* softened Vincent's face. "Fine," he said.

Demelza looked at them all. "We're going to need to change."

ELEVEN

BLY TRIED TO LOOK SULTRY AND SEDUCTIVE as she walked toward the door of the fortress. Demelza had given the rest of the group glamour spells—candied rose petals to turn their eyes gray. She'd also given them all an even rarer spell: the delicate strands of a spider's web that could create any garment the caster imagined. The others had spelled themselves the purple and red clothing vampires favored.

Bly had imagined a golden gown when she spoke her spell— she remembered Kerrigan saying he liked his snacks wrapped in gold—but she'd pictured the color too deep; it had taken on a coppery gleam instead. It looked more like Kerrigan's hair than gold.

The waterfall of material dropped between her breasts, leaving visible her pale white skin that never saw the sun. The skirt was a flowy cascade of silk, but it had two cuts up either side of her legs that went almost to her waist. The dress was held up by straps that were nothing more than threads, with billowing sleeves that hung off her shoulders and opened in wide slits to show her arms underneath. The important part, however, was that she'd designed wide cuffs at her wrists, held together with black buttons, to hide the player marks and the spells she needed.

Emerson had blanched when he'd seen the transformation.

But Demelza had reminded her that she needed to look like a vampire whore—someone who wanted to take Kerrigan up on his offer.

Bly had cringed at her wording.

She tried not to tug on the dress as she walked, and she tried not to care that the loose flaps of material were exposing the sides of her breasts. She focused on walking in the boots she'd conjured that laced to her knees and had sharp heels that made her even taller.

She couldn't stop the wobble, but she hoped anyone who noticed would think she was drunk. The others had already gone into the fortress, hopefully finding the empty dressing room to wait in. Bly needed to go in separately, and she wanted to attract attention, not blend in with the vampires.

She kept her chin raised and her hands loose at her sides as she strutted past the two guards that flanked the entrance. They eyed her and one guard winked, but they didn't stop her.

She walked alone down the familiar hallway, half wishing that she had Seraphine and Sebastian to guide her, but she wasn't alone. One of the doors cracked open and Demelza's head popped out slightly, giving Bly a nod before disappearing back inside, just like they'd planned. It'd be the first door on the right if she was heading in the other direction. What she didn't want to do was lead him to the wrong room, to be alone with him with nobody to ambush him at all, but not because she thought he'd kill her—because then she'd have to let him feed off her and pretend to like it.

Bly took a deep breath and entered the ballroom.

It looked similar to the party before the trial. The golden maze of brambles was filled with vampires and humans milling around, but already the room smelled of spilled blood and wine, the scents mingling into a sharp sweetness that clogged the nose and made Bly want to back out of the room again.

This party was different from the last. There were more vampires than before, and even though their clothes were magnificent, they weren't as stunning as the trial. This party must have been open to all of Vagaris. There seemed to be more humans than before as well. Some of them wore fancy clothes with easy smiles on their faces as they leaned into vampires, offering a wrist here or a neck there—the bleeders who lived in Vagaris and sold blood straight to the fangs. But others were dressed like they'd just come from the Gap. Bly passed a girl dressed in torn, muddy skirts, holding a plate of tiny cakes in front of her. A vampire stood behind her, his mouth pressed against her neck. The girl shoved a whole cake in her mouth and chewed like she didn't even notice.

Bly had always known that Havenwhile and Vagaris were open for anyone to visit during the Games, but she never imagined actually going to either place. Well, maybe she had when she was a child, before she knew that vampires and witches were responsible for the way humans lived. Before she knew people who'd died at their hands.

But she also hadn't grown up hungry.

She'd spent the last year with her stomach grumbling while she skipped meals to trade for spells, but that was not the same as living your whole life with an ache in your stomach and no memory of what it felt like to be full.

Her eyes stung at the thought of being so hungry that you didn't feel fangs in your neck while you ate pretty cakes.

She had a feeling Nova and Vincent knew that type of hunger.

An old familiar spark flickered to life: the rage at things that weren't fair and the desire to do something about it. But how could she? She was caught in the same cycle as everyone else, playing a game to fix her own problems. At least she wasn't trying to keep the money. That would go to someone who needed it more.

She'd gotten good at foraging. She could keep doing that when this was over and give her vampire earnings to someone who needed it. Because she'd never try to buy a pretty dress again, that was certain.

But she was getting ahead of herself.

There was nothing she could do for the girl in that moment, so she forced herself to move past her, weaving through the crowd, looking for a head of copper hair. She didn't see him.

A woman with chestnut hair grabbed Bly's elbow. "A coin for a sip from your neck?" She flashed her fangs in a smile as she pressed a coin toward Bly's hand.

"No." Bly pulled back. "I'm not . . . I'm not selling."

The woman raised her eyebrows, eyes scanning Bly's dress and then her neck. Bleeders wore chokers with a single ruby blooddrop at their center to indicate they were allowed and willing to sell blood. Bly had forgotten that any human could be here tonight and not just bleeders. She should have stayed in her own clothes to avoid confusion.

"My mistake," the woman said. "But if you change your mind." She backed away with a wink.

Bly's heart sped. She had a feeling that not every vampire in the room would take no for answer. She scanned the crowd again.

He wasn't here.

"Bly?"

She spun at her name.

Seraphine and Sebastian stood in front of her. They were no longer dressed in rich gold, but they were no less stunning. Sebastian wore deep purple pants and a black doublet over a white shirt. Seraphine's flowing skirts matched Sebastian's pants. Her black corset laced over a billowy white shirt that hung off her shoulders. Her black hair was braided back, exposing a neck that would've attracted every vampire in the room if she were human.

The relief she felt at seeing two friendly faces surprised her.

Seraphine grinned at her. "It is you."

Sebastian raised his eyebrows. "What are you doing here?"

She bit her lip, her earlier relief fading. Seraphine had seen how squeamish she'd been at the thought of being bitten. Surely she'd see through her lie that she was there to get a taste of what Kerrigan had offered—or rather, let him get a taste of her.

"I still want a sponsor." The new lie was easy, and it perhaps made more sense than her just being a girl who wanted fangs in her neck. She could play into her desperation—that part was painfully real.

Sebastian shook his head. "Not against the rules, but not likely. You could've had everything you wanted if you'd just killed the witch." He didn't hide his bitterness.

Seraphine shoved her shoulder into his. "Well, I think it's nice you're still fighting." She shot her brother a glance. "Can't hurt, right?"

Seraphine wrapped an arm around Bly's shoulders, spinning her around so they faced the room together. "Hmm," she said, tapping one finger against her red-painted lips. "You'll probably need to get someone to put you on a team they've already sponsored, which means you wouldn't be winning immortality because someone's already planned to claim it, but money's still nice, right?" She sighed. "But most teams have already left."

"What about Kerrigan?" Bly asked. "I thought he might . . . change his mind . . . but I don't see him."

"Doubtful," Seraphine said. "There." She pointed a finger toward a blond vampire with his face buried in a girl's neck. "Benedict actually picked a team this year, and he loves biting things if you're willing to get over that little hang-up? You really need to bring something else to the table after what you did in the trial, and let's just say Benedict is easily distracted by pretty things." She laughed.

Bly glanced at Sebastian and he shrugged. "He's your best bet, but I doubt you'll win. Nobody believes he's taking this seriously. He probably just got bored and picked a team on a whim."

They all watched as Benedict wrapped a hand around the wrist of another woman before releasing the neck of the one he was already drinking from. Spinning to the new woman, he laughed and brushed her long hair over her shoulders before sinking his fangs into her.

Bly swallowed. Kerrigan wasn't here, and Benedict had liked her even if he passed her by after the trial. Plus this was even better than Kerrigan, because trapping the vampire that had been kind to her, no matter his reasoning, had been nagging at Bly.

"Donovan's still here," Sebastian added. "He likes the challenge of giving everyone a head start."

Bly tried not to cringe. "I think I'll take my chances with Benedict."

"Good choice." Seraphine gave her a push in that direction. "Go get him!"

Bly moved through the crowd until another blonde stepped in front of her.

Jade looked at Bly with her head cocked slightly, and Bly took a step back before stopping herself.

Jade was a royal. She'd work just as well as Benedict. Maybe even better. She wouldn't lose sleep over turning in the vampire who'd bitten her.

The blond bloodsucker moved so close that she had to look up at Bly.

"I confess, I'm surprised to see you here." Her eyes were on Bly's neck. "Nobody picked you at the trial. Did you come to another arrangement? Who's biting your lovely neck in return for helping you? I love your little dress."

Bly swallowed and Jade's eyes darkened.

"Nobody. That's why I'm here. I was hoping there was still a chance."

Jade sighed. "I suppose you think you still have a chance with Kerrigan."

"I'm looking for whoever's interested." Bly swallowed again. "You liked what you tasted."

Jade smirked. "You're desperate. I like that. I don't usually play—too much time with humans. I like to drink and forget about you." Her eyes gleamed. "But maybe another taste will convince me." She reached out and grabbed Bly's wrist, but Bly stepped back. She had no doubt that Jade intended to drink her almost dry and then leave her without sponsoring, but that didn't matter.

"Not here." Bly glanced around her at the other humans being bitten.

Jade laughed. "You can't be that shy."

This was the weakest part of her plan. How to get them to follow her? The only thing that was on her side was that she'd been here for their trial. They had no reason to believe she was working with the witches and that she wasn't here still trying desperately to snag a sponsor.

"I just . . . I don't like blood. I'm feeling faint. How about one of the changing rooms just down the hall?"

Jade's eyes narrowed. "And you want to be a vampire?"

Bly gulped, but this time Jade's eyes didn't darken. She was suspicious.

"My friend did. I just want the money."

Jade nodded, her wariness fading. A human being desperate for money was always believable.

"What did you catch?"

Bly jerked toward the deeper voice, the red hair instantly filling her with relief until she realized it was bright red and not a softer copper. Donovan stared down at her.

"The rabbit from the woods," Jade answered.

Donovan blinked down at Bly, and then a wide grin spread across his face. "The one that got away."

"Not from me," Jade chirped.

Donovan gave her a dark look. "And you know I've been jealous ever since."

"She wants to be bitten if you'll sponsor her."

Donovan cocked his head. "Well, my team could use one more. You want a share of the cash?"

Bly's mouth was too dry to speak.

Jade spoke for her. "She's shy. She wants to be bitten in private." She laughed lightly as if joking about the weather, but joking about blood was probably just as casual to a vampire.

"Do you mind?" Donovan asked.

Bly looked at him, but he wasn't talking to her.

"She's all yours." Jade dropped her wrist.

And then Donovan's hand was at her back, his other hand lightly gripping her upper arm, leading her toward the open door of the ballroom. His touch was soft, but it felt like ropes against her skin, ready to pull tight into a snare at a moment's notice.

He was never her plan. Kerrigan seemed like the safer option, the type of vampire who might hesitate to kill even once he realized he was in a trap. And even the vicious Jade, with her petite frame, seemed like an easier choice, but everything about Donovan screamed ruthlessness, and she was leading him straight for Emerson.

But she didn't have a choice anymore.

They were in the hallway. She stepped toward the line of doors, hoping she could get him to the right one.

But Donovan's grip tightened on her arm, pulling her in the other direction, down a hallway that didn't lead to her trap.

"Aren't there rooms right here?" she stuttered.

"I prefer my chambers."

"I . . ." She started and stopped, glancing back over her shoulder. If she screamed, Emerson would hear her. But so would all the other vampires in the ballroom. She'd give them all away. Her mouth clamped shut. She wouldn't do that. She wondered if Donovan would let her change her mind. He might, but did she really want to?

Her breaths came too fast and short as she counted the steps that led her farther and farther away from Emerson until she forced herself to slow each intake of air.

She wasn't helpless. There was a pocket in the cuff of her dress with a sleeping spell tucked inside. She could slip it out and spell him if he was distracted.

If she let him bite her.

Her pulse skittered again, and she gave up trying to fight him. He'd probably like that anyway.

Eventually, they turned down a wide hallway where the floor

was deep black stones mixed with gray ones, all cut into squares and alternating so that each step took you from the night sky to a cloudy overcast day. Alcoves lined the walls, each holding a different statue depicting people and vampires tangled up in intimate embraces that made Bly's chest feel hot just looking at them. She glanced down at her feet even though she was supposed to want that embrace, or at least one that ended with fangs in her neck.

She didn't even notice they'd paused.

"Brother," Donovan said.

Bly's head snapped up. She couldn't stop the relieved exhale of breath that left her lips.

Kerrigan blinked down at her. He wore black velvet pants and an emerald silk vest over a flowing shirt of the darkest purple. Green vines were embroidered on the lavender scarf at his neck.

"Heading to the ballroom?" Donovan asked. "There's plenty to pick from down there."

"What are you doing with her?" Kerrigan's eyes hadn't left Bly's.

"Ah, yes. I forgot you seemed to have a soft spot for this one. We all know that's not going to end well—for you or for her. Better let me have her."

Donovan moved, tugging her forward a hair before stopping again because Kerrigan hadn't budged.

"To do what with?" Kerrigan asked.

"Whatever she wants, and I believe what she *wants* is to secure a sponsor."

"Leave her to me then," Kerrigan said.

"You don't play the Games."

"I want her," Kerrigan bit out, his voice finally losing its cool.

"To set her free again?"

"Not if she doesn't want to be."

Donovan looked between Bly and Kerrigan, his eyes narrowing as he stared at his brother. "Fine, but you owe me." He gave Bly a push toward Kerrigan that made her stumble. Kerrigan's hands caught her upper arms, his grip harder than Donovan's had been. He spun her around, shifting his hold to her wrist and pulling her down the hallway.

Donovan chuckled behind them.

Bly felt torn. She'd liked the idea of handing over the vampire who'd toyed with her.

But this was better. Safer.

Trying to seduce Prince Donovan would be like trying to charm a snake. She'd end up bitten for sure, but also probably dead.

Eventually they reached a heavy wooden door. This one was carved with a sea of overlapping flowers—more types than Bly could even name. In its center was a gleaming copper knocker that was melted to look like a ring of leaves. It was one of the loveliest things she had ever seen, and she had to stop herself from reaching out to touch it.

Kerrigan twisted the copper doorknob, intricately etched with the same array of flowers. Bly expected he would pull her in after him, but he let go of her, glanced down the hallway where Donovan had disappeared, and then stepped inside without her, twisting back to look down at her.

For a moment he simply stood there, arms folded across his chest, as he seemed to consider what to do next. He stepped back slightly. "Come on in then," he said. "If that's what you really want." It wasn't a question. In fact, it sounded more like a threat.

One that made her heart beat just a little bit faster.

Which made his stare drift down to her very naked chest. His eyebrows shot up. "I guess you got over your fear of bare skin." He laughed. "You're good at playing the damsel in distress, I'll give you that, but that didn't work, so you've moved on to the next plan, I suppose." His gaze turned black. "I like this version better, I think. It's truer."

She almost backed right out of the room, but she stepped inside instead.

The walls were the blackest stone she'd ever seen, as if they were swallowing every bit of light around them, but it was like a perfect night sky behind a whole world the vampire had collected. Gold-framed pictures covered almost every inch of the wall: gloomy lakes at sunrise, silhouettes of trees, a deer in a meadow, couples kissing under moonlight. Sconces peppered the wall between the pictures, holding flickering red candles that filled the room with the heavy scent of cinnamon. The smell reminded her of home, and Elise baking apple bread before dawn. It eased a little of the tension in her chest.

In the center of the room sat a red velvet chair and a simple wooden table with an ornate lamp beside it—a smaller mirror of the ones that hung from the banquet hall with a golden stand of vines that curved at the top where it gave way to tiny lit orbs clustered like berries. They glowed with the light of spells, casting everything in hues of seduction. Beyond this room, she could just make out a bedroom with the same design and a bed frame of golden berries.

Kerrigan drifted over and sat in the chair. He picked a berry from a gleaming gold dish on the table and popped it into his mouth. As he poured red from a pitcher into a glass, Bly braced herself for the smell of blood, but all she got was bitter wine. He eyed her as he sipped from the cup.

She ran her hands nervously down her dress and licked her lips, biting her bottom one in a way that she hoped made her seem eager.

He laughed. "You can stop that."

She froze. The spells under her sleeve felt like burning beacons.

"You're not the first one to try and convince me to pick them to sponsor using"—he waved a hand up and down her body—"inventive ways." A lazy grin stretched across his face. "You're welcome to try, though. Just so we're clear, I will not change my mind, but we might both enjoy you giving it your best shot. And before you think about going back to my brother, he already has a team, and I doubt he'll add you to it, regardless of what he promised. I did you a favor."

At least he didn't guess what she really wanted.

As he waited, his eyes wandered over her until her whole body felt like it was blushing. He smirked at her hesitation.

So she folded her arms behind her back in a way she hoped looked sexy, and not like a girl trying to free a weapon, and took slow steps toward him until she stood between his knees, her legs brushing the velvet of his chair.

"Actually, you said if I wanted to know what it was like to be bitten to just ask. Here I am . . . asking."

His eyes widened.

She'd surprised him. Good. Hopefully it threw him off-balance.

She leaned forward and let her hands rest on the arms of his chair, her spell carefully hidden between her fingers.

His lips curled but his eyes looked flat, as if he weren't actually enjoying this. They weren't black like they had been a moment ago. Maybe he had more control than she thought.

She tried not to let that bother her. She just needed to distract him—not actually win him over.

Leaning in, she put her lips next to his ear, letting her neck sit stretched and vulnerable just inches from his mouth. "Maybe I'll taste so sweet that you'll be begging to sponsor me," she whispered and swung her hand that held the sleeping spell toward the bare skin of his neck.

The spell's word hadn't even left her lips when fingers closed around her wrist, crushing the bone so hard that her grip sprung open. She cried out, pulling back as much as she could.

A thin sliver of dried mushroom landed on the velvet of his pants.

"Well, that was actually surprising," he said.

He pushed himself to his feet, knocking her backward so quickly that she would have fallen if not for his fingers clasping her wrist. In an instant, he'd spun her, one arm wrapping around her chest, pressing her back against him as he lifted her so her feet barely touched the ground. His other hand gripped her chin, twisting it so that the side of her neck was exposed. His fangs pricked her skin without breaking it, and her whole body thrummed with panic before he pulled back slightly.

"Playing both sides, which means you're desperate for the money or just greedy. Which is it?"

She strained against the crush of his arm. She didn't owe him an answer.

"Greed then," he said for her.

His fangs brushed her neck again.

She gasped, squirming in his grip. His arms were iron around her, but it didn't stop her from fighting. His fangs scraped her skin each time she struggled, but she didn't care.

If she died, then Emerson wouldn't keep playing. He believed the dead should stay dead—he'd always said that. And even though that had been before Elise died, she doubted his thoughts had really changed all that much. Emerson never changed his opinions just to suit his own desires. And he'd made it perfectly clear that he didn't want to be a vampire.

Her death would mean Elise would never live again, and Emerson would soon follow her into the ground.

Knowing all that wasn't enough to help her break free.

So she stopped, letting tears fall—for them. None of them were really for her, and she trembled with the realization of how little her own life had begun to mean to her. She'd become a person without her own dreams. A person willing to die to get what she wanted: her sister back . . . and perhaps some level of forgiveness for herself, too.

She let out a tiny choked sob.

The hand holding her chin loosened, and suddenly the

vampire's fingers were on her cheeks, playing in her tears. She jerked at the invasion of it, and his fangs slid away from her neck before she could cut herself on them.

"So you do want to live. You do value your little life . . . but you've realized it too late."

"I don't give a damn about my own life." She twisted her face away from him, and this time he let her, but his hand settled on her neck. His grip wasn't tight, but she knew he could snap it in an instant if he decided to.

"Oh?" he said, as if her words were a lie.

She hated that.

"I want to bring back my sister." Her voice broke as she said it because she was trapped and hopeless, even more than she was before. She could feel Elise slipping further and further away, and she was about to join her, wherever she was.

But her feet touched the ground again, and firm hands spun her around. "What did you say?" The vampire stared down at her, brows drawn together.

"I just want to bring my dead sister back." She could feel the hot tears still running down her face. She tried to turn her head away so he couldn't watch, but his hand found her chin again, though this time his grip was soft as he turned her face back to him.

"But you were here . . . at the vampire trial. Why, if raising the dead is what you want? We create the dead; we don't raise them."

"My . . . my best friend is death cursed. I want to save him too. I want to save everyone." Softer, she said, "I don't want to be left alone."

He flinched back from those words.

She hadn't meant to admit that last part—the selfishness in it. She needed to save herself just as much as she needed to save them.

Kerrigan stared down at her for a long time. There was something in his eyes that tore at her—it was like looking in a mirror, but that didn't make sense. What could she and a vampire possibly have in common? Everyone he knew was immortal and powerful and safe.

"What's your name?" he finally asked.

"Bly," she said, startled.

"Then I'll come with you, Bly."

Her mouth popped open. "What?"

"My life is yours. I'll give it for your sister."

She backed away from him, and his hands fell from her arms.

"Don't play with me," she said quietly.

But his face held startling sincerity. There was sadness in there and resignation, and also an odd light that she didn't understand.

"I'm not," he said.

"Why?"

"I am done with this life." Kerrigan glanced around his room, and Bly did too. It was clear he had access to everything he could desire, except whatever he wanted to escape.

"Why?" she pressed again.

Something flickered across his face. Pain? Regret? Something unpleasant. His face turned to stone the second after. "My reasons mean nothing to you."

He wasn't wrong. At least, he shouldn't have been, but Bly found herself desperate to know, to understand what reason an immortal prince would have to feel so unsatisfied with his life that he'd give himself over to captivity and death.

But she wasn't going to say all that.

"I don't trust you," Bly said instead, despite the fact that he'd had her by the throat a second ago and she was still in one piece—she wasn't even bleeding.

His eyes were still black. It must have taken incredible strength not to bite her.

He blinked at her as if trying to clear his hunger.

"I suppose you shouldn't," he said slowly. His hands clenched at his sides, knuckles whitening. "You're smart for that."

It took everything in her not to swallow.

Silence stretched between them until his eyes traveled from her head to her toes and back up again, settling on her neck for so long that her cheeks heated. He closed the gap between them so that they were almost touching, but she didn't want to give him the satisfaction of stepping back.

Her nose almost brushed his chest. He smelled like the same cinnamon that overpowered his room, and it made some ridiculous part of her want to lean into him, to get lost in that smell, to give herself over to good memories and forget about this moment. Forget that she needed this vampire to die to erase all her mistakes.

Her nostrils flared as she let herself breathe too deeply.

Even though they still weren't touching, she could practically feel the subtle shift in his body. The tension.

He sighed, his breath brushing the top of her head, so she knew he was staring down at her even though she wasn't looking up.

"I have tried everything." His voice cracked with emotion, and the surprise of it made her finally tilt her chin to look at him.

His eyes were wide like it had startled him even more, and they weren't black anymore. They'd returned to a dark gray rimmed in green, but as he and Bly stared at each other, the black pulsed in and out. One of his hands hovered between them. A fingertip brushed her skin at her shoulder, and he watched her reaction.

Nothing was holding her here, this close to him. He'd already let her go so many times before, she knew he would again. This little touch was a question.

His eyes went pitch black again when she didn't move, and he traced the sensitive line of her collarbone to the center of her chest between the swell of her breasts.

"I have tried every pleasure." His lips curved with seduction, but his face resembled one of his paintings, something not quite real no matter how perfectly rendered. Whatever this moment was, it was more vulnerable than just a moment of attraction.

Bly pushed that realization away. She was here to manipulate, to catch a prize, not to feel a connection.

Kerrigan's smile abruptly fell away as if he knew she could see through it. "I've tried every pain." He grimaced and pulled his hand away as if a memory had bitten him. "But nothing . . . nothing has done anything to dull the memories."

Bly's mouth was dry, but not from lust—from the deep feeling of understanding between them. Memories haunted him just as they did her. And if she thought that time might release her, here was proof that that would never happen. Kerrigan had all the time in the world, but he hadn't found anything to dull whatever caused the pain that clung to his face now.

She felt her choices dwindle even more. If she wanted any life at all that wasn't constantly running from her past, she needed to erase it.

She needed Kerrigan.

And not to share their losses together, not to feel out whatever thread connected them.

She needed him to stay drowning in the same hopelessness that she was running from so that he'd sacrifice himself for her sister.

"I believe you now," she said.

He nodded.

"Then you'll let me take you." Her hands drifted toward the other spells tucked in her dress, but his fingers closed around her wrist before she could even touch them.

"I do not like being trapped," he said coldly.

"But . . ."

"No. I have rules. I'm coming willingly. I won't be led like a hog tied for the slaughter."

Bly nodded.

He stared at her for a moment. "I'll need blood."

She swallowed, unsure if he meant from her or not, but her head seemed to nod all by itself.

"And . . ." He hesitated. "I want you to talk to me on the way there. I want you to tell me about your sister."

She took a step back in surprise.

"The blood didn't scare you, but that does?" He raised an eyebrow. "I want to know who is going to live in my place," he said softly.

For some reason, tears pricked the edges of Bly's eyes, and her chest expanded with a painful kind of hurt and hope. She nodded. She could give him pieces of Elise if it meant Elise would be standing in front of her whole and alive at the end of it.

"Then let's go, love." He stepped forward and wrapped an arm loosely over her shoulders, his hand hanging down just above her breast without so much as grazing it.

"What are you doing?" she said, voice squeaking.

"Walking us out of here." He propelled her through the door and into the hallway, moving her back the way she'd just come.

This wasn't the way she imagined this going—she thought they'd be trying to drag him out of here unconscious, not strolling as if they were lovers enjoying the night.

"Relax a little," Kerrigan said. "You look like I've abducted you, which is suspicious. Everyone knows I prefer very enthusiastic partners whether that's for blood drinking or . . . other things."

She blushed, tensing even more.

He chuckled a little at her response. "Sorry," he said, but he didn't sound sorry at all. "At least put your arm around me?"

She slid an arm around his back. Her hand hung awkwardly in the air for a moment before she finally let it rest against his waist.

She swore she could feel him silently chuckle.

But then she felt him tense, too.

Her eyes, which had been half dazed, focused in on the person approaching them.

Donovan again.

"Relax," Kerrigan said, even though she could feel the strain in his body. He leaned down slightly toward her ear. "May I touch you a little more?"

Her mind tumbled over what exactly he meant, but she didn't really have time to ask.

"Bly?" he said softly.

She nodded.

His arm slid across her shoulder until his hand cupped the side of her neck.

Breathe, she told herself. *Look like you like it.*

"Brother," Kerrigan said, his voice light and airy.

Donovan smiled widely as he stopped in front of them, but his eyes trailed over Bly critically, focusing on the hand on her neck and then her face, giving her more attention than he had earlier.

She wasn't quite sure what expression she was supposed to be wearing. Lust? She almost grimaced because she wasn't even really sure how to look like that. She tried to smile demurely instead.

"I was just coming back to see if you kept her or not," Donovan said.

Kerrigan shrugged. "I like her."

"I know," Donovan said darkly. "Are you playing?" There was

a hint of hope in his question.

"Just enjoying. Turns out she wanted other things that she didn't need to play for." Kerrigan's fingers stroked Bly's neck before his hand drifted up to gently tug on her earlobe.

She gasped. Her stomach bubbled with an uncomfortable heat.

And for a second, she thought she'd given it away, but Donovan chuckled. "I'll let you go enjoy your evening."

Apparently she didn't need to pretend to like it.

Donovan moved past them, but not before Bly saw something else in his eyes: worry.

She wished she hadn't seen it. Whatever she thought of him, she knew what losing a sibling would do to someone, and she wouldn't want to inflict that on anyone, not even a vampire who saw her as nothing but blood and bones.

She tried not to think of it.

Kerrigan's hand slid back down from her neck and hung over her shoulders again in a pose that was a little less intimate. She told herself she was relieved. But every part of her was aware of the way he kept glancing sideways at her as they walked.

She told herself it was because she was grateful to him.

That was all.

But she needed to remember what Emerson had said: a vampire was a vampire. He had his own reasons for doing this, and it wasn't because he liked her.

No matter how he looked at her.

Nobody bothered them as they walked past the ballroom and into the hallway that led out of the fortress.

Bly stopped in front of the first door on the right.

"What is it?" Kerrigan asked.

"The rest of my team's in there. They were supposed to ambush . . . whoever I brought back."

"Did you plan on it being me?" He cocked as head, searching her face in a way that warned her that he'd know if she lied.

"I was willing to take another, but . . . yes."

He nodded. "Why?"

"You seemed . . . nice."

"Weak, you mean."

"You seemed like someone who wouldn't be missed," she added. Jade had called him a traitor.

He flinched, and she regretted her harshness.

"You may be right about that," he said.

She waited for him to say more, but he didn't.

He pulled open the door and waved her forward. "After you."

She stepped inside and his arm wrapped around her shoulder again.

"You can come out now," he said lightly to the racks of clothes her team hid behind.

Emerson appeared first, striding toward them like Bly wasn't standing next to a deadly creature.

"Wait." She held up her hands. "I got him."

"It looks like he's got *you*," Demelza said. She'd stepped out with the twins on either side of her.

Emerson hadn't stopped. His knife settled against Kerrigan's neck while Kerrigan didn't lift a finger to stop him.

"Back away from her."

Kerrigan chuckled.

"Emerson, stop. He's with us," Bly said.

Emerson's eyes darted to her in confusion before narrowing back on Kerrigan.

"You've been tricked," Demelza said. "And he's probably going to kill you before I can spell him." She didn't sound particularly sad about that.

Kerrigan's head snapped in Demelza's direction so quickly that blood trickled from his throat where he'd hit Emerson's blade. "Are you a witch? You may have vampire eyes, but I can spot a witch from a mile away."

Demelza glared at him but didn't deny it.

"You didn't tell me you had a witch," he said to Bly.

She stared up at him, hoping that wouldn't make him back out. His expression was unreadable as he glanced at her and then back to Demelza.

"Well, witch, if I wanted to kill her, I already would have," Kerrigan said slowly. "Lower your weapon or I'll change my mind." He turned his head slightly toward Emerson. His arm had shifted too as he spoke, so quickly that Bly hadn't registered the movement. His hand had curved around her throat, fingers digging into the front of her neck with a force that was just shy of being painful. But his thumb at the back of her neck, hidden from view, traced a soft circle against her skin.

She hoped that was a sign for her—that he didn't *really* plan on killing her.

He just wanted Emerson to lower his weapon.

"I'm fine," she said to Emerson.

He shook his head at her like they were kids again and she was doing something entirely reckless.

"Listen to me," she snapped. His eyes met hers. "I am *fine*."

He removed the blade from Kerrigan's neck. He didn't retreat, though.

"I knew they weren't smart," Vincent muttered. Neither he nor Nova lowered their own daggers an inch.

Kerrigan let go of Bly's neck and draped his arm across her shoulders again. "That's better. Let's get going, shall we?"

Nobody moved.

"Go where?" Emerson asked.

"To my doom, of course," Kerrigan said.

"Why would you . . . just come with us?" Nova finally asked.

"Bly is very convincing."

They all looked at her. She shrugged. "He wants to do something nice for someone," she said weakly.

"Die?" Vincent's voice held the disbelief on everyone else's faces.

"The ultimate sacrifice," Kerrigan chirped. "Paying the price for my evil life. Redemption and all that."

"Since when do vampires worry about redemption?" Demelza spat.

"You wouldn't understand it, witch." Kerrigan's voice grew cold.

It was jarring how quickly he could switch between masks, and yet none of them was the boy she'd just been alone with in his rooms. But she couldn't say that.

"I trust him," she said instead.

Emerson let out a huff she was all too familiar with. She knew she had him. He'd go along with this.

"Well, I'm not going to say no to a vampire who wants to die," Demelza said with a shrug. "But I want you bound. *I* don't trust you." She shot Bly a condescending look.

"No," Kerrigan said. "Bly and I have a deal, and it involves me going on my own, and her keeping me company on the road."

Demelza was shaking her head. Nova and Vincent exchanged worried glances, and Emerson looked as though he wanted to lop Kerrigan's head off.

"We're doing this," Bly said. "Unless you want to part ways?"

"Fine," Demelza said. "At least he'll kill you first when he decides he's done playing."

Her voice sounded a little too hopeful.

TWELVE

KERRIGAN WALKED BEHIND EMERSON
and in front of Bly. She kept waiting for him to demand her
attention but all she got was the occasional glance, a narrowing of his eyes, or sometimes a slight smile, as if he could gather
something about her just from a look.

Leaving Vagaris was simple with Kerrigan in the group, unrestrained and looking like a sponsor, not a prisoner. The guards at
the gate even nodded at them as they left.

They walked for a couple hours before stopping. There were
fewer screams now, as if the killing lessened the closer dawn
came.

They made camp quickly. Demelza was the only one with a
small tent she unpacked from the long slender bag she'd been
carrying. The rest of them had bedrolls that they spread around
the hidden fire before pulling out their packs of food.

Kerrigan shook his head when Bly offered him a handful of
dried apples.

"I hate to say it, but I need to eat something else," he said.

They all froze with food halfway to their mouths. Vampires needed to drink blood daily or their strength would dwindle rapidly, and they'd become less and less tolerant of the sun.

"You didn't bring anything with you?" Demelza snapped.

He shrugged. "It was a bit spur of the moment."

"Usually we don't bother feeding captives," Demelza said. "You don't really need to keep your strength up."

"But I'm not actually your prisoner, am I?"

"You could be."

They sat in tense silence for a moment.

Maybe they could overpower him, but if he decided to fight them for any reason, then surely some of them would die.

Vincent glared at Bly, and he didn't need to say a thing to accuse her: she was the one who'd thrown out their original plan. They could've had a bound, unconscious vampire, but now they were sitting around in a circle with someone who could easily kill them if given the upper hand.

"Well, you're not getting a drop of my blood," Demelza said.

"I wouldn't drink witch blood even if I were dying," Kerrigan said, which didn't make sense at all. Vampires loved witch blood. It was one of the reasons they had the Games, after all.

Kerrigan suddenly smiled, eyeing each one of them in turn. His gaze slid back to Emerson. "You're particularly handsome, so I'm sure you'd be wonderful."

"No," Emerson said.

Kerrigan shrugged. He turned to Vincent and Nova. "You both look like you'd be . . . bitter."

Vincent looked one second away from decapitating him.

"Although I do like your feistiness," Kerrigan added, winking at Vincent.

He glanced down at Bly. "And you . . ." He trailed off, like he'd forgotten what he wanted to say about her.

Bly's mouth went dry, but she spoke anyway. "I'll do it," she said.

"She hates blood," Emerson interjected.

Bly shook her head, but Kerrigan was already frowning at her.

"For crying out loud," Nova said. "I'll feed the damn vampire. I've sold blood my whole life. A fang can't be different than a needle."

"I can make it different," Kerrigan said, his voice seductive, but he wasn't looking at Nova; his eyes were still on Bly.

He only turned away when Nova plopped next to him on the crumbling tree trunk he sat on, rolled up her sleeve, and held out her wrist. He sighed as he took it, but he placed it in his mouth and started drinking like it was nothing. Bly tried not to watch as he drank, but she couldn't help herself, and every time she looked his way, he was staring at her.

Nova looked bored.

When he finished, he ran his tongue quickly across his lips. The corner of his mouth tugged up as he noticed her staring again.

But when Bly caught Emerson's eye, the disgust on his face was clear.

She didn't look at Kerrigan again.

◆ ◆ ◆

The morning came swiftly. Light sunk through the canopy of trees and coated the ground in mottled gold. The air was hungover with cold, and Bly's breath puffed out in heavy clouds as they prepared to start their long walk.

Demelza eyed Kerrigan. "You walk between Vincent and Nova today."

"I'm going to walk with Bly," Kerrigan said, straightening his cloak. He'd brought nothing with him but the cloak he'd grabbed from one of the changing rooms on their way out and had slept with his back against a tree. Demelza had insisted they take turns watching him.

"We'll bring up the rear," he added.

"No way am I having a vampire at my back."

"Nonnegotiable," he said.

Demelza's fingers twitched like she was one second away from reaching for her spells.

"I made that bargain," Bly said. "He just wants to talk to me."

Emerson was shaking his head.

"Why would he want *that*?" Demelza folded her arms across her chest.

"She's the most interesting, and I don't like being bored." Kerrigan shrugged.

"You can't be bored if you're unconscious." Demelza's voice was soft and deadly.

"Try me, witch." Kerrigan's voice was a deeper mirror of Demelza's.

Bly stood slightly between them both, and she thought maybe she should get out of the way.

Instead, she took a deep breath and stood her ground. "We're doing exactly what I agreed to. This is my plan."

Demelza's face reddened. Bly thought she might murder her and then Kerrigan.

"That's fair," Emerson said gruffly. Bly shot him a look of thanks for having her back this time, but he didn't look the least bit happy about it. All he did was give her a slight nod before turning away. "Let's move," he said.

"Agreed," Vincent added. "If she wants to risk being an afternoon snack, that's her problem." He strode past Bly without looking at her, as if to emphasize how little he actually cared.

They were being ridiculous anyway. If Kerrigan wanted to kill her, he'd had his chance.

More than one.

As everyone else pulled away, Kerrigan held out his arm.

She hesitated at that. Talking was one thing; strolling together arm-in-arm was another.

He lifted a brow as if daring her to decline.

She didn't like saying no to a dare—at least, not in theory. As a kid, she'd always tried to goad Elise or Emerson into challenging her to do something outrageous, but they never would. She always ended up daring herself, which was a lot less fun.

She slipped her hand around his arm, resting her palm easily against it.

He stood still for a second, letting the others get a little distance on them before following.

"So tell me about the sister who you love enough to stroll through the woods on the arm of a despicable vampire."

"I wouldn't call you despicable," she said.

"Your friends seem to think so." He paused. "What would you call me then?"

"Sad." She said it without thinking, but it was the first word that dropped into her mind.

Darkness flitted across his face. "Enough about me. You have a deal to uphold. I know you loved your sister, but tell me why."

Bly opened her mouth, expecting every detail that made her sister special to come pouring out easily. After all, Elise had been a constant presence in her mind for the past year, haunting Bly's every waking thought, but when she reached for the details, her sister slid through her fingers like the ghost she was.

"We can start with something easy," Kerrigan said softly. "What did she look like?" There was a hint of sorrow in his voice, but it wasn't his own. She thought it was for her, as if he knew exactly why she was struggling, but how could he? And how could he know that even that question was difficult? What color had her eyes been?

Finally, Bly opened her mouth to answer. "She was . . . beautiful." That word alone was a tangible thing that helped Bly begin to picture her, really picture her. She let herself get lost in the image. "She had hair like the sun and a personality just as warm."

She glanced up at Kerrigan. He was nodding, a slight smile on his face, as if he could see her too. Because Elise was the kind of person who could draw a smile from anybody, even in death.

"And?" It was all he said, letting her take the conversation wherever she wanted.

"She was the kind of person who always put others first," Bly said. "Especially me. I hated working with both my parents. My dad is a tanner, and my mom is a healer, and Emerson wasn't lying . . . I hate blood."

He chuckled softly. "That's fair."

"But Elise was always volunteering to work with both of them. She excelled at it, and I used to think that she loved it, but sometimes I wonder if she did it just to take the pressure off of me—maybe she was playing the role of dutiful daughter so I didn't have to."

And then the one time Elise had done something reckless, that had been for Bly too. A wave of guilt crushed her, and her hand tightened on Kerrigan's arm for a moment, but he said nothing about it.

For a second, they walked in silence, with Kerrigan occasionally brushing aside a hanging branch of pine.

"Tell me something she did that made you laugh," he said eventually.

Bly's mind went painfully blank again. Elise had been soft smiles and patience, not wicked laughter—that had been Bly. She let her mind wander into the forest, focusing on the leaves instead of the past until a memory came to her like a gift.

"This one time when she was baking apple bread—she was always baking apple bread anytime we could afford the apples—but anyway, this one time I woke up late, as usual, and I walked over to our kitchen table and she'd sat this apple there. She'd carved a little face into it with this ridiculous grin, and I picked it up and I loved it instantly, and it made me love her more. Because she knew it would delight me—that silly little face on that silly little apple. I burst out laughing and she did too. We laughed so hard that our mom came in from outside just to check on us, and when I showed her the apple, she just looked at us like we were strange and went back outside, and we laughed even harder. Because we were strange. Or at least I was, and Elise loved me for it."

The story made Elise so real that Bly could almost touch her. It made the ache to have her back even stronger, but Bly didn't mind because the longer they walked, the closer she was to making the aches go away forever.

"She did that for me too once."

Bly blinked. She hadn't noticed that Emerson had fallen back within earshot. He was looking over his shoulder with a distant smile on his face—a smile caught in the past with just the echo of it in the present.

He slowed even more until he was on Bly's other side. "More than once, actually. She'd carve a weird face on one and leave it impaled on one of my knives in my forge, so I'd see it first thing in the morning. Always green ones. I used to think they were too sour, but she always said the best way to start the day was with something tart and a laugh to sweeten it. Eventually they grew on me." He laughed then, deep and booming, the kind of laugh that she thought he used to save for her funny little stories. Apparently Elise had managed to make him laugh too.

And it was Elise's memory that drew the laugh from him now.

It warmed her. How long had it been since she'd heard that sound? Elise was coming back to them; even Emerson felt it.

So she kept talking until Kerrigan's arm beneath her hand felt like the most natural thing in the world. She gave him story after story and detail after detail until she knew that he could picture her sister despite never having met her. Because Elise *was* alive in her memories again. Bly hadn't even realized how she'd blocked out all the good memories with the wall of one painful one, but now they crashed through that wall, and while she still felt that rubble at her feet, she didn't want to rebuild it. It was okay to let herself remember and miss all the good things about Elise.

She was almost done missing those things, anyway. Soon she wouldn't have to.

Eventually they stopped talking, and Emerson moved to walk ahead of them again, like he'd come back to his senses and realized he was sharing something precious with a vampire.

Kerrigan didn't press her for more.

He seemed too quiet, as if his mind had left for his own perilous memories.

"Tell me about your brother," she said, because it was the polite thing to do. She really didn't want to know about Donovan at all, but even if she thought he was evil, he probably meant something to Kerrigan.

She felt Kerrigan's arm tense beneath hers. "Why would you ask about him?"

"I just . . . thought we were sharing."

He stopped and turned toward her, forcing her hand to drop from his arm. He smirked at her as if trying to put back on that casual charm he seemed to use like a shield, but this time there was cruelness in it. He looked more like Donovan. "We're not sharing. You're entertaining me on the journey. I just wanted to have a little fun because you're pretty and I like the sound of your lovely voice." He reached out a hand and tugged at one of the curls around her face. "That's all. We're playing a game within the game until we get there."

A ball of hurt clogged her throat. He'd made her believe that he cared just for the fun of it.

But as she looked at that halfhearted smirk that didn't reach his tired eyes, something told her he was pretending now, not then, but it didn't lessen her anger.

She slapped his hand away. "This isn't a game to me."

The smirk dropped in an instant. "And you think it's really one to me? I'm heading to certain death, remember?"

"Well, you're not acting like it."

"And how *should* I face death? Would you rather me fight and scream?"

She tensed. She wondered if he knew that it might not be death that he faced—that the witches kept some of their prisoners alive.

"I'm guessing you wouldn't like that. I'm very good at pretending, and that's all I want for my last day—to pretend that I'm taking a walk in the woods with a pretty girl I fancy and maybe even pretend I'm human again. Would you deny me that?"

"Of course not," she whispered.

"Good." He held out his arm again.

But she didn't take it. She stared up at him—a new fear beating in her chest, drowning out her hopeful heart.

"You're not going to change your mind, are you?" she asked. All this talk of Elise after a year of missing her and having no one to talk to had conjured a ghost so real that Bly knew it would kill her to have that ripped away again.

And it all depended on the beautiful vampire in front of her keeping his word.

Kerrigan's expression darkened. "There's only one thing I want more than getting your sister back, and I can't have that. So no . . . I won't change my mind. You have my word."

"And why is my sister so important to you?" Obviously he wanted to escape something—that much was clear—but there were other ways to do that besides marching to a terrible fate. There had to be more.

He looked away and back at her. "I've always tried to help humans, and you've given me a final chance."

"She's one girl." Bly cringed at her own words, because to her, Elise was everything, but if Kerrigan cared about humans, there had to be so much more he could do than giving his life for a girl he'd only ever heard about. "You're a prince. You have power."

He gave a dark laugh. "And I tried to use it once. I failed."

"That's why you're a traitor."

He nodded.

When she opened her mouth to ask for more, he shook his head. "I couldn't save many, but I can save one." He held her eyes. "Or two," he added softly. "And I won't change my mind. That's all that should matter to you."

She shivered, partly from relief and partly from the cold. A thick fog had rolled in, draping over them like a curse.

Kerrigan took off his cloak. She opened her mouth to protest, but he'd already swung it across her shoulders, clasping it around her neck without touching her. The soft fur warmed her in an instant. The dark green stitching that wound in leafy patterns across the black velvet was the type of thing she'd once dreamed of wearing. He'd wrapped her in a sliver of the dreams she once had.

It felt like a promise, and she knew she shouldn't accept it as such, but she needed something to comfort her for once.

She opened her mouth to ask what he wanted that he couldn't have, even though she knew he wouldn't like it. But she couldn't fight the desire to get to know him as well, which was incredibly foolish.

He guessed her question before she could utter a word, though, and shook his head. "Enough. I'm pretending I have no past."

She held her tongue. They had a bargain, and it involved him getting to know her, not the other way around. She started to turn. The others had slipped through the brush, and it wouldn't be long before Emerson did look back again, but Kerrigan's hand gripped her elbow.

"You love your sister."

He said it in present tense. The change made her heart swell— he was saying her resurrection was imminent.

"But that's not everything, right?" he asked. "Love drives people to wild acts of bravery." He hesitated. "But guilt drives people to their death."

She wasn't sure they were talking about her anymore, so she said nothing.

"Let the love drive you," he said.

"I'm not planning to die."

"Good." A flicker of relief crossed his face, and she couldn't help but wonder why he cared so much.

THIRTEEN

THE WALK BEGAN TO FEEL TOO EASY.
They could still hear an occasional distant scuffle, but nothing that came near, and the silence that surrounded them most of the time started to feel as if it were waiting for something to fill it.

Kerrigan had gone quiet. Bly still walked beside him, but she no longer held his arm.

"Not many bounty hunters playing today," Bly whispered, wanting to break the lull that had descended.

"Off getting paid," Emerson said from in front of them, voice dripping in disgust.

"Or they wouldn't dare attack a group with an unrestrained witch *and* vampire," Kerrigan said.

"Exactly." Demelza glanced back at Kerrigan for the first time with a look that wasn't quite pure hatred.

In one thing they agreed: whoever attacked them wouldn't live to tell any tales about it.

It made Bly feel more relaxed and more on edge at the same

time. Some bounty hunters were desperate. Others made a career out of hunting the desperate, but she didn't want to watch either one bleed out in front of her. Not again.

So when Kerrigan paused with his head tilted to one side, Bly's heart raced with fear for herself and whoever was coming.

Nova stilled, listening. "They're coming straight behind us, and they're not even trying to be quiet."

"That's not a good sign," Vincent grumbled, but there was a slight smile on his face as he tightened his grip on his sword.

Demelza and Kerrigan wouldn't be the only ones to kill without a second thought.

Bly met Emerson's eyes. Whatever tension was between them, she knew he valued human life. She knew he'd think twice about killing, even if the other person had a sword at his heart.

She loved that about him.

But her instinct told her to stay next to Kerrigan.

She saw the couple first—the ones who'd won the vampire trial. The girl still wore her hair in a high bun that looked immaculate for someone who was walking through the woods. The boy wore a hungry sneer on his face. They each had a bow made of wood polished to an almost black gleam. Each bow already held an arrow tipped in red and purple feathers. Vampire bows.

And she remembered who'd chosen to sponsor them.

Donovan stepped out of the woods and stood between them, his own bow at the ready. Behind him, two other vampires emerged with drawn swords, dressed in the red uniforms of guards, their faces grim and eyes shifting as they took everything in.

Donovan's bow lowered a fraction when he saw his brother. "Kerrigan." His eyes slid to Bly, eyebrows raising with surprise. "The little bleeder convinced you to play after all? Why didn't you tell me? We could've done it together." His eyes slid to Demelza. "And you've already got a witch. Why are you heading toward Havenwhile?"

Kerrigan was silent for a moment. For some reason, his focus shifted to Bly. There was a different kind of pain in his eyes. He hadn't planned on this moment. He hadn't planned to see his brother again at all.

"Because I'm the captive, not the captor."

"You're not bound." He stared at Kerrigan's free limbs before his bow rose again and shifted to point at Demelza. "What new witchery is this? I've never heard of a spell that could take away free will."

"There is no spell," Kerrigan said gently.

Something flickered in Donovan's eyes. Bly thought it might have been understanding, but whatever it was, he shoved it away. "You're not making sense."

"I'm done with this life, brother. I want to give myself up for something good." He glanced at Bly. "I want to save someone else."

The way he looked at her made her think he meant her, not Elise.

But Donovan's attention was on her too now and the tip of the arrow in his bow pointed her way. He turned back to Kerrigan. "What game has this little human been playing with you?"

"No games," Kerrigan said. "I just saw something in her that . . ." He trailed off, and Bly wasn't sure if it was because he didn't want to share or he didn't really understand why he seemed to like her.

She felt too many stares on her, as if everyone was wondering the same thing.

"Then drain her and move on. Don't get human on me again," Donovan snapped. "I'm not going to sit here while you toss your life away for a pretty neck."

"It's not up to you," Kerrigan said.

"The hell it isn't." He nodded at the other two with him.

Three bows pointed at Bly, pulling back. She wondered exactly where they were aiming . . . an eye? Her neck? Maybe her heart? For some reason she hoped it was the last one. Her heart had been in pain for so long that she probably wouldn't even feel an arrow through it.

"Bly!" Emerson screamed. But she didn't turn toward his voice. She couldn't see anything but Donovan's wicked smile.

She needed to at least pick a direction to dodge. She couldn't just stand there—not with Elise still in the ground.

Donovan pulled the bowstring back just a little more.

Someone's arms closed around her from behind, pressing her against a muscled chest before spinning her around so she faced the unthreatening trees, turning their own body into a shield.

The body at her back jerked once. Twice. Three times while the strong arms held her tight and kept her hidden from the arrows. She struggled to free herself.

The line of trees became nothing but a blur as she panicked. She choked on Emerson's name. She'd always wanted him to be the hero in her story, but not like this. Not a dead one. She tried to yell at him again to let her go, but the fear of seeing him die kept her voice trapped.

Finally, his arms loosened, and she twisted around to face him. Her hands automatically reached up, searching his chest for wounds.

A chest dressed in an emerald silk vest.

Bly's hands froze as her chin jerked up.

Kerrigan stared down at her, his eyes wide and confused, as if he were just as surprised as she was to find himself saving her.

Blood trickled down the side of his lip.

His arms were still wrapped around her as he started to slump, pulling them both down to their knees.

Behind them, Donovan roared. "Fools! You shot my brother!" He tossed his bow on the ground and slid his sword from its sheath.

"You shot him first!" screamed the girl. "And we're supposed to be hunting a witch, not your brother who seems to have a death wish—"

Her head dropped from her shoulders, hitting the ground first, and then the body fell next, and Bly was certain she'd never forget that horrible detail.

Bly hadn't even seen Donovan's sword move—just a girl with a head and then a body without one.

The boy's mouth gaped as he stared at the head. His eyes already held an unbearably haunted look. A look Bly knew well.

The same expression was on his face when his head fell too.

"Stop him or he'll kill you all," Kerrigan rasped out. He wasn't even facing that direction, but he seemed to know what was happening, as if he were familiar with the sound a head made when it hit the ground.

But Bly couldn't let go of him. His arms had slipped from her back and hung limply at his sides, and at some point her arms had instinctively closed around his waist, and she could feel him tilting on the brink of collapse.

Donovan stepped toward them, sword raised as if he'd strike Kerrigan down, but Bly knew who he was really coming for. Her shield was half dead, and some ridiculous part of her wasn't going to let Kerrigan take another wound for her. More blood bubbled at his lips, and all she wanted to do was fix him.

Protect *him*.

But that made no sense at all. *She* was the one trying to hand him over to certain death. *Donovan* was the one trying to save him. Who was the hero and who was the villain in Kerrigan's life? He was her hero, but she was his villain.

Donovan closed the gap between them, his face a mask of rage. He looked like the real villain, because in Bly's story he was, but she'd waited too long to act. She let go of Kerrigan, trying not to care as he slumped sideways. The soft crunch of him hitting leaves made her cringe as she fumbled at her waist for a speed spell.

Donovan's sword was raised above his head.

Ironic that she would die because she wasn't fast enough to reach the spell that would make her faster. Her fingers pulled a wooden case from her pocket that protected the spells from snapping. She drew out a slender blue feather.

Swords clanged above her head as she spoke the spell and

snapped the feather. She followed it with a strength spell, and the blood in her veins seemed to surge, demanding that she move: run or fight.

Emerson's arms shook as he held his sword against Donovan's. Demelza must have managed to get him a strength spell, but he wasn't going to last long.

Bly darted to her feet, drawing a binding spell from her sleeve. She fumbled for her dagger, freeing it only to drop it. Donovan's eyes were already on her, like holding Emerson at bay was nothing, like he was just waiting for her to get closer and then he'd kill Emerson in a flash, followed by her, too. She didn't have the element of surprise. She didn't dare reach down for her lost dagger.

A whisp of red behind Donovan's shoulder caught her attention.

But Donovan must have noticed the movement of her focus. One of his hands left his blade as he shifted, holding Emerson at bay with a single arm while the other struck backward and closed around Demelza's throat.

Demelza smiled at him, her arms still down by her sides. She wasn't allowed to harm him, and he wasn't allowed to harm her. His fingers twitched like he might change his mind, and Bly worried that if she tried to stab him with her own spell, he'd snap the witch's neck on instinct.

She needed to destabilize him—do something he wouldn't expect.

Bly lunged forward, limbs as light as air, launching her body into Donovan's like it was the only weapon she needed. To her surprise, he fell and she tumbled with him, both of them

landing on top of Demelza. The binding spell in her fist snapped
before she could use it and something else snapped next to her
ear. His teeth. She tried to scramble away, but for a second they
were all a tangle of writhing limbs, and Bly wasn't sure which
hands were trying to kill her and which weren't until someone
pulled her from the fray. Emerson let go of her and placed his
sword against Donovan's neck where he still lay on the ground,
but he wasn't trying to rise. Demelza was extracting herself from
his magic-bound limbs.

Demelza smiled down at him.

"I know you spelled me, witch," Donovan snarled. "I heard
you mumbling. You won't get away with breaking the rules."

Demelza shrugged. "I didn't spell you. She did."

Bly tried not to look shocked. Donovan's eyes landed on her,
and his expression said he didn't believe it. But she held up the
broken birch stick in her shaky hand—the broken spell that she
hadn't gotten a chance to use, but she didn't need to let him
know that.

She looked away so he wouldn't see the lie on her face.

The twins stood in the distance over the bodies of the vampire guards Donovan had brought with him. Bly wondered how
much help Demelza had given them, but she tried not to look
too closely. She really didn't want to know if they were dead or
bound or unconscious, but they weren't making noise.

"Help him." The plea drew her back to Donovan. For a second his voice sounded almost soft. It made Bly stare at him for a
moment—the hate in his eyes had mixed with worry. She wondered if whatever Kerrigan had been through had impacted his

brother, too—made him cruel where it had made Kerrigan sad.

"They like their vampires alive, don't they?" Donovan snapped.

Bly twisted and ran, dropping back down to where Kerrigan lay on his side. His eyes were glassy.

"Remove the arrows so he can heal," Donovan said.

"I know," Bly snapped. Her hand reached around Kerrigan's back, wrapping around the shaft of the arrow. He groaned as she jostled it. Shifting, she pulled him slightly onto her lap so she could grip the arrow in two fists. His back was drenched in red. Her eyes blurred as she tried not to look. She yanked. The arrow lurched and stopped as Kerrigan hissed. She glanced up at Demelza. "I need something to help with the pain." Because she *had* the strength spell still in her—she could rip them out, but she kept tempering each yank. She didn't want to hurt him more even though she needed to in order to save him.

"I don't have anything," Demelza said calmly.

Bly glanced up at her face. She was staring right at Kerrigan's wounds. She wasn't smiling, but there was something about her expression that made Bly think that smile was barely hidden.

"Lying witch," Donovan said.

Bly had to agree.

Emerson knelt down and grabbed an arrow, snapping the tails off with ease. "These are practically through the other side of his chest already. Easier to take them out that way."

"What?" Bly's voice went high.

"I'll do it," Emerson said. "Unbutton his shirt."

Bly's fingers shook as she fumbled with the buttons of his

vest and then the shirt underneath. Kerrigan's lips quirked as if he wanted to make a joke, but he said nothing as she bared his chest. She nodded to Emerson.

Bly wanted to turn away from the blood and leave him to it, but a cold hand touched hers, and she found herself gripping Kerrigan's fingers, squeezing them as she nodded at Emerson to do it.

But Emerson wasn't looking at the arrows anymore. His brows drew together as he stared at Bly's hand in Kerrigan's.

"*Emerson*," Bly said sharply.

He turned to the arrows without looking her in the eyes.

He gave no warning, just pushed one through the rest of the way before reaching around to pull it out the other side.

Kerrigan screamed, fingers crushing Bly's so hard that she gasped, and Emerson looked like he'd stab the arrow back into Kerrigan just to make him let go of her. But Bly bit her lip and shook her head.

Emerson yanked out the others with no gentleness.

Bly's eyes found Donovan's. "How long until he heals?"

"Why do you care? You might as well drag him by the ankles like the prized blood bag he is to you."

She tried not to show how much those words hurt. She was handing him over to the same people who took Elise. But Kerrigan wanted to go.

He did. That made it different. *He'd* had *her* by the throat—she'd been his captive, but he surrendered to her.

She'd already prepared herself to live with guilt and regret after the Games for the things she'd be forced to do. It was the price she'd pay for getting Elise back.

He wasn't a prisoner.

And she wasn't going to drag him like he hadn't chosen this.

"How long?" she asked again.

"Minutes," Donovan spat at her.

She was surprised he'd even answered.

She started to pull away from Kerrigan, but his fingers clung to hers. His grip wasn't that tight anymore, just a gentle pressure, a question that asked her to stay.

She swallowed and stared at him. His eyes were closed, but his face was pinched in pain. Healing hurt.

She looked up. The twins were heading into the woods, probably checking for anyone else who might have drifted their way at the commotion, looking for an easy steal from an already attacked group—there were many strategies in the Games, and most of them involved preying on the weakest.

Emerson and Demelza had moved away, and then Bly watched as Emerson lifted his hands to Demelza's throat. For a second, she thought something had gone wrong—that she'd tried to hurt him, and he was grabbing Demelza to stop her— but his fingers seemed light and gentle. She tilted her chin as he looked at the blue fingerprints forming from Donovan's hand.

Bly's limbs were still airy from the speed spell, but the rest of her felt weighted.

He was only being kind—just like she was only being kind.

She glanced back down at Kerrigan.

"Is he awake yet?" Donovan asked.

Bly shook her head.

Worry creased Donovan's brow.

Blood still coated Kerrigan's lips and Bly couldn't tell if it was fresh or not, so she reached down and grabbed his ridiculous scarf and traced the outer edges of his lips with the tail of it.

"What are you doing?" Donovan asked.

"Just trying to help him." She glanced up at Donovan.

He frowned at whatever he saw on her face, and she looked back down, leaning closer to Kerrigan's ear.

"Wake up, please. I need you."

"Promise not to let go of me and maybe I will." Kerrigan's voice was a little raspy, but his signature charm was still there.

Bly jerked back. Her fingers slid from his grip.

"How long have you been awake?"

He grinned. His eyes drifted to her hand still clenching his scarf. "Just milking the moment."

"You're an ass," she grumbled, letting his scarf fall back against his naked chest.

"I'm an opportunist." He chuckled, then winced a little as he lifted a hand to touch the silk she'd just let go of it. His fingers drifted to his lips as he watched her.

She stared at his chest, at the bloodstains on it.

"I'm fine, love. Just a scratch. I'll be in beautiful condition to hand over. The best captive they've ever seen." Was there strain in his voice? She opened her mouth to tell him that that wasn't why she cared, that it wasn't just about using him, but wasn't it?

She turned her head away in case he could read her face and make sense of the emotions that she couldn't.

"Are you okay?" Genuine worry was in his question, and she

met his eyes and saw the same thing there—unnamable emotion.

He'd taken three arrows for her. She wanted to ask why. Of course he didn't seem to care whether he lived or died, but even so, stepping in front of flying arrows for someone wasn't nothing.

Unless it was.

But he was staring at her like it meant everything.

"I'm fine, thanks," Donovan said.

Kerrigan sighed and turned away from Bly to face his brother. "I'm sorry I didn't say goodbye. It was weak."

"No. What you're doing now is weak. Running from the past? You think being locked in a dark cell while your blood gets drained again and again will make you forget?"

So he did know. He knew there was a possibility of a fate worse than death.

"Maybe it's not about forgetting anymore," Kerrigan said softly.

"You're making no sense. Have you been reading poetry again? I told you to stop that. It makes you insufferable."

Kerrigan laughed. "I love you, brother."

"Then don't do this to me. *You* made the choices that put me here. You can't leave me."

There was pain in Donovan's eyes—the kind of pain that came from looking at the person you loved most in the world and knowing they were as good as gone. Bly had wanted someone to look at her like that when she'd said she was entering the Games, like her loss would be unbearable, but her parents hadn't. Emerson hadn't—his instinct had been to calculate the risk and reward. He'd told her not to go, he'd offered to go in her place because that was the type of person he was, but he didn't look at her like her loss would be unbearable.

If Elise had been alive, she would have looked at Bly like that.

Bly was destroying Donovan's entire world to save hers, and she hated herself even if she hated him, too.

Kerrigan had been silent for a long time. When she looked back at him, she found his eyes were on her.

"I need to," he said softly without looking away from her.

She glanced back at Donovan, who was staring at her too now, but with a loathing that made her want to crawl behind Kerrigan again.

Nova and Vincent burst through the trees. "We've got company heading our way, but they're slow. We should still move."

Demelza nodded. "First, we bind him."

Bly glanced at Donovan, already bound, before she realized that Demelza had meant Kerrigan.

Bly rose to her feet at the same time as Kerrigan. He wobbled slightly, and she knew he probably needed to feed to make up for the blood loss. What he didn't need was to be bound.

"You can't be serious," Bly said.

Demelza raised her eyebrows. "I most definitely am."

"That wasn't the agreement, and I think he's proven that he's coming with us willingly."

Donovan huffed.

"We'll move faster if he can walk himself," Emerson said.

Bly gave him a grateful nod, but she wasn't sure if he was siding with her to back her up or because it was just logical. He was giving her an odd look, and she realized she'd shifted. She stood in front of Kerrigan now, like *she* was willing to take an arrow for *him*.

She was just paying him back.

Demelza sighed. "I'll do just his arms."

"No," Kerrigan said.

"You're too weak to fight me, vampire," Demelza said. "And I trust you less now that your brother's making sad eyes at you. How do we know you won't change your mind and murder us in our sleep?" She stepped as if to move around Bly, but Bly shifted too. A slow smile spread across Demelza's face. "I don't think you want to cross me either." A flash of brown made Bly glance at Demelza's hands. Had it been a death curse? All she saw now was a slender shoot of birch. Had she imagined there was something else?

"Fine," Kerrigan said. His eyes were on her hands as well.

Bly didn't budge.

"Bly," Kerrigan said. "It's fine." His hands closed around her shoulders and pulled her to the side.

Demelza stepped toward Kerrigan, but he held up a hand, and she let out a low hiss of frustration.

They all froze. Perhaps Donovan *had* gotten to him, but he wasn't looking at Donovan. His eyes had hardened as he stared at Demelza. "Release my brother first. I'll not leave him to get picked up by scavengers."

Demelza snorted. "So he can try to rip us to pieces again?"

"He won't. He's alone now."

Demelza scoffed. "No way."

"Then I'll take him home myself." He didn't say what he'd

do with the rest of them—how it would end if they fought him.

Bly swallowed. "Just do it."

Demelza looked like she wanted to just decapitate them all and be done with it. But she glanced over her shoulder at Emerson, as if wondering if that would make him hate her.

"Let him free," Emerson said. He glanced between Kerrigan and Bly. "I actually believe him."

"Then you're a fool," Demelza snapped, but she turned around and knelt at Donovan's side, pricking him with a piece of birch that had been burned over a fire—the release spell. She stepped back as he launched to his feet with a growl.

"Brother," Kerrigan said.

Donovan jabbed a finger at him. "I don't care about ranking. I'm not taking orders from you anymore."

"You'll take this last one. Go home."

Kerrigan had stepped up beside Bly, and for a second, she thought that Donovan might attack again.

Instead, he stepped back. "I'll hate you for eternity."

Bly could practically feel the change in Kerrigan, as if the words had punctured a hole in him. "Then it will be like always," he said.

Donovan's own face collapsed in defeat. He stared at Kerrigan for one second longer before spinning on his heel and running.

FOURTEEN

THE NEED FOR REST HIT THEM SWIFTLY.
Speed spells made you fast but they did nothing for your energy
levels. And even healed from the arrows, Kerrigan had begun to
sway on his feet. They found a hollowed patch of forest where
several trees had fallen across each other, crumbling with time
as if nature itself had tried to build a small fortress.

"He needs to feed," Bly said. Kerrigan sat on one of the toppled trunks, legs spread out in front of him, head drooped and
staring at nothing.

She half expected some glib comment about whether or not
she was offering, but Kerrigan just nodded and looked up briefly
with vacant eyes. Something told Bly the vacant stare wasn't just
from blood loss. His past pulled at him. Perhaps it was just the
recent exchange with his brother, but she suspected it was something from a long time ago.

Nova rolled up her sleeve and stepped forward, but Bly shook
her head. "I'll do it."

Emerson's head jerked in her direction, but he didn't say a

word, just turned quickly away.

She sat beside Kerrigan on the log, folding her hands across her knees for a moment before realizing that she needed to give him an arm. She thrust one in front of him, and he reached up, arms still bound at the wrists in front of him, and gently cradled her hand in his. "You don't have to do this. I am used to bitterness. You don't owe me anything."

"I know," Bly said, even though she was about to owe him everything. She was going to see Elise's eyes again, and this time she'd memorize the color.

"Are you sure?" Kerrigan squeezed her hand. She glanced sideways at him. He looked like he wanted to protest more, but he also tilted slightly as if he were one strong breeze away from crashing.

"I'm sure," she said. Even though she didn't mean it. Her mind rolled back to all the pricks in her arms from selling the blood that had gotten her here. Tiny needles were not fangs. And she barely remembered Jade's bite because she'd lost consciousness so quickly. She wasn't weak with blood loss now. She'd feel every single moment. She squirmed slightly at that realization and felt Kerrigan's hesitant eyes on her again, so she nodded.

He still didn't move, but she reached over and pulled up her sleeves. The shock of cold air on her skin made her jump as if she'd already been bitten, but this time he didn't notice. His hands had shifted awkwardly so his thumb could trace a small circle on her wrist, and the movement made her breath hitch until she realized what he was looking at.

The mark of a vampire player. His voice dropped so low that

she could barely hear him. "You could get yourself killed. You should stop after you've handed me over."

"You know I can't," she said. She'd already told him about Emerson's curse. He couldn't have forgotten.

"Let him die." The words made her try to rip her arm away, but his grip hardened, holding her next to him.

"I can't do that." She followed Kerrigan's stare over to Emerson, who turned away as if he'd been watching them even though he was out of earshot.

"You're in love with him." The words sounded like an accusation.

Bly's mouth dried, and for some reason, she couldn't say the words to confirm his suspicions. She'd been thinking them for so long that they should have fallen from her lips easily. Instead, she said, "I can't imagine my life without him. It would be just as unbearable as . . ." She didn't need to say that part. He already knew.

"I'm not giving my life away just so you can die afterward."

"Who says I'm going to die?"

"The odds."

She almost told him that he sounded like Emerson.

"Why do you care?" she asked instead.

His face pinched as if he didn't know the answer or didn't want to give voice to it, which was exactly why she'd asked it.

He shook his head, lifted her wrist to his mouth, and pressed his closed lips over the berry etched there. She thought he might be trying to distract her from his lack of answer. It was working. His tongue flicked across her skin as if he were tasting the fruit. She let out a small gasp at the softness of it when she'd been expecting a bite. His fingers folded over her palm squeezed tighter as he shifted ever so slightly toward her so their hips and legs pressed together, and only then did his teeth graze her skin followed by the prick of fangs, which didn't make her cringe like she thought it would. The slight pain made her shiver in the same way that his tongue had. His fangs pulled out after only a second, and his mouth settled against her skin, tenderly sucking.

Her breath went shallow. What in all the curses was wrong with her? She was positive she wasn't supposed to be feeling . . . *this*. It certainly hadn't looked like Nova felt anything at all— she'd looked like she'd been having her blood drawn by a needle. But Bly felt *everything*—the brush of his lips, his hip against hers, the pressure of his fingertips on her hand, the painful throbbing of her own heart, and the burning inside of her that wanted him to keep taking. She was dizzy from too many sensations all at once.

He pulled back in what seemed like both moments and hours, and it was only then that Bly felt the sting of the wound from his fangs, and she longed for the press of his mouth again that had somehow hidden the pain.

"Thank you for saving my life," she said to distract herself from the moment, to remind herself that she was deep in the woods with a vampire, a witch, two people she didn't trust, and the boy she wanted to run away with. She didn't need to be thinking about lips and fangs. She'd almost died earlier, and things would only get more dangerous.

Kerrigan's hands clenched and unclenched where he still held her. "You said that wasn't why. I wouldn't have taken blood from you if I thought that you were doing it because you owed me."

"That's not why."

He gave her a hard, searching look and seemed to believe her.

"Why then? Curiosity?" He flashed her one of his disarming smiles, but it felt out of place between them. Even though they barely knew each other, they knew each other's pain deeply enough that it was like looking in a mirror. And maybe part of it was that he'd saved her life, and part of it was curiosity, but most of it was just that . . . she'd wanted to.

"It's none of those things," she said, half lying, half telling the truth.

"Then why?" He bit his lip and then leaned down, brushing a bloody kiss where he'd bitten her, and her skin itched with healing.

She swallowed. "I'm not sure." It was the most honest answer she could give.

"I want to talk to you about your plan," he said.

Bly stood up so quickly her head spun. He'd still been holding onto her arm and hand, and his fingers trailed down her skin as she pulled free of him. She held her wrist to her chest as she pushed down her sleeves. "It's not open for discussion."

She stormed away before he could say anything else. She didn't want someone telling her what she couldn't do. She *did* want someone to care whether she lived or died, but not the vampire who she was handing over to the people she hated most in the world.

She needed to stop. Stop seeing him as . . . a friend. Like

something more than a means to an end. Everyone looked at her when she reached where the others had set up camp, as if they could sense her shame at the way her wrist still throbbed from the pressure of his mouth. She could feel herself blushing and was thankful for the dark.

"Should we be leaving him all alone over there?" Nova asked.

Kerrigan had moved farther away, sitting on the ground with his back against a massive oak.

"He's not going anywhere," Bly said.

"And what makes you so sure?" Demelza asked. A hint of acid dripped in her voice. "And do any of us believe his brother won't make another try for him?"

Bly just stared at her.

"We'll take turns watching him tonight," Vincent said.

Emerson rose from where he was crouched in front of the fire. He brushed his hands over the thighs of his pants before turning to Bly. "Can we talk for a moment?

"Of course." She didn't know why the words sounded so distant and formal. She didn't know what was happening with them. When he'd first agreed to come with her, she had thought the gap between them would slowly start to close, but it felt like it was pulling farther apart.

"Alone," Emerson added, and without waiting for a response, he turned and strode into the woods. She followed him to a darker spot in a cluster of tiny oak trees.

"What are you doing?" His voice was as cold as the harsh breeze that ripped through the trees.

"What you mean?" She knew, of course, but she didn't want

to admit that. She wanted to pretend that there was nothing to understand.

"Bly." He said her name like an admonishment, like he'd done so many times before. It was one of the few things that she *didn't* like about him—his ability to make her feel ashamed just by the way he said her name. But she knew his protectiveness came from what had happened to his sister. Before he'd been there to catch Bly when she fell from the trees, but after, he'd asked her not to climb them at all. He just wanted to keep her safe.

But maybe this time she did need someone to call her back from the dangerous place she was climbing.

"You're going to make me say it?" he asked.

She bit her lip.

He cleared his throat like he was uncomfortable, and she prepared herself for one of his famous lectures, the kind she'd gotten many times before when she went too far into the woods. She'd hated that too, actually, but that annoyance had always been overshadowed by joy at knowing that he cared enough to lecture her with all his logical reasons why she should play it safe. But this time was different.

"We're so close." His voice cracked on the words, startling Bly. This was not the calm and collected Emerson who rarely showed emotion. "When we first started this, I thought we had no chance. I thought . . . I thought I was just making sure that you didn't die alone. But we're so close, Bly." Her name turned into a plea. "We actually have a way to go back to how it was before, and I know that's not really possible—it'll never be exactly the same, but it feels that way, right?" There was a painful hope in his voice, the kind of hope that had kept her going. A hope that she wasn't sure he'd felt before, and her chest practically burst at the thought that he could feel it now. They *were* close, and whatever was pulling them apart now wouldn't matter once they'd won.

She reached out, her hand closing around his, but he yanked it back. The suddenness of it startled her.

"You have to hand him over."

She ground her teeth. He could tell her she shouldn't get close to the vampire, but suggesting she wouldn't do what was necessary to save her sister was a step too far. "I know that," she bit out, struggling to keep the anger out of her words. He was in pain. Hope could hurt, especially when you'd just found it. So she tried to gentle her voice. "I'll do what needs to be done."

"I've seen the way you look at him." Revulsion pulsed in his voice. "I don't know why he took those arrows for you. I wish it had been me. But maybe it's part of his game. Maybe all of this is just a game to him and he has no intention of following through."

"He wouldn't do that to me," Bly said.

"There," Emerson said. "That right there is the problem. You think he cares about you but he doesn't."

Bly opened her mouth to defend him, but all it would do was help prove Emerson's point that she was getting too close to Kerrigan.

"Just don't fall in love with the idea of a good-hearted vampire."

"*Fall* in *love*?" Bly actually laughed. "You can't be serious."

"I know you, Bly. I know you like to make up impossible fantasies that can never be real. It's what makes you . . . you. But it also makes you vulnerable."

It hurt that he saw her dreams like that. That she was just a silly little girl to him, even now when he was admitting that her dreams had led them here—so close to retrieving what had been stolen from them.

"You don't know me at all," she whispered in a sudden moment of clarity.

He huffed. "Of course I do."

She shook her head. "If you knew me, then you'd know it was *you* I was in love with. It's always been you."

She didn't know what she expected, but it wasn't nothing. The leaves rustled as if trying to break the awkward silence. The cluster of trees around them seemed to tighten, wrapping them in an awkward cocoon.

"Say something," she said.

But she knew him, and he'd stay quiet for ages if he didn't know what to say. In fact, she thought they might never speak again.

But he didn't leave. At least he stood there and faced her confession with a look on his face that suggested it was torture. Finally, he said, "I didn't know." A simple statement of fact. Nothing more. No declaration of similar feelings. She couldn't even read anything in his voice. It held no inflection.

It made her angry. "Well, now you do."

More silence.

"That's it?" she asked.

"Bly . . ." There was finally something in his voice: hesitation. She tried to read into it more—a nervous hesitation? An awkward one?

"Maybe we can talk about this later. When all of this is done. We don't even know if I'll be alive a year from now. I can't think of anything else until I know I'll still be here."

"Right," she said. There was pain in the word. She needed to regain her footing. She needed to lash out. She glanced over her shoulder at the others before dropping her voice to something less than a whisper. "And what about *you*? Can you follow through?"

"What are you talking about?" He seemed genuinely confused.

"Demelza," Bly hissed. "She's powerful. She's exactly what we need. You're not going back on the other half of the plan, right? Just because she helped you once?"

"Isn't once enough?"

"Kerrigan helped me more than that."

The moon didn't give enough light for her to read his face, but his pause said enough.

"You like her," Bly said.

"I owe her."

"She's still a witch."

"Emerson," Demelza hollered. "I think we need a little more wood for the night. Will you come?"

Bly glanced pointedly at Vincent and Nova, who were perched on a fallen log right next to Demelza, not doing anything at all.

But Emerson didn't seem to care. He left Bly for the witch, and she'd thought she'd seen a flicker of relief on his face. But what was she supposed to do? Chase after him and beg him to say it back? In all the times she'd imagined the moment when she'd finally tell Emerson how she felt, it had never been like this— with a witch and a vampire both wedged between them.

FIFTEEN

Nova woke Bly an hour before dawn.
Bly was supposed to be the final shift for the night.

The other girl hesitated as Bly sat up in her bedroll.

"Do you want me to wake Emerson instead?" Nova asked.

"What? Why?" She blinked up at sky, its darkness showing just the barest hint of giving way to the light. It was definitely her turn.

"Emerson told me to wake him for your turn."

Bly sighed. Before last night, she would have thought he was just being kind, but she knew what it really was: he didn't trust her.

The ache in her chest that had been there since their conversation last night grew a little bit deeper. She glanced at Kerrigan, still sitting upright against the tree, his eyes closed, mouth parted slightly in a way that made him look young.

"Thanks for waking me," Bly said.

And trusting her, unlike Emerson. Even though she didn't say the words, Nova seemed to sense the unspoken.

"We both have too much at stake," Nova said, turning and walking away to her own bedroll, hunkering down without a single glance back.

Bly lay on her back, staring at the sky through the canopy of branches.

"Finally," Kerrigan whispered as soon as Nova's soft snores joined the sounds of the night.

Bly jerked in his direction. His eyes were open and alert like he hadn't been asleep at all.

"Can we talk now?" he asked.

"Not about my plan. I don't need someone else telling me I can't win."

"I wouldn't dare."

"You just tried to talk me out of it last night."

"I apologize. That was my own fear talking because there's always a risk, and I'd rather you not take it. But if anyone can win both prizes, I'd bet my life on you. I *am* giving my life because I believe in you."

I believe in you. Her eyes stung at the words. She wasn't sure anyone had ever said that to her before. Her parents thought she was throwing her life away. Emerson thought he was just coming along to die with her, and even now, when she'd proven she could get this far, he still thought she was weak.

Even back before Elise had died, nobody had taken her dreams seriously. Nobody had believed in her but herself.

It made it hard to accept that Kerrigan was the one person who did.

"Why?" she said softly.

"Because I've seen how strong you are. The first time I saw you in the woods, you fought back. And in the trial, you reached that witch first. You moved like your life depended on it. More—like someone else's life depended on it."

"But I couldn't kill her." She could have done better.

"That was a different strength," he said. "A kind I might not have had."

Hot tears ran down her face. It felt like some of the hurt she'd bottled in her chest was leaking out, as if Kerrigan's words had gently pierced something that needed to be bled.

"Unbind me," he said. "We have an hour until the sun is up, and I want to teach you how to hold a knife. That's all. I just want to help you."

Demelza had given her some of the unbinding spells—part of the condition of Kerrigan allowing them to bind him at all.

"Fine," she said, "but I want something from you."

"You want more than my life?"

"I want to know the life I'm taking. I want to remember you." She was asking for more hurt, she knew that, but she needed to have something of him to hold on to when he was gone. When she was with Elise again, she'd wrap Elise's arm in hers and tell her she was right about the vampires. It was a vampire who'd saved her.

He let out a huff, then sat in silence for a moment before answering. "Deal."

She freed him, and they snuck away from their camp until they came to a small clearing hedged in by clusters of manzanita.

Kerrigan turned to face her. "May I see your knife?"

She handed it to him and watched as he balanced it on his fingers before flipping it in his hands and catching it easily by the hilt. "A good weapon."

"Emerson made it."

His eyes flicked to her face. "But he didn't train you with it?"

She shrugged. She didn't really want to explain that they hadn't been on speaking terms before entering the Games.

He gripped the blade in his hand and offered her the handle. "Not too tight," he said as she wrapped her fingers around it. "You don't want to cut off your own circulation with your grip. You need to be able to feel it."

He nodded as he watched her. "Good."

"When do I get to ask a question?"

"How about when you draw blood?" His teeth flashed white in the navy blue of the lightening night.

Her knife flashed too, but he was too busy smirking to notice until it nicked his thumb.

His eyebrows shot up. "Well, someone's not playing."

"I did warn you this wasn't a game to me," she answered, although somehow, just in this small moment, it felt lighter.

"Ask away," he grumbled.

"How long have you been a vampire?"

"Four years."

Not long. Somehow she thought it'd have been longer—he seemed full of so much pain that she'd thought he'd collected it over a long immortal life—not a life that hadn't been much longer than her own.

"Were you turned at eighteen or did you win the Games?"

"I was orphaned as a human and raised by the vampires. I chose to become one at eighteen, but you didn't earn two questions. Don't push your luck again."

"Then teach me something."

He laughed and bent down, reaching into his boot to lift out a dagger with a handle gilded in gold and embellished with a vine of tiny emeralds.

"Demelza would not like to know you're armed."

"I'm a vampire. I'm always armed whether I've got a blade or not—and that's your first lesson. You'll never win against us in a one-on-one fight, so run. We have built-in weapons and we're quicker than you, but immortality makes us lazy. You're fast, so we might not bother chasing."

"So I should just run? I can do that."

"Now, if you're boxed in and bolting is out of the question, keep your legs wider, crouch down a little. Nothing's more important than your balance. If you're on the ground, you're probably dead." He tapped her leg with the flat side of his dagger. "Widen your stance."

She did.

"Good. You'll need to move, of course, but keep this stance in mind and fall back to it if you can. You don't want your own feet to tangle together." He shifted to stand in front of her. "Now take a swing at me."

He was well within reach of her, so she swung her blade in an overhanded slash without hesitation.

He dodged it easily. "That's all you've got?" His voice held a restrained laugh.

"Well, I thought you were going to teach me something besides standing."

He set the laugh free. "Fair enough, love." His expression shifted to something more serious. "You need to assume your attacker will dodge your first swing, so follow it up. Watch me."

Kerrigan became a blur of movement and flashing steel.

It was Bly's turn to laugh. "You're going to have to move at human speed if you want me to catch that."

"Right. Two slashing movements, and then follow with a thrust." He did it slower and then waited for her as she tried it.

Shaking his head, he stepped toward her. "Let me show you." He positioned himself behind her, his right arm sliding around so it caged in her own arm. His fingers wound around her wrist, and she wondered if he could feel the pounding of her pulse.

He must have, because he hesitated. "Are you . . . comfortable?"

"Sure," she rasped.

"Hmm," he mumbled as his other hand gripped her left shoulder. "Keep this one back. Lead with your right side so that you can get more range when you strike." He moved his foot between hers, tapping her heel with his toes.

She didn't think he'd meant to bring their bodies so flush together, but her breath caught at the closeness. He cleared his throat, but he didn't step away. "Right foot forward, widen your stance."

She did, and then he led her hand through a downward slash that traveled back up and then down again in the other direction. He ended with a short jab.

"You could've just told me to make an *X*."

He chuckled, still so close to her that she could feel it. "Where's the fun in that?"

She spun in his grip, looking up into one of his flirty smiles that didn't seem quite real. The darkness was succumbing to the dawn around them, but his eyes were black.

She slid her knife up between their too-close bodies and scratched his throat. His eyes widened as he stepped back from her. His finger touched his neck, and when he pulled it away, he stared down at the blood on it.

"You fight dirty."

"I don't need to be taught that."

"I suppose you want another question."

"Who are you really? You act charming, like nothing's serious to you one moment, and the next you're sad and . . . valiant." He raised his eyebrow at that, and she cringed. "You know what I mean."

He looked away into the trees as if he wouldn't answer. "I'm both." He turned back to her. "I used to be this vibrant kid who could make a whole room light up. People told my parents I was witty, but things changed, and then I thought if I pretended, then maybe I would eventually be that boy again." He shrugged. "It worked for a while, and now . . . sometimes I still want to be him, if only on the surface."

"What happened to change you?"

"That's a question with too many answers, and I already paid the price for this cut." He pointed at his neck, but it had already healed.

"I don't want to play the game anymore. Just answer."

He beckoned her forward. "Show me the move."

She slashed at him without holding back, but he dodged her easily.

"Don't thrust out the knife with such force. Make it more of a jab—you don't want to hit so hard that you bury the blade in your opponent too deep to retrieve it . . . unless you have a kill shot. Again."

She moved, stabbing at him over and over again. Each time he dodged her easily.

He clearly didn't want to let her make him bleed again, but she needed more.

He blocked the next thrust of her blade by grabbing her wrist, but instead of backing away and practicing the same move again, she spun so her back was against his chest, his hand still holding her arm. She slid her foot between his legs, hooking it behind his ankle, and then she threw herself back against him, sending them both toppling to the ground. He pulled her arm with the knife out beside them as they fell so she couldn't stab one of them, but he loosened his grip as the air whooshed out of him on contact.

She flipped around on top of him, and his hands gripped her waist as if to lift her off, but she pulled herself up, resting her elbows on his chest so she could peer down at him. The tip of her knife sat in the hollow of his throat.

"I don't *really* want to cut you again."

"I appreciate your mercy."

She could feel his body relax beneath her, as if he were tired of fighting everything, not just her.

For some reason, she wanted to melt too. Sit the knife down, flip onto her back beside him, and watch the morning sun vanquish the rest of the night.

He gazed up at her, his eyes wandering over the different parts of her face like it was a constellation of stars he'd never see again.

Her mouth parted, and his stare tracked the movement.

"But I still get another question," Bly said.

Both their chests moved with his gentle laugh.

"And I don't want you to think that makes me weak if I don't cut you." She needed to talk because her lips wanted to do something much different. "I'd stab this in your throat right now if it'd bring my sister back," she added.

She thought that would end it, this pull between them, but he still didn't look away from her lips.

"I know," he said, reaching up and tucking a stray curl behind her ear. "I know you would."

Her own body relaxed against his. *Kerrigan* understood her. *He* saw her as a threat. Unlike the boy who'd known Bly her entire life who thought she'd give her own *sister* up for a vampire. But Emerson was right about one thing: there was something between her and Kerrigan.

He felt it too. But only his expression was acting on it, and maybe his hands gripping her waist a little tighter than needed.

"What is this?" The voice was deep and familiar, and Bly jerked in its direction.

Kerrigan hissed, and she realized she'd accidentally drawn blood after all.

"I thought we agreed that was unnecessary," he grumbled, but she wasn't looking at him anymore.

She would have scrambled up, but Kerrigan's grip on her waist tightened.

"Let go of her." Emerson's sword was already out.

Kerrigan laughed. "*I'm* the one with the knife to his throat."

The others crashed out of the woods behind Emerson.

Vincent scowled. "You shouldn't have left her alone with him," he said to Nova.

"She has a dagger to his throat," Nova said. "I don't think she was running away with him." But Bly thought she saw a sliver of distrust in her eyes.

Kerrigan shifted his grip on her waist, helping her slide off him to stand.

"Relax," Kerrigan said, brushing a hand down his silk vest. "It was just a little knife practice. Shall we go?" He walked over to Demelza and held out his wrists. "I assume you want to bind me?"

Demelza took out her sliver of birch and muttered the spell, but her calculating eyes stayed on Bly, not Kerrigan, as if Bly were the one she wished she could bind.

SIXTEEN

KERRIGAN DIDN'T INSIST THAT BLY WALK WITH him when they left, but Bly sought him out. Because she'd drawn more blood, and a deal was a deal.

He smiled as she slipped beside him. "I suppose you came to collect."

"I'm just trying to think of how to phrase the question so I get all the details I want."

He sighed. "Well, I'm a little tired of bleeding on this trip. How about I just answer your last question about what changed me? I think it'll be worth the blood you drew."

She nodded. She got the sense that he wanted to tell her.

"As I mentioned, Donovan and I were taken in by the vampires when we were children." He paused, the silence weighted with the beginning of the story that he wasn't going to tell: what happened to his parents. "Human children taken in by vampires . . . it's not a normal life. They see humans as weak, and to make them worthy of becoming vampires, they have to mold them from a young age into something harder."

He swallowed, and Bly wasn't sure if she should ask what that entailed or not. She could tell by his face that it was nothing good. "That sounds unpleasant," she finally said, leaving it open for him to tell her more or move on.

"Yes." He glanced at her and nodded as if deciding that she could handle what came next. "They trained us to fight with our hands and with every weapon available—even spells—and once we were physically strong, that's when they turned to making our hearts hard. They'd make us face off with each other in the arena, and only the winner would eat that night. They said it was to make us understand that without force and ruthlessness, we'd grow hungry. They wanted to show us why vampires needed to treat humans the way they did: it was just survival."

"Well, that explains vampires like your brother," Bly mumbled.

"No." Kerrigan's voice was so sharp that Bly jumped, and Emerson glanced back at them. "No," he repeated, softer this time. "Donovan was a good kid. He was the kind of kid that would find a frog hopping through the muddy streets and walk it back to the edge of the forest because he was afraid it'd get stepped on. He was . . . better than me. He never wanted to fight. But I thought the vampires were right about one thing: that humans were weak, and I didn't want to feel that way ever again. I pushed Donovan to train, and when they eventually pitted us against each other in the arena, I beat him again and again, making him go hungry because I thought I needed to make him stronger. One day, he finally snapped and he beat me, and then he never looked back. He embraced the hardness I pushed him to."

He stared at her again, searching her face as if he wanted to find some condemnation in it. He blinked at whatever he saw there before continuing. "I ended up being both queens' favorite because of how ruthless I was in pushing my own brother to the breaking point. And I was very good at fighting. At eighteen we were given the same choice as all the children raised by vampires: be turned or leave for the Gap. It was all I wanted: power and safety. I was made a vampire with Queen Melvina's blood, as was Donovan the year after."

"So what changed you?" Bly hadn't even realized she'd spoken the question, but she was trying to see the path that took Kerrigan from what Donovan was to the vampire beside her, walking toward his death to save a human he'd never met.

"I'm getting to it. I thought you were hungry to know me?"

"Sorry. I am."

He gave a soft, distant smile that told her he was more in the past than with her.

"All the royal children are given jobs, and I was assigned one of the highest in the city: I oversee the guards that patrol the Gap and the woods surrounding it. They thought I was good with a blade and that my heart was also made of steel. I thought that too. But seeing how the humans lived and were treated . . . all it did was crack open the memories of the human life I'd tried to forget. Then one day I was patrolling the woods with a couple of vampire guards, one of them a friend who'd been raised alongside Donovan and me . . . Gregory." He paused. "He was Jade's brother—the two of them were every bit as ruthless as I was." There was guilt in his voice, and Bly had a feeling this story explained why Jade seemed to hate him even more than the other vampires.

"We came across a group of humans trying to make it past the woods patrolled by the witches and vampires and into whatever lay beyond. Normally I would've just taken them and turned them over to our council for punishment and wiped my hands of whatever fate waited for them, but these humans refused to surrender. They'd prepared for a fight but they still didn't stand a chance. We overpowered them, but then Gregory grabbed a young girl who wasn't much older than us and bit into her neck as she screamed and fought. I ordered him to stop, but before he did, she managed to sink a knife into his throat. He threw her to the ground and prepared to take her head with the swing of a sword, and she held her chin high and spit at my feet. My own sword was blocking the killing blow before I'd even realized that I'd moved, and when Gregory spun on me, I . . . killed him. Him and the other guard. And I wasn't sure if it was to save the girl or because he'd seen me act human . . . weak. But I'd just witnessed strength that surpassed my own, and it was from a group of worn-looking humans. I escorted the humans to where the patrols stopped, but they didn't all leave. Some of them, including the girl who spat at me, were a rebel group that worked to help people escape. The girl, Bianca, convinced me to join them. I even recruited a few vampires who I knew sympathized with the humans, and we helped more than twenty people escape."

"Did you love her?" Bly wasn't sure why she'd blurted out such a question.

Kerrigan's eyebrows rose in surprise. "Bianca?" He laughed

for the first time. "I wasn't her type. She was an ally and a friend—someone I respected, but nothing romantic."

He went quiet for a moment. Perhaps lost in the few good memories he had.

"So what happened?"

"We got caught. All the rebels were slaughtered, but I was spared because the queens loved me, and Bianca was spared because I pled for her life. So instead of killing her, they left her with nothing beyond their city walls, in the part of the forest that crawled with banished vampires. I even kept my title and position, although the queens assigned Donovan to be my right hand. Donovan runs the guard now, even though I still hold the title of commander. He hates that, and he hates me for what happened to Gregory. I told people that humans killed him, but after I got caught helping them, he figured I had something to do with his death—as did Jade.

"And that's why nobody likes me," he said with a grin. "Including my own brother." His joking smile faded.

"Well, it makes me like you even more," Bly said, and she meant it.

He'd been full of dreams once, just like her, and he'd paid for them, just like her.

But she was still dreaming, still fighting, whereas he'd given up.

"Did you ever look for Bianca?"

"I did. My *mothers* had me dragged back and threatened to banish Donovan if I ever tried again. That was when I realized that they didn't spare me because they loved me—they did it because they wanted to keep their pet in its cage, and they knew leaving me trapped would be its own punishment. And so I play the part of the party boy who doesn't care anymore, because if I didn't, they'd punish me through Donovan." He cleared his throat. "But if I'm handed over in the Games, they can't blame him."

He was silent after that. And when they stopped for the night, he sat against a tree away from them.

It'd taken a toll to tell her about his past.

And even though she joined the rest of them around the fire, she kept glancing back at Kerrigan. She barely noticed when Demelza asked Emerson to help her with firewood again.

"Don't make this messy for us," Vincent said, startling her out of her thoughts. The threat in the words wasn't even hidden.

Bly turned to him. She needed to stop watching Kerrigan. "I don't know what you're talking about."

He said nothing, just stared at her until she felt like he had his sword pointed in her direction. She glanced around for Demelza and Emerson, but she couldn't even hear them.

"I'm hungry again." Kerrigan's flirty voice was out of place in the tense moment.

"You just ate last night," Vincent snapped.

"But I worked up an appetite yesterday saving everybody and getting mortally wounded for you little humans."

"Not for us," Nova said. "For *her*."

She glared at Bly too. Whatever tentative trust they'd had was slipping. It was clear that they thought she had something with Kerrigan as well. She wanted to scream that she couldn't care less about the vampire. He was a way to get her sister back, nothing more. But that was a lie, and she couldn't explain that her feelings didn't matter. Only Kerrigan seemed to understand that.

"I thought you were on the same team," Kerrigan said sweetly. "Saving one is like saving all of you."

"It's not," Vincent said coldly.

"I want Bly anyway." He was still smiling with his ridiculous charm, but his eyes were on Bly. Beneath the smile, something about his expression seemed off.

She took a step toward him.

"You don't owe him anything else," Nova said. "You know that, right?" There was sincerity in her eyes, along with her disdain, like she actually wanted to help Bly.

"I know," Bly said. "Thank you," she added.

Nova sighed like Bly was beyond help before ripping into a piece of jerky. She could feel their stares on her as she walked back to Kerrigan. Her legs felt like liquid, and her heart thudded a little too quickly, but she couldn't tell whether it was because she feared the puncture of his bite or because she craved it. The thought made her stomach tighten. But it was just a physical thing—her body reacting to a sensation. It didn't mean anything at all. She crouched down next to him and unbuttoned her sleeve with the witches' mark. She started to lift her wrist toward Kerrigan's mouth.

"I want your neck," he said.

She froze. "No."

"Pretty please?" He winked at her.

"No," she said again, but this time her voice was light and raspy. She cleared her throat, pulling back her arm. She had some boundaries. She couldn't imagine Emerson coming back and finding her with a vampire's mouth against her neck.

"Bly." His voice was soft and the frivolousness in it was gone. She realized that she hadn't met his eyes since she'd walked over. They were hard. They held no hunger or lust or joking. "We both know you owe me," he said louder with all the charm back in his voice as his eyes still said something else.

He'd never use those words—say that she owed him any of her blood or body. He'd said the exact opposite just yesterday. Her eyes narrowed. There was something else going on here.

She knelt down beside him, trying to figure out how to get closer to him without crawling onto his lap.

"Come now, love. Just lean into me. I'll do the rest."

Easier said than done. His hands were bound in front of him. His long legs were spread out. Bracing a hand on each of his shoulders, she leaned in, tilting her head to the side, until she felt the barest touch of his lips.

She knew he wasn't actually going to bite her, but for a second, he just sat there, and she wished she could see his eyes—if they were black with hunger.

Finally he spoke. "I don't like the way the witch is looking at you. I've been watching her all day." His lips brushed the side of her neck as he murmured, and she sucked in a sharp breath, shuddering before she could even try to dampen her reaction. Her fingers dug into his shoulder.

He drew in his own breath at her reaction, pulling her already tingling skin against his lips. It felt like a kiss.

"Sorry," he breathed out, making it worse.

Her knees trembled and her arms shook as she tried to hold herself in the awkward position.

"I'm going to fall over," she said.

"You could always sit on my lap." His voice was a low rumble against her pulse, prompting it to speed. This time his flirting was quiet, not for show. Real.

"I don't think that will help," she practically choked out.

He chuckled.

"That doesn't help either."

She forced herself to breathe. This wasn't the moment for this. What was wrong with her? She'd just confessed her feelings to Emerson last night and he'd walked away. But he hadn't said no. Should she be affected so much by another man only a day later? Kerrigan believed in her, but Emerson had always been the overly cautious one. She couldn't fault him for being himself.

But already she was trying to forget with another fantasy— or, at least, her body was.

Bly's own whisper was strained when she finally spoke. "I think Demelza likes Emerson a little too much." The witch sure looked at him a lot.

"And you're in the way." He'd pulled back just a hair, so his lips no longer touched her. But his breath still did.

"I'm not," she said. Bitterness leaked into her voice. There was no way he hadn't heard it.

He hesitated. "Well, she thinks you are." His voice darkened. "I know what murder looks like in someone's eyes."

Murder? That seemed extreme, but then she thought of Elise's body being rolled onto a stretcher by witches acting like they were on a joyful stroll.

"Don't go to sleep tonight," Kerrigan said. "She wanted me bound for a reason. She's been planning something for a while, but tonight she looks like a coiled snake. You'll need to unbind me."

Curses. She'd need to reach into her skirt's pocket for that, and she didn't know how to do it without giving up their ruse.

"Are Nova and Vincent still watching?"

"Yes."

"Then I'm going to crawl onto your lap."

His breath exhaled on her neck. "Please do." Then louder, he added, "Get closer so I can heal you."

Shifting, she swung a leg over his waist to straddle him.

He bent his knees so she could balance herself with his thighs. His bound hands snaked up between them, grabbing her chin and tilting it up, drawing her neck closer so his lips brushed the center of her throat before pulling back. "Okay?" he asked.

She wanted to nod so she wouldn't have to hear the rasp in her own voice, but his hands under her chin wouldn't let her. She murmured something she hoped sounded like consent before slipping her hand into the pocket with the spell and bringing it up to his hands.

Pricking his skin, she said, "Release."

He lowered his hands from her neck, keeping them pressed together at the wrist so they still looked bound.

She slid off him and stood, smoothing down the creases in her dress.

She didn't look down at Kerrigan. Instead, she eyed the dark as if the owls would see her embarrassment and carry the gossip back to Emerson.

She spun and walked away.

"I'm enjoying the rewards of saving you," Kerrigan hollered after her. "Please try to get shot at again!"

He sounded like the version of himself he showed to others again, but she thought she heard a note of sincerity in his voice that wasn't there before.

When she reached Nova and Vincent, she could feel the heat in her cheeks. They both wore matching scowls.

"You move fast," Nova said, eyebrows raised in judging arches.

Vincent huffed in a way that might have been a laugh . . . for a person who'd never tried it before.

Bly ignored them.

And she ignored Demelza and Emerson when they came back as well. When it was time to sleep, she unwound her bedroll closer to Kerrigan than Emerson, despite the fact that she could feel Emerson's stare on her. Lying down, she rolled onto her side and faced the vampire. She was too far away from him to make out his expression, but she could tell he was awake. And she knew he could see her stare too, and for some reason she wasn't shaking with fear at the thought of Demelza trying to kill her, because he was watching.

Eventually, he closed his eyes, but she could feel it—the awareness in him.

She let her breathing go deep and shallow. The night seemed to still with waiting.

She didn't even hear her coming. One second she was counting shadows, and the next Kerrigan was standing overtop her, grabbing someone. Bly twisted in time to see a knife leaving her own throat and Demelza's hair glowing in the moonlight. And then Kerrigan flung the witch against the tree he'd been leaning on moments before.

He crouched down beside Bly, hands running over her neck.

"Are you okay?" he asked.

Her heart thudded with a delayed response as she nodded, and then he was on his feet again, eyeing the witch heaped at the base of the tree.

SEVENTEEN

"WE NEED A BINDING SPELL," KERRIGAN said to Bly. "Check her pockets. I can't be the one to actually spell her."

Bly scrambled over to Demelza, lying on the ground, hair covering her face, and began to check the folds of her skirt. Bly had her own binding spells, but there was no sense in wasting them when she could take one. The number of spells hidden beneath the cascade of fabric leaves that made up Demelza's skirt stunned her. She pulled out more than enough strength spells and spells for warmth she'd claimed not to have enough of.

"What the hell is going on here?" Nova asked from behind them.

"I suggest you lower your weapon," Kerrigan said softly.

"She's switching sides," Vincent growled. "She'd running off with this fucking vampire."

Two sets of footsteps inched closer as Bly's fingers finally found the binding spells sheathed in the inside waste of Demelza's skirt.

"What happened?" Emerson's groggy voice joined them.

"Take another step," Kerrigan growled.

Vincent laughed. "We don't need a fucking spell to kill a vampire. We're stronger than you all by ourselves."

Bly shuddered. She'd seen him decapitate one in the trial. Nova had been spelled but not Vincent. He was capable. But Kerrigan was a prince.

"Your girlfriend is running off with another man . . . or creature." There was a sneer in Vincent's voice.

"She's not my girl—" Emerson stopped as if realizing that wasn't the point. "Bly?"

Her heart hiccupped. The denial that he wasn't *with* her was the first thing to leave his mouth—not a defense of her. She was surprised at how little that part stung, but then saying her name like a question, asking if it were true, even after what she'd confessed? He really didn't know her at all, and that gutted her the most.

"I knew this was going to happen," Vincent said. "Weak little bitch with a taste for getting fed on. You know he's probably going to drain you dry and leave you rotting with the fallen trees in the forest."

"You're about to lose your tongue," Kerrigan said calmly.

But Vincent just turned his rant to Emerson. "You know she let him suck on her neck while you were in the woods earlier?"

"What?" Emerson's voice was hurt. And she knew it wasn't because he was jealous. It was because he hated vampires, and she'd seen the good in one. She'd seen that they weren't all evil. Some of them wanted to help. Some of them had tried. If

Emerson knew what she knew about Kerrigan, he'd see that too.

But she couldn't explain all that in a single moment.

"Bly?" This time the voice was Kerrigan's, soft and prompting.

She'd frozen. Her hand was in the air, binding spells in her shaking fingers, but their words were turning her to stone. She took a breath and spoke the spell as she pricked one of Demelza's limp hands and then her ankle. Her limbs tied themselves together with invisible cords.

"I'm going to kill you *after* I kill your vampire," Vincent said to her. "Killing you will be so easy, like dessert after a meal."

"Wait," Nova said.

But Vincent glared at his sister. "*You* said we could trust her."

Nova didn't defend Bly again.

"Hey." Emerson's deep voice steadied with resolve. At least he didn't want Bly dead.

"Silence!" Kerrigan's voice rang out above everyone's, sharp and commanding—the kind of voice that made people stop what they were doing on instinct. Everyone stilled. "The witch tried to kill her."

"Who?" Nova asked.

"Me," Bly said softly as she finally turned to face them. She tried to step up next to Kerrigan, but he shifted slightly, angling his shoulder in front of her so she'd stay behind him.

When she took in the hate-filled faces of Nova and Vincent and the way their weapons were held for violence, she decided to stay there.

Emerson was different. There was no hate on his face—just hurt and confusion.

And even though she felt terrible about it, his wounded expression made her feel better. She wanted him to feel a little bit of the way it'd hurt her every time he doubted her.

"That makes no sense," Nova said.

"Makes sense to me," Vincent muttered, eyes on Bly. "She probably saw you escaping."

"I wasn't escaping!" Bly screamed, her voice piercing the night around them. Everyone stared at her in shock. When she spoke again, she was quieter, but she let her voice vibrate with rage. "I don't care about any of you as much as I care about my sister." She locked eyes with Emerson, and he glanced away. "Nothing will stop me. Not any one of you, and not the witch that tried to kill me. Nobody." She looked up at Kerrigan, and he held her stare and nodded down at her.

A hard silence sat between them, but nobody questioned her.

"That's not even her," Emerson finally said.

Everyone stared at him.

"That woman's hair is darker. Look."

Bly glanced over her shoulder, careful not to turn her back on the twins.

The girl on the ground had long hair like Demelza, but it lay fanned in a beam of moonlight, and where Demelza's hair had been honey mixed with a drop of blood, this hair was a deeper-than-blood crimson.

"That's not possible," Bly said. "I . . . she was right above me. It was her. She had a knife to my throat, and . . ."

"Why would a witch use a knife? Fuck. Demelza's probably been captured by another group, and we're all standing around over the body of some other player," Nova said. "We need to get her back."

"Wait," Vincent said. "We're almost there. We still have the vampire—do we really need her anymore?"

Bly almost had to admire his ruthlessness.

"It's her," Kerrigan said slowly. "We need to tie her hands to the tree so she can't reach any hidden spell. Even bound, she could slip them from a pocket. Do we have rope?" He looked at the others like they were on the same team again.

"Can you *not* see?" Nova snapped. "That's clearly not her."

"She was glamoured," Kerrigan said. "A glamour won't hold if the wearer loses consciousness."

"All this time?" Vincent's voice was skeptical.

"Why?" Emerson asked. "I met her over a year ago, and she wore the same glamour."

"Because she's somebody important. She probably wore a glamour for protection." There was a hollowness in his voice as he looked back at her. "Get some rope," he commanded.

The moment filled with tension as the question of whether or not they would still work together rattled unspoken between them. Finally, Nova lowered her ax, went to her pack, and brought back a rope.

Kerrigan held out his hand for it, but she shook her head. "I'll do it."

Nova hauled the body against an oak and into a sitting position before pulling the witch's hands above her head and tying them. When she was done, she grabbed a fistful of red hair and pulled the girl's chin up.

Her face was thinner than Demelza's, with sharp cheekbones instead of soft round ones, a narrower nose, a squarer chin. Still pretty but not the same.

Kerrigan sucked in a breath.

Emerson was watching him, noticing first what the rest of them hadn't. "You know who she is."

Kerrigan was silent for a moment. "She's the head witch's daughter." He took a step back, his face pale in the moonlight.

Bly couldn't help it—she turned to Emerson. A vampire prince *and* the head witch's daughter. They didn't just have what they needed to save Elise; they had what they needed to save *him*, and Demelza had just tried to kill Bly. Surely whatever loyalty Emerson felt toward her would end with that.

"We still don't know if that's Demelza or not," Nova said.

"She'd have access to all the spells she needed to maintain a glamour," Kerrigan said.

The girl moaned. Her head lifted, blue eyes the same as they'd been before, the same as every witch. She searched out Emerson first, and Bly knew, without a doubt, that it was her.

"The vampire attacked me," she sputtered. She pulled at her hands bound above her head, looking for the first time at all of them. "What's going on here?"

"You tried to kill me," Bly said.

"They're lying." Demelza shifted her stare from Emerson to Nova to Vincent, looking for an ally. "They attacked me out of nowhere."

Nova and Vincent shared a look, as if deciding something between them.

"Your face was a lie," Vincent said.

Demelza sputtered, and her lips looked like they'd form another plea, probably another lie, but then she glanced down at her hair. Her mouth closed, and her eyes hardened. "Do you know who I am?"

"Una," Kerrigan said.

Demelza cringed at the name.

Kerrigan glanced at the rest of them. "Named after your grandmother—"

"I prefer Demelza," she interrupted, lifting her chin—only royalty could make demands while tied to a tree.

"—and the daughter of an evil witch," Kerrigan added. Everything about him was tense: hands fisted at his side, jaw tight, body leaning forward as if ready to strike.

Demelza laughed. "Well, that's one way to describe my mother. Let me go or you'll see just how evil she can be."

"I already know," Kerrigan said. There was hate in his words, and it wasn't just the rivalry between vampires and witches, because Bly thought she heard sadness in there too, an ingredient for the worst kind of hate.

Whatever else haunted Kerrigan, the thing he'd left out of his story, it had to do with Demelza's mother.

"Why'd you try to kill me?" Bly asked.

For a second, it seemed like Demelza would deny it again. Then she laughed. "I thought if I stabbed you and then screamed, it'd be easy enough to blame a bounty hunter."

Bly's stomach lurched. "I asked why, not how you planned to do it."

"I find you annoying. Those sad eyes darting between Kerrigan and Emerson, like you're torn between two lovers, when one of them is willingly marching to his death, so can't like you all that much, and the other doesn't seem to feel a damned thing for you despite knowing you his entire life, which seems a little sad, doesn't it?" She raised her eyebrows, smirking.

Bly sucked in a breath and then wondered if she had to let it back out again, because breathing suddenly felt like too much. Kerrigan was looking at her and Emerson wasn't, and she didn't know which was worse.

She wasn't going to answer Demelza's stabbing question. She was going to hit back. "I'm not the only one with unrequited feelings."

Demelza's smirk disappeared.

"This seems pointless," Vincent said. "Let's leave her and finish this ourselves." He glanced at Nova, who nodded, and then turned back to Bly. "Our partnership with you still stands."

It wasn't an apology, but Bly knew it was the best she was going to get.

She wanted more from Demelza though. Not remorse, of course, but an admission of why she'd really done it. Kerrigan was right. She was jealous of Bly. She'd wanted Bly out of the way.

Even if she really didn't need to be. Bly glanced at Emerson. Being protective of someone didn't mean they saw you romantically. She should have accepted that a long time ago.

Everyone started packing up except for Kerrigan, who seemed to be in a staring contest with Demelza.

"We can't leave her," Bly said. "We need her."

Nova turned around with a frown. "I thought you could handle yourself with the spells? Clean her out and you can be our witch."

Bly cringed at the wording. But instead of answering, she pulled at her sleeves.

"Bly," Emerson warned.

But it was too late. She held up her bare wrist and watched Nova take in both marks with narrowed eyes. She already knew, but her expression said she hadn't planned on Bly bringing it up, because that's what Bly had promised.

"Vincent," Nova said.

Her brother turned, taking a second to focus on what his sister was looking at. "So you're liars too. The most honest one among you is the fucking vampire." He spit in the dirt.

Bly shook her head. "We were just going to turn in Kerrigan like we planned and then go our own way to capture a witch. We didn't lie." She didn't mention that Nova already knew.

"Why?" Vincent asked. "I thought you wanted your dead sister back. You want to be immortal so you can outlive her and watch her die again?"

"Not me." Bly looked at Emerson.

A muscle in his jaw ticked. She knew he didn't want to show any vulnerability. He wouldn't want people to know why they needed a witch too, but the only way out of this was honesty. She saw his eyes settle on a choice and then he unbuttoned his sleeves, revealing the marks on his wrist. Then he kept going until he reached his elbow; even in the moonlight, they could see the silvery black of the death curse in his veins. It had spread since the last time she saw it.

"Lots of people die," Vincent said with a shrug.

Nova glanced at her brother and then gave them both a sympathetic look. "We can't help you. You did what was best for you, and now we will too. We take the vampire to Havenwhile like we all agreed. Maybe the witch will be here when you get back." She shrugged. "Or you find a new one. Not our problem."

But Demelza would never be there when they got back. Someone else would find her, and as she was the head witch's daughter, that someone else would win the immortality from the vampires even if Bly and Emerson did manage to get another witch.

"Help us and we'll give you the vampire prize money too," Bly said.

"Don't need it," Vincent said, but Nova turned back around, and for the first time, Bly saw something else behind her eyes besides survival, something familiar—a dream. Vincent and Nova clearly had a big family. One prize was enough to lift them out of poverty, surely, but was it enough to dream?

"Think of what you could do with it," Bly said. "More than just enough money to not be hungry—enough to really *live*."

"Too risky," Vincent said, but then he looked at his sister, and Bly saw something soften in his eyes. He could see it too, that wanting for more than was in their reach. This was the closest they'd ever be again. Deep down they probably knew that.

"We're so close to Havenwhile," Bly said. "You could stay and guard Demelza while we take Kerrigan and hand him over."

Why did speaking those last words out loud feel like she was stabbing herself in the chest? "And then the four of us take her back. You're right—I know all the spells. I can get us back safely."

"Emerson," Demelza said, a slight plea in her voice.

Emerson's face collapsed. Demelza didn't say anything else, but she didn't need to. The way she said his name was a reminder, a debt being called. And Bly knew he'd feel an obligation—Demelza had saved him, and Emerson valued a balance in things, even if their world terribly lacked it, or maybe because of that.

He might still try to save her.

At the very least, he'd want to hear her out. He turned to her. "Why would you do it? That's not you. You said you hated seeing the death in this world, but I guess I should've known that was a lie the second you wanted to be a sponsor. Because that's all these Games are: death." He looked at Bly when he said that last part. As if he still didn't believe in what they were doing, even if he wanted the end result as much as she did.

"Because you cost me everything!" Demelza cried. "When I found you searching for that girl after she died, I thought it was romantic. I wanted to help because I'd seen you in the woods with her once before, kissing her, and then the way you risked everything just for her body? I've never once had someone love me that much, not even my own mother. So I helped you. But I got caught. A guard saw me and told my mother."

A black haze lingered over Bly's vision. Her heart pounded so hard it swallowed every other sound. She couldn't have heard it right. Demelza had seen Emerson and Elise kissing before Elise died. A lie. Demelza was lying. Hadn't she proven that through and through? Bly blinked until she could focus again, and then she turned to Emerson. *Emerson wouldn't lie to her*. But that thought tilted. It didn't hold the weight it did a moment ago because his face said it all.

Guilt.

She wasn't sure she'd seen the expression on him before, her friend who always did the right thing.

For a second, she tried to make some other story fit. But Bly had never seen him with any other girl but her and Elise, leaving her with the awful truth: Emerson *had* broken into Havenwhile after Elise had died, but it wasn't for Bly.

None of it had ever been for her.

Emerson grimaced and turned away from Bly to face Demelza again. "You're lying," he said, and Bly expected him to deny that he'd ever kissed Elise. Even though his face had already confessed, she desperately needed him to, but instead he said, "You had the same glamour on when you saved me. How could someone report you to your mother if you didn't look like . . . you?"

"I wear glamours out all the time," Demelza snapped. "It's to keep me safe from those who want to hurt my mother enough to go through me." She glared at Kerrigan. "Even with my own people, I only show my true face at parties and rituals. But my mother's guards always know what I look like. I thought I'd given them the slip that day, but I should have known better. I could barely do anything without their eyes on me—or at least that used to be the case. I'm not sure my mother cares anymore." She laughed, soft and bitter. "Now she says I'm too much like my grandparents, that I'm weak for wanting to help a human. She's been threatening to stop training me to take her place as head witch and replace me with my cousin. But she's waiting to see if I can prove myself." She paused, a broken look on her face. "When I saw you in the trial, I came up with a plan to get my mother's respect back. Deliver a high-ranking vampire *and* the boy I'd shown sympathy for. That would show her I could be ruthless, that I'd learned my lesson."

"But why'd you try to kill Bly?" Emerson asked. His voice was cold and odd, almost like a stranger's, but Bly barely registered it. Her mind buzzed, still trying to take in things it didn't want to accept.

"I knew Nova and Vincent would go along with my plan if I offered them money." Her eyes narrowed on Bly. "But I knew *she* would get in the way."

Bly finally focused on Demelza. The hate on her face, directed at Bly. But Demelza's betrayal meant nothing. Bly turned to face Emerson.

She'd built her dreams around someone else's reality. Her sister had been living at least a piece of the life Bly had wanted, while Bly had sat in the low branches of trees and dreamed about it.

She felt small and foolish, like a child who'd been allowed to dream too long.

And she'd always thought she was the link between Emerson and her sister, the core that held her group together, when in reality she'd been on the outside.

"You and Elise?" She said it like a question, knowing it wasn't, but it let her have just a moment to hope that she was wrong.

"We only kissed that one time, just before she died," Emerson said, then hesitated. "But I'd loved her for longer than that."

The words were a blow. But of course, she already knew it was more than just a kiss to him. He had risked everything for Elise when he tried to get her body back.

"And Elise?" she asked.

He seemed confused by the question.

"Did she love you too?"

"I . . . I don't know." He shook his head, not looking at her. "She's the one who broke our kiss that day. She said we couldn't . . . and then she ran away from me." He looked at her then. "I think she might have been worried about you, but I never got a chance to ask her."

Another truth hit her. She thought he had entered this competition for her, because she needed to get Elise back to live again and because she couldn't live without him too, but it had never been about that. He wanted Elise back for himself, not for her.

"Bly," Emerson said, but she shook her head. She didn't want whatever would come after her name. An apology? A defense? She didn't know which would be worse. And she didn't have room to process it because there was one more piece of the truth that was ricocheting around her heart like a thorn, tearing it to pieces.

"You lied to me. Hiding a truth is a lie," she said, her voice as shallow and weak as the voice of a girl dying from internal blood loss. She raised her hand to her lips and brushed them, half expecting her fingers to come away wet and bloodied, because there had to be some physical wound for the pain she felt. How could anything but torn flesh make someone feel this badly?

"I didn't want to hurt you." Emerson grimaced as if *his* insides were getting ripped apart as well, but she didn't want to see his pain. Not when he was the one wielding the blade. He'd caused this. With Elise. The two of them had already become entwined in her mind as one deep hurt.

"Why would it hurt me?" she asked. "For you to just be honest? Why would you think that?" she asked—but then she realized, "You guessed." Emerson looked away in shame. "You guessed that I had feelings for you." She shook her head. A sob she hadn't even known was building broke through her, and she heard the crunch of leaves beside her. Her head turned in that direction.

Kerrigan had stepped closer to her. Although he didn't quite look at her, as if he knew that she wouldn't want him to. He was right. She'd forgotten about everyone else but her and Emerson and the ghost of Elise. But somehow, everyone was still present. Nova and Vincent stood stock still, watching. Demelza still sat trapped against the tree with a slight smirk on her face. But Kerrigan was the person she most needed right then.

And like a magical light flickering to life, Bly suddenly understood: Emerson had always been just a dream. Kerrigan, though something new, was also something *real*.

Kerrigan had pulled her back to herself, away from the shadow she'd become in the last year. She'd thought she'd loved Emerson for so long that she was mistaking this hurt for a broken heart. But her heart had never pounded at Emerson's touch the way it did at Kerrigan's. Emerson had never looked at her and seen her as she was: a girl who could accomplish anything she dreamed. Kerrigan did. The feelings she was beginning to build for Kerrigan were already far greater than the fantasy she'd built around Emerson.

With Kerrigan beside her, she no longer wanted to run into the woods and never look back, but the hollowness left in her from the gutting of the truth had begun to fill with rage. Because this wasn't about love. It was about secrets. She pointed a finger at Emerson. "It's your fault she died."

"What?" Emerson's voice held no inflection, as if his emotions were shutting down even more than usual.

Bly laughed. The sound was cutting and cruel and nothing like it had ever left her lips before. "The reason I went into the woods," she said. "I never told you because I thought it would make you hate me and hate yourself for something that wasn't your fault. But it *was*—it *was* your fault." She drew the deep breath of someone about to release a truth they thought they'd carry to their grave. "We went out into the forest for you. *I* went for *you*."

Emerson just shook his head, because of course he didn't get it. He'd never wanted to know how she really felt about him, so instead he pretended as though it didn't exist.

"I thought I needed something for you to see me as more than a friend." She laughed again, and this time it wasn't cruel, just broken. "I wanted to collect mushrooms to buy myself a pretty dress and a matching ribbon." Her hand drifted reflexively to the fraying threads on her wrist, and Emerson's gaze followed as a new understanding crept onto his face. "I thought it would only take a dress—that the problem was that you saw me as just a friend. And if you saw me in something beautiful, it would make you realize that I could be more. But it wouldn't have made me my sister . . ." She trailed off.

Elise would still be here if he'd told her the truth. Elise would still be here if *Elise* had told her the truth. Bly had confessed her feelings straight to her sister's face, and she'd still said nothing. That hurt the most, she decided. A violent thought tore through her. Elise had caused her own death. *She deserved it.* The thought almost made her double over with self-hatred, and that was the tipping point. She hated Emerson. She hated Elise.

And she hated herself most of all.

All that hate was too much for a body to hold, and it clogged her chest until she felt as if she were drowning, and her breaths came shallow and sharp until a steady hand pressed against the small of her back. For a horrible second, she thought it was Emerson. But he still stood across from her, watching her with a pained expression on his face, like he could feel everything she suffered, but she doubted that was true.

The hand belonged to Kerrigan, and the touch drew her back to herself. She trembled from the cold air that suddenly seemed impossible to bear. But it also reminded her that she was alive. And Elise was still cold in whatever grave she'd ended up in. Regardless of whatever hurt Bly felt, the absence of her sister was still the biggest one.

"Well, that was entertaining," Demelza said.

Bly stared at Emerson. "We finish what we started. We win

both prizes, you and Elise get to have your happily ever after, and I'll . . ." She'd meant to come up with something. Dream something else for herself that would make everyone watching stop looking at her with unbearable pity.

She had nothing.

Because Kerrigan's hand on her back was temporary comfort.

"It can still be like what it was before," Emerson said, but his words were weak and empty, because Emerson was too smart to actually believe them.

"We have a vampire," Bly said. "And we have a witch." She looked at Emerson, daring him to say that he wouldn't give up Demelza even after she tried to murder Bly.

He nodded.

"No," Kerrigan said.

Bly was suddenly aware that his hand had left her back.

She turned to him, and he looked at her with a coldness in his eyes she'd never seen before.

"You don't have me."

EIGHTEEN

BLY'S HEART HAMMERED IN HER CHEST AS she tried to make sense of his words.

Emerson drew his sword without hesitation, as if he'd been waiting for this moment.

"I wouldn't do that if I were you," Kerrigan said to Emerson.

Nova and Vincent had drawn their weapons too.

"Wait." Bly held up her hands. "What do you mean?"

"He's going back on his promise," Emerson said, spitting the words. "Just like a vampire."

"He's not," Bly said, hating how small her voice sounded. Kerrigan's eyes snapped down to hers, and a grimace tightened his mouth.

"I'm not going back on my deal," he said. "But I want something in exchange." He glanced down at Demelza.

"Her?" Bly asked.

"Her mother," he growled.

Emerson's voice took on its own dangerous rumble. "We're not going to help you start some war because you see an opportunity to get your head patted by one of your mommies."

Bly had never heard Emerson talk like that. Rage bubbled in his voice.

"My reasoning is none of your concern," Kerrigan snapped.

But Bly knew that it wasn't just a political move to take out the head of his enemies. This was personal—she could see it all over his face, the memories that were nipping at him. He appeared to be one second away from tearing Demelza's head from her shoulders.

"What's your plan?" she asked softly.

His head whipped in her direction as if he hadn't expected her to consider what he wanted. She wasn't sure that she should, but she felt like she owed him at least that.

"I don't know why we're negotiating." Vincent nodded at Bly. "Like you said, we have both prizes. We're done. We just need to hand them over."

"But I can get you the head witch," Kerrigan said. "We trade her daughter for her."

Demelza laughed. They all jerked at the sound but she said nothing.

"We don't need the head witch," Vincent said. "Do we really think that someone's going to top her daughter?"

"You're forgetting my original statement," Kerrigan said slowly. "You don't have me."

"You're standing right here." Emerson turned to Bly. "You were right. We take them both."

"Do I look restrained to you?" Kerrigan's voice was the softest whisper, like a breeze rustling the leaves right before a storm rips the limbs away. It made the hairs rise on the back of Bly's neck.

"You promised," she said.

Emerson scoffed. The sound held every warning he'd given her about trusting a vampire.

But Kerrigan's eyes softened when he looked down at her. "And I'll keep that promise." He turned back to Demelza. "But first I want revenge."

* ✦ *

They walked in silence until those familiar green hedges rose in front of them.

Kerrigan stepped forward and pulled open one of the small wooden doors and held it as if politely waiting for Bly to go first. When she didn't move, he seemed to understand exactly why. He nodded with a grim expression on his face and offered his hand instead. When she didn't take it, he wiggled his fingers. "Come on then." He smiled, but she saw the tension in it. "You need to pretend you like me, remember?"

"I'm a little angry with you."

"But you know I'm right. It makes more sense if I'm on your side longer and help you deliver a witch first."

"You're doing this for you, not me. Otherwise, we would've just taken Demelza."

He gave her a hard look. "That's part of it."

She was the other part. He wasn't lying—it would be safer to turn him over last, let him help her deliver a witch and save Emerson. But trying for the head witch was a huge risk.

And every moment she didn't hand over Kerrigan as the prize to save Elise was a moment she might lose him.

She patted the binding spells still folded into the pocket in her skirt. She could bind him as soon as they got inside, hand him over, and then take Demelza to the vampires. But somehow it felt like a betrayal, even if it was what he originally agreed to. She couldn't do it to him. Not now.

She'd already agreed to his plan. Bly had taken all the spells she could find on Demelza, including a stash of glamours. And now she and Kerrigan had blue eyes and clothes patterned to blend with the forest around them. They'd enter the city, pretending to be a witch couple enjoying the festivities, and then they'd get close enough to deliver a message to Halfryta: trade yourself for your daughter.

Bly didn't like it. Her mind said it was a risk she didn't need to take, but her feelings told her she did. She needed to give Kerrigan something in return for what he was giving her.

His eyes narrowed as if he knew that there was a part of her wavering from their new plan.

So she stepped forward and let his fingers close around hers before he pulled her through the wall of leaves. Havenwhile was just like it was last time, bright and cheerful and warm and cozy—all those things that Bly longed for but did not want to see in a place she despised. It was empty compared to last time in the bustle of morning. And for a second, Bly wanted to imagine that this was a quaint little village lost deep in the woods where humans could live without the cost of blood. She pictured a boy with copper hair smiling at her in the sun, but just as she relaxed into that fantasy, a man stepped out of one of the cottages built around a tree and lifted a hand in their direction. His deep blue eyes crinkled with a smile.

Kerrigan lifted a hand in answer, but his other hand tightened around Bly's. Hers tightened in return, each crushing the other with their own trauma.

As they walked in farther, she understood why this section was empty. Music and laughter drifted from the lake. Kerrigan had explained that there would be some type of festival happening. Both the vampires and witches loved to host parties while the humans fought tooth and nail in the Games for a chance to live like them.

It seemed dangerous to let loose during the one time of year humans had an ounce of power.

"Why do you all throw these parties?" Bly asked as they walked. "Why not just hunker down and hide?" Even the humans that foraged in the woods regularly never stepped in them during the Games, and they definitely weren't throwing parties.

Kerrigan shrugged. "Boredom? With the treaty in place, there's not a lot of threat to us—at least not legal threat. Some will break the law and kill each other if we happen upon one of our enemies in the forest, but for the most part that doesn't happen. Punishment is swift on both sides. So maybe we need to feel that danger to keep feeling . . . human."

"And that shows just how far away you all are from being human," Bly said darkly. "Death isn't a thrilling, distant danger to us. It's our entire existence."

"I know," he said. "It's not fair. This world is far from it."

"But you've given up on trying to fix it."

He turned to study her. "Don't you want me to? I wouldn't be here if I hadn't."

She didn't answer. Needing was different than wanting.

The road around them began to fill with witches, and their hands gripped tighter again as they let go of the hurt between their people to focus on the one pain they shared.

"Remember, we need to look like a couple in love," Kerrigan said. "Not like a couple of players masquerading as witches. If anyone gets suspicious, we'll end up knocked unconscious and tied to a tree trunk outside for the bounty hunters to find. At least that's what they'll do to you. I might just disappear. Technically, they're not supposed to keep me if I'm not an official captive handed over by players, but witches have been known to break the rules."

"I got it," Bly said tightly.

Kerrigan burst out laughing as if she'd said something hilarious. She practically jumped at the suddenness of it. His free hand reached out, and he ran his fingers across her chin as they walked, tilting her head in his direction. He smiled down at her as if all he wanted was to see her face for a moment, and the look of admiration in his eyes was so real and startling that her steps faltered. Catching her, he pulled her into his chest. His fingers feathered into her hair, and for a second her heart stopped, thinking he would kiss her—and he did. But it was only a featherlight touch on her head just below her hairline.

"Please pretend you liked that," he whispered before he pulled back.

She smiled up at him. She knew she probably appeared

flustered, but hopefully she looked the kind of flustered of a new love.

"You're perfect," he said loudly. Then, quieter, he added, "But I'm better at pretending."

Pretend. The romance was as real as his witch-blue eyes.

A masquerade. And it needed to stay that way no matter what was under the surface.

He wrapped an arm back around her shoulders, tugging her down the same path that she'd walked with Emerson not long ago. She tried not to dwell on that memory. Or Emerson in general.

Eventually they reached the lake that shimmered with silver in the moonlight. It looked nothing like it had the day of the trial. The place was stunning and magical and more than Bly ever could have dreamed up on her own. She heard a soft gasp and realized that it had come from her.

Each gazebo that ran along the edge of the water had been strung with ropes of tiny lights, creating a twinkling wonderland that cast golden glows that mingled with the moonlight in the lake's reflection. Lights dotted the trees as well, making everything appear as if it had been dipped in the sun.

The platform in the lake where they'd done battle for the trial was still there, but instead of horror, it held a second elevated stage at its center. On top of it, a group of witches played flutes and violins, and the music rippled across the water and surrounded everything in a soft lullaby of magic. Around the musicians, people danced, lilting back and forth perfectly in time with the music. The small wooden boats floated everywhere again, but this time each one had a lantern hooked onto its bow. Couples sat in the boats, laughing and kissing or sometimes even trying to dance. She watched as one boat toppled over and two men fell into the water, disappearing for a moment before their heads popped up again, laughing and smiling, kissing each other as they tried to climb back in.

Most of the witches had foregone their usual browns and greens and wore bright, vibrant colors—breeches the color of sunflowers and skirts that whirled like pink rose petals. Flowers crowned everyone's hair.

A young girl appeared in front of them. Her dark brown hair fell to her waist in two braids sprinkled with tiny purple wildflowers. She wore a dress of white rose petals dusted in streaks of pink, and she smiled up at them with wide eyes that were so earnest that for a second Bly forgot they were witch eyes and smiled back at her. The girl balanced a wooden tray in front of her that had been polished to a gleam and held candied flower petals filled with swirls of whipped cream and sprinkled with something pink.

"May I offer you a little taste of magic?" she asked. Bly's mouth watered before the reality of where she was snapped back into her. She almost cringed away, but Kerrigan's arm pulled her even tighter against his side.

His other hand reached out for the treats, plucking a lavender petal from the tray. "I never say no to magic." Even though Bly wasn't looking at him, she could hear the winking charm in his voice. He *was* good at pretending. "Love? Aren't these your favorites?"

Bly shook herself. "Right," she mumbled, reaching out a hand she prayed wouldn't shake. She pulled back a light pink petal and held it in her fingers while the girl stood smiling at them as if waiting to watch them eat it.

So she did. And it *did* taste like magic. Like sunset and sweet mornings. Like a memory of happiness. She lost herself in the sensation until Kerrigan's hand ran up her arm.

"Bly?" he asked. "Did you like it?"

"Yes." But as she spoke, the sugar turned sour in her stomach like a dream morphing into a nightmare. Because that's what this place was to her. It should have been everything she longed for. It *had* been once. But now it was tainted.

Bly looked for the girl to choke out her thanks, but she had disappeared. Bly and Kerrigan were alone again. "No," she added truthfully. "I hated it."

"I did too," Kerrigan whispered.

He shifted, letting go of her for a moment so that he could cup her face and tilt her chin up to look at him. "Pretend with me," he said. "Pretend this is just a dream—that we're not two broken people trapped in the world that broke us while it celebrates the pain. Pretend it's just us and we're really just two people in love in a place where magic is free and blood doesn't pay for it." His voice broke a little. He wasn't as good at pretending as he thought he was. "It's just a dream, Bly. Dream with me." He ran his fingers across her cheeks again and again as if his cloud-soft touch could help her find that dream.

And somehow it worked. Despite his tainted eyes, she looked up at him and saw a boy who had the power to make her dream again. Something she didn't think was possible, not after Elise's death. And definitely not after Elise's and Emerson's betrayal. Because in that moment, it had felt like any hope or dream would be just beyond her grasp for the rest of her life. But this vampire was looking at Bly as if *she* were the dream. Like he wasn't pretending at all when he looked at her.

She let out a soft rasp of air as her hands reached up and closed around his wrists while his fingers still stroked her face.

"There we go," he said. "Now you look like you're in love with me." He smirked.

Her heart practically stopped in her chest as if he had sunk a dagger through it with his words. Her hands clenched at his wrists as his fingers stopped tracing her cheeks. His grip on her face tightened, as if she were something he was afraid of losing. His eyes roamed over her, and his expression shifted to shock at whatever he saw in her eyes.

They were letting this go too far.

The pretending.

"You must really be in love." The woman's voice startled them.

Kerrigan's fingers didn't leave Bly's face, but they loosened enough for her to tilt her head toward the witch in front of them. She was older, with white hair streaked with faded brown, and she held the hand of a little boy at her side. The witch waved at them. "The fireflies. They're drawn to true love."

"Mom says that's a myth," the little boy piped up.

"Your mother's just a cynic," the witch said with a laugh. "But your grandmother's going to teach you better."

Bly glanced around them. She hadn't noticed the tiny cluster of lights that were dancing around her and Kerrigan's heads like a storm of magic.

Kerrigan chuckled. "I believe it," he said.

Pretend, Bly reminded herself.

"Well, kiss her then," the old witch said. "Don't keep us waiting."

Bly started to shake her head, but Kerrigan's hands pressed harder against her cheeks, trapping her. He stared down at her with questioning eyes. They had to do this, but he wasn't going to without her permission.

She needed to say yes. But even more so, she *wanted* to.

A commotion broke out at one of the gazebos, jerking everyone's attention away from them. Kerrigan dropped her face and wove his fingers through hers as they turned toward the sound too. A person lay in a heap on the ground, and a young man bent over them. Someone else crept up behind the young man, swinging one of the same wooden trays they'd just plucked treats from. The tray thudded against the young man's head, and he collapsed on top of whoever he'd been checking on.

People flipped him over, and someone pulled open his eyelids.

"Glamoured!" someone yelled.

Witches cheered.

They gathered the limp humans, pulling them onto stretchers as they laughed at their victory.

Bly's stomach lurched. Her chest tightened until she could barely breathe. The past unfurled with the present, and she knew she was one second away from passing out and giving them away.

If she lost consciousness, her glamour would fade. She'd end up easy prey for a hunter, and Kerrigan . . . he would die without the redemption he so clearly craved.

She couldn't do that to him, but her body felt like something outside of her control. The pain inside her was alive again, and it would squeeze her lungs until darkness greeted her. For a second she wished for Emerson's warm fingers at her wrist. That thought only made it worse.

People still cheered as the stretchers with limp bodies passed them. They were going to come right by them.

"Well," the older witch was saying. "Back to what's important . . . love."

Bly wanted to gag. Lights danced before her eyes, and they weren't from the charming little bugs.

Kerrigan chuckled. It sounded tense. He pulled her into his chest, wrapping his arms around her so tightly that it almost stopped her shaking. She hadn't even realized she *was* shaking until his hold lessened it. She kept her nose buried against him, but she lifted her arms and let her fingers grip the collar of his shirt.

"She's a little shy." Kerrigan's voice was a rumble against her chest pressed flush with his. She could feel the hardness of his muscles, tense and ready. She was putting them in a precarious situation.

The witch huffed.

People cheered as the parade of bodies passed them.

And Bly finally lifted her chin.

"Yes," she breathed softly, only for Kerrigan.

Because if his arms could stop the shaking, maybe his lips could push back the darkness.

He didn't hesitate. His head dipped next to hers so that the corners of their mouths whispered together for a moment before he moved his lips over hers, just barely brushing them, like two people who'd never kissed before.

But that wasn't what they needed.

Bly stood on her tiptoes and let her lips melt into his. He froze for one second before he let himself go too. His hands slid from her back and into her hair, tilting her head to deepen the kiss. They crushed into each other until the cheers began to fade. Until Bly couldn't breathe for a reason that had nothing to do with the panic in her chest.

Her fear had faded to a dull hum as every bit of her focused on the way her lips just wanted to keep moving, to take everything Kerrigan would give her and offer anything at all in return.

There was a slow clap, and it wasn't for the parade of bodies—they were long gone. It was the old witch. "That's what I like to see."

"Gross," the little boy muttered. "Can we go find some cake now?"

Bly and Kerrigan broke apart.

The witches were walking away. The older one gave her a wink as they left.

They'd fooled them. Bly had even fooled her own body. Her lips tingled, wanting more.

Kerrigan still bent over her, hands in her hair. She wondered if his eyes would be black if not for the glamour.

"Are you hungry?" she blurted.

His eyes widened. "That's what you're thinking about?" His voice was low and raspy.

"I . . ." She wished she hadn't said that.

"I'm always hungry," he said.

She felt like she should move away from him but didn't.

He finally let go of her, but it looked like it hurt him to do so.

She cleared her throat. "So I take it you know what Halfryta looks like?"

Bly had seen her at the trial, but those moments had become a blur in her memory.

"I do." The words were clipped. Whatever was between them cooled off in an instant as his past came rushing back to haunt him.

Part of her wished she could undo the question and not let reality in.

But she'd also needed a reminder of why they were here.

"Where do we find her? Demelza said that they always locked down during the Games."

Kerrigan shook his head. "Half-truths at best. There's no way that the head witch wouldn't be present for the parties. Or at least make an appearance. Not coming would make her look weak, and she'll have guards, so the risk would be nonexistent. But we're not trying to capture her here. We just have to wait."

He pulled a note from his pocket and passed it to her. "I prepared this while you were fleecing Demelza. We're not even going to speak to the witch. We hand her this and slip away."

She unfolded a worn-down piece of browned paper with

words written in rough charcoal in elegant script: *Your daughter is being held in the woods. Dead north of the center entrance. Come alone to secure her release. If anything happens to us, she dies.*

On the back of the paper were charcoal sketches—a chubby-faced baby surrounded by other kids of various ages, including a boy with a wide smile on his face that prevented Bly from recognizing him at first: Vincent.

"What's this?" Bly asked.

Kerrigan snorted. "Nova was the only one with paper on her. Can you believe she likes to draw? I really can't imagine her doing anything besides cutting things into pieces."

It shocked Bly, too—to be holding a little reminder that Nova was human too and not just a girl with an ax. She held a piece of Nova's motivation. Winning wasn't just about Bly—other people had things at stake.

"How's she going to know we're not lying?" Bly asked.

Kerrigan held up a strand of Demelza's real hair tied in the ribbon she'd been wearing. He took the letter back from Bly and folded the hair into it. "She'll believe us."

Bly glanced around them at the party. She didn't think she could pretend for much longer. "What do we do until then?" she asked.

"A boat?" Kerrigan looked out at the lake as he started to lead them down one of the paths that wound the perimeter of the water.

It would give them a little space, but her stomach turned at the idea. It reminded her of the trial.

She shook her head.

She let her eyes glaze over as they walked again so everything would be a blur. She couldn't take much more beauty, and she trusted Kerrigan to stop her from stumbling into the water.

His hand gave hers a soft squeeze after another minute of walking. "How about we wait there?"

It took her a moment to realize he was pointing up.

An ancient oak towered on the edge of water. Its branches fanned out in a perfect half-circle that dipped to the ground on one side and brushed the surface of the lake on the other. Each branch, down to the smallest twig, was wound in soft lights. It looked like half the moon had fallen from the sky and landed here.

Strung up in the branches were hammocks.

The whole sight was stunning and romantic, and she squeezed Kerrigan's hand tighter without really thinking about it. He must have taken that as a yes because he started pulling her toward the tree. They passed through the lowest branches to dozens of staircases spiraling into the branches above.

Kerrigan searched for a free hammock as Bly blushed at the sounds of kissing coming from some of the ones closest to the ground. Most of them held two people, but it appeared a very uncomfortable fit . . . or a cozy one.

Her nerves screamed at her to run, but her heart thudded with want.

She needed to stop thinking like that. She followed him as he pointed to an empty hammock that hung out over the water.

"Okay?" he asked.

She swallowed in answer, but he didn't wait for words. He waved for her to go up the staircase first. The steps were small and almost impossible to climb, and her hand gripped the smooth wooden railing. She was too aware of Kerrigan at her back, but when she reached the top of the staircase, she had no choice but to focus because the hammock was still ten steps away, and each step was a small wooden board on a branch barely the width of a single foot. But Bly had spent her life in trees that didn't have steps.

She didn't hesitate as she made her way to the tiny platform that was the last step before the hammock. She glanced back at Kerrigan, balancing with his arms spread out at his sides as if he thought he might take flight, his eyes glued to his feet.

A giggle bubbled to Bly's lips before she could stop it.

"Oh, you think this is funny, do you?" He didn't look up.

"A little bit," Bly said as Kerrigan jumped the last few steps to land on the small square platform with her. He wrapped his arms around her waist as he teetered.

"It's not going to be funny when I take you down with me," he said.

She dropped her voice to the barest whisper. "I thought vampires were supposed to be coordinated."

"On the ground," he grumbled, but he smiled as he said it.

They both grew quiet as they stared down at the hammock.

"Looks a little tight," Bly squeaked.

Kerrigan cleared his throat. "Looks delightful."

She could tell he was trying to sound flirty and casual, but the strain in his own voice gave him away.

He glanced around. "We could find separate ones?"

"I think we should stick together, don't you? I mean . . . that would be the most practical thing."

"Right. Practical. I'll get in first," he said. "Since I'm bigger." He sat down and awkwardly rolled into the hammock, which shook back and forth in the branches. Bly tried not to laugh as he adjusted his long frame into the tiny space.

He cleared his throat. "Your turn."

She tried to climb into the sliver of space beside him but ended up flat on top of him instead. "Sorry," she mumbled as she tried to wiggle her way to the side.

"No need to apologize." His voice sounded even more strained than before.

She finally squeezed to the side, but her arm and one leg were still draped over his legs and chest. She struggled to rearrange herself.

"Feel free to touch me as much as needed or as much as you'd like." His chuckle moved his chest against her hand.

"You're impossible," she said.

"I've been told that before."

"That's the most believable thing you've ever said."

He laughed, and it was real and startling, not his silly little chuckle that she thought was half a charade. She loved the sound, the openness of it, the boyishness, a glimpse of the person he'd said he'd been once, and she tilted her head to look at his face. He was staring up at the lights in the trees.

He sighed as his laughter faded. "I wish we could really forget for just a minute because this is . . . magical."

The lights above them shined against the backdrop of stars beyond, so it looked like they were soaring through night sky. If she were a different girl, and if Kerrigan were just a boy, then she might've felt weightless and free hanging in this hammock. She might've been a girl on the verge of feeling true love for the first time.

But she wasn't that girl. And Kerrigan had fangs behind his soft lips. She turned from the stars and glanced back up at him, her head resting on his upper arm, her chin bumping his chest. He wasn't looking at the stars anymore. He was staring at her with the same sense of wonder on his face. She didn't look away and neither did he as her fingers splayed wider on his chest where her hand rested, and she felt the little catch in his breath beneath her touch.

"Bly." Her name sounded like both a warning and a plea on his lips, and she wasn't sure which one she should listen to.

"We're just pretending, right?"

"Yes," he said, voice hoarse. "And the stars are still watching us." She felt him swallow. "We wouldn't want them to give us away."

"Definitely not." Her hand fisted in his shirt as she pulled herself up to him, and his arms closed around her as his lips met hers again. And this time, with no witches watching and only the stars as their witness, their lips moved in a way that wasn't pretend at all. It was all gentle exploring and wonder, and when they broke apart, neither one of them moved away, and their soft breaths mingled. Bly's hand had crept up to his throat, and her thumb brushed gently against his bare skin. His hand that clasped her waist drifted up, and he trailed his fingers along her side and back down again.

"You're beautiful," he said.

Her heart swelled and ached at the same time. She'd imagined those words being said to her before. She imagined herself in that sky-blue dress with the ribbon in her hair, and Emerson looking at her the way that Kerrigan was looking at her now, with those words coming from *his* mouth. It hurt to hold that freshly shattered dream in her hand while looking at a boy who was a dream that could only be shattered too.

Why was she hurting herself again?

A tiny tear trailed down her nose.

"Hey," Kerrigan said, brushing it away with his finger.

"What are we doing?" Bly asked. He opened his mouth, but she shook her head before he could speak. "Don't say pretending."

It'd be a lie—they both knew it.

And that made it so much worse.

"I have to kill you," she said.

He didn't answer. There was no good answer. He closed his eyes as if he couldn't look at her any longer. After a while, his breathing grew shallow, and she wondered if he'd fallen asleep.

"Will you tell me what happened to you?" she whispered. Not the things he'd already told her—the hurt he held deeper than that.

"To make me this handsome?" The corner of his mouth quirked up. He was awake then, just avoiding her. And she should've let him.

"Kerrigan."

"Don't you need to draw blood first?"

"*Kerrigan*," she repeated.

He sighed as he opened his eyes to look at her. For a moment, she thought he'd refuse, but he closed his eyes again as he started talking, and she wasn't sure if it was because he didn't want to see her face as he told it or because it was his way of hiding from the memory.

"I was seven and Donovan was five. We were poor, so poor that my parents decided we should go into the woods to forage, and that it made the most sense if we all went, so that we could carry back as much as possible and not have to go again—at least for a while. Our parents told us to stay in sight of them while we gathered, but I . . . even though we were always hungry, I wasn't a kid who feared things. I let myself get caught up in the task, following the mushrooms where they were the thickest, dreaming about asking my parents to buy me and Donovan an orange to split, and they'd have to say yes because I'd found mushrooms the size of my palm. But when I looked up, I saw the hedges of Havenwhile. My parents called my name, and I yelled for them, and when my family came out of the woods, I felt this relief spread through me—this lightness that said everything would always be okay because they'd always find me. I don't think I've ever felt that way again.

"A caravan of witches came out of the woods a moment later. It was Halfryta. She looked at each one of us. I remember that part. She met my eyes and still did what she did. She said we were so close to their walls that we had to be trying to break in, which gave her the right to punish us however she saw fit. She had my parents brought to their knees. They didn't fight because they were pleading their case, as if she were someone who could feel compassion. They even pointed at us and pleaded for our sakes, their children who needed them to survive, and she didn't even give them the courtesy of answering. She just nodded at two of her people. They didn't use a neat little spell—they came up behind each one and slid a dagger in and out of their throats, and they didn't even try and take the blood. They didn't need it. Red ran down the front of my mother's blue dress—she only had two dresses, and that was her favorite. I remember thinking how sad she'd be that it was ruined before I realized she wasn't going to feel anything at all. As the blood began soaking the ground at my parents' knees, Donovan broke free from the witch holding him, and grabbed onto our mother as she slumped to the ground. Then I was just standing there. My dad was looking at me, his mouth opening and closing without words as blood gurgled from his lips, and then he fell too, and I never even broke free. I don't think I even tried."

Bly's heart bled for him. She didn't think it was possible to hate the witches more than she did. But she *hated* Halfryta.

Kerrigan cleared his throat. "I remember a little girl that was with them. She had the same dark red hair as Halfryta, and she laughed when my dad fell forward onto his face. Demelza laughed. And then they just left us there. And eventually we tried to find our way home, but we ended up finding vampires instead. And that time I finally acted—I charged right at the group of them and yelled for Donovan to run, but they scooped us both up easily and took us to the queens, and apparently my courage impressed them." He laughed, the sound bitter with self-loathing. "They thought I was courageous enough to be one of them. And that's why I trained so hard, how I ended up in charge of the guard—I wanted to make sure I always fought back."

"You were just a kid," Bly said. "You *were* courageous."

"I wasn't. And I was the reason we were so close to this cursed place."

"You were just a kid," she said again. It was different than her own guilt—she'd been childish, but she should have known better.

"Tell that to my brother. He blamed me for wandering. And then I froze when I should have tried to do something. *I* could've been a distraction. Maybe they could've gotten away. I should have been the only one to pay the price."

"You know that's not true. They would've killed you all."

"And maybe that would've been better," he said darkly.

"No," she said. "No. It wasn't your fault."

"And it wasn't your fault either." She knew he was talking about Elise.

"That's different."

"But it's not, Bly, it's not. It's this whole bloody world's fault."

"You want me to let go of my guilt while you keep yours?"

"Don't you *want* me to keep mine?" he asked.

She was silent for a long moment. His guilt was the reason he was helping her, giving his life to fix his mistakes and her mistakes. It felt as if she were being ripped into two different wants.

This boy in front of her and what his life could buy her back. She was really crying now.

"Please don't," he said. "Please don't. I'm not changing my mind."

That made her cry harder.

He shifted so that they were both on their sides facing each other and his hands were on her wet cheeks, and his lips were on her mouth again, and she met them with her own aching tenderness, as if they were both trying to bandage each other with a kiss, and it might've worked if they were different people. They might have held each other together forever.

All they got was a moment suspended in the stars.

A new commotion down by the lake broke them apart. Cheering again, but more than last time.

"That's her," Kerrigan said.

Bly nodded.

Still, they clung to each other for a second longer. Because once they left this hammock, the pretending that wasn't really pretending was over.

NINETEEN

KERRIGAN INSISTED ON DELIVERING THE note himself. Although he told her that he knew she could do it multiple times, Bly could admit that she wasn't good at pretending. After the story Kerrigan had just told her, she was certain her disgust would be all over her face. He was better at keeping his hate off his face and locked in his heart.

She was surprised at how easy it was though. Halfryta's guards didn't stop him from approaching. He had the eyes of a witch, after all, and he'd had the glamour turn his copper hair a light brown. Plus, many witches were approaching her, handing her gifts before bowing their heads in respect. Kerrigan had plucked some wildflowers from the side of the lake and placed their note in the petals. Halfryta's eyes had flashed as she'd read it. She'd glanced at her guards, but she'd said nothing. After all, the note said her daughter would die if anything happened to them, but Bly had held her breath regardless. Some parents wouldn't care, and Demelza had said as much about Halfryta. But the witch let them walk out of there without anyone trying to stop them.

They cast glamour spells to undo their witch eyes as soon as they entered the trees. Bly was grateful Demelza had so many on her, and they could use another to reverse it instead of waiting for sleep to take the spell away. She wanted to look human for what came next.

Her mind was such a whirl of relief and dread for what was to come that she hardly noticed the mushrooms she crushed beneath her boots as they made their way back to camp. She barely registered anything at all until Kerrigan put his arm in front of her.

She stopped and followed his nod to someone behind a tree, fiddling with a rope. Bly crept past Kerrigan, using the cover of trees so she could get a closer look. A young man was on the other side of the tree, head slumped to his chest. A few feet away a girl was tied to a slender pine, her brown hair hanging in a curtain over her drooped head. The couple who'd been knocked unconscious inside. A bounty hunter had already found them.

"Hey," Bly called, already stepping out from behind the tree without hesitating. She had a vampire at her back, after all—one who'd risked his life for humans before. Perhaps this could be his last act as a rebel: to save a couple more people.

The person behind the tree stood and turned toward them, and Bly stopped. She recognized her: dark brown skin, long black hair striped with gray, witch-blue eyes. Bly searched her memory for her name.

"Hazel?"

The woman smiled warmly. "I'm glad you're still alive."

Everything about her seemed sincere, just like it had in those moments of kindness she'd shown Bly earlier.

But she was also standing behind a human with a long blade in her hand.

"I'm sorry I don't have much time," Hazel said, turning back to the man.

Bly looked over her shoulder at Kerrigan, and he stepped up beside her as his eyes scanned the woods for other witches.

Hazel knelt down, knife moving toward the man's wrist.

"Stop," Bly said.

The witch's knife flashed. Kerrigan had already taken two long strides toward Hazel, but then he stopped.

The rope fell away.

She bustled around to the other side of the tree to work on those bindings too.

"Are you stealing him?" Kerrigan asked.

"I'm freeing him," Hazel said without looking up.

She moved on to the girl, cutting her free before reaching into her pocket and holding something under the girl's nose. "Wake," Hazel said. The girl started to stir as she moved on to the man, performing the same spell before moving to stand by Kerrigan, who stared down at her with his eyebrows drawn together.

Hazel pulled two binding spells from her skirt. "Just a precaution if they need to be restrained again," she said. "Most of them are grateful and run the second they awaken, but some of them still want a witch and think I'm old and an easy target." She smiled. "I'm not."

The man and woman stumbled to their feet, reaching for each other and clasping hands. They took one look at Kerrigan and Hazel and ran off through the woods.

Bly turned to Hazel. "You risked a lot to help them."

Hazel shrugged. "I'm not the only one." She glanced around them. "I'm afraid I have other work to do today. Good luck." She winked as she turned and spun around, disappearing into the trees.

A witch risking her life for humans. Bly stood next to a vampire that had done the same, was still doing it. She'd already accepted that, but she hadn't wanted to believe Hazel the first time she'd told her that all witches weren't the same. But now she had proof.

"I like her," Kerrigan said slowly.

"Me too," Bly said.

It might have complicated things, but she wasn't capturing just any witch to hand over.

Halfryta deserved whatever happened to her. Demelza did too.

✦ ✦ ✦

They were back with the others, waiting. It was almost time.

"You've made a mistake," Demelza said with a laugh as the sky turned a watered-down blue. "My mother doesn't love anyone more than herself. At best, she'll come with backup to wipe you all out for daring to take me, and if I die in the process . . ." She shrugged.

"Put your sword on her throat and kill her if the witch doesn't come alone," Kerrigan said to Vincent.

"I'm not your servant, vampire." Vincent scowled.

Nova sighed and got off the stump she was sitting on next to her brother, then strode over to Demelza before loosely holding her ax at an angle that could definitely switch from casual to decapitation if the need arose.

Bly couldn't help but glance at Emerson. His expression was stormy, but he said nothing to stop them. Demelza had confessed her plan to betray him, after all. Whatever he owed her for saving him once was void.

The sky shifted to a dull gray with tinges of soft pink. It made Bly think of diluted blood. She used to love a pink-laced sky, but blood had saturated her existence even more than before, and she didn't think she'd ever see the world through a lens that wasn't bloodied.

She decided not to care.

At least not right now.

"I told you . . . " Demelza started, but her voice trailed off.

Halfryta stepped out from behind a giant oak trunk as if she'd been standing there for some time. Her hair, the same dark auburn as Demelza's, was braided into a crown as if reminding them of who she was even without her finery.

Demelza's eyes went wide. She scanned the woods as if waiting for an ambush. When no one else jumped out behind Halfryta, the shock on Demelza's face shifted, leaving something raw and vulnerable—a look of relief when you were sure it wouldn't come.

Bly almost felt a pinch of feeling for her. Almost.

Halfryta just raised her hands. "I'm here as you so eloquently requested. Release my daughter."

"Bind yourself first." Kerrigan's voice held barely contained fury.

"Don't, mother," Demelza said. "The vampire violated the rules already. He knocked me unconscious. We can call for his blood."

"Only because you were going to murder your own human player," Kerrigan hissed.

"Lies," Demelza said with a smile that made her look more like her mother—whatever vulnerability she'd shown a second ago had been replaced.

Halfryta's eyes flashed in Kerrigan's direction. "Vampire. You're playing a dangerous game. Give me my daughter and we'll forget about your indiscretion."

"No," Kerrigan said simply. "I'd rather see you die."

Halfryta eyed him more closely. "This is personal."

"Yes," Kerrigan said.

He opened his mouth to say more, but she lifted a hand to stop him. "No need to elaborate. I assure you that I do not care about whatever you think you suffered at my hand."

Fists clenching, Kerrigan took a step toward her.

She smiled, and Bly could see the resemblance to Demelza even more—the smiles that held no warmth at all.

"Please do come closer," Halfryta said.

If he attacked her, this wouldn't end well. Nova might kill Demelza, but would Kerrigan survive a fight with Halfryta?

"Kerrigan." Bly took a couple steps toward him, turning her back on Halfryta so that she could face him. She couldn't exactly stop him if he decided to strike, but she could make him have to move past her to do it. "I need her alive."

His eyes were a fire on a rainy day—hot pain and endless sorrow.

"Please," she whispered.

His stare flickered to her and away again, and he seemed to shudder with the fight to control himself, but his hands flexed in and out of fists and his nostrils flared.

Bly sent Nova a look.

The other girl tightened her hold on her ax. "Bind yourself, witch, or I take her head."

Halfryta's eyes flickered between each one of them, and then finally settled on her daughter. She gave a disappointed sigh that made Demelza look down before she reached into a pocket of her shirt and pulled out the familiar twigs. "Bind," she said, pricking her finger and then her leg.

Her limbs melded together, and she fell to her knees but somehow didn't topple.

Kerrigan let out a sharp breath, and Bly wished that she could reach for him to hold his hand as the memories came rushing back in this moment that he'd waited a lifetime for—the witch who'd killed his parents on her knees in the same helpless position she'd murdered them in.

"We should kill Demelza anyway," Vincent said. "We don't want her chasing us."

"No," Kerrigan said. "We keep our word." He swallowed, and Bly knew he had to be remembering the little girl who'd laughed as his parents died.

Bly didn't think she'd be so generous to the witches who'd laughed at her sister's body.

Nova backed away from Demelza, ax dropping to her side with something like disappointment.

"You *should* kill me," Demelza said to Kerrigan. "I'll bring war down on you. You laid hands on me, remember?"

"Shut up, silly child," Halfryta said.

Demelza went silent.

"Can you carry the witch?" Kerrigan asked, turning away to Emerson and Vincent. "I don't want to touch her."

Halfryta laughed. "As if you *could*."

The words didn't hit immediately.

Nova turned around first, ax raised, darting back toward Demelza. Vincent's sword scraped free next, followed by Emerson's.

But they weren't fast enough.

The witches peeled away from the trees they were hidden in like bark scraping loose, and they were on them in seconds, forming lines in front of Demelza and her mother. Their hands held an array of spells and weapons meant to kill and maim, and Bly knew instantly that they didn't stand a chance.

They'd lost.

Because they'd expected the witches to honor the rules of the game. Invisibility spells were illegal in the forest.

"You cheated," Bly said weakly.

"And you can't say a thing about it," Halfryta said. "Because the vampire touched my daughter first. You're lucky I don't kill every last one of you." She tilted her head as if she were reconsidering as one of her people unbound her, and she stood. She turned to Kerrigan. "Say hello to your little orphan brother." She grinned. "I do recognize that hair of yours. I remember how sweetly your mother begged for me to let you live. Don't make me regret that favor again."

Bly saw what he would do before he even moved. Her hands closed around his arm, and for a brief moment, she held him, but it wasn't enough. He roared, ripping free of her as if she were nothing.

He was on the witches before she could even turn. Or rather, they were on him, swarming him like ants. It only took a second for him to go down, legs and arms bound together. They gripped him and hauled him into the trees without even looking back at them.

"Kerrigan!" Bly screamed. She tried to run after him, but Emerson grabbed her, yanking her back so hard that she crashed into his chest. She smacked her fist against him before trying to rip herself free. "Let me go!"

"It's not worth it!" Emerson yelled back at her.

"They're going to kill him," she panted.

His eyes flashed with confusion. Of course they were going to kill him, but that shouldn't have mattered—that had been their plan all along.

"And we won't have Elise back," she added. But it was too late. She saw on his face that he knew that wasn't the first thing she'd thought about. She'd only thought about saving him.

She turned to Nova and Vincent. "We need them both."

"If we're dead, our family loses everything," Vincent said.

"Do you really have enough for them to all live? Your little siblings? How many do you have? Seven?" Bly cringed at her own words, the manipulation in them. They hadn't told her how many siblings—she'd guessed from Nova's sketch.

Nova's face looked bleak. "We can go catch someone else."

"No," Bly said. "Another prince? We'll lose. What's the point if we can't win?"

"Where's my brother?" They all jumped at that deep familiar voice. Bly jerked toward Donovan as Emerson dropped her arm to raise his sword. Donovan looked like death with fire for hair. Behind him, in the woods, she glimpsed multiple sets of gray eyes. And a girl with white-blond hair. Jade.

She never thought she'd be happy to see these particular vampires again.

"The witches have him," Bly said.

Donovan unsheathed his sword. "Then the four of you won't live to see your prize," he hissed. The other vampires crept closer.

"Wait." Bly held up her hands. "We didn't hand him over. He changed his mind and ours. He was working with us to capture a witch. We had Halfryta before they ambushed us."

Donovan's face morphed into something even more terrifying. "My brother had the head witch?" Respect leaked into his voice. Bly had a feeling it might have been for the first time. "Then help me get them both back, and you can still have your prize for the witch."

"Let's just kill them first. We don't need their help." Bly hadn't noticed how close Jade had crept to her.

Donovan ignored her. "Where?" he barked at Bly.

She pointed a shaking finger into the woods, and the vampires took off without waiting.

She tried to follow, but Emerson still held her arm.

"You heard what he said. We can still have the prize." She turned her pleading eyes onto Nova and Vincent. "Please," she said to them.

Vincent shook his head. "Fighting alongside fucking vampires." But his grip tightened on his sword.

Nova twisted her grip on her ax and looked at him. "For our siblings," she whispered.

He nodded.

They took off after them, and Emerson's hold finally loosened enough for Bly to run.

She knew he'd follow—despite everything.

The scene was chaos when they caught up with them. The witches had their speed spells and the vampires had their natural speed, and both danced around each other, dodging behind trees and branches, each trying to get close enough to wound the other.

"This is a breach of our treaty," Halfryta was screaming.

"You breeched it first," Donovan roared back at her.

They stood in the center of the battle. The witch held Kerrigan in front of her like a shield.

"Give me my brother and we'll end this with peace intact."

"Will we?" she sneered.

"You have my word."

"The word of a vampire means less than dirt to me."

A witch screamed as a vampire landed a killing blow to the neck. Donovan and Halfryta didn't even glance in that direction.

Bly snuck along the edge of the battle.

"You know giving him to me is really your only choice," Donovan said.

Halfryta snarled. Another witch went down with an agonizing cry.

Two bodies crashed into the brush where Bly crept. A tumble of witch and blond vampire, until Jade's legs and armed twined together. The witch girl straddled her, pressing a blade to Jade's throat.

Bly stabbed a binding spell into the witch's arm, and she collapsed on top of Jade, who was waiting with an open mouth. Her fangs sunk into the witch's bare throat and the girl screamed, thrashing against the bite as blood poured onto Jade's face.

Bly gagged as the witch slowly stopped moving.

Jade blinked at Bly with her blood-soaked face. "Thanks, but that won't stop me from killing you later. I may be here because I love Donovan, and I know losing his brother would kill him, but I still love seeing Kerrigan suffer, and something tells me your death would do that." She snapped her teeth as Bly crawled past her, on her hands and knees now, through the thick brush.

"Hand him over now or her head rolls." Nova's clear voice rang out above the fray.

Through the leaves, Bly could see her standing with her ax against Demelza's back. Vincent's sword was in the air, prepared to make a deadly sweep across her neck. Demelza's hands were up, an unused death curse pinched in her fingers.

Nobody bothered to stop fighting, but Halfryta sighed. "Always a disappointment." She looked at Donovan. "Your brother for my daughter."

He nodded.

She shoved Kerrigan away from her and he crashed into Donovan, who almost dropped his sword as he caught him.

Nova and Vincent had dropped their weapons from Demelza.

Bly knew Donovan wanted the witch, but not at the cost of his brother.

But Bly still *needed* the witch. Her hand crept out from her hiding spot, and she pricked Halfryta's ankle. The witch crumbled. Her eyes met Bly's in shock as her head hit the ground. Bly bound her hands before she could cast her own spell.

Silence fell.

Vincent's roar broke it.

Demelza stood over Nova, who was on the ground, black vines climbing over her skin as she writhed. Vincent had dropped to his knees at her side. Bly ran toward them, but the expression Vincent turned on her made her steps falter. She'd never seen so much hate on someone's face before.

"That's for being a traitor," Demelza said coldly, but Bly was certain neither twin could hear through their pain.

Demelza's eyes fell on her bound mother. Hurt flickered on her face, but she turned and bolted into the woods without a word.

The last of the witches died horrible deaths.

Bly backed up, shaking. Emerson knelt beside Vincent.

"Help her," Vincent said, standing, twisting to look at each of the vampires. "Turn her."

"You know we can't," Donovan said coldly.

Vincent turned to Kerrigan, thrusting a finger at him as if it were a sword trying to kill. "She was cursed coming to get you."

Vincent turned on Bly, his face a mask of pure rage. "Convince him. This is your fault. We should've let them do their own bloody battle." His voice broke and he growled as if trying to hide the emotion.

All Bly could do was shake her head. She could barely bring herself to glance at Nova, a girl who'd been fighting for her family just like Bly. And she was paying the price while Bly escaped it again.

"Vincent," Emerson said gently.

Nova's hands clawed at the ground. This was no death curse that took a year. This was just death. Her voice rasped out with more and more distance between each labored effort.

Vincent dropped to his knees again and took Nova's hand until she finally went still. Bending, he rested his forehead against hers for a moment before reaching around her neck and pulling off a piece of twine that held a small stone encased in wire. He put the necklace on, his eyes dry.

"Well then," Donovan said. "Let's get going, shall we?" His voice was casual, like they were all just heading out for a walk, not like there were bodies and death all around them.

"We're not leaving her here," Kerrigan said.

Vincent looked up at him, his face blank.

"You can't be serious," Donovan replied.

"I am. She has a family. We take her home to them."

Donovan sighed. "Always the bleeding heart, but never bleeding hearts. Good to have you back, brother." He looked past him to Halfryta on the ground. "And you actually did something this year. I'm proud of you." His voice was demeaning, as if he were the older brother talking to a child.

Kerrigan didn't answer.

Bly watched his shoulders sag under the weight of the past. Capturing the witch hadn't changed the burden he carried. She could already see it. She wanted to reach for him, but she didn't.

TWENTY

THE BOUNTY HUNTERS WERE OUT IN FORCE, but the two groups that stumbled upon them took one look at the vampires and ran in the other direction. Bly was relieved. She didn't have another battle in her, not that it would be much of a fight with her current companions. Her limbs were tired from keeping up with the vampires, and the journey had taken an extra day because of their detour to take Nova's body home. They'd all camped outside of the Gap while Vincent insisted on carrying the body the final leg by himself. He took so long to return that Bly thought he might have abandoned them, and it was only Kerrigan's insistence that kept Donovan waiting. Eventually, he had come back and said nothing, just walked past them in the direction of Vagaris.

Bly wanted to be done. She wanted to sink into a warm bed until her tired limbs could feel again. She groaned when someone stepped out of the woods in front of them, just before the walls of Vagaris, but she assumed whoever it was would run the other way like those who'd come before.

But Donovan, who was leading the group, halted, and Bly looked up at the man who stood before them.

No. Not a man—he wore an outfit of startling bright red. He had white-blond hair and a grin that seemed jarring against the solemness of the woods.

Bly stopped just behind Donovan's right shoulder, and Kerrigan stood to her left. Jade was at Donovan's other side, and Emerson and Vincent stood behind them with two guards carrying Halfryta on a stretcher. The other vampire guards were out of sight, patrolling the woods at Donovan's command.

The vampire's stare zeroed in on Bly, though, and he cocked his head. "Hello, Bly," he said. "Aren't you a lovely surprise—I didn't think you'd make it this far."

She jerked at Benedict's recognition, startled the vampire would remember her.

His eyes slid behind them to Halfryta. "Is that . . . ?"

"The head witch," Bly said.

Donovan glared down at her, but she didn't care. She remembered what Benedict had said to her at the trial. "Looks like you picked the wrong player."

His grin widened. "I'm delighted you proved me wrong."

He seemed like he meant it.

She peered at him, but he'd already focused on Donovan again.

"Benedict," Donovan said. "What are you doing out here? Away from your lounge?"

"I hate to do this, my friend, but I'm going to need to take your prize for myself." Benedict raised a hand and waved with two fingers. The three hulking men Benedict chose after the trial stepped out behind him.

Donovan laughed. "Waiting until the end to pilfer someone else's spoils? Very unsporting of you. Although I'm surprised you're still playing at all."

Benedict sighed. "The things we do for love."

Donovan chuckled. "Love—with whom?"

"You know."

"Still infatuated with your human pet?" Donovan shook his head.

Benedict shrugged. "What can I say? I want to love her forever and ever."

Kerrigan snorted. "It'll be someone else within the month."

"Nobody asked you." All the charm had disappeared from his voice.

"But he's right," Donovan said.

Benedict placed a hand over his heart in mock hurt.

"Move along, friend." Donovan didn't so much as reach for his sword, and somehow that felt like a threat.

The men behind Benedict tightened their grips on their sheathed weapons.

Donovan sighed. "I'm weary of your games. Normally I wouldn't mind a fight between friends, but it's already been a particularly long day. You know you don't stand a chance. Take your little group and pester someone else."

Benedict grinned. "Did I mention they've been spelled with vampire fangs?"

Kerrigan shifted, positioning himself in front of Bly.

"Stop being tedious," Donovan growled. "It's not enough."

"I'd like to see, nonetheless." His eyes settled on Jade. "Sister?"

Bly wasn't sure how she hadn't seen it before, the white-blond hair and the slim features.

"You could have warned me of your plans," Jade said, glaring at Benedict.

He shrugged. "You love surprises. Besides, I wasn't looking for you lot specifically. But this *is* a happy coincidence. So how about switching sides, Jade?" His expression grew harder even as he smiled, and his stare shifted from his sister to Kerrigan. "Or perhaps Kerrigan would join me? He does so love betraying people."

Jade frowned at her brother, glancing between him and Donovan. Finally, she sighed. "I *do* love a slaughter." She turned to Donovan. "Sorry love, blood comes first." Her eyes flicked to Kerrigan. "You understand."

She stepped to the other side to stand by Benedict.

"Whose prize is she anyway?" Benedict asked.

"Mine," Kerrigan said.

"Even better." Benedict's hand settled on the hilt of his sword.

"My dear friend," Donovan said, "think this through. We have the head witch. Do you really *want* to win the prize?"

Benedict paused, sword half out of its sheath. Something unspoken passed between the two vampires, and then Donovan whistled.

"Darling, who's not being sporting now?" Jade pouted as the rest of the guards trickled out from the woods around them where Donovan had ordered them to walk.

Benedict took them all in and shared a calculating stare with his sister. Turning to the spelled men behind him, he said, "I don't suppose you feel like dying today?"

One of them spun around and bolted into the woods.

Benedict sighed. "I don't want to either." He raised his hands. "I surrender."

"I thought you might," Donovan said.

Benedict shrugged. "Well, I only promised I'd try, and you clearly have the upper hand." He strode over and wrapped his arm around Donovan's shoulders. "I could use a drink. No hard feelings, right?"

Donovan laughed. "None."

* ✦ *

Once they had entered the city, word seemed to spread. By the time they reached the gates of the fortress, the streets were lined with jeering crowds who pointed and laughed at Halfryta. She never glanced right or left, just held her chin in the air as if she were above every last one of them. Donovan waved and nodded as they yelled his name, assuming he'd been the one to capture her. Kerrigan was a solemn figure walking beside Bly. Barely anyone yelled out his name, but he didn't even acknowledge the few that did.

This was not a victory parade for him.

Bly understood the feeling. Even handing over someone who'd done unspeakable things to the people she cared about left an uneasy pit in her stomach. But Halfryta had a hand in keeping the world what it was, and Bly was only playing by *their* rules.

As they finally made it through the fortress gates, Kerrigan let out a tiny sigh of relief before he straightened and pulled back his shoulders. He turned to the two vampires who held the witch. "Deliver her to the queens and tell them we expect to claim the prize at midnight because it's impossible for anyone to beat us now."

The vampires nodded and disappeared.

Kerrigan sagged as soon as the witch was out of his view. Bly started to reach for him as easily as she would have in Havenwhile when they were only pretending, but Jade slid in front of him without bothering to toss Bly even a glance.

"Don't hurt Donovan again," she told him.

If she wanted a promise, she didn't get one. Kerrigan stared at her, his expression giving nothing away until she gave up and spun around, snarling at Bly as she shoved past her.

Kerrigan turned over his shoulder to look at Vincent and Emerson. "I can take everyone to their own rooms until the queens summon us for the ceremony. I believe they'll do it tonight as I've asked."

"I'll find my own place to sleep," Vincent said, stalking off without waiting for a response.

Nobody tried to stop him.

"Brother," Donovan said. He'd moved to stand in front of them. "May we speak?"

Bly started to step back, but Kerrigan reached out between them and lightly touched her wrist with a single finger. She stayed despite the look of exasperation Donovan gave her.

"I'm proud of you," Donovan said. "We could have done it together, though—all these years we could have been working together to capture her." His eyes slid to Bly and away, and she didn't miss the jealousy in them. "I thought you didn't care."

"I always cared," Kerrigan said. "You know it's why I chose this life in the first place."

"But you threw it away."

"By trying to save people? Maybe you should try it."

The old wound between them was palpable in the silence.

"I am what you made me, brother," Donovan said. "I embraced the life *you* pushed me toward, and you were right to do it. Saving people won't change what happened." His eyes flitted to Bly, but for once there wasn't maliciousness in them but sorrow.

Kerrigan looked tired. "I know that."

Donovan seemed to deflate. And for the first time, Bly thought he looked like the younger brother, someone who just wanted their sibling to see them. "Anyway, I'm just glad you came to your senses." He glanced at Bly again. "Whatever the reason."

Kerrigan nodded but said nothing, and for a second Bly thought they might hug, but Donovan twisted on his heels and stomped off. Kerrigan didn't move until Donovan disappeared from sight, as if it were the last time he'd ever see him.

When he finally glanced down, he caught Bly studying his face. Worry needled her, and he seemed to see it instantly.

"Don't worry, love, I haven't come to my senses." He smiled sadly.

Her chest expanded, but it wasn't relief; it was a new desperation warring with the other familiar ones.

She didn't want to let him go.

Part of the reason she'd agreed to his plan to trade Demelza was to buy her more time with him, delay the inevitable, but that time was whittling away, and each moment lost carved a little something away from her.

She thought she'd feel whole again once she got Elise back, but that would never happen now. She'd never feel that way again—it was just a matter of which version of her broken self she wanted to be.

And she wasn't going to choose a vampire whom she'd only known for days over the sister she'd grown up with. There was no choice, even if it felt like the choice was killing her.

So she said nothing.

Hurt flashed on his face before he glanced over his shoulder at Emerson, who was watching the exchange. "Come on, I'll show you to some rooms."

They arrived at two rooms, and Kerrigan nodded at each. "Here we are," he said, and he stood there until Emerson disappeared without a word. Bly took a step toward her own room just as Kerrigan's hand landed on her arm. "Wait."

She turned to him, but he stared at his boots.

"I miss our pretending." His voice was barely a whisper. But she heard the words easily. It was as if they were already echoing inside the hollowness of her chest, and he'd merely given voice to them.

She let the silence stretch between them for what felt like an eternity to her but was probably nothing to a vampire.

Finally, he looked at her, eyes pleading. "Pretend with me a little longer?"

But they both knew it wasn't pretend, and it was much more dangerous than any game. She'd planned to gamble her life, not her heart.

She nodded anyway.

He reached out and took her hand, weaving his fingers between hers as they made their way back to his rooms. If anyone gave them a second look, she didn't notice. Her body felt numb as if she were half asleep and toeing the edge of a dream.

She entered his room in a daze, and as the door clicked shut behind her, she moved to one of the walls of paintings, eyes drifting over them without seeing a single one. The only thing she was truly aware of was him, standing behind her, watching.

She turned to glance at him over her shoulder. "Do you have a favorite?"

"I didn't used to." He hesitated and tilted his chin in the direction of the wall that led to his bedroom before walking over to stand with his hands behind his back, staring up at a painting above the doorframe. She moved over to his side, letting her shoulder lean against his upper arm as she looked up.

A wolf stood silhouetted against a sky the color of near-dark. The animal howled up at a sliver of a moon while surrounded by trees rendered in such deep browns and greens that the branches looked like blackened claws reaching for the light. It was beautiful and haunting.

"It reminds me of you," he said, shifting to stand behind her, so close that she could feel his chest moving with each breath. "Alone and desperate." He reached up, and his fingers ran the length of her neck. "But beautiful and strong."

Her pulse skittered, just like it had that day in the woods when she'd been trapped, but that time it had been from pure fear—from being seen as nothing but an animal to be hunted. This time . . . the fear was still there, but it was a different type.

This fear came from being seen and desired and vulnerable.

He pulled his fingertips away from her skin, leaving them just shy of touching.

"Are you afraid?" he murmured.

"Yes."

His hands dropped away, and she spun around so that their chests were almost touching.

"But not of you," she said. It *was* him, though, just not the way he was thinking.

His eyes went black with hunger, and he turned his head slightly as if he didn't want her to see.

But the darkness didn't make him look like a monster to her—it lit up the ring of green around his irises that never went away.

"You're hungry," she said.

He cleared his throat. "I can call for something to be brought up. I'll get it under control."

She grabbed his chin and pulled him back to face her. "Feed on me."

He shook his head. "I don't need to do that. We're not in the woods anymore."

"It's not about need. I *want* you to."

He stared down at her with his black eyes as if trying to gauge whether or not she meant it.

She did, and it wasn't because she owed him an endless amount of gratitude. She couldn't pretend that was the reason anymore.

It was because her whole body felt like it lit on fire with the idea of it.

He didn't believe her, though. He grimaced as if it took every ounce of self-control not to taste her.

So she reached up and let her hands wind into his hair as she pulled him down, guiding his lips to her neck. He let out a sharp breath that made her shiver, but still he didn't bite.

"Are you sure?" His question was light as silk against her skin.

"Please," she answered.

His hands held her waist, tugging her to close the tiny gap that was still between them.

She tensed for the prick of his fangs, but instead she got the press of his lips, soft at first, and then hungrier as if he wanted to consume all of her, not just her blood. He traveled up the side of her jaw until his fangs scraped her earlobe.

She let out a soft gasp, and his fingers squeezed her hips in response.

Her own hands drifted to the sides of his face, trying to pull his mouth to hers, but he let go of her, hands clasping her own, gently pulling them away. He gripped her wrists in one of his hands. "Let me take my time." His voice was a low growl, but his free hand cupped her chin gently as he softly added, "Okay?"

All she could do was nod.

He backed her up slightly until she hit the doorframe. He lifted her hands just above her head, eyeing her carefully as if making sure she hadn't changed her mind.

Her heart pounded so hard that she thought she might faint, but all she could do was focus on his lips, on wanting them against her once more.

He seemed satisfied with whatever he found on her face, and his mouth found her neck again as he continued to hold her captive. His free hand wound into her hair, thumb tracing the curve of her ear. His kisses trailed to the edges of her lips and away until she thought he might intend to spend eternity teasing her, but she'd never had eternity, and now, neither did he.

Finally, he drew a shuddering breath and moved his lips to hover above hers.

She crushed into him with a hunger that rivaled any vampire's.

He seemed almost shocked at first, pulling back slightly, but she bit his bottom lip in response before letting go.

"Okay?" she asked, her voice barely more than a rasp.

He chuckled, the sound electric between them. "Bite me as much as you'd like."

And she did. Their kisses went from sharp to languid and back again. She tasted blood as she nicked herself on his fangs, making him groan, and his grip on her tighten, but it did nothing to stop her.

It wasn't until her lips felt swollen and raw that she pulled back slightly and looked at his black eyes. "What are you waiting for?"

He set her hands free, and she immediately gripped the front of his shirt. She thought her knees might collapse without him, but his arms folded around her, and he half carried her to the bed until the back of her thighs hit the silky black bedding.

She hesitated, her eyes widening.

"I just want you to be comfortable. Do you trust me?"

She nodded and he guided her back, lying on his side before pulling her down beside him. He gave her a light kiss on the lips.

"Flip around," he said.

Once she had, he pulled her back against his chest until her head rested against his bicep. His free arm draped over her breasts, and his hand cupped the front of her throat.

His lips found her neck again, trailing kisses, but he didn't draw it out. His mouth parted after a moment, and the sharpness of his fangs settled against her skin. His tongue darted out, flicking the spot where he was about to bite.

"Yes," she said, in case it was a question.

The pinch of his fangs made her body shudder, and she sucked in a sharp breath. His fingers traced gentle lines up and down the front of her neck as his mouth closed over the wound, drinking.

Some small part in the back of her mind told her that she should be revolted. Humans were vampires' prey. They weren't supposed to enjoy getting caught, but all she wanted to do was stay in this moment.

He pulled back too soon, and she grumbled.

He laughed. "You're hungrier than I am."

He touched her neck, healing the small cuts with his own

blood, but she didn't feel like someone who'd been wounded—all she felt was the healing.

She twisted in his arms so he could kiss her, and he did, slowly, as if they had all the time in the world, as if tomorrow wouldn't come.

But eventually he stopped, pulling back slightly even as she still reached for him.

"I can't," he whispered.

"What?" She could hear the confusion in her own voice.

"I can't keep pretending," he said.

"Oh." She moved to sit up, to leave. She understood the pain they were inflicting on each other by letting themselves have this moment.

"No." His hand enclosed hers, stopping her from standing, pulling her back down so that she was in his arms, looking up at him. "I don't mean for you to leave. I don't want you to ever leave." His throat bobbed. "I want . . . I want you to claim the immortality at midnight. I want you to stay here with me . . . forever. I've never really wanted forever before. I . . ." He turned and stared at the ceiling as if he couldn't bear to look at her. "I can picture it now."

She burned with her own want. She could imagine it too, being here with him, staring at paintings all day—it wasn't the dream her heart had been full of for so long, but she knew without a doubt that she could make a new dream from this.

Her throat ached with the possibility.

"Emerson's dying," she said.

"I know," he said with a sigh.

"You could change me yourself. I know the punishment of turning a vampire without permission is death, but . . . the queens let you live before." She couldn't believe she was even speaking the words but perhaps she'd already been burying the thought, because even if he said yes to turning her, she still needed him to die to save her sister.

He shook his head. "They'd punish my brother in my place. I know it. It's what they've already threatened."

"I can't live with the guilt of taking this from Emerson. You can't really be asking me to . . . and Elise . . ."

When he turned back to her, she expected him to look at her with sadness, or at least disappointment. After Elise had died, all she'd seen in her parents' eyes, and eventually Emerson's, were horrible mixtures of those two things. But when she twisted in his arms and stared up at him, she saw neither.

She saw forgiveness. And longing. He wanted to beg her; she could see it all over his face. But he wouldn't.

"It's okay," he said.

A tiny sob broke from her chest at those simple words.

"I'm not abandoning you." His face dipped down to hers, and his lips brushed away one of the tears on her cheek. "I'm not abandoning your sister either. I'll sacrifice myself for you any day. And her too. All I've ever wanted is to go back in time and give my life to try and save my parents. It's why I tried to help Bianca."

Bly tensed. "Do I remind you of her?" She'd wondered a thousand times why it was her he'd decided to help. What if it wasn't about her at all? What if she reminded him of a ghost from his past?

He must have felt her unease because he reached out and gripped her chin. "In some ways, yes. You're fierce like her, but you're not the same. You're someone else entirely. I don't want you to think I don't know that." He ran a thumb across her cheekbone. "But Bianca gave me a way to help people, and you're giving me the same. You're giving me that gift."

"Death is not a gift," she choked out past the sorrow that wracked her body.

"It is for me."

She knew that wasn't true. Maybe it was before, when she'd first met him, but he'd just asked her to live forever with him.

He *wanted* eternity.

But he'd give it up for her.

Her heart felt like it was expanding then shattering over and over again; it was somehow a thing of wonder and pain all at the same time, and she thought it might be love. She'd never felt anything like it before. She'd thought she was in love with Emerson, but she'd only fixated on him as a logical building block for the future she'd imagined.

This wasn't logical at all. She'd only just met Kerrigan. It defied every bit of reasoning in her mind, but what she felt was in her bones, a yearning that made her want to press her body as close to his as possible. She even longed to feel her blood leaving her body to nourish his—something that would have made her squeamish before. But she wanted every part of him. Even the dangerous ones.

His lips were still trailing over her cheeks as if he could kiss away her pain.

Each tender touch was another breaking of her heart.

She couldn't do this.

"Wait," she said.

He pulled back and looked down at her with worry in his eyes.

"What if we capture another vampire?" she asked. "Why does it have to be you?" He stiffened in her arms, but she kept going. "You could help. There are rules about how much you can help your team when capturing a witch, but what about helping capture one of your own?"

"There are no rules because that's unthinkable," he said, his voice as tense as his body.

"Why?" She pulled back a little so she could stare at him, but his face gave away nothing. "We can buy Elise's life back with someone else. We'll worry about turning me later."

Kerrigan didn't answer for a moment, and the silence let her mind run away with hope. "I couldn't do that," he said finally. "I couldn't condemn someone who didn't want that. There's a reason I never play."

"You captured Halfryta."

He flinched. "She was evil," he said simply, but she could see the turmoil in his eyes—that getting revenge was never going to be a thing that healed him. It haunted him already.

"Surely there's someone in this city who deserves it?"

He shook his head. "We banish those who are truly terrible. I know that doesn't mean there aren't still evil vampires among us, but finding one? Being sure that they deserve that punishment?" He swallowed. "No. I can't do it."

"What about the banished? In the woods beyond Vagaris?"

"There's no time for that."

She swallowed the painful knot forming in her throat. "Then we wait until next year." She couldn't believe she was even saying those words, but at her core maybe she was still the selfish girl who went into the woods to chase her own wants without worrying about the consequences. As much as she wanted to be as selfless as Kerrigan, part of her was still scrambling to have everything she wanted: her sister back *and* the threads of whatever new dream she might weave with Kerrigan.

But his face held no hope for a future between them. Whatever moment of weakness had led him to ask her to stay with him was gone.

"I won't let you do that," he said. "The banished are dangerous. I'm not going to let you die to save me." He hesitated, and the light in his eyes grew suddenly distant. "Not when I don't want to be saved."

She knew what he was doing—letting his past overwhelm him again, letting whatever bit of sadness she'd managed to chase away snake around his heart once more. He was leaving her even as his arms clutched her tighter, tucking her into his chest so that his chin rested on the top of her head.

So he wouldn't have to see her.

She didn't try to hide the way her body shook, though.

She wanted him to feel what his loss would do to her.

He needed to die knowing that.

TWENTY-ONE

THEY WERE LED TO ONE OF THE FAR
sides of the fortress along a curved hallway with windows that
showed off the shore of the lake. They reached a dead end of
two bloodred doors. Bly swallowed, glancing up at Kerrigan,
but he wasn't looking at her. He'd barely looked at her since the
midnight summons had arrived. She'd fallen asleep, and he'd
woken her with a kiss to her forehead, but that was the last trace
of affection he'd given her. They'd walked the whole way there
with an arm's length of cold space between them.

All she wanted to do was close the gap.

Emerson and Vincent already stood waiting, both with dark
looks on their faces, and part of her was surprised each one had
come—especially Emerson. Guilt bit at her. She should have
checked on him last night. Despite what had happened between
them, he was still her friend.

The guards swung the door open before she got a chance to
speak to him, and they entered the throne room.

Finally, Kerrigan closed the distance between them himself,

his arm gently grazing hers.

The room was stunning. Pebbles the size of fingertips created the floor—a sea of white with black stones forming tiny swirls across the entire expanse. It made Bly dizzy, as if the room had come to life, and she'd be pulled into the floor with one wrong move. The far side of the room was open arched windows that let in the cool breeze from the forest beyond. It made it look as if the sprawling pines and oaks had been captured and framed, as if the rulers sitting in the center of this magnificent place actually had that power.

They looked like they did.

In the center of the room, on a raised platform, sat two stone thrones—one a startling snow white and the other the perfect blackness of a moonless midnight. A woman lounged in each one. The one in the white throne had sleek black hair cropped to her chin, porcelain white skin, and sharp but dainty features. She wore a black silk gown that hung in loose waves from a golden chain around her throat. The woman on the black throne had tight blond ringlets that hung wild around her shoulders. She wore a golden corset that hugged her small waist and flared out into full red skirts sprinkled with flashing rubies that grew more numerous at the bottom until the gems became a solid sparkling band.

The queens appeared almost frozen as the group walked in to stand in front of them, and Bly wondered if that was what happened when you lived forever—you forgot you were a creature that moved.

After a long moment, the blond queen raised a single eyebrow as her gaze settled on Kerrigan. "My son." Kerrigan cringed at the words but she didn't seem to notice. "Your brother tells us that it was you who captured Halfryta. I have to say I'm a little surprised." Her eyes shifted to taking in the rest of them. "These are your humans?"

Bly could almost feel Emerson frowning even though she wasn't looking at him.

"Yes . . ." the queen continued. "I'm very surprised."

"I am not. This is why we didn't banish you. You've become exactly what we wanted." The other queen's voice was low and gravelly, and when Bly looked in her direction, she was still staring straight ahead like she hadn't spoken at all.

The blond queen lifted a dainty shoulder. "Well, I'd always hoped you'd come around again. What changed?" She looked Bly up and down and then cocked her head as if that might help her see the situation in a different light.

Kerrigan shrugged. "I got bored."

The blond queen burst into laughter. "Now, that I can believe." She leaned back in her chair as if that answer had put her at ease. "Well, let's move on with it, shall we?"

Kerrigan nodded and then finally glanced at the rest of them, his eyes trailing over them as if he weren't really seeing anything at all. He bowed slightly to the golden-haired vampire queen first. "This is Queen Melvina." He shifted to bow to the other. "And this is Queen Allena."

"Son, are you forgetting your place?" Melvina's eyes focused on where Kerrigan's elbow just barely touched Bly's upper arm, and a spark of interest shone in them before she looked back at Kerrigan.

Kerrigan hesitated for only a moment before leaving Bly's side and stepping forward, moving to stand to the right of the thrones.

Melvina rose from her chair and steepled her hands in front of her as she assessed them with a crinkled nose. "And who is the lucky mortal who is claiming an eternity with us?"

Vincent and Bly both glanced at Emerson, but he was staring forward as if in a daze.

Emerson finally turned to look at Bly. His lips were set in a grim line.

Her stomach dropped.

He couldn't say no—not when they'd fought so hard to get here. But he'd been saying all along that he didn't want this. And Emerson wasn't one to change his mind.

Bly moved, and Kerrigan's head snapped up, eyes flashing with hope. Her steps faltered from the weight of his longing, but she forced herself to look away from him and go to Emerson.

There was a hint of surprise on Emerson's face, like maybe he thought she didn't care anymore what happened to him.

Maybe she shouldn't have.

"I won't do it," he said plainly.

She opened her mouth to beg him to do it for her, because a week ago those were the words she would've been certain would convince him.

But those pleas died on her lips.

"Do it for Elise," she said instead. "I don't want to bring her back and have to explain how you died trying to help me do it. How's she going to walk among the living again while carrying that with her? Her life will be ruined before it restarts."

His eyes narrowed. They both knew what life was like without the person you cared about most.

Maybe *Emerson* was that person to Elise. Not Bly. She didn't know since Elise had never told her how she truly felt, even when she had the chance that day in the woods.

"Are you going through with it then?" he asked.

"What?" The question startled her.

Annoyance pinched his face, as if she should know exactly what he meant. His stare shifted pointedly over her left shoulder, and she didn't have to turn around to know exactly who he was looking at.

"I won't spend eternity without her," he said. "I knocked on the door of your room last night. I needed . . . my friend to tell me again that I had to go through with this. Where were you, Bly?"

She sucked in a breath. "You *still* don't think I'll let him go," she whispered. The accusation was a slap, even though she'd wavered with Kerrigan's arms around her just hours before. That was a single moment of weakness when she'd done nothing but fight for this. Because regardless of the anger she felt at Elise and Emerson's lies and despite the soft dreams that had begun to whisper between her and Kerrigan, she still loved her sister more than anything. Elise's death was still a constant hole of guilt inside of her. And even though she'd tried to shift some of that blame to Emerson and Elise, she was the one with the ribbon on her wrist, paid for with Elise's death.

The blame *still* fell on her shoulders. She felt it there like a suffocating cloak she was desperate to shed.

Kerrigan's affection couldn't change that.

But his sacrifice would.

Bly's sacrifice.

She would give someone she might love to bring back the person she and Emerson both loved.

She had thought that bringing back Elise would let her dream again, but it would only ensure that she never could. But that horrible understanding wasn't enough to stop her.

"I'm bringing my sister back." She put all the resolve in her voice that she could, and then she let a thread of ice slip through. "And don't you dare question my love for her again."

He looked at her for a long moment. "I'm sorry," he finally said. "You're the one who got us here. I . . . I'm the one who never thought it was possible. I never would have even tried, but we've done it." He shook his head as if he still couldn't quite accept it, but then he said, "I believe you."

Her chest swelled. Even if she'd never needed his belief to keep going, she'd wanted it.

She reached out and squeezed his hand, and he nodded sharply. "For Elise then."

She tried not to cringe at the reminder that this wasn't for her. Instead, she breathed a sigh of relief and stepped aside as Emerson strode forward toward the queens.

Queen Melvina glanced from Emerson to Bly to Kerrigan. "He's the one?" she asked, her knowing stare sliding again from Bly to Kerrigan.

Kerrigan said nothing, just folded his hands together in front of him while keeping a blank expression on his face.

Melvina shrugged before stepping down from her throne, the jewels on her gown making uncomfortable scraping sounds across the pebbles of the floor as she moved. She stopped in front of Emerson. A guard came forward, unbuttoning the sleeve of his uniform, but the queen held up a hand, halting him. She looked Emerson up and down. "On second thought, I like the looks of you." She turned over her shoulder to address Queen Allena. "What do you think? He looks like a prince to me."

Allena eyed him coolly but said nothing at all.

"Then it's settled," Melvina said brightly.

"I don't—"

"You don't what?" Melvina cut Emerson off.

Kerrigan shook his head, and Bly held her breath, but she saw the shift in Emerson before he even spoke. His eyes went from cold to calculating. There was even a brief flash of something dangerous—that rebellious heart that had been buried since his sister died. Being a prince would give him more power to use.

"Nothing," he said without inflection. "Thank you."

"My pleasure," Melvina said, like nothing at all was wrong. "You'll need to feed on me at the exact moment I feed on you. Drinking your blood will enhance the power in mine while you drink it. The effect will not be instantaneous. It'll take days for the spell in my blood to transform you." She eyed Emerson. "You'll be weak in the meantime and should rest."

"I'll be fine," he said coldly.

Allena let out a soft laugh. "Finally, someone who seems worthy of our gift."

Melvina nodded, pulling a gold-plated dagger out of the waist of her dress. Emerson didn't so much as flinch, and she raised her eyebrows at him. "I suppose he'll make a good vampire."

That made him wince.

Melvina cackled and drew the blade across her arm, freeing a stream of blood. She held it out and waved at him to give her his own wrist.

His jaw tightened but he didn't hesitate. He'd already decided, and once he settled on something, that was that. He took her wrist and placed it in his mouth as she sunk her fangs into his in return.

He looked as if it meant nothing more than an exchange at the market, but Bly could feel the tension coming off him.

It went on for a horribly long time. Even Vincent looked away. Bly didn't though. She wanted to be there for him, but he never glanced her way.

Eventually the queen freed his wrist with a sigh. "I do enjoy that part." She gave Emerson a dismissive look. "Welcome to our city." She turned to Kerrigan. "And we'll talk tomorrow about *your* reward. Your mother and I agree that you deserve more responsibility again given what you've just accomplished with so little." She chuckled as her eyes flitted over Bly and Vincent again. "But leave us for now. The night is young and we have other fun things to do. Enemies to play with." Her smile turned deadly, but it was Allena's slow grin that sent a chill down Bly's back.

Kerrigan dipped his chin at the queens. They gave him a bag that clanked with coins, and he passed it to Vincent as he ushered the rest of them out.

"How do you feel?" Bly asked Emerson as the doors shut behind them.

"Fine."

She wanted to keep asking him questions, but he scowled before his expression softened as his eyes held hers. "Thank you," he said.

She nodded. The words were more than she expected.

"Well then, on to the last little task," Kerrigan said. His voice sounded like he was trying to be light with humor, but bleakness leaked into it.

"Should we wait until morning?" Bly asked. *Could we keep pretending just a little bit longer?* She wanted him to see that unspoken question in her eyes, but he refused to meet her stare.

"No point," he said. "Plus we don't have that much extra time to spare."

The words pricked her. She drew in a shaky breath that she hoped nobody noticed.

Emerson was watching her, though. She saw the flash of sadness on his face—for her, because he finally understood all she was willing to lose to win.

Bly turned to Vincent. "Are you sure you want to go on? We wouldn't blame you if you wanted to go home."

Vincent's hands tightened on his bag of gold. "And miss this easy money?" He jerked his head at Kerrigan. "My family will need it more than ever with Nova dead." His words were blunt, but Bly understood the harshness in them. Vincent didn't have the luxury of wallowing in his loss. He had the living to protect.

"Plus I want to see you hand the vampire over," he added, voice hard and cruel.

Bly flinched. "Let's go," she said, even as half her heart begged her to stay.

TWENTY-TWO

EMERSON DIDN'T LOOK WELL. EVERY DOZEN steps he paused to lean on a tree.

"You don't need to come," Bly said as she glanced at him. "Go back and wait for me." It wasn't like he was going to be helpful in a fight anyway. And the woods were quiet. Most players would have already turned over their captives, which meant bounty hunters would've given up too.

Emerson let out a huff and glared at her. He didn't need to say it. He wasn't going to miss the moment Elise came back.

She glanced at Kerrigan, who was marching along behind her as well, a passive expression on his face, as if he hadn't had his lips pressed to her neck just hours before.

It hurt that she hadn't even caught him glancing at her once. Nothing.

Maybe all of it *was* pretend if he could turn it off so easily.

She drew in an unsettled breath. She needed to let it go too.

Vincent was nowhere to be seen; he'd drifted out beyond their sight as soon as they'd reached the woods. It made the hairs on the back of Bly's neck stand up, knowing he was probably watching them even though Bly couldn't spot him.

She glanced right and left, but all she could see were the dense vines sagging under the weight of berries. She shivered at the memory of getting caught picking them, of Kerrigan's surprisingly kind eyes. It seemed like a lifetime ago. A long and hard life.

But she was so close to starting a new one.

She stepped into one of the rare breaks in the bramble, a clearing with soft grass, framed by trees, the sky unusually clear above. She could even feel the kiss of warmth from the sun. Every exhausted inch of her wanted to collapse into the grass and bathe in it, but there would be time for that later.

"Bly." Kerrigan's voice startled her dreaming. For a moment, she was just glad he was talking to her again. She'd half turned to him when he shouted, "Run!"

Adrenaline blazed through her, making her limbs shake before she even knew what was happening, but she didn't let it propel her into flight. She twisted the rest of the way around just in time to see Donovan sweep his legs behind Kerrigan's, knocking him on his back, arms bound in front of him. He slammed his foot down on Kerrigan's chest to keep him from rising.

She didn't see Emerson anywhere.

"Where is he?" Bly asked, as her fingers fumbled for a strength spell and then a speed spell. For the dagger at her waist.

Donovan noted her movements but didn't bother stopping her. He scowled. "The other one?" He shrugged. "Unconscious. I would've snapped his neck but killing a transitioning vampire seemed wrong. And I only had one binding spell on me since I was in a bit of a rush after I checked Kerrigan's rooms. I was coming to celebrate with you." He twisted his heel against Kerrigan's chest.

Kerrigan wheezed. "Could you let up a little?"

Donovan stared down at him. "I'm disappointed in you."

"So nothing new."

"I thought you'd turned a corner."

"I have," Kerrigan said softly.

"The wrong one then. Because of her." He lifted his head to look at Bly. "Another girl leading you down the wrong path."

"She means nothing." Kerrigan's voice was passive. "It's not really about her at all."

Bly winced. He was too good at acting.

Donovan stepped off Kerrigan and was in front of her in a second.

She was ready. Power pulsed all the way to her fingertips. She swung the dagger with all her strength and speed—her own and what magic gave her—slicing it in the X Kerrigan had taught her.

Donovan dodged her, and when she tried to finish with the jab, he caught her wrist easily, eyebrows raising as she held her own for the briefest moment before he bent her arm back at a painful angle. She gasped, but she still managed to swing her other hand. "Bind," she said.

But he grinned, catching her other wrist before she could land the spell.

"I'm used to a witch's tricks. And even with your little spells,

I. Am. Stronger." He squeezed her wrists with each word until the unused spell and her dagger dropped from her hands. "Reach into a pocket again and I'll snap your neck." He let go of her, stepping back slightly so he could assess her.

"Don't touch her again, brother." Kerrigan's tone was light and conversational, but he stared at Donovan's back as if he were two seconds away from ripping his heart from his chest.

The look sent a shiver through Bly. And a wave of relief. That wasn't the look of someone who cared nothing for her.

Kerrigan struggled to his feet, arms still bound.

Donovan wagged a finger at him. "Move and I kill her before you even reach me."

Kerrigan froze. He seemed to be calculating the distance between them, and he chose not to move.

Donovan chuckled as he stared at Bly without bothering to glance behind him at Kerrigan. He began to circle her, as if he were a wolf and she were once more the rabbit he'd claimed her to be. "She looks human enough, but she seems to have cast a spell on you." He stopped at Bly's back, leaning over her shoulder so that their cheeks almost touched. "Perhaps a witch in disguise then?" He stepped around to her side, eyes on her as he talked to his brother. "You've always been careless but never a fool. Joining rebels is one thing, but marching to your death when you've finally gotten the revenge we wanted is another. It makes no sense." He reached out a hand, letting it hover just under her chin. "Not unless she's a witch." His fingers pressed under her jawbone, digging in until it hurt.

She tried to hold her head steady, but he grinned like he

enjoyed the fight before finally forcing her chin up.

Kerrigan snarled, but Bly didn't glance at him.

She stared into Donovan's narrowed eyes.

"Do I see a fleck of blue behind that pretty brown? Only one way to know for sure." He dropped her chin. Her skin throbbed from the release of pressure.

He pulled a blade, and she started to lunge away, but his hand gripped her upper arm so tightly she thought her bone would snap. He was going to stab her, kill her right when she was so close to winning. Her eyes flicked to Kerrigan's panicked face.

She searched the woods for Emerson. And she found Vincent's cool gaze hidden in the space between two bushes. He didn't look like he was in a hurry to help.

But Donovan wasn't going to stab her, at least not yet. He raised the blade over her head hilt-down to knock her unconscious, but who knew if she'd wake up from a blow like that. She tried to pull away from his iron grip even as she closed her eyes and braced for the impact.

Instead she was jerked so hard she thought her arm might pop off. Her eyes opened as she fell and hit the ground, limbs tangling around her. Growls rumbled in her ears as she tried to orient herself.

"Run, Bly." She blinked up as Kerrigan pressed against her and she felt the shift of Donovan beneath her, trying to break free from the weight of bodies on top of him. And then Kerrigan rolled off and she scrambled away from Donovan, who hadn't grabbed for her again . . . yet.

His expression, contorted in anger, was focused solely on Kerrigan.

Bly rose to her knees and then her feet. Her legs shook so badly that she had a hard time standing.

She glanced back at Donovan. Even spelled, each of her moves would be half as strong as his, and he'd already pulled himself to his feet. His focus narrowed back onto her.

It was too late to run.

Kerrigan still lay on the ground, and he swiped a leg out, catching Donovan by the shins and dropping him to the dirt once more.

"I said run!" Kerrigan's yell was a half snarl. It wasn't the voice of a kind knight who was saving her. It was the sound of an animal that would kill her himself if she didn't listen.

Fear took over. She wasn't a girl anymore; *she* was the animal, and instinct turned her shaking legs into lithe limbs that knew just what to do. But it wasn't to run. The Games had hardened her. She was the wolf, not the rabbit. Her instinct was to fight, even knowing she didn't have the upper hand, and anyway, when had she ever?

She dove at Donovan before he could make it upright. His back hit the dirt with her on top of him, the air whooshing out of him, but even with the element of surprise, his fingers closed around her neck in an instant.

"Bind," she choked out just as she thought he'd rip her windpipe from her throat.

His eyes widened as the magic ripped his hand away, winding it with his other at the wrist. She scrambled down and bound his ankles, too.

Donovan growled like a captured bear. But there was a look of begrudging respect in his eyes. "I might see why you like her—if she were a vampire, she'd be something to behold."

"She's something right now." Kerrigan looked at her for the first time since they'd left, eyes naked with feeling.

His expression made her want to go to him. It made her want to run.

She understood then why he'd stopped looking at her.

Seeing how he felt made this impossible.

Donovan was glancing between them. He let out a low whistle.

"I told you to run," Kerrigan said softly, a hint of anger on his face.

"I'm sorry," she said, and she knew he thought she was apologizing for not listening to him.

But she was sorry for what she was about to do.

She knelt down where he sat in the grass, hands still bound. Leaning across his lap, she brushed her lips softly against his. His mouth parted in surprise before he moved toward her, but she was already pulling back, grip tightening on the spell hidden in her hand.

She pricked him with it and murmured a word he surely wasn't expecting. *Bind*.

Confusion flashed across his face as his ankles cinched together. He shook his head, as if trying to understand, just as Emerson burst through the tree line, leaning on his drawn sword as he took in the scene with wide eyes.

Vincent stepped out from his hiding place.

"Thanks for your help," Bly snapped.

Vincent shrugged without a hint of remorse on his face. "Playing the odds."

"Do you have a blanket we can use as a stretcher?" Bly asked him.

He frowned but nodded.

"Good. We're going to need it."

Bly turned to Emerson, who nodded as well. He'd already guessed her plan. She wasn't surprised. In a way, she was doing exactly what he'd feared all along.

"Bly," Kerrigan said slowly with a dawning horror in his voice.

She swallowed down the lump in her throat, refusing to look at him. She turned to Vincent, the only one who didn't know what she was up to. "We need to find a place to hide Kerrigan so he's safe until the binding spells wear off. And then we take Donovan instead."

For a second, Vincent looked like he'd protest, but then he gave a harsh laugh. "Fine. Even better—the vampire will hate you as much as I do."

"Don't." Kerrigan's voice was ice cold.

Bly knew she had to look at him, but she didn't want to.

"I'll never forgive you for this." The harshness in his tone said he meant it.

It crushed her.

But so would handing him over. She couldn't keep going like she had for the past year, knowing that someone she loved was dead because of her.

Better to have him alive and hating her. She could live with that.

"Please, Bly. Don't do this to me." A sob caught the end of his words, and that finally made her turn to him.

His expression held so much pain that it felt like her own heart was ripping out at the sight of it.

"Donovan's a bad person," she said weakly.

Donovan's laugh broke out behind them. "She's right about that." He kept chuckling as if his evilness was the funniest thing he'd ever encountered.

"No," Kerrigan said. "He's just been hurt."

Donovan went silent.

Bly shook her head. "It's not an excuse."

"You still have me," Kerrigan pleaded. "You can still take me."

"But I can't." She could feel the hot tears on her cheeks. "I can't."

"She makes a better vampire than you, brother," Donovan said. "Ruthless."

Bly glanced at him. There was even more respect in his eyes.

Perhaps this wasn't the right thing at all, if the person she thought deserved death more was looking at her as if she were someone he admired. Unease bit at her.

But she didn't care.

"Bly," Kerrigan started, but she didn't let him finish. She couldn't let his words soften her resolve, so she cast one more spell on him and put him to sleep.

TWENTY-THREE

"I'M GLAD YOU'LL BE OUT OF MY BROTHER'S life, at least." Donovan spoke for the first time since they'd left. It had been a long day of silence between them all. The trees were silent too. The echoes of the dying had ceased. Most people had turned in their captives by now or had died trying, and the bounty hunters had made enough money not to bother any stragglers. They'd passed more than one body in the woods missing and arm or two.

Even the birds were absent, probably having fled the sounds of horror. She wondered how long it would take them to come back—to forget the terror that had driven them away to begin with.

She wouldn't blame them if they never returned.

The smell of death clung to everything. One minute fresh pine would lull you into peace, and the next the breeze would shift and leave your stomach rolling with the truth of what these woods had seen lately.

"Happy to die for that," Donovan added when nobody had

acknowledged him. With his fate looming ahead of them, he must have decided to get in a few more jabs.

Bly was carrying the cloth stretcher at Donovan's feet, and she glanced over her shoulder at him. "I'm just happy you'll be dead."

"I don't think so. I've changed my mind—you're not ruthless, you're scared. I was that way once. Maybe you'll be ruthless one day, but my death will haunt you."

"They're probably not going to kill you anyway. Maybe they'll keep you alive and drain you forever."

He took a long moment before answering. "Well, that would be worse, wouldn't it."

The trickle of fear in his voice *did* make Bly's stomach pinch with guilt.

But maybe he wouldn't be there forever. The queens seemed formidable. They could negotiate to get him back, perhaps. The rules of the Games probably didn't apply to princes.

Or maybe she was still playing pretend.

Emerson opened the door to Havenwhile as he wiped sweat from his brow. He hadn't been able to carry Donovan at all. He'd barely stayed on his feet this whole time. He looked as if he were caught somewhere between the living and the dead. Gray already pulsed around his pupil. She'd miss the dark brown, but at least the outer ring of his true color would stay.

Witches watched with curiosity as they walked down the street, heading for the lake, where Bly assumed they'd be gathered. She looked up at the almost noon sun. Yes, the Games were ending soon. They would be gathered.

Some of the witches walked up to them to peer down at Donovan, who hissed at them like a trapped cat. Most of them jerked back, but some laughed in his face. Their glee grated on Bly's nerves.

She hated to give them something they desperately wanted.

A crowd had gathered around the lake as she predicted.

For once, she pushed herself through the fray of witches without hesitation. The hurt they had caused her was about to be a thing of the past. They would undo it for her because she'd played their bloody game and won. She wasn't afraid anymore.

As the last of the crowd parted for her, Bly hesitated before a new structure that had been erected. Three small platforms carved from solid white stone stood side-by-side, with the one in the center slightly lower than the other two.

One platform held a human girl with green eyes ringed in dark circles, standing between two witches. The other held a vampire who looked like he'd be snarling if his mouth weren't gagged. The girl had to be the current winner whom Bly was about to unseat. Her eyes were wide and terrified, like she already guessed that Bly would steal the victory from her.

Demelza stood on the center stone. Pink roses crowned her head. Vines dangled from the floral crown and tangled in her long hair, holding the strands at wild angles so that the sun made the red in her hair blaze as if she'd caught fire. She no longer wore her glamour. A simple white dress hugged her tiny waist before cascading out to her bare feet.

Of course, she would be the head witch now that her mother was . . . gone.

Her shoulders were squared and her chin was high. She appeared to fill the role with ease. A witch Bly hadn't seen before stood behind Demelza. The women had a bird's nest of wild blond hair littered with tiny white flowers that matched a gown of stitched white petals that outdid Demelza's simple attire. Her eyes were cast down. Whoever the other witch was, Demelza was clearly in charge.

Demelza's face pulled into a snarl the second her eyes lighted on Bly.

But the witches in the crowd were beginning to whisper, and that whisper quickly turned into a cheer as more and more people crowded in to glance down in the stretcher Bly and Vincent carried.

Because they recognized Donovan. They knew what a feat it was to capture a prince.

Demelza's face turned to stone before she carved a stiff smile onto it. She couldn't do anything to harm them—not in front of her people. Not without breaking the rules and raising questions she probably didn't want to answer.

She glanced up at the sun as if she might be able to disqualify them for being late, but they had made it.

Demelza's eyes pinched with annoyance before she spoke. "It would seem you've captured quite the prize. Let me see."

They stepped forward, and Vincent moved from behind to stand even with Bly so that Donovan was stretched between them. Then they lay him on the ground.

Demelza's eyes widened, and she cackled with glee as she turned to Bly with a shake of her head. "A bold move." There was a hint of respect in her voice that made Bly sick. "A prince," she said louder to the waiting crowd. "I believe we have a new winner. Escort the other humans out."

Bly hadn't noticed them before, but a sharp wail jerked her attention to another team with a vampire bound at their feet. They'd clearly been waiting to collect the prize. They weren't people she remembered—a trio of boys barely older than her and a girl with dark brown hair cropped close to her ears. The girl was the one with tears falling freely, and Bly ached for her—whatever death she'd wanted to reverse would haunt her for at least another year.

A couple of the boys glared at Bly and Vincent as they were hauled off.

The girl was too caught in her grief to see them.

The vampire was taken in a different direction.

But they forgot to remove the girl on the platform. Her expression hadn't even changed. And the other platform still held a vampire. Who were they? Uneasiness tightened Bly's throat, but she didn't have time to unravel it.

Demelza dusted her hands as if ridding herself of pesky bugs.

She glanced between them all. "Now, which of you will claim the resurrection?"

Bly stepped forward.

"I will."

TWENTY-FOUR

BLY'S MOUTH WAS OPEN, BUT THE WORDS hadn't been hers.

Her heart stalled as she turned to Vincent, who'd stepped up as well.

"I claim it," Vincent said.

"No. It's mine," Bly said as she glanced back at Demelza. Demelza knew their deal. The prize was *always* supposed to be Bly's, but Demelza's face held a look of pure giddiness that made Bly's chest tighten. The witch would not help her.

She spun back to Vincent. "We had a deal."

"We made that deal when Nova was alive." Vincent's eyes burned with pure hatred. "And now she's dead because you liked getting your neck sucked by that fucking vampire."

Some of the witches tittered.

Bly jerked back at the bluntness of his words. "But you need the money. It's an even split of the prize."

He shrugged. "I already have some money, and I need my sister more." His hard voice cracked a little. "*You* take the money."

Bly felt a twinge of sympathy, but it would never be enough to make her back down. "The prize is mine, and you know it." She directed her words to Demelza.

Demelza smiled. "I care not for the broken word of humans." She glanced between them. "You'll fight for it."

She'd barely finished speaking when Vincent yanked out his sword, and Bly couldn't stop herself from stepping away from him. Her knife would do little against his weapon.

But Demelza held up her hand. "No weapons." She turned her focus on Bly. "And no spells. It will be a fight of strength. You'll have staves and nothing else. The first person to hit the ground will lose. Agreed?"

Vincent answered with a violent grin.

Bly shook her head; it would hardly be an even fight. Demelza had already chosen her winner.

Bly searched for Emerson, who was leaning on his sword with a bleak look on his face. For a second, she wondered if he should lay claim, fight instead of her, but he could barely stand, and he wasn't entirely human anymore—they'd never let him.

Emerson gave her a nod, but his eyebrows were drawn, and his mouth pulled down at the corners.

He looked like someone who'd given up.

She drew in a shaky breath as she handed over her dagger to the witches, accepting the long wood staff they gave her. The wood was rough and full of knots that could surely do significant damage to a body with each hit, and Bly was imagining them hitting her, not Vincent. Already she was thinking like someone who'd lose, but she wasn't Emerson. She didn't care about the odds of something happening. She'd always let herself live outside of logic; she lived in hope, even after everything. It had gotten her this far. She needed to believe she could do this—that belief *was* her upper hand.

Plus she had one more advantage. She'd been using strength spells on herself for the journey here to help carry Donovan. She hadn't given any to Vincent, whose arms were bulky with muscle.

But she could already feel that familiar tingle of exhaustion that came when the spell was fading. A few more moments and she'd only have her own abilities.

So she couldn't let this last more than a few more moments.

She tightened her grip on the staff and charged at Vincent without waiting for Demelza to command them to start.

Demelza's trickling laugh was the only sound of approval.

Vincent backstepped in surprise as Bly swung her staff for his head. One blow. She just needed her first blow to land, and this would all be over.

But Vincent's staff rose just in time, taking the impact even as it made him stumble.

Vincent's eyes widened and then narrowed as he pushed back, and Bly held her own, even though her arms shook from the strain of it. They buckled as the rest of the spell left her.

Vincent shoved her, and it was Bly's turn to stumble, twisting away as he swung after her.

He moved relentlessly, swinging the staff above his head and down again, and even though Bly was faster on her feet, she had nowhere to go but back until she found herself pressed against the edge of the crowd. She recoiled from the brush of witches' hands on her as Vincent brought his staff down again.

Bly raised hers. Wood cracked so loud that it sounded like a tree splitting in the forest. Vincent bore down slowly as if savoring the moment, and her arms bent in surrender as he closed the space between them until his snarling face was inches away.

Vincent reared his head back before smashing his forehead into hers.

Pain exploded in her nose, spreading through her face as she crashed backward into the crowd.

One set of hands grabbed her under the armpits, hauling her roughly to her feet before she hit the ground. Pain pinched at her shoulder as she struggled to find her balance and pull away from the steady grip that still held her.

"Don't lose this." The familiar voice made her heart plummet and speed at the same time.

Kerrigan's hands pushed her back into the ring.

"That's not fair!" Vincent had backed away to scream up at Demelza's impassive face. "She would've fallen!"

Bly didn't hear what Demelza said, but the witch wouldn't stop the fight, not with a crowd hungry for it.

She'd turned to look at Kerrigan, his face a horrible mixture of hate and worry. He seemed to force himself to look away from her. His eyes flipped to rage, and she knew he'd turned his attention to his brother.

She felt like she'd already lost.

But he'd told her not to. Some part of him cared. He'd run here, after all. They'd been slow, hauling Donovan between them, but even with that, Kerrigan had to have used every bit of his vampire speed to get here.

He probably needed to feed, but this wasn't the moment to worry about him.

Vincent roared, the sound drawing closer and closer until Bly had to turn her attention back to the broken person thundering toward her, staff raised above his head.

She set her feet, raising her own staff in front of her to try and hold the blow.

But something felt different. The staff felt lighter and steady in her arms that had been shaking moments before. Her senses sharpened on the tingling sensation speeding through her that she'd mistaken as fear. She felt as if she could move in a blur if she ran fast enough. She'd been spelled with strength and speed.

That was why he'd grabbed her.

She desperately wanted to look at Kerrigan again. She desperately wanted to run to him and throw herself in his arms and thank him.

But she had to finish this. She needed to be careful, though. She couldn't let on that she'd been spelled.

Vincent was almost on her. His expression held no mercy.

But Bly didn't deserve it or want it. She threw her staff at Vincent's face, leaving her without a weapon if this didn't work.

Vincent's weapon raised up and blocked it. Bly's staff didn't so much as hit him, but she didn't need it to. She just needed his staff to raise for a moment.

She barreled toward him, diving low so her shoulder sailed into his stomach while her arms grabbed his waist. Vincent teetered, his staff coming down on her back with a force that made her grunt, but the pain didn't matter because Vincent fell. His back hit the ground as she came down on top of him.

Bly rolled off him with a groan, staring up at the sun, letting the brightness burn away everything else.

She'd done it. She started to heave herself up on her elbows when Vincent straddled her, hands clamping around her neck before she could even comprehend what was happening.

Her legs flailed as her vision wavered with black at the edges. She wanted to scream that Demelza couldn't let him kill her. It wasn't fair. But why would she expect fairness? She'd cheated first.

Someone knocked Vincent off her and Emerson knelt beside her, leaning over her as he shouted up at Demelza. "Bly won! Stop this!"

Bly couldn't see what the witch said, but Vincent let out a roar that rattled inside Bly's fuzzy head as Emerson helped her to her feet.

Each breath she took burned her throat, but her vision cleared as Emerson murmured in her ear, "You did it, Bly. It's over."

She finally managed to lift her chin to meet Demelza's cold expression. "I assume you've brought something of your loved one."

Her clumsy fingers moved to her neck where she pulled free a necklace.

She held it out where Emerson could see it. A tiny wooden daisy on a string—it matched the wooden rose that Bly always wore around her own neck.

"Oh," he let out softly. There was a hint of surprise in the sound.

"She must have forgotten to put it on that morning," she said. She had found the necklace under Elise's pillow after she'd died. "I've been carrying it for this moment." The fact that you needed something of the person who'd died for the resurrection spell, something they'd touched, was the only thing anyone really knew about it. The winners who'd witnessed it were sworn to secrecy. Anyone who told that secret disappeared, and so did your whole family and maybe your neighbors and anyone else you might have spoken to. It happened once, years ago. People didn't make mistakes like that twice, even if they had only heard a tale of the consequences.

Emerson's hand drifted out to touch one of the wooden petals.

"Do you want the prize or not?" Demelza snapped.

Bly fought a scowl as she moved forward and lifted the necklace. Demelza's face pinched in disgust as she took it, but Bly ignored her. *This was it.* Her body vibrated with anticipation. It'd been so long since she hugged her sister, and she was finally going to hold her again.

A slow, cruel smile spread across Demelza's face as she addressed her people. "I know it's customary to use prisoners already in our possession for the spell, but shall we make things more interesting this time?" A few witches laughed and cheered. Some shuffled, sharing confused glances.

Demelza turned to the group of witches restraining Vincent. "Replace the human sacrifice with him." She turned and nodded at the witches guarding Donovan. "Replace the vampire with him." She turned back to Bly, and some of the cold harshness in her expression melted for a moment, leaving behind pain. "This is for my mother." She winced on the last word.

For a second nobody moved.

"You want to sacrifice the prince?" asked one of the men holding Donovan upright. He didn't look much older than Demelza, and he had the same burgundy hair she shared with Halfryta. His eyes were sharp and judging, and Bly wondered if they were related.

Demelza's smile faded slowly as she stared down the man. "Was I not clear?"

The moment stretched with tension until someone in the crowd shouted, "Kill the prince!"

The words were a jolt. Of course, she'd known she was bringing Donovan to die, but in the back of her mind she'd held on to the story of how they kept some alive and hidden. She didn't want to believe she was actually bringing him to be murdered, but he was being pulled up onto the platform as the other vampire was dragged down. They shoved him to his knees so hard that Bly could tell it took effort for him not to cry out.

She looked at the other platform, at Vincent also on his knees, shoulders trying to jerk away from the hands that gripped him. One of those hands held a knife flashing in the high noon sun. And then she noticed a detail she'd missed before: a chute leading from each higher platform to Demelza's.

Horror dawned on Bly. Spells took blood. And the strongest spells took human *and* vampire blood.

Demelza addressed the crowd. "The resurrection spell is the

most powerful of all—the only spell that requires a body's worth of blood from a human, a witch, and a vampire to restore the life of another."

"No," Bly said softly.

"You can't stop this," Emerson said beside her. There was disgust in his voice, but also a hint of begging. He didn't *want* to stop this. He'd been against it from the start, but standing here now, he must have felt just how close they were to having Elise in front of them.

"Vincent," Bly choked out.

She was supposed to be sacrificing a vampire—not a boy with a family at home—a family that wouldn't have either sibling return to them now. Bly thought of the faces on the paper from Nova's sketchbook—the pain they'd feel. Donovan was one thing. He was cruel. She could live with his death, but Vincent's? He was all rage and brutality, but he wasn't evil. He was hurt and doing whatever was necessary to save his sister. And Bly was buying her sister's life with the life of someone fighting for their own family.

Vincent fought to tear himself free.

"Stop!" Bly screamed over the crowd that had started to cheer with anticipation.

She couldn't go through with this.

Demelza looked at her. There was no joy in her expression, but there was resolution. And Bly knew no amount of begging would stop this. Demelza would give her exactly what she'd wanted all along, and the price would be Bly's humanity.

She'd be just like the worst of the witches and vampires—

someone who used human life to get what they wanted.

"Please!" Bly yelled, but her voice sounded weaker in her own ears, as if she were already a sliver of the person she was just moments before. "I don't want this."

Nobody seemed to hear her—not even Emerson next to her, who looked ahead with nothing but resignation on his face.

Demelza didn't look at her either. She raised her hands out to the side, palms up to the sky.

"Stop!" Another voice rang out, loud and commanding. "Use me instead."

Bly spun as Kerrigan stepped forward from the crowd. Witches peeled away from him, as if just noticing the vampire in their midst.

"Absolutely not," Donovan shouted from where he knelt. He wasn't even trying to get up. His face held a grim resolve.

"Please," Kerrigan begged, speaking first to Demelza then to Donovan. "Let me make up for my past. Let me be the one to die this time."

"Listen to me." Donovan's voice was firm. Whatever Bly thought of him, she had to respect his ability to stay calm with a dagger at his throat. "You do not have anything to make up for. We were both kids." He paused, the only sign of emotion. "I just needed someone else to blame. It wasn't fair to you. It wasn't really even about you."

"Touching," Demelza said. "Perhaps vampires do have feelings."

The crowd's laughter was sickening.

Kerrigan turned to her again. "Let me take his place."

She seemed to consider it, and her calculating eyes met Bly's, and Bly knew what she was actually thinking about: which would hurt her more. After all, it was Bly who had cast the binding spell that brought Halfryta down.

Bly wasn't sure what the answer was anymore. She thought killing Donovan would be easier, but she was breaking Kerrigan in a way that was worse than death. Kerrigan had done all of this to save Bly from her guilt, but she wasn't saving his life by handing over his brother; she was putting him in the same hell she'd played the Games to escape: his brother would be dead at the end of this, and it was because Kerrigan had trusted her. Donovan would be alive if he'd never helped her.

She thought she was finally being selfless, giving up her own dreams with Kerrigan to give Elise back her life, but in the end she'd tried to have everything again.

She felt as if she'd been ripped into a thousand pieces, and each tear had been her own fault.

Demelza turned her gaze back to Kerrigan. Then she turned to one of the guards. "Restrain him without binding." She smiled but it seemed distant. "I want to see him struggle."

Witches closed in on him, and he didn't fight as hands gripped him.

"No," Bly said. "*No!* I didn't give him to you!" she screamed up at Demelza.

But Demelza wasn't even looking at her. She waved a hand at Donovan and then Vincent. "Kill them."

Everything stilled for one horrible moment.

A blade crossed Vincent's throat. His eyes blinked in surprise as red streamed down his neck. He slumped forward onto his face, and one of the witches kicked him to the side so they could all see his gaping mouth struggling to draw air.

Kerrigan roared, fighting to get to Donovan as a witch stabbed a dagger into his brother's throat.

The witches dragged Kerrigan to his knees. He clawed and fought, but there were too many of them.

Donovan didn't flinch as the dagger entered his neck and stayed there. With no way to pull it out, he would bleed to death, but his face said he wasn't afraid. Blood streamed from the wound, but he stayed upright for a horribly long time, watching Kerrigan fight to reach him.

He tried to say something, but only a bubble of blood came out of his mouth, and then he fell too.

The witches pushed him to the edge of his platform in the same position as Vincent.

The witch behind Demelza stepped forward, kneeling. Her hands shook at her sides, but her expression was horribly empty as Demelza placed a hand on her shoulder. "I'm sorry. You may not have been strong enough to create spells, but your blood will," she said before opening the witch's throat with a blade, sending a waterfall of red down the delicate petals of her dress. After a moment, she crumpled into a heap.

Vampire and human blood slipped down the chutes to Demelza's feet, mixing with the witch's blood. Demelza watched it pool with a blank expression until finally nudging the witch's body to the side so she could kneel in front of the gathering blood, dropping Elise's necklace into the sacrifice.

Bly's stomach lurched painfully. She didn't know what to feel. Tears pooled in her eyes. Kerrigan was still yelling to her left, and Emerson breathed heavily to her right, eyes glued on that puddle of red that was going to bring back the person they both loved the most.

This wasn't how she'd imagined this moment. She knew she'd have to be ruthless to win, but she'd never thought it would be at the expense of someone she cared about.

Her whole body trembled with her warring emotions: the Bly who felt guilt about Vincent's death, the Bly who felt pain for Kerrigan's loss, the Bly who just wanted to hug her sister.

She just wanted to hug her sister again.

She tried to drown out everything but that thought.

Kerrigan's cries still pierced her, though.

Demelza was chanting, hands in the blood, eyes closed.

Suddenly she stopped, blinking. "I can't feel her."

"What do you mean?" Bly asked. "Find her. Her name's Elise. Blond hair, dimples, brown eyes . . ." She trailed off, unsure if more details helped or not.

"She's not dead," Demelza snapped. Her eyes seemed to struggle to focus, but she turned her head in Bly's direction. Bly almost stepped back. The lake blue of Demelza's iris had bled into the whites of her eyes, making it look as if she were drowning inside.

"That's not possible." Panic lanced through her. Something was going wrong. She felt for her necklace, as if she might have given hers instead of Elise's, but she brushed the familiar rose carving. Demelza had the right one. "You're lying."

"I'm not." Demelza's voice was strained. She lowered it to barely a hiss. "Do you think I want to look like I can't do this spell? *She's not dead.*"

There was an earnestness in her voice. She was telling the truth—it wouldn't look good for her to fail. The realization hit Bly like a slap. Her sister wasn't dead. She tried to let the words sink into her, but all they did was bring up her sister's unblinking eyes, the vines reaching up her arms, the way her body flopped as the witches rolled her onto their stretcher. She hadn't imagined that.

"I saw it," Bly said. "She died."

Demelza scowled. "Do you have someone else?"

If Elise wasn't dead, then where was she?

Nowhere good. She would have come home if she could've.

That new truth took hold of Bly, becoming a painful hook in her chest that threatened to pull her heart right out. Elise wasn't dead. How long had she wanted to say those words? But now it felt like an awful new reality she didn't want to face.

"I need someone else," Demelza ground out. "Now."

Bly blinked. She glanced at Vincent.

"It can't be him," Demelza said. "His blood's powering the spell. He might not even be dead yet."

Bly winced.

Her sister wasn't dead. The thought tried to derail her once more, but she didn't have time to dwell on it. Not yet.

Bly ran to Kerrigan, reaching to grab his arm through the witches that stood around him but weren't holding him as tightly any longer. He was still on his knees, head bowed slightly.

He let out a low growl when she touched him that made her skin crawl with regret.

"Your parents," she said. "Do you have anything of theirs?"

"Bring one of them back so they can see their dead son?" He lifted his chin, face filled with disgust. "So they can live knowing what bought them their life?" He jerked his arm free of her, and she turned her back on him, because she didn't have time to argue and he was right. She couldn't change who was dying to cast the spell.

Her eyes fell on Vincent, and she ran to him.

"I told you I can't bring him back," Demelza bit out.

Bly pulled the dagger from her waist and reached for Vincent's neck. She didn't have time to be squeamish about the gaping red line of his throat or the stream of blood running from it. She reached for Nova's necklace and pulled it forward, cutting the twine with her blade.

Bly froze as Vincent blinked. Her stomach lurched, but she didn't have time to wonder if he was conscious enough to understand what was happening. Bly hoped he was. She hoped he died knowing his sister would live.

"Bring back Nova." Bly tossed the necklace at Demelza, who dropped it in the puddle of blood. She sunk her hands into it and began to chant again until her eyes started to flutter, and her head tilted up to the sun and her arms shook. She lifted her hands slightly, and the blood started to rise as if evaporating into a bloody steam that shifted, swirling around itself until it began to take shape, forming limbs, a torso, a head. Then the red smoky shape seemed to harden until a naked girl lay there.

Demelza's chanting stopped. The sudden silence was disarming.

Demelza slumped to the side, catching herself on her elbow before pushing to her feet. Her limbs shook, and her already pale skin held no color as if the spell had stolen her life too. Crimson covered the lower half of her dress. She held out her hands at her side, bloodied palms out.

Whispers shivered through the witches. Some of them bowed their heads in respect, and Bly realized this had been a test for the witch, proof that she was powerful enough to take her mother's place, and she was.

And her sharp gaze had zeroed in on Bly.

Nova sat up with a gasp that sounded like she'd been stabbed. She drew in ragged breaths that swallowed every other noise around her. Pushing herself off the platform, her feet slid from under her. She fell to her knees, eyes wild as she held out her arms and stared down at them. Tiny streams of blood covered her, making it appear as if her veins ran on the outside of her skin. She started to run her hands over herself as if feeling for wounds.

Bly took a faltering step toward her, but Emerson beat her there, grabbing Nova's elbow and helping her stand. She wavered on her feet like a tree in a storm.

"Vincent." Her brother's name was barely a croak.

Her eyes landed on Bly, then Emerson, before finally finding her brother.

"*No.*" The word echoed—or maybe she repeated it over and over again as she took wobbling steps to the platform Vincent was splayed out on. She pulled at his body, dragging him into her arms. She fell back from the weight of him so that she was on her knees again, holding him against her chest, fingers dancing around his slit throat as if she weren't sure if she should try and push the gaping flesh back together.

"What." Her teeth chattered around the word that didn't even sound like a question.

But Demelza was all too willing to answer. "He fought Bly for the prize to raise someone. He lost, surprisingly, so I used his blood for the spell, but it turns out Bly's sister wasn't dead after all, so Bly brought *you* back. I guess you can thank her for your life . . . *and* for your brother's death." Demelza looked at Bly.

Nova's eyes landed on her as she softly lay Vincent on the ground.

"I didn't kill him," Bly said. "I didn't." But her denial didn't even sound confident to her own ears.

Nova stood up. Her steps became more and more sure the closer she got to Bly, but her eyes had gone hazy and vacant, and it reminded Bly of the way the resurrected Mabel in the market sometimes looked. But Mabel at least had Ackley to bring her back to herself. Who would do the same for Nova? Certainly not Bly—whatever comradery they'd shared had surely died with Vincent. Emerson stepped in front of Nova, saying her name, but she shoved him to the side and Emerson stumbled, falling to the ground.

Bly scrambled, grabbing one of the abandoned staves and clutching it in her hands, but Nova didn't even register the weapon. She just kept coming.

Nobody was going to stop her.

All Bly's death would be to the witches was an encore.

She tried to steady her shaking hand. She needed to take the first swing because she could already feel the spells fading away again and leaving her weak. But her own guilt was like a manacle around her wrist. Maybe Nova had every right to hurt her.

Nova's hand closed around her arm.

Her face held no emotion as she plucked Bly's weapon free with her other hand. Emerson pushed himself to his feet behind her, but he couldn't save her.

He'd never been the one who could save her.

Nova raised the stave.

A hand closed around Nova's wrist just before she could land the blow. Another hand closed around her throat and squeezed, lifting her off her feet for a moment before tossing her back. She landed hard on the ground next to Vincent's body. She strained to raise herself, but then it seemed like something gave out within her. She lay there and turned her head to look at her brother's still-open eyes.

Someone should've closed them.

"Vampire," Demelza said.

"Witch," Kerrigan returned. He stood beside Bly. It took her a moment to even realize that he'd been the one to stop Nova. She stared up at him, but he didn't look back at her.

She turned to see the witches that had been guarding him now pulling themselves up from the ground where he'd left them. They stalked toward him again, but Demelza held up a hand to stop them.

"Take the knife out of my brother. Maybe he can still heal.

You know a vampire can come back from nearly anything."
Kerrigan's voice was calm as if he were done begging.

Demelza's eyes flitted, taking in the crowd around them for a
moment before settling back on Kerrigan. "I can't do that."

"Please." Kerrigan's voice broke on the word.

And something in Demelza's expression seemed to crack
as well at the raw pain in his voice. Her face twisted into a
grimace.

Bly reached a hand out for Kerrigan's, ready to pull him away.

"Take it out," Demelza called down to the witches nearest
Donovan.

"Una." The young witch who challenged her before stepped
forward again, glancing into the crowd at a group of solemn
witches with shrewd blue eyes. They had to be part of the
council.

But Demelza seemed to be her mother's daughter in one
way. Her face hardened as she spun toward the man. "Do not
question me. You know my mother would have done the exact
same thing. A live prince is worth more than a dead one. Do
it. Now."

Nobody else challenged her. The witch scowled before bending and yanking the dagger out.

Demelza turned back to Kerrigan. "Do not mistake this for
compassion. He will not leave here with you today."

Kerrigan took a step toward her, and she lifted a hand.

"You're a long way from home." Her calm words carried a simple threat.

The crowd stirred around them.

"Give him to me," Kerrigan demanded.

"Your brother was handed over fairly." She stared pointedly at Bly.

"I know." There was bitterness in his words.

"But if my mother is still alive, I would consider a trade."

The crowd murmured. Bly glanced around. Some nodded, but not everyone wanted Halfryta back.

"Don't do it." Donovan's voice was raspy. He'd pushed himself to his knees. Blood still trickled from the healing wound in his neck. He stared only at his brother. "Don't free her."

"A brother for a mother," Demelza said. "It's your choice." She scanned her people as she spoke. Bly thought there was fear in her eyes, but she held her head high as she stepped down and walked toward them, stopping first at Nova. She held out a gleaming bronze key to her. "A key to Havenwhile, as promised." She walked to Emerson next. "I would give you one, but you won't be welcome here much longer, I am sad to say." Emerson grimaced as she turned away and stepped in front of Bly. She smelled of sharp blood and sweet roses, and Bly could barely stop herself from gagging. She held out the key, and as Bly took it, she leaned in close. "I would not make a habit of using this." Her smile as she pulled away promised a million different revenges. She faced the crowd. "Let us celebrate." She glanced back at them. "Leave."

"Wait," Donovan croaked. "I want a word with Bly."

Demelza glanced between them. "Fine."

Kerrigan stepped forward.

"Not you," she said.

He growled but Demelza barely glanced at him. "Now or never," she said to Bly.

Bly swallowed and then walked over to Donovan. It was hard not to gag just looking at him. Red covered his entire front. One side of his face was sticky with it from where he'd lain in his own blood.

She opened her mouth to say she was sorry, even though she wasn't sure if it was a lie or not, but he shook his head.

"Don't apologize. That's weak, and I've started to like you." He laughed, and blood gurgled from his lips. "I know where your sister is."

Her mouth popped open. Whatever she expected him to say, it wasn't that.

"Elise, right? Blonde with dimples and brown eyes."

He was only being cruel, repeating the details she'd just given Demelza to get her hopes up. She started to turn away.

But then his lips curved as if he knew exactly what she was thinking. "Tiny crescent scar on her chin?" he added.

She froze. Elise had fallen during one of their many races, cutting her chin on a stone so badly that even their mother couldn't totally erase the scar.

He leaned closer as if to tell her a secret. "Pesky little death curse?"

Her heart sunk to her toes. Her sister might have been unconscious and not dead that day in the woods, but Bly hadn't imagined those black vines of death. Her sister was still alive, but how long did she have before the curse stole her away?

"Where?" she could barely breathe the word out.

He grinned, his teeth bloody. "Get me out of here before my brother can turn over that bitch who killed our parents, and I'll tell you."

"Please—" she started, but he shook his head.

"Take him away," Demelza said.

Two witches hauled Donovan to his feet. Kerrigan tried to move toward them, but Demelza stepped in front of him.

"No," she said simply.

"I will—"

"You'll what?" A handful of witches closed in. "Get out. Now. Or I'll spill your blood too."

"Try it." He took another step, and Bly rushed back to grab his arm, but he shook her off so hard that she stumbled.

Anger flashed in Demelza's eyes. She really didn't want to hurt him. He wasn't a prize from the Games, which meant killing him could start a war. But he was pushing her into a corner in front of her own people.

Making her look weak. She'd just shown her power performing a difficult spell, but Bly caught how she continued to sway slightly on her feet from the way it had drained her. She couldn't afford a fight.

Demelza nodded at Bly. "You have ten minutes to get her out of here, or it will be *her* blood I spill, not yours."

Kerrigan finally looked at Bly then, and there was so much loathing on his face that she thought he might just tell Demelza that he didn't care.

"You're wasting time you could be spending getting to my mother before she's dead," Demelza said coldly.

Kerrigan grimaced and grabbed Bly's arm, tugging her through the crowd.

"Emerson," she managed to get out.

"He's behind us."

She tried to turn around, but he was practically dragging her, knocking her against witches that looked like they were itching for permission to cast a death curse on her.

But they were allowed to leave.

And she knew she had Kerrigan to thank for that. A couple of human winners that never came home? Nobody would've cared about that. Another missing vampire prince? That was different.

Kerrigan's grip on her didn't loosen until they were out of Havenwhile and deep into the forest, standing in a tiny clearing of bright green grass overrun with pops of white mushrooms. Even now, her chest tightened at the sight of them, and her legs numbed as she gulped down a few forced breaths. They were still the image of the worst moment in her life. And she still didn't have her sister back, even after doing the impossible.

It was all supposed to be fine after she'd won.

And now the boy she had thought she loved was kneeling on the ground, retching as his blood tried to turn him into a vampire, and the vampire she knew she was falling for was staring at her like he wished her dead.

"Kerrigan," she started.

He shook his head. "Don't. You tried to condemn me to the same fate you were trying to escape. How *could* you? I saw so much pain in you that I was willing to die to try and fix it, and you . . . gave it to me." He sucked in a breath and looked up at the sky.

Vultures circled high above them, searching for the dead.

Bly hurt too much to be dead.

"I'll help you get him back," she promised.

"Why should I trust you? What did he say to you?"

"That he knows where my sister is, and that she's still death cursed."

Surprise flashed through the hate in his eyes, but it was brief. "Ah, so that's why you want to help me. It'll get you what you want." His bitter laugh made her want to take a step back from him, but she stepped forward instead.

"Please," she said, and she wasn't even sure what she was begging for. Forgiveness? How could she ask that of him when she couldn't even forgive herself?

It didn't matter anyway. He turned away from her.

"Wait," she said.

He kept walking.

"Emerson needs help getting back."

Kerrigan stopped. He turned around and helped Emerson to his feet, bracing him under his shoulder. He didn't look at Bly as he did it, as if he wanted her to know that he wasn't doing it for her.

Emerson began to hobble off with the very vampire he'd told her not to trust. Of course, it had turned out that she was the one who couldn't be trusted. Kerrigan had never betrayed them, but she'd betrayed him.

Emerson looked back at Bly. "We need to find her," he rasped out.

She nodded as they disappeared into the trees, leaving her in the drowning sea of bleak white.

She'd free Donovan and find her sister. Finding what she'd lost and returning what she'd taken from Kerrigan were tied together now. Maybe he'd see that with time. Or maybe he'd never speak to her again.

She couldn't let that matter.

Elise was the only one who'd ever loved Bly as much as Bly had loved her, and now she was the only thing Bly had left in this world.

Her sister was trapped somewhere, alive but unable to come home, and her heart was a ticking clock. How long until it stopped?

Bly would find her before it did, and she'd curse anyone who got in her way.

ACKNOWLEDGMENTS

I usually sit on my book ideas for a long time before writing them, but *The Revenant Games* was different. I was already deep into another book proposal when the story came to me, but I couldn't shake my desire to write it immediately.

I'm so thankful to Rebecca Podos—you were the first one I shared my new idea with, and your encouragement and excitement for it told me that I was right to want to chase it.

Thank you to Sarah McCabe for trusting me to write a second world fantasy that was a departure from my first two books. Thank you for pushing me to dig deeper into my characters. They truly come alive with your guidance.

Thank you, Anum Shafqat, for all of your sharp insights. The spelled vampire fang you suggested became one of my favorite spells in the book!

Thank you to the entire team at McElderry Books for continuing to believe in my stories and get them into the hands of readers: Justin Chanda, Karen Wojtyla, Anne Zafian, Bridget Madsen, Elizabeth Blake-Linn, Chrissy Noh, Caitlin Sweeny, Lisa Quach, Bezi Yohannes, Perla Gil, Remi Moon, Amelia Johnson, Ashley Mitchell, Saleena Nival, Trey Glickman, Elizabeth Huang, Emily Ritter, Amy Lavigne, Lisa Moraleda,

Nicole Russo, Nicole Valdez, Christina Pecorale and her sales team, and Michelle Leo and her education/library team.

A special thanks to Debra Sfetsios-Conover and Andrew Davis for creating a cover that so perfectly captures this story.

Thank you to both my in-person and online writing groups for your constant support. I've been blessed with so many new writing friends since I started that I'm afraid to list everyone from fear of missing someone, which, for a very shy person, is a problem I never thought I'd have. A special thanks to Eliza Langhans for giving me feedback on this book when I needed it. Jess Creaden, I'm so excited to see how our writing careers both continue to unfold. I'm lucky to call you my friend. Sana Z. Ahmed, I always look forward to our chats—you're a constant source of encouragement. Angela Montoya, I'm writing this the day *Sinner's Isle* came out, and I'm just so thankful to have you and your wonderful books in my life. Bailey Gillespie, Christy Cooper, and Portia Hopkins, you've been my friends from the start, and I know you'll always be there for me. Stephanie Garber, our writing days are the best workdays. You're the friend I can always turn to for invaluable advice in this industry.

To my mom and dad: I wouldn't be able to survive on this career path without your constant love and support.

To my nephews, Lucas, Liam, Gabriel: you're all so creative and clever and a constant source of inspiration. I love you.

To my readers: I can't thank you enough for picking up my books. Every kind message I've ever gotten has been my inspiration to keep writing.

MARGIE FUSTON

grew up in the woods of California where she made up fantasy worlds that always involved unicorns. In college, she earned undergraduate degrees in business and literature and a master's in creative writing. Now she's back in the woods and spends all her time wrangling a herd of cats and helping her nephews hunt ghosts, pond monsters, and mermaids. You can find her online at MargieFuston.com.